Books by Judith Miller

www.judithmccoymiller.com

*with Tracie Peterson

THE
CHAPEL
CAR BRIDE

JUDITH MILLER

BETHANY HOUSE
a division of Baker Publishing Group
Minneapolis, Minnesota

© 2017 by Judith Miller

Published by Bethany House Publishers
11400 Hampshire Avenue South
Bloomington, Minnesota 55438
www.bethanyhouse.com

Bethany House Publishers is a division of
Baker Publishing Group, Grand Rapids, Michigan

Printed in the United States of America

Library of Congress Cataloging-in-Publication Data
Names: Miller, Judith, author.
Title: The chapel car bride / Judith Miller.
Description: Minneapolis, Minnesota : Bethany House, [2017]
Identifiers: LCCN 2016041083 | ISBN 9780764230110 (cloth) | ISBN 9780764219054 (trade paper)
Subjects: | GSAFD: Love stories. | Christian fiction.
Classification: LCC PS3613.C3858 C48 2017 | DDC 813/.6—dc23
LC record available at https://lccn.loc.gov/2016041083

Scripture quotations are from the King James Version of the Bible.

This is a work of fiction. Names, characters, incidents, and dialogues are products of the author's imagination and are not to be construed as real. Any resemblance to actual events or persons, living or dead, is entirely coincidental.

Cover design by LOOK Design Studio
Cover photography by Aimee Christenson

Author is represented by Books & Such Literary Agency.

17 18 19 20 21 22 23   7 6 5 4 3 2 1

To Carolyn Poe
who graciously loaned me her research books
and documents that helped to make this story
of the chapel car ministry come alive.

CHAPTER

1

Hope Irvine clutched a handful of leaflets and picked her way toward the rear of the swaying train. Pushing open the heavy door, she grasped the waist-high railing of the train's rear platform with her free hand. Her lips curved in a bright smile as she leaned forward to toss flyers from the Herald of Hope, the chapel car entrusted to her father's ministry.

But where were the children who usually ran after the chapel car when they pulled into a town? Had she miscalculated the time of their arrival? Were the children still in school? Rather than little girls with pigtails flying in the breeze and young boys waving their caps, the only folks watching the train were a few surly-looking men lolling about outside a tavern near the railroad tracks.

When several of the men hooted and shouted catcalls in her direction, Hope startled, loosened her grip, and toppled backward, landing on her backside with skirts splayed out. Too late, she clapped her right hand to her head. Her ribbon-bedecked hat that was a perfect match for her red claret suit sailed from the back of the train like a kite on a windy day. Quickly swiping her skirt back in place, she clung to the rear railing and pulled to a sitting position. A rush of anger assailed her as she watched one of the scalawags crush the fashionable hat onto his head, then jump in the air and click his booted heels together. She narrowed her eyes and scowled.

Before she'd regained her footing, her father stooped down beside her, his eyes filled with concern. "You're hurt! I'm so sorry, Hope. From now on I'll toss the flyers."

The train lurched as he helped her to her feet, and both of them grabbed for the railing before they toppled to the platform. He pulled her close to his side.

"I'm fine, Papa. The only thing damaged is my new hat and my dignity."

He tightened his hold around her shoulder. "I've made a mistake bringing you with me. This train isn't a proper home for a young woman. I shouldn't have been so easily convinced."

Her father wasn't stretching the truth when he said he'd been easily convinced. Hope had been caught by surprise when he agreed after only a few hours of arguing her case. No doubt, the loneliness he'd written of in his letters over the past years had influenced his decision, as well. If she didn't allay his concerns, this silly incident might cause him to seek another solution to her living situation before they'd even arrived at their final destination.

"Pshaw." Hope smiled at her father. "What about the wives who have been accompanying their husbands on other chapel cars for many years now? I'm not going to endure any hardships that haven't already been overcome by those fine ladies."

Her father sighed. "Whether you care to admit it or not, there is a vast difference between a married woman accompanying her husband and a minister's daughter of nineteen years who has never experienced the hardships of life. Besides, you're no more than a wisp of a girl. A strong wind could topple you."

A hairpin fell from her riotous reddish-brown curls and nested in the navy trim that accented her full skirt. She yanked the pin from the decorative cording and thrust it into her curls before flashing a smile at her father. "Nothing you say about those unruly men or the hardships of living in a chapel car will change my mind. I believe the Lord wants me at your side. Those men and their rude comments haven't discouraged me in the least." With a quick swipe, she brushed the soot from her skirt before stepping back inside the chapel car. Though her father wasn't one to end a conversation until he was ready, she hoped her final remark would put an end to this discussion.

Her father followed on her heels as she navigated the narrow aisle that centered the rows of wooden pews in the chapel portion of the railcar. "You can walk away, but we aren't through talking, Hope." He pointed his thumb toward the window. "I shouldn't have given in and let you come with me. If I'd had time to consider the idea thoroughly, I would have insisted you remain in Pittsburgh."

She continued onward until she entered the cramped living quarters at the rear of the car. She squeezed through the slight space between the berths and dining table, sat down, and gestured for her father to take the seat opposite her. "I believe that if you weigh the good against the bad, you'll soon agree that this is where I should be, Papa. Besides, you agreed that you needed someone to help with the children, and while you're a gifted preacher, we both know that the Lord didn't grace you with an abundance of musical talent."

Her father grunted and lowered his lanky body into a chair and met her eyes. "That much is true. And having you along to play the organ and lead the singing will be a great help. But I've managed without you, thanks to the gramophone and an occasional volunteer in some of the towns. You've already proven your talents are useful to me and the church's ministry, but at what cost?" He shook his head. "I think you should return home. We're going to be in a mining town, where life will be quite different from anything you've ever experienced."

His words had been spoken with such conviction that Hope was left momentarily speechless. Eyes wide, she stared at him and waited to hear him recant the statement. But the only sound in the swaying car was the clacking of the wheels as the train labored up the forested hillside toward the next small town. When she could bear the silence no longer, she reached across the narrow table and clasped her father's rough hand. Not the hand one would expect of a preacher, but Layton Irvine had been a carpenter and builder before he'd accepted his first preaching position many years ago. Since then, his life had been as much about building churches as preaching in them. Each time he'd returned to visit Hope at Aunt Mattie's clapboard cottage in Pittsburgh, he'd repeated the same tale. The life of a traveling missionary wasn't acceptable for a growing young girl. And she'd accepted his explanation—until now. She was no longer a growing young girl, but a full-grown woman.

"What home would you have me go to, Papa? Aunt Mattie is dead, and we've disposed of her belongings. She didn't even own the house where we lived."

She was surprised to see a multitude of gray hairs appear when her father raked his fingers through his mass of wavy dark brown hair. "I know. I know." He waved toward the passing scenery. "But traveling on this chapel car with me isn't the answer. If you would return to Pittsburgh, I'm sure they'd rehire you at the department store. I'll stay long enough to help you get situated in an affordable boardinghouse. I imagine there are several located within walking distance of the store. If you don't have to ride the trolley to and from work, it will reduce your expenses so you can purchase some new bauble from time to time." He blew out a short breath. "And with your sweet disposition, you'll have no problem making friends with the other boarders."

Hope's stomach churned. Her father was talking as though she'd already agreed to his idea. No doubt his mention of her sweet disposition was an attempt to discourage any argument from her. While she understood his desire to protect her, she was far more likely to encounter difficulties living on her own in Pittsburgh than she would under his watchful eye. Instead of speaking of her desire to help him with his ministry, she decided to recount the perilous situations that sometimes confronted single young women working in the city.

"Papa, Pittsburgh is the last place I want to live. Even though I walked to the trolley stop in full daylight during the summer months, the sun was blocked by the haze caused by the surrounding steel mills. The city is blanketed in darkness both day and night. I'm sure you haven't forgotten the inescapable murky shadows that stretch over the streets in every direction." She'd spoken the truth, but hoped the word picture would convince her father. She didn't want him to feel guilty for leaving her with Aunt Mattie after her mother died eleven years ago. Hope had been only nine years old and he'd wanted her to have a stable life while she finished her schooling. But her education was complete, and Aunt Mattie was dead. Now, more than ever, she wanted to be with family. And he was her only family. Couldn't he see that she needed him?

When he didn't respond, she continued her graphic tale. "In the winter, it was even more frightening. The ice and snow made for treacherous walking, and more than once I was hounded by beggars. When I didn't toss them a coin, they shouted threats at me." In spite of the warmth inside the car, Hope shivered. It hadn't been necessary to embellish those encounters. Truth be told, fear had caused her to change her route to the trolley stop on several occasions.

"I didn't know. I'm so sorry." He bowed his head and stared at his weathered hands. "I'm still not convinced this is the best life for you, but I suppose I shouldn't let one incident sway me." He leaned back in his chair. "I want your assurance that you'll come and tell me if you encounter any sort of problems with men in the towns where we stop. And remember, even some of the men who work for the railroad can be a rough lot." He hesitated a moment. "I want you to tell me if any of them bother you in any way."

She nodded and smiled. "Thank you, Papa." She glanced through the door toward the rear of the train. "And I do hope you'll allow me to continue tossing tracts from the train until we arrive in Finch."

"We'll see." He turned his attention to the window. "This is Brookfield. We'll be stopping soon. The brakeman told me he was sure some of the railroad workers will want to attend a ten o'clock meeting after they finish their stint tonight. We'll need to be ready for an early meeting with the townsfolk tomorrow morning, as well. Our car will be pushed onto a spur once we arrive in Brookfield."

The distance from Pittsburgh to their final destination in Finch, West Virginia, was less than three hundred miles, but they'd already been traveling for more than a week. And from her father's account, they'd be traveling for at least two more weeks before they reached journey's end. She'd quickly learned their progress was determined by the railroad companies and their willingness to attach the chapel car to the rear of their trains. Most of the companies along the route from Pittsburgh to their final destination were more than willing—but at their convenience.

Hope sighed. "I didn't realize it was going to take us so long to get there. I'll need to do laundry while we're here."

Her father's eyebrows dipped low above his dark eyes. "Remember, we must be thankful for the cooperation of the railroad and make no complaints."

There was no choice but to accept these stopovers, yet it was difficult to remain thankful when they were pushed onto a spur for days at a time. Granted, such stops gave her father an opportunity to preach and minister to folks in the small towns along the way, but Hope was eager to reach Finch. Besides, being pushed onto the spurs could be painful. At one of their first stops after departing Pittsburgh, Hope had been awakened from a deep sleep when their car was switched during the night. The jarring motion had thrust her body forward and she'd banged her head against the end of her berth. A knot the size of a goose egg had emerged beneath her auburn hair and remained for days. Upon hearing her complain later in the day, one of the trainmen had been quick to tell her that those who traveled for free shouldn't complain.

After the worker marched off, her father had taken Hope aside and explained that when a chapel car was attached to a train, the railroad provided the service at no cost to the missionaries, and the rail passes that permitted them to ride for free were an act of goodwill offered by the railroad officials. She hadn't realized that a complaint about layovers or traveling conditions could result in the withdrawal of such charity. Since then she'd attempted to withhold her complaints, but occasionally she still slipped up.

Hope peered out the window as the fringes of the small town came into view. There was no telling exactly how long they'd be here. At extended layovers, her father would put his preaching and carpentering skills to work among the people, though Hope was eager to get to Finch where they would truly begin their work. Before accepting his assignment in Finch, her father had been advised the town was without a preacher and the need was great. He'd agreed to remain as long as the association believed his services were required in the small coal-mining town.

Although some of the chapel cars stopped for only a few days in each town before continuing onward, others remained for extended periods in areas where there was no church. Sometimes the chapel car preachers remained until a permanent parson arrived or until a church was constructed. According to Hope's father, a few of the preachers had remained in the same town for several years. She wasn't certain she wanted to live in Finch for years, but she was eager to be in one place for more than a few days.

"We'll hold services here at seven o'clock. Now, I'm going into town to see if there's a church and permanent preacher." Her father pointed out the window. "Looks like they'll move us onto that spur once the baggage is unloaded."

Hope pushed up from the table. "May I come with you? I can pass out tracts and invite folks to attend tonight's meeting. I didn't get many leaflets thrown from the train, so unless we go and invite folks, we may not have much of a turnout." She gave what she hoped was a convincing smile. "Besides, I'd like to see the town, and school should soon be out. It will give me a good opportunity to invite the children to my class."

She longed to do everything she could to prove her presence would be a help to him and to the chapel car ministry. Thus far, her father had been particularly pleased with her assistance in the musical portion of the services and with the children, but she also hoped to do her part to encourage attendance at their meetings.

Before Hope joined her father on the chapel car, the small organ that sat in a corner near the pulpit had remained silent, and her father had relied upon a gramophone to assist with the musical portion of the service. After one of their first services together, he said he thought folks came to hear her organ playing even more than to hear his sermon. Hope had been quick to say he was mistaken, yet his compliment had given her great joy. For so long she'd missed having her father near, and his praise had warmed her heart.

Each evening after she played the final strains of the closing hymn, Hope's thoughts shifted from music to the children. Her father enjoyed youngsters, but keeping them quiet in the cramped railcar was difficult, so he'd readily agreed to her proposed classes for the children. His consent had furthered her prospects of remaining with him and given her the opportunity to use the skills she'd acquired while teaching children at the church she and Aunt Mattie had attended each Sunday. Using Aunt Mattie's Bible teaching and the instruction she'd received in Sunday school and church, Hope's lessons with the youngsters had proved a success at their first stops.

She'd been especially thankful for Aunt Mattie's instruction to trust Jesus and find joy in all circumstances. That lesson had served Hope well during the first months after her own mother's death. And because of Aunt Mattie's teachings, Hope had been able to share and encourage several motherless children she'd met since their departure. She'd gone on to tell those children how Aunt Mattie would sit by her side while she read the Bible aloud each evening. Hope encouraged the older ones to read the Bible every day. While they likely didn't have an Aunt Mattie to sit alongside them, she told the children to think of God sitting at their side and to know He would be pleased with their devotion. Just as her faith had deepened through the years, she wanted the same for all of these children, especially those who had suffered loss and were hurting.

Her father gathered a stack of flyers and divided them in half. He smiled and nodded at one of the mounds. "You take those and I'll hand out the rest. Looks like we're going to have good weather for the rest of the day."

She nodded. "No need to ask about using the train station for my lesson with the children." On the rare occasions when the weather hadn't cooperated, they secured permission to meet in the train stations. But the clear skies and billowing clouds overhead indicated perfect weather.

Together, they stepped off the train and headed into town. Her father's tall frame still made her feel like a little girl when she walked at his side. She reached up and placed her hand in the crook of his arm. As they crossed the train tracks, she glanced about. After seeing those men at the tavern, Hope wasn't sure what to expect, but she was pleasantly surprised as she and her father walked the main street of town. Though few in number, the buildings that lined the brick street in the main portion of town were reasonably maintained. And, if one could judge from the wares displayed in the windows and crates in front of the Brookfield businesses, the stores were well-stocked.

Hope displayed a bright smile as they handed out tracts and visited with folks. When she spotted a young woman with two small children in tow, Hope asked for directions to the schoolhouse and inquired what time the children would be dismissed for the day. As four o'clock approached, she gained her father's approval and headed off toward the school located on the outskirts of town, with his admonition to be careful ringing in her ears.

The woman's directions had proved accurate, and Hope spied the schoolhouse in the distance—a rather small frame building in need of repair and a fresh coat of paint. She'd mention the project to her father. No doubt he'd have it in fine shape before they departed. While the few schools she'd visited since leaving Pittsburgh didn't resemble those she attended as a child, she soon learned that families placed a higher value on physical labor than education. Consequently, schools were constructed where they would gain maximum attendance from the surrounding farms and from the families living and working in the small towns.

The late April sun beat down with unseasonable warmth, and the scent of honeysuckle and lilac filled the air. Hope's shoes sunk into the soft ground as she trudged toward the school with her skirt swishing the tall grass. How she longed for the wide brim of her hat that had gone flying into the hands of those rowdy men earlier in the day. That hat would have blocked the sun from her eyes to perfection. Certain she heard voices in the distance, Hope stopped short and tented one hand above her eyes, then glanced toward a grove of pawpaw trees. There had been no ringing bell to announce the end of the school day, and there were no children in sight.

Her heart pulsed a beat that resounded in her ears. She tamped down her fear and glanced over her shoulder. There was no one in sight. She sighed in relief as she stepped forward. Likely she'd heard nothing more than some birds nesting in the trees. Keeping her attention fixed on the uneven ground, she started as a flash of red fabric flew in front of her and landed near her feet. Her hat!

She gasped and clutched the remaining flyers to her chest.

CHAPTER

2

Four men jumped from their hiding place among the trees and greeted her with loud guffaws. They pointed to the remains of her bedraggled hat lying on the ground. The wide claret ribbon that had formed a fan-shaped bow along one side of the hat now hung from the brim as a limp and lifeless reminder of the men's rough handling, serving as a warning of the treatment she might receive if she wasn't careful.

Hope's heart continued to race. She took a deep, calming breath. Best to keep a level head and begin with kindness. "Good afternoon, gentlemen. I see you've been checking on the pawpaws." She forced a smile. "Doesn't look like they're ripe just yet."

One of the men spit a stream of dark juice into the tall grass. "You know all about pawpaws, do ya?"

"I know they turn from green to brown as they ripen, and when you shake the tree, they'll fall to the ground if they're ripe. My aunt once told me that a pawpaw was ripe the day it hit the ground and was eaten by a raccoon."

The men burst into laughter, but their howls soon subsided.

The tallest of the foursome hooked his thumbs in the straps of his overalls. "You ain't from around these parts. We seen ya on the train."

She wanted to say that she'd seen him outside the saloon with her hat smashed on his head, but she didn't want to do anything that might stir them up. No doubt they still had plenty of liquor in their bellies. "I'm traveling with my father. He's a preacher and we've been holding church services in some of the towns we pass through. We're having services tonight down near the train station. You're all invited to join us."

"I'd like to join you, but not at no church meetin'," one of the men jeered. They jabbed each other in the sides with their elbows and once again broke into raucous laughter.

Hope ignored the remark and leaned down to pick up her hat. She tucked the ribbon inside the crown of the hat. With a bit of work she might be able to salvage enough ribbon to make the hat presentable, but that all depended on whether she could get away from these men.

"I hope you won't think me rude, but I need to get to the schoolhouse before the children head off to their homes." She prayed for enough courage to get by the men without incident.

Easing to her right to distance herself from the men, Hope took several steps forward. As if joined at the hip, the men moved in unison and stopped directly in front of her.

The tallest of the group ogled her with narrowed eyes. "No need to rush off, pretty lady. What's your name?" His lopsided smile revealed a row of uneven yellowed teeth, obviously discolored by the wad of tobacco pouched in his jaw.

Beads of perspiration trickled down her back, and in spite of the heat, Hope shivered. How was she going to get away? The thought had barely crossed her mind when the sounds of shouting children and the peal of the teacher's school bell rang through the afternoon air. When the men turned, Hope raced toward the school, waving the flyers overhead while calling to the children.

She'd expected to feel one of the men grab her wrist or catch her by the waist, but once she took flight, she didn't hesitate. Her shouts challenged the teacher's clanging bell. "Chapel car services tonight at the train station! Come get a flyer to take home to your parents!"

Soon she was surrounded by the children, all of them clamoring to learn more about the church service. Only then did she dare look back at the grove of pawpaw trees. While the men had disappeared from sight, she couldn't be sure if they'd merely returned to their hiding place or headed back to the saloon. Her stomach knotted. She'd soon need to retrace her steps, and those men could be waiting anywhere along the way.

"Good afternoon. I'm Lillian Stanley, the teacher here at Brookfield School."

Hope turned toward the soft voice. The quiet tone didn't match the sharp-featured woman with pale skin and eyes as dark as raisins. Her shoulders were held erect, and a few strands of gray colored her dark hair. "I'm pleased to meet you, Miss Stanley. I'm Hope Irvine. My father is a pastor assigned to the Herald of Hope chapel car. We're going to be in Brookfield for a few days and we'll be hosting church services. I hope you'll be able to attend." Hope stretched her arm in a wide arc to include the children. "All of you, as well as your parents." She extended one of the flyers in Miss Stanley's direction. "This tells a bit more about my father and the chapel car ministry."

While the teacher scanned the tract, the children scattered and hurried toward their homes.

Miss Stanley tapped the flyer. "I'm certain everyone will be delighted to have the chapel car visit us for a while. The pastor of the small church in town moved away almost a year ago, leaving a void in the town and surrounding farms. The church was the gathering place for community events. Seems no one is willing to organize anything now that the preacher's gone." She sighed. "Some of the farm wives thought I should try to organize some picnics and such, but my time is as busy as everyone else's during the school year. Once school is out for the summer, I plan to go home to visit my family, so I won't be around. But it would be wonderful if we could get a permanent preacher." She arched her brows. "Any chance you and your father might stay in Brookfield?"

Hope shook her head. "My father has a commitment to remain with the chapel car ministry, Miss Stanley, but I'm sure he'd be willing to send word of the need back home to the association headquarters. That might help. Why don't you come and talk with him after services this evening?"

Miss Stanley tucked the flyer into her pocket. "I'll plan to do just that. If you're not in any hurry to return to town, do you mind waiting until I've locked up the school and I'll walk with you?"

Hope nodded. Earlier, the arrival of the children had curtailed any further advances from the four raucous men. And now Miss Stanley would be at her side on the return to town. If the men were still hiding in the trees, she doubted they would show themselves since she wouldn't be alone. Her prayers had been answered.

She followed Miss Stanley up the two wooden steps into the schoolhouse. Rickety tables were being used as desks. Benches bordered the tables and looked as though they would collapse under the weight of more than one child. A broken window was covered with oilcloth, though Hope doubted it would keep out much rain. "Looks like the inside of the school is in need of repair as well as the outside." She immediately clapped her hand over her mouth. "I'm sorry. That was unkind."

Miss Stanley shrugged. "No need to apologize. You haven't said anything I haven't already told the school board. They say there's no money to repair anything right now, so we must make do. I'm hopeful they'll at least find sufficient funds to repair the window before next winter. Unfortunately, the school isn't much of a priority to the residents of the county."

"My father is an excellent carpenter. I'll speak to him and see if he can help."

They chatted and walked side by side until the rooftops of the buildings that fronted the main street of town came into view. Only then did the tension ease from Hope's stiff shoulders. Thankfully, there had been no sign of the four men on their return. She tightened her grasp on the brim of her upturned hat and moved it to her left hand.

The teacher pointed at the hat. "That's a beautiful color. A perfect match for your suit, though it appears the ribbon has come loose."

"Thank you. I'm hoping I can repair it." No need to tell Miss Stanley about her encounter with the bullies, especially since they'd safely arrived back in town.

The teacher waved toward a white clapboard two-story house near the far end of the street, not far from where they stood. "That's my boardinghouse, so I believe this is where we'll part ways. I'll see you this evening, and I look forward to speaking with your father about repairs to the schoolhouse."

"Oh, yes—of course, but you might want to arrive early. After services, he's sometimes busy talking to folks until time for the late meeting he holds for the railroad workers."

"Thank you. I'll be there by half past six at the latest." Miss

Stanley gestured toward Hope's hat. "I do hope you'll be able to fix the ribbon."

She realized then that her father would question how she'd regained possession of the hat. Hope wanted to keep it, but how could she? Her thoughts whirred as she searched for a solution that wouldn't be a lie. And then it came to her. She could tell him she'd found it lying on the ground on her way to the schoolhouse. After all, the hat did come flying from the trees and landed at her feet. A stretch of the truth? Perhaps, but still the truth. At least that was what she told herself.

.............ཻ.............

As expected, her father noticed the hat, but he'd easily accepted her explanation and had even accompanied her into the milliner's shop, where the owner quickly refashioned the ribbon and tacked it back in place. Though the bow wasn't exactly the same, it was far better than anything Hope could have re-created. Upon learning how the hat had been damaged, the shop owner refused payment.

"The opportunity to hear you preach will be compensation enough, Pastor Irvine. We've been praying for a new preacher for over a year now." The milliner arched her thin brows. "Maybe the Lord will reveal that this is the place where you should settle with your daughter and wife?"

Hope didn't miss the expectation in the woman's voice, nor did her father. He shook his head. "My wife died years ago, but my daughter and I will be continuing on to Finch for a period of time. I don't know where the chapel car ministry will take us from there. While we can't remain here, I'm pleased to have a short time to preach and pray with folks. Perhaps I can help with some necessary repairs to the church building so it will be in good condition when the Lord sends a preacher to Brookfield."

Though the shopkeeper appeared disappointed, she bid them a cheery farewell and promised to attend the evening service. Once outside, Hope slipped her hand into the crook of her father's arm. "When I was at the school today, I met Miss Stanley, the teacher." Hope detailed their conversation regarding the town's need for a preacher, as well as a list of repairs for the schoolhouse. "She's planning to come to the chapel car at six thirty and visit with you."

Her father slowed his stride and looked down at her. "I hope you didn't promise her that I would stay until they've located a preacher. While I can likely complete the repairs you've mentioned, we need to continue on our journey."

"I made no promises. I only said I would tell you of the problems, though I did say you might possibly write or telegraph the association headquarters and mention the need for a preacher." Her eyes met his. "Was that wrong of me?"

He shook his head. "No, that was an excellent answer, and I'll be happy to do at least that much. No town this size should be without at least one church where the folks can gather to worship. I look forward to meeting Miss Stanley."

When they returned to the chapel car, Hope glanced at the clock. She had planned to wash clothes, but the task would have to wait until tomorrow. For now, she needed to cook supper and then prepare her materials for the children's class.

She let out a sigh when she opened a cupboard and two metal lids tumbled to the floor. Rather than putting them in the rack where they belonged, she'd shoved them atop a small skillet after drying the dishes last night. *"A place for everything and everything in its place."* Her father's first instruction when she'd stepped into the chapel car had once again been affirmed. She knew the rule, but sometimes she simply didn't take time to wiggle and jiggle each pot, book, or jacket into its proper position.

While their railcar was certainly handsome and a worthy addition to any train, living in a space that measured only eighteen feet long required adjustments. She sometimes wondered whether a little more of the seventy-seven-foot chapel area would have been designated as living space if a woman had been in charge of the railcar's design. The toppling lids were a reminder that she needed to heed her father's rule. Stooping down, she picked up the two lids and carefully slid them into the wooden rack.

She'd already become accustomed to the wide-eyed stares of visitors when they viewed the compact quarters that accommodated their two berths, a dining room with fold-up table, a study with typewriter, desk and library, a kitchen with range and closet, an ice chest, pantry, wardrobe, toilet room, and a heater that was supposed to heat the entire car, though her father admitted it was a poor excuse for a heater. She hadn't asked him what they would do when winter arrived in West Virginia, for she feared it would give him even more reason to believe that she shouldn't travel with him.

Supper this evening would be simple—fried potatoes, eggs, and a small piece of ham. More like breakfast than supper, but her father never complained. He was always appreciative of anything she placed in front of him. For that she was grateful. And she was also grateful that as soon as she began her meal preparation, her father moved to the sanctuary of the chapel car to read his Bible, pray, or work on his next sermon.

She hummed as she peeled and sliced potatoes and then scooped them into a grease-coated iron skillet. When the potatoes were almost done, she fried a piece of ham and then cracked eggs into the sizzling skillet. Leaning toward the doorway that led to the sanctuary, she called to her father. "Time to set up the table, Papa."

He stepped into their living quarters, removed the table from behind his desk, and unfolded the legs. Moments later, they were seated at the small yet surprisingly sturdy table. Her father gave thanks for their meal and then forked a slice of potato. "You did a fine job in such a short time." He smiled across the table at her. "I've been praying that we'll have a good turnout this evening. How did the children respond? Did they appear eager to attend?"

She nodded. "Eager and curious. They all want to see the chapel car. They've never heard of such a thing, so they were very interested. I think we'll have a good number attend. Miss Stanley mentioned that many of them live on farms, so I don't know if their parents will be willing to hitch horses and wagons for the drive into town. I told them we would probably be here on Saturday and Sunday, as well. If they don't come this evening, I'm sure most of them will attend some time while we're here."

"I know I can't expect everyone to come to all of the meetings, but it would be nice, wouldn't it?" His eyes glistened with excitement. "I wish I could spend the time to preach of God's love at every stop on our journey."

"We would never arrive in Finch if we spent time at every stop, Papa." Hope sopped a piece of bread in the creamy egg yolk and put the bread into her mouth.

"I know, but I often wonder about the people in the towns we pass by." His words bore a note of melancholy that contradicted his smile. He pushed back from the table. "No time to fret about such things right now." He nodded toward the window. "Is that Miss Stanley approaching?"

"Yes." Hope stood. "Please go and greet her while I clear up the dishes. I don't want to have them waiting for me after the meeting tonight."

...............✿...............

When she finished the dishes and everything was back in its proper place, Hope retrieved her Sunday-school supplies from a box beneath her father's desk along with several tarps, then stepped from their living quarters into the chapel portion of the car. Her father and Miss Stanley sat on one of the pews near the rear.

"Don't let me interrupt. I'm going to find a shady spot and set up for the children."

She was thankful for the grassy area along the far side of the spur where their car had been moved while they were in town. When she spied honeysuckle vines climbing a nearby tree, she inhaled a deep breath. As soon as her arms weren't full, she'd pick one of the blooms and tuck it into the eyelet that trimmed her white high-collared blouse. The fragrant blossoms and the far-reaching tree branches provided a perfect place to spread the tarps. She couldn't ask for a better spot to conduct the children's class. After placing a stack of Sunday-school papers beneath her Bible, Hope plucked one of the blooms and tucked it into the eyelet. No doubt it would soon wither, but she could enjoy the scent as she sauntered back through the tall weeds and grasses. She swiped at the perspiration that trickled down the side of her face, thankful she'd left her suit jacket inside.

Her breath caught when she returned. The platform outside the train depot was filled with folks waiting to be directed to the chapel services. The conductor was sending them across the expanse of tracks, his forehead creased with irritation.

"Papa, are you still inside?" Hope glanced toward the rear platform of the train as she called to him.

Her father and Miss Stanley appeared moments later. After

one look at the depot platform, he loped down the steps and gestured to the rush of folks crossing the tracks. "Right this way!" He continued to wave them forward. "Children, remain with your parents or along the outside of the car until after the singing. Then you'll go with Miss Hope for your own special meeting."

Miss Stanley remained on the rear platform, and Hope hurried up the steps to join her. Miss Stanley followed her inside while Hope retrieved her jacket and hat. For this first meeting with the townsfolk, she wanted to be properly attired when she sat at the organ. After she'd pinned her hat in place, Hope turned to Miss Stanley. "I hope your meeting with my father went well."

"Your father is most kind. He's agreed to contact his supervisors in Pittsburgh to see if they can locate a preacher who might be willing to take over the church here in Brookfield." Her lips curved in a generous smile. "And he's going to come to the school tomorrow morning to see what he can do to help with repairs. He's hopeful that one of the merchants will agree to donate the necessary supplies to complete the work." She gave an approving nod when Hope pinned her hat in place. "The ribbon looks most attractive. I'm pleased to see you were able to repair it so quickly."

"The lovely bow is thanks to the owner of the millinery shop here. Wasn't that kind of her?"

"Indeed, it was." Miss Stanley stooped to look out one of the train windows. "I better choose my seat. It looks like the pews will soon be filled."

Hope took her seat at the organ, which sat adjacent to her father's pulpit at the front of the car. At each of their stops she'd enjoyed sitting on the small stool, watching the variety of people who poured through the car's narrow doorway. The early arrivals had first choice of seats, but there were always those who preferred to sit near the back—and those who wanted the first row. The oak pews were the same, except that those along one side were wide enough for three and the ones along the other were wide enough for only two, causing the view from the front of the car to appear somewhat lopsided.

From her vantage point, she could see a number of the older boys standing outside the car, but the younger children sat perched on the laps of their parents, anticipation etched on their faces. The youngsters had never before attended a church service inside a railroad car. Since the pews had filled, the remaining folks gathered on the train platform and along the outside where they could hear through the open windows.

Once her father had entered the car and was making his way down the narrow aisle, Hope gestured to the crowd. "There are hymnbooks in the racks beneath your seats. We'll begin with 'Rock of Ages' on page thirty-six." Hope waited for a moment, struck the opening chords, and in a clear soprano voice led the group through each verse of the hymn.

After the final verse had been sung, Hope stood and looked out over the crowd. "Children should file out the back of the car and join me outdoors for their lesson." She waited while the youngsters scooted from their parents' laps or off the wooden pews and made their way to the rear door.

After leading the children to the tarps spread beneath the nearby tree, Hope chose one young boy and one girl to hand out Sunday-school papers. "If you look at the back side of the paper, you'll see there's a story. Those of you who can read might want to follow along." Hope smiled at a group of younger children. "And those of you who haven't yet learned to read can listen with both ears." She touched her index finger first to her left ear and then the right.

"I promise I'll listen with both ears, too."

Hope jerked around toward the menacing voice. Her breathing turned shallow when she caught sight of the men who'd been hiding in the pawpaw grove. *Please, Lord, make them go away.*

Luke Hughes glanced at the hand-painted sign hanging over the front door of the store. Black-and-gold stenciled letters declared the business to be the Brookfield Department Store, a highfalutin name for what had been Waverly's General Store until just a few years ago. When a wealthy investor from Charleston purchased the place, he'd changed the name and hung the flashy new sign. Back then folks thought they'd soon see an expansion of the business and a greater offering of goods, but their expectations soon faded. The new manager, a fancy cash register, and a slight increase in prices had been the only changes. None had been welcome.

Truth be told, the locals now laughed at the pretentious name. While bustling cities boasted large department stores with sparkling displays and a bounty of merchandise, the goods for sale in the Brookfield store sat on newspaper-lined shelves or tumbled from wooden bins shoved into every nook and cranny. Luke yanked his hat from his head, raked his fingers through a thatch of light brown hair, and squinted his bottle-green eyes.

Had the sign been an inch lower, Luke would have had to duck his head to get inside the store without injury.

A lanky man with a pair of spectacles perched on the tip of his nose came from behind the counter and greeted Luke. "Need help finding something in particular?"

Luke nodded. The store might not be what folks had hoped for in Brookfield, but it offered far more than the company store run by the mining company in Finch. Over his twenty-two years, he'd been in this store only a handful of times.

Working and living in a coal-mining town meant using their credit and purchasing their goods at the company store. Seldom did any of the mining families have cash. Instead, the men's wages were allocated to pay the rent for their company-owned homes and toward their credit at the company store in Finch. Choices were limited and needed goods frequently unavailable, a fact the miners and their wives were forced to accept without complaint. But Luke wasn't willing to let his mother suffer simply because Finch didn't have what his sister needed to make a birthday gift, so he'd made the long train trip to Brookfield.

"I need a needle for my ma's sewing machine. It's a Success machine, if that matters," Luke added.

The man shook his head. "They're all pretty much the same." He crossed the store and picked up a tiny red packet with black print and waved it toward Luke. "They come two to a package. Can't break 'em up. Fifteen cents."

The man waited beside the shelf, apparently unwilling to carry the envelope back to the counter unless he was sure Luke was going to buy them.

"If you got nothing cheaper than fifteen cents, I'll take them."

The man frowned and strode back across the room, the floor-boards creaking beneath his black thick-soled shoes. "If I had anything cheaper, I would have said so." He slapped the packet onto the counter. "Anything else?"

"Fabric. For a dress." Luke turned to the bolts of cloth to his right. "My sister said to be sure it's material that can be washed and won't fade or shrink. If you have a rose color, she said that would be good. If not, maybe lavender or blue."

The man's smile was so tight, his lips nearly disappeared. He gestured for Luke to follow him. "I'm guessing you want the cheapest instead of the best quality?" A note of disdain tinged the question.

If he hadn't promised Nellie he would purchase the needles and fabric, he would have promptly marched out of the store. "If I wanted the best quality and highest prices, I'd go to Charleston, now wouldn't I?"

The man glared at Luke, who immediately regretted his rude response. He wasn't a man given to impolite behavior, but he'd met with one problem after another since arriving in Brookfield, and the merchant's comments had cut to the quick. The store owners in Brookfield made it clear they believed themselves better than the miners who worked in the local mining camps. And they could afford to be rude to the miners and their families. Little of their business depended on the loyalty of miners, who were required to purchase most of their necessities at the stores owned by the mining companies rather than at privately owned businesses.

The merchant stepped to an array of fabrics and nodded. "I'll leave you to make your decision."

Luke stared at the stacks of material. His knowledge of fabric was nonexistent. He was going to need help choosing what would be appropriate for a dress. He shouldn't have angered the merchant. He sighed as a woman about his mother's age drew near. She touched a piece of patterned fabric and smiled up at him. "Looking for something special?"

"It's a surprise for my mother's birthday." He glanced toward the merchant, who was busy helping another customer. "A fabric that can be easily cared for, in a rose or lavender shade."

The woman traced her hand down the stack of yard goods and tugged a piece from one of the piles. "These are end pieces from the bolt. They're always a few cents cheaper, so it's where I look first. How many yards do you need?"

He shoved his hand into his pocket and withdrew a folded piece of paper and handed it to the woman. Holding the end of the fabric in her right hand, she moved the fingers of her left hand further up the cloth, touched it to her nose, and stretched her right arm to full length. Luke frowned, uncertain why she would stretch and smell the fabric.

The woman had obviously noted his confusion and grinned at him. "The length from the tip of my nose to the end of my outstretched arm is one yard."

Luke had never heard of such a thing. "Is that a fact?" His tone was more skeptical than he'd intended, but the concept was somewhat difficult to believe.

The woman *tsk*ed and shook her head. "When Mr. Jennings measures the fabric on that yardstick nailed to his counter, you'll see I'm right." After six quick movements, she gave a nod. "There's a little over six yards in this one. He won't cut the end pieces so you'll have to pay for the extra, but it's still less expensive than paying full price for some of these. And the color is lovely." She held the cloth close to her face. "It will bring out the roses in your mother's cheeks."

Luke was certain it would take more than a bright pink dress to put color in his mother's cheeks, but perhaps the gift would momentarily erase the deep creases caused by years of worry and hard work. He hoped so.

He reached for the material and gathered it into his arm. "Thank you for your help."

He heard the woman's footfalls behind him as he walked to the counter and turned to look down at her when she moved alongside him. "I want to be here when you see that I'm correct about the measurements."

For the first time that day, Luke laughed aloud and placed the fabric on the sleek oak countertop. The two of them were still smiling when Mr. Jennings returned to the counter. Before Luke could speak, the woman placed her palm on the fabric. "Please measure this. It's from the stack of end pieces."

Mr. Jennings flashed the woman an annoyed look. "I know it's from the end pieces, Mrs. Goodson." He plied his hand through the material until he located the end of the piece and then carefully measured the fabric against the worn yardstick. "Six and seven-eighths yards. I don't cut end pieces. Seven cents a yard. Six cents for the seventh-eighths of a yard. Take it or leave it."

"I'll take it. And the needles." Luke pointed to the red packet sitting near the cash register.

Mr. Jennings heaved a long sigh. "I know you want the needles."

Mrs. Goodson nudged Luke. "Those are sewing-machine needles. Did you want regular sewing needles or needles for a machine?"

Mr. Jennings glared at Mrs. Goodson. "Are you hoping to take over as manager of the store?"

The woman straightened her shoulders until they were as stiff as a starched shirt. "Indeed I am not, but since I didn't see you offer this young man any assistance with the fabric, I doubted you'd helped him with anything else."

Mr. Jennings punched the cash register keys and pulled down

the lever. "That'll be seventy-five cents. Sixty cents for the fabric and fifteen cents for the needles."

Luke dug in his pocket, retrieved the necessary coins, and placed them on the counter.

"They were only twelve cents the last time I purchased them." Mrs. Goodson reached across the counter, picked up the packet, and pointed to a spot that had been scratched out and replaced with a new figure. "See here? They've raised the price. Everything in this store has gone up in price since the new owner took over. It's a sin the way they take advantage of poor folks."

Mr. Jennings wrapped the fabric and needle packet in brown paper and tied it with a piece of string before looking up. "If there's nothing else, please excuse me. I must go and find my Bible. I want to see if I can locate any passages that refer to my sinful nature."

Luke met the man's harsh look. "If you begin by reading Proverbs 29:7 or Proverbs 22:22, you'll discover only two of many verses that rebuke mistreatment of the poor." He turned and thanked Mrs. Goodson for her help, picked up the bundle, and rushed from the store.

If he hurried, he wouldn't miss the train. At least that was his silent prayer as he ran toward the depot. The tracks were close enough to the main street that he should have heard a whistle or rumbling of a train, and he'd not heard either. Missing the train would mean he'd be stuck in Brookfield for at least two days since the trains to Finch were limited. The railroad was willing to come in and hitch up the coal cars, but they didn't worry about keeping a regular schedule for passengers. Just like everything else in the coal camps, folks had to adjust—whether they liked it or not.

He yanked open the depot door and dashed across the room and out the far door to the platform. A trainman stood leaning against a metal post. "If you're lookin' for the train to Finch, there's no need to hurry. It's running late. You've got at least a half hour." The trainman nodded toward a spur on the other side of the tracks. "Probably got enough time to hear most of the preacher's sermon over at the chapel car if you've a mind to get some Bible teachin'." The man waved his hand toward the car. "They got so many folks over there, they can't fit 'em all inside."

Luke peered across the tracks, his eyes landing on the shiny black railroad car. A group of men and women packed the rear platform, and others had gathered outside near the open windows of the railcar. The late-afternoon sun glinted off the black car. He tented one hand above his eyes. *Herald of Hope* had been painted on the side of the car in fancy gold letters. Luke dropped his hand to his side and turned to the trainman. "Never heard tell of a chapel car."

The trainman spit a stream of brown tobacco juice onto the track bed and hiked a shoulder. "Me neither. Not until today. I ain't been over there, but one of the conductors told me it's a traveling church. He says a small part is set up as living quarters, and the larger end is like a church with pews and even an organ. I didn't believe him, but I heard the organ music a little while ago." He pushed his cap back on his head. "They're holding a late-night meeting for us railroaders who work the second shift. Think I'll go over and take a listen." He nudged Luke's arm. "You should go over. Might never get to see such a thing again. You'll be able to hear your train coming long before it gets here."

Luke stared across the expanse a moment longer and then nodded. "Think I'll take your advice." He stepped down onto the track bed and picked his way across the tracks. He shortened his long strides when he neared the car and looked for a space where he might draw close enough to see inside. He wanted to hear what the preacher had to say, but his curiosity to see pews and an organ inside a railroad car caused him to perch on his toes to gain a better view.

A hawk-nosed man peered down at him from the open window, and Luke took a backward step and moved to the rear of the car. He had hoped there might be a little space so he could get a look inside, but even the iron rail surrounding the rear platform had become makeshift seats for several men. He circled to the other side of the car and located a spot where he could hear the preacher, though he couldn't see inside. He'd not been there very long when the sound of children's laughter drifted from a grove of nearby trees.

A young woman wearing a ruffled white shirtwaist, deep maroon skirt, and matching hat moved among the group of children, her face alight with amusement. His breath caught. Though she appeared strangely out of place, wading through the overgrown grass and weeds in her fancy hat, her loveliness was unexpected. Was this the wife of the preacher? She didn't appear much more than eighteen or nineteen, perhaps younger. But the pastor might be a young man, as well. From his earlier vantage points alongside the chapel car, Luke hadn't gained a view of the preacher.

He strained forward, hoping to hear what she was teaching the children, but decided against moving any closer. He didn't want to cause a disturbance now that the children had ceased laughing and were listening to her every word. Maybe if he backed away, he could return to the chapel car and hear a little more of the preacher's sermon. Besides, he'd like to get a look at the man fortunate enough to win the hand of such a beautiful young bride.

He'd taken only a few backward steps when two men poked

their heads above a stand of elderberry bushes. The young woman gasped, then frowned deeply.

The two men came around the bush, and the taller man moved closer. "I see you got your hat all fixed up real fine. My friend thought he'd like to try it on for size."

The other man guffawed, yanked off a dirty cap, and ran his fingers through matted brown hair. "I always did think I'd look purty in a nice red hat."

The men started toward the young woman. She straightened her shoulders and pointed at them. "Stay right where you are."

The taller of the two took another menacing step in her direction, and one of the boys cupped his hands to his mouth and shouted toward the train. "Hey, Pa, Samuel Fields and his brother are out here. Come and take them inside the train. I think they're lookin' to find Jesus."

The boy's effort was valiant, but his small voice went unheeded across the distance. The shorter of the two turned his gaze toward the boy. "We ain't lookin' to find Jesus, Johnny Wilson, so shut your trap afore I shut it for ya."

The young woman appeared to bristle at the man's remark, and she took a step toward the men. "How dare you speak to a youngster in such a mean-spirited manner."

Luke grimaced. If she wasn't careful, she was going to be within arm's distance of the men. He could see that she needed more help than a group of young children could offer.

He rushed forward. His pulse pounded in his temples. What would he do if the men didn't take off running? "Get out of here!" His voice boomed across the short expanse.

Startled, the two men backed up, but then stopped and eyed Luke. The shorter one grinned. "What you gonna do if we don't? There's two of us. You think you can handle us both?"

Luke strode past the teacher and group of children. He should have thought this out before he made his move, but he couldn't back down now. He took several long strides toward the men, then shoved his right hand beneath his jacket and let it rest there. Eyes narrowed, he tightened his jaw and hoped he looked more forbidding than he felt.

When he was close enough for the men to hear him speak in a low voice, he nodded toward his right hand. "I don't want to pull this gun in front of the children. I'd hate to shoot one of you with these youngsters looking on. It might scar them for life." He arched his brows. "'Course it would do more than scar you."

The taller man glowered. "You can't shoot us both afore we take ya down."

"Trouble is, you don't know which one of you I plan to shoot. At this distance, I might even be able to get both of you before we're done." Luke kept his eyes fastened on the men. "I think both of you need to turn around, go home, and sober up before someone gets hurt real bad." They hesitated and glanced at each other. Luke gave another nod toward his right hand. "Go on now, before the church service ends and those men inside discover what you're up to out here."

The two of them mumbled, turned, and ambled away. Luke sighed and let his hand drop from beneath his jacket. What would he have done if they had called his bluff?

A train hooted in the distance, and Luke glanced over his shoulder at the young woman. "Your husband should keep a better lookout for you, ma'am."

Before she could reply, he loped through the field and crossed the tracks toward the depot.

CHAPTER

4

Kirby Finch stood in front of the building in downtown Pittsburgh that housed the offices of Finch Mining and Company. From an early age, Kirby had known he was expected to become the "and Company" portion of the business. Back then he hadn't aspired to fill the position. He still didn't. While he enjoyed the benefits that his father's business afforded him, Kirby had no interest in the company. Or in work of any sort, for that matter.

He much preferred to spend his days and evenings partaking in amusements of various sorts, primarily gambling—an illegal activity, yet one at which Kirby excelled. At least most of the time. He cared little whether it was horse racing, playing cards, or wagering on fisticuffs.

Kirby turned to the policeman, who remained close to his side. "You sure we can't work something out? If you wait down here, I'll be back in no time with the money to cover my fine."

The officer shook his head. "The only reason you were released is because your father is Milton Finch. If it was my son who'd broken the law, he'd be in jail until I put up the money to bail him out."

There was enough bitterness in his voice that Kirby didn't argue further. Side by side, the two of them ascended the marble steps leading to his father's office. This wasn't going to be pleasant. Kirby's last escapade had resulted in an ultimatum from his father. If he couldn't convince his father otherwise, Kirby would be on a train to Finch, West Virginia, in the very near future.

The policeman knocked on his father's office door, then nodded to Kirby. "Don't just stand there. You heard him say 'come in' and so did I."

Kirby turned the brass doorknob and forced a broad smile. His father's expression of pleasure swiftly turned to one of surprise and then anger. He pushed away from his desk and closed the distance between them in record time. His eyes burned with rage. "What have you done now, Kirby?" His attention moved from Kirby and lingered on the policeman.

The officer released his grasp on Kirby's arm. "Your son was among a group of men who were gambling in the back room of an establishment on Penn Avenue. We got a tip there were some high-stake games taking place most every afternoon. Guess they thought we wouldn't suspect anything illegal was going on before dark." He shook his head. "We're not as uninformed as most criminals think we are."

Milton Finch's jaw twitched. "So you were arrested? For gambling? Again?" He punched each question like an angry boxer going for a knockout.

"So long as I pay the fine, the judge says he'll release me to your supervision. I assured the judge he won't see me in court again. I've learned my lesson. I promise it won't happen anymore, Father."

"I've heard that promise before. I'll pay the fine, but this time you'll pay the consequences of your behavior." He turned to the policeman. "How much? I'll write out a check to the court."

Minutes later, the policeman tucked the check into his pocket and strode past Kirby on his way out the door. Kirby hesitated, uncertain whether he should sit down before being invited.

His father shoved his large leather-clad checkbook into the center drawer of his massive desk. "Don't just stand there staring out the window. Sit down. We're going to have a long talk about your future."

Kirby dropped into one of the chairs opposite his father. "I know it's time for me to take hold and do my part."

"Stop right there, Kirby. You're not going to smooth-talk yourself out of trouble this time. The last time you got yourself into trouble, I told you to be prepared to make a move to our coal mine in West Virginia. I plan to keep that promise." He leaned back in the chair and folded his hands across his midsection. "I'm going to send you down there to work. There's unrest brewing among the miners. Maybe you can help discover who's causing the problem. We can't afford a strike, and I sure don't want the union coming in there and organizing the men. You've proved you're talented in sniffing out illegal activity. Let's see if you can use that same ability to find out who's causing the trouble in Finch."

Kirby drew in a sharp breath and prepared to battle the decision, but his father immediately waved him to silence.

"I'm not changing my mind. You can argue as long as you like, but you'll be on a train to Finch by week's end."

"Since I'm being forced to leave home, I'm sure you'll want to increase my wages."

His father laughed. "Quite the opposite. You'll be paid only enough to cover room and board with a little extra to purchase necessities, but not enough to bankroll your gambling habit."

THE CHAPEL CAR BRIDE

"That isn't a fair exchange. I'm being sent off to live in a boardinghouse with strangers in a town where I don't know a soul, and now you tell me you're going to pay me next to nothing."

"What isn't fair is the way you've squandered every cent you've been given since coming to work for the company. You've never given me an honest day's work, and now you complain I'm being unfair." His father shrugged. "If you don't like the arrangement, you can go out there and make your own way in the world."

Kirby winced. He couldn't carve out a place in the world. He didn't even have enough money to buy his dinner. If only he'd saved a portion of the wages he'd been paid since coming to work for his father. But he hadn't—not a cent. And now he'd pay the price for his careless choices and illegal activities.

"How long do I have to stay there?" Kirby rubbed the kink in his neck.

His father stood. "Until the problems are solved."

...............ૠ...............

Hope fretted for the five additional days that she and her father remained in Brookfield. With each passing day, her fears had deepened. If her father learned of her encounters with the local hooligans, she had no idea what he might decide about her future. Every time she taught the children, she felt more assured that she belonged at her father's side doing the Lord's work and she didn't want that to change. Two days ago, the railroad company offered to hook the chapel car onto a train going to Finch, but her father had refused. He'd promised to complete the much-needed repairs at the schoolhouse before they departed. And her father wasn't a man who would break his word.

Today the chapel car had been moved from the spur and coupled with a train going to Finch. Hope wouldn't breathe a sigh of relief until the train had departed the station. Her father exited their car and stepped to the rear platform. He gestured to several of the workers and called out his thanks for joining their car to the train. One of the men chuckled and shook his head. "You shoulda let us hook you up to the train going to Finch a couple days ago. This here locomotive couldn't pull a settin' hen off her nest. Gonna take you a lot longer to get through the mountains." He tipped his cap. "Good luck to ya. Enjoyed your sermons and hope to hear ya preach again. You maybe oughta whisper a few prayers afore you head up those mountain passes."

Another trainman nudged his friend in the side. "Stop trying to scare him, Henry. Ain't no snow this time of year, so they'll get through the passes just fine. Maybe a little slower than most, but just fine."

The men's banter could be heard through the open windows of the chapel car. Hope winced. She had hoped to relax once the train left Brookfield, but now she wondered if they'd ever make it to Finch.

The train belched a cloud of black smoke that slowly drifted to the rear of the train and through the open window. A long whistle signaled their departure as the chapel car lurched, jerking Hope forward. Her father held tight to the iron railing while he stepped inside and dropped into his chair. "Well, we're on our way." As the train chugged away from the station, he shot her a bright smile. "I thought you'd be singing for joy." His smile faded. "Something troubling you?"

"Didn't you hear the men at the station? It sounds as though the locomotive on this train is far from reliable. What if we get stuck in the mountains?"

"Those trainmen were joking. We may not arrive in Finch as quickly as we might have with another locomotive pulling us, but we'll arrive safe and sound. You can use the time to prepare some new lessons. We'll be in Finch for some time, and you won't want the children to tire of hearing the same stories over and over."

Hope opened the desk and flicked through the folders her father had received from the ministry headquarters. She clasped her hand around a bulging folder labeled CHILDREN and lifted it from the drawer. Along with the preprinted tracts and lessons, there were designs to make crafts as well as short skits for children to perform. Unlike their other stops along the way, they'd be in Finch long enough to make use of these ideas. Her excitement mounted as she considered the possibility of the children performing a Christmas pageant, or the joy they'd experience giving their mother or father some special gift they made in her Sunday-school class.

Images of the success she would have once they were able to establish a routine in the mining town flashed before her. She pictured towheaded boys and girls dressed in their Sunday best, flocking to the chapel car. Or maybe there would be a church like the one in Brookfield that was in need of a preacher to fill the pulpit. Wouldn't that be grand! Folks wouldn't have to squeeze into the chapel car for meetings, and she might even have a special room where she could teach the children.

The train slowed and panted for new life before gradually chugging up another steep incline. With each ascent, Hope's breathing turned shallow. When they finally arrived at the top, she blew out a breath. "I hope that's the last mountain. I don't think this train will make another climb."

Her father gestured for her to turn and look out the window. "I believe we're coming down into Finch right now."

Hope twisted around in her seat and peered out the window during their descent. "Look at those houses. They look like they're clinging to the side of the hill. I'm amazed they don't topple over and wash away in a rainstorm."

Her father closed his Bible and put it inside the desk. "I'm sure they're quite safe. Some of them have probably been on that hillside for many years."

No doubt he was right, but the ramshackle wooden houses looked no stronger than a row of matchsticks. There was nothing appealing about the sight, and she now wondered if the main portion of the town would be any more attractive. Their earlier stops had been in small towns, most of them somewhat impoverished, but they'd all had access to the main rail lines and weren't so isolated. This coal camp was serviced by only one railroad trunk line, which catered to the coal company rather than to passengers. Of course, the coal camp was the end of the line and they'd come through only one other small town on the way. Still, Hope hadn't expected to be surrounded by nothing but wilderness. Her father had assured her there were other small communities to the north and south, yet she wondered if he was merely attempting to appease her worries.

Hope smiled weakly. "Looks like we're in for quite an adventure. Somehow it feels as though we've departed civilization."

Her father chuckled. "I wouldn't go quite that far. I'm sure we'll both have a bit of an adjustment, but I think folks here will be much the same as those we've encountered since leaving Pittsburgh—glad to have a preacher and his daughter arrive in town."

When they'd departed Brookfield, she hoped they might move into a real house and temporarily leave their cramped quarters in the chapel car. However, one look at the wooden houses perched on the surrounding hillsides had changed her mind. Their limited space on the railroad tracks wouldn't be as worrisome as living in one of those houses.

A loud hoot announced their arrival, and soon one of the trainmen stepped into their car. He nodded toward the depot. "Not much of a station here." He shot them a wry look. "'Course it ain't much of a town neither, but I guess you knowed that or you woulda gone somewhere else. Just wanted to let ya know we'll be moving your car onto that spur before we load the coal cars and head out. If ya don't want to suffer through all the jostling, ya could take a walk into the main part of town. Ain't much to look at, but ya might meet a few folks at the company store."

Hope stood and reached for her father's hand. "Oh, please, let's go, Papa. I need to stretch my legs for a while. We can hand out leaflets to folks while we're walking through town." Before her father could answer, she stepped to a storage crate near the desk and removed a handful of the flyers.

Her father pushed up from his chair, retrieved his hat, and grinned at the trainman. "It looks as though we're going into town."

The worker tipped his hat before jumping down from the car. "Next time the train's in Finch, I'll try to attend a meetin'. You folks take care." After shouting his parting words, he scuttled off and disappeared from sight.

Hope handed the flyers to her father, then pinned her hat into place and made a futile attempt to finger-press the creases from her skirt. She sighed. After sitting for several hours, wrinkles were to be expected. Perhaps the walk into town would relax the fabric a bit. She wanted to make a favorable impression upon their new neighbors, but not enough to take time and change or press the offending creases from her skirt.

Not far from the train depot, they made a left turn onto the county road that had developed into the main street of Finch, as well. Hope scanned the crooked line of wooden structures that constituted the Finch business district. It was a far cry from Pittsburgh. Instead of bustling into the new century, Finch looked as if it had ceased progress decades ago. Her stomach tightened. The other small towns on their route between Pittsburgh and Finch hadn't offered the amenities of a large city, but she'd observed a sense of pride in the communities and an urgency to expand and grow. Finch appeared tired and worn, like an abandoned settlement left to die a slow death.

Hope circled around a deep rut in the road. "From the look of things around here, folks don't take much pride in their town."

"There's usually a reason, my dear. Perhaps folks don't have the funds to keep their homes or businesses in good repair. My carpentry skills can be put to good use here in Finch. I think the Lord is providing me with an opportunity to become acquainted with lots of folks who need help."

"I suppose that's a good way to look at things, but it would take a lifetime for one man to get this town presentable." She looked toward the houses perched on the hillside. "And another lifetime to get those houses repaired and painted." She gave her father a sideward glance. "But knowing you, I'm sure you'll do your best to get it all done in less than a month."

"Oh, I think I'll need at least six weeks." Her father's laughter was contagious, and Hope joined in. He lightly grasped her elbow and directed her to the other side of the street. "Let's begin at the general store." A wooden sign hung at a lopsided angle over the front door. Chipped white paint announced they were about to enter the Finch General Store.

Hope leaned close and kept her voice low. "I hope the inside is in better condition than the outside."

Her father patted her hand. "We need to have a spirit of

kindness, my dear. Over the years I've discovered that most folks do the best they can with what they're given. We won't win the hearts of people if we are critical, now, will we?"

Heat rose in her cheeks. With his quiet comment, he was reminding her why they'd come to Finch. For her to point out shortcomings was neither helpful nor becoming. "I'm sorry, Papa. You're right."

"No need to apologize. Finch can't compare to Pittsburgh, but you must remember I warned you that life would be very different and much more difficult."

She bowed her head in a slight nod. How could she forget the cautionary tales her father had spun as he'd attempted to deter her from joining him? Hope had initially decided his claims of a difficult life in the railcar and small towns were exaggerated and she'd quickly pushed them from her mind. While life in the railcar hadn't been particularly pleasant, living in this town might prove to be more of a challenge. A thought she would keep to herself.

Once inside, her father glanced around the store, then turned to Hope. "Do you see the proprietor?"

Hope craned her neck to the left and then to the right before moving toward the right side of the store. "I don't see any customers, either." She gestured to the left side of the building. "Why don't you go that way and I'll look over here?"

She'd passed the canned goods and fabrics when she heard her father's voice. Apparently he'd located the owner. She soon found the men and stepped to her father's side. He looked at the older gentleman. "This is my daughter, Hope. Mr. Woodbine." He looked down at her. "Mr. Woodbine owns the general store, so you'll be seeing him when you purchase our supplies."

"It's a pleasure to meet you. I'm sure I'll enjoy doing business here, Mr. Woodbine. It looks like we've come at an opportune time since you're not particularly busy." She glanced toward the counter at the front of the store. "Perhaps we could leave some of our flyers on the counter and you could give them to your customers."

Her father cleared his throat, and Hope turned toward him. His forehead creased into tight wrinkles, his brows dropping low. She'd obviously overstepped.

She inhaled a deep breath. "Why don't I look around the store while you and Mr. Woodbine finish your conversation?"

Her father reached inside his jacket and withdrew an envelope. "Better yet, take this to the post office and mail it for me." He handed her the envelope and two one-cent coins to purchase a stamp. "Mr. Woodbine tells me the post office isn't far."

Thrusting his thumb toward the far wall, the older man gestured to the west. "Jest go outside, turn in the opposite direction of the train depot and keep walking until you see the sign. It's on the other side of the street. You'll pass the livery and hotel afore ya get there."

"Shall I return here after I've posted your letter? Or perhaps I should stop at some of the other shops and ask to leave our pamphlets?" Hope tucked the change into her pocket and looked up at her father.

"That will be fine, but stay on Main Street so I can find you when I've finished speaking to Mr. Woodbine."

The store owner laughed. "This ain't no big city, Preacher. Most any business you want to visit is on Main Street." He hesitated a moment. "'Course you might want to take your preachin' to some of the folks who frequent the speakeasies outside of the small towns in these parts. Liquor's not legal anymore so they say there's only dancin' and such going on, but I think they may enjoy a little moonshine, too." He winked at the preacher.

"I may want to visit those establishments in the future, but I don't want my daughter inside such places." He turned a stern look on her. "You understand, Hope?"

"Of course, Papa." After her problem with the hooligans in Brookfield, Hope wasn't about to chance a meeting with men who might be drinking liquor.

Pamphlets in hand, she lifted them in a quick wave and strode outdoors. The afternoon sun was bright for springtime and warmed her back as she headed off toward the post office. Along the way she stopped at the bank, a barber shop, and several other small shops where, along with her flyers, news of their arrival had been welcomed.

Like most folks they'd met on their journey, the residents of Finch had never heard of a chapel car. She invited them to attend the meeting that evening and remained patient as she responded to the same questions she'd answered at each stop along the way. After walking farther than she'd anticipated, Hope wondered if Mr. Woodbine had played a trick on her. She'd passed the livery and the hotel, but she still hadn't seen the post office. She was about to ask an approaching young woman when she spotted the structure tucked between a boardinghouse and a hardware store.

If her father hadn't met her by the time she left the post office, she would stop at both places once she posted his letter. Unlike Pittsburgh, there was no line at the Finch post office, and it took only a few minutes to purchase her stamp and mail the letter. Her request to place a small stack of flyers in the business was met with enthusiasm. She departed, pleased with the reactions she'd received thus far.

She was intently counting the number of flyers in her hand when she approached the hardware store and didn't notice the rakes and shovels leaning against several wheelbarrows outside the store. Her foot came down on the tines of a rake that instantly popped forward, hit her head, and then sent the remaining rakes and shovels clattering to the wooden sidewalk.

Her hat tipped to the side as she rubbed the lump that was now rising on her temple with one hand and reached down to retrieve one of the fallen rakes with her other.

"Trouble seems to find you wherever you go, doesn't it?"

Hope looked up and was met by a lopsided grin and eyes the color of lush spring grass. Her head throbbed. She'd seen this man before, but where?

He stooped down, picked up the rakes and shovels, and leaned them against one of the wheelbarrows. "You met up with some trouble in Brookfield, too."

She gasped. This was the man who had chased off the ruffians. "I remember who you are. You hurried off before I could thank you for helping me while I was teaching the children in Brookfield."

He nodded and picked up several rakes. "Luke Hughes."

"Hope Irvine," she said with a slender smile.

"Nice to meet you. I rushed off because I didn't want to miss my train. I live here." He glanced toward the hardware store. "Well, not here. I mean, I don't live in the hardware store. I live in Finch."

She giggled, but her laughter caused a sharp pain in her head. She touched the tips of her fingers to her temple. "I believe I'm going to have a terrible headache."

He leaned closer to her. "You may have more than a headache. Given the size of the lump and where the rake hit you, I think you may have a black eye by evening."

"Oh, no. How awful. What will people think if they see me with a black eye at the meeting tonight?"

He grinned. "Your husband's a preacher. I doubt they'll think he's at fault. Maybe you can tell folks what happened before you begin the singing."

She massaged her temple and stared at him. He wasn't making any sense. Had the blow to her head muddled her brain? "My husband? Whatever are you talking about?"

CHAPTER

5

Luke looked deep into the young woman's eyes. Maybe she needed medical attention. Her memory seemed flawed. She had recalled who he was, yet confusion had taken hold when he mentioned her husband.

He frowned and continued to stare at her. "Maybe you should see a doctor." He pointed down the street. "Doc Burch might be in his office. I can walk you over there. If he's not around, maybe you should go back and rest."

"Unless the doctor can do something to make this lump disappear or stop the possibility of a black eye, I don't think I need to see him." She touched her hair. "I'm not bleeding, am I?"

"No." He leaned down and swooped up her hat, brushed a smudge of dirt from the brim, and handed it to her. "At least not that I can see. Would you like me to take a closer look?" He lifted his hand toward her mane of reddish-brown curls.

She pulled back a step.

"Watch out!" Luke pointed at the tools he'd restacked only minutes earlier. "Sorry. I thought you wanted me to check if you were bleeding. I didn't mean to be forward." Hoping to assure her, he shoved his hand into his pants pocket. "Where's your husband? I can fetch him if you'd like."

Hope sighed and gave a slight shake of her head. "Why do you keep asking about my husband? I don't have a husband."

For a moment he remained silent and attempted to digest what she'd said. It made no sense. A proper young lady wouldn't be traveling alone with a man who wasn't her husband, and a preacher wouldn't bring along a woman who wasn't his wife, would he?

"You're not married and you're traveling with a man? Without a chaperone?"

He shouldn't have been so bold, but she needed to know that folks living in the hills of West Virginia would be as disapproving as those living in large cities. Hadn't she and the preacher encountered any questions before now? Or had people simply assumed they were married? Was he the first to ask? He lowered his eyes to look at her ring finger. She was wearing gloves, but he didn't see any sign of a ring beneath the cotton fabric.

"I hope you won't fault me for accompanying my father without a chaperone." Red splotches colored her cheeks, but there was a defiant tone to her voice. She lifted the flower-bedecked hat to her head and gave a firm tug to its brim.

Her explanation left him momentarily speechless. Luke hadn't been able to get a close look at the preacher back in Brookfield. He simply assumed the preacher was her husband. Embarrassment seized him, but was quickly replaced by a sense of unexpected exhilaration. This lovely young woman wasn't married—wasn't even betrothed. At least he didn't think she was. There he went again, jumping to conclusions.

"I-I'm very sorry." He bowed his head. "I hope you'll accept my apology and we can start over." He looked up and grinned. "Maybe become friends? I'd be happy to show you around town."

"From what Mr. Woodbine over at the general store told me, a grand tour won't be necessary. He said all the businesses except a couple of taverns are located right here on Main Street."

"That's true, but there's more to Finch than Main Street. I thought you might want to meet some of the folks who live here." Luke gestured toward the hillside. "Of course, there's the mine, but I don't think you'll want to spend much time there. You'd get pretty dirty if you went over there to do any visiting. Besides, management frowns on uninvited visitors."

"Hope!"

Miss Irvine turned and waved at the tall gentleman striding toward them. The man's eyes narrowed as he drew near her side and looked at him. Concern etched his face. "I hope there isn't any problem?"

Hope shrugged. "Not unless you consider knocking over a pile of shovels and rakes a problem."

Her father let out a short gasp and turned toward the window of the hardware store. "I'm pleased to see there's no broken glass." He offered Luke a narrow smile. "If there are any damages, I'll take care of them for my daughter."

Luke shook his head. "I don't own the store. I don't even work here. I just happened to come along when the mishap occurred and I offered a bit of help." He tapped his finger to his temple. "Your daughter took a good hit to the side of her head. I figure she's gonna have a pretty bad headache and maybe a black eye, but she said she didn't want to see the doc."

The preacher twisted around and lifted his hand to his daughter's head. "Let me see, Hope." He frowned. "I believe Mr. . . . ." He extended his hand toward Luke. "We haven't even met, have we? I'm Pastor Layton Irvine. And you are?"

"Luke. Luke Hughes. I work for the mining company. My family lives up there." He nodded toward the hillside.

"Well, thank you for coming to my daughter's assistance, Mr. Hughes. We've brought our chapel car and hope to hold meetings . . ."

Hope touched her father's arm and stayed him. "He knows, Papa. Mr. Hughes was in Brookfield when you were holding meetings there."

"Ah, well that's good to know. Perhaps you can help us spread the word to your friends and neighbors that we'll be holding a meeting tonight at the chapel car. It's short notice, but we'd like to begin our ministry as soon as possible. If the folks who attend tonight enjoy the meeting, I hope they'll encourage others to come in the future."

Luke smiled. "I'll do what I can, Preacher, but you need to know that folks around here don't take to strangers. There's only a few reasons for anyone to come to Finch, so folks are mighty suspicious of new arrivals."

"I'd like to learn whatever you're willing to share about the town and the folks who live here, Mr. Hughes."

Luke pushed his cap back on his head. "If you call me Luke instead of Mr. Hughes, I'll tell ya what I can."

"Agreed," the preacher said. "If you have time, we could go back to the chapel car and visit." He glanced at his daughter. "And you, my dear, can rest and perhaps take some headache powders." He patted Hope's arm. "I'm hopeful you'll be able to help with the music this evening, and teach the children."

"I don't need to rest, Papa, and I'll have no problem conducting classes for the children this evening. You're going to discover I have more resilience and determination than most women."

Luke glanced at Hope. She'd directed a smile at her father, but Luke didn't miss the grimace that followed. There was little doubt she was in pain. Did she believe revealing her discomfort made her appear weak? He'd judged her to be a meek and obedient young woman, but perhaps he was mistaken.

"What about it, Luke? Do you have time to visit with us?" The preacher arched his brows.

Luke accepted the invitation. He wanted to remain in Miss Irvine's company, but if her father had his way, Hope would likely go off to rest once they returned to the chapel car. Still, he knew the preacher would be more quickly accepted in Finch if he had an understanding of the challenges he'd encounter, and he wanted to do all he could to help the people of this town find hope in the Lord. Luke decided to do his best to explain things. And if he was completely honest with himself, he wanted the opportunity to get to know Miss Irvine much better.

On the walk back to the train station, the preacher detailed their journey from Pittsburgh to Finch. "The two of you must enjoy traveling. What other states have you visited, Miss Irvine?"

Before she could answer, the preacher shook his head. "This is the first time Hope has traveled with me." There wasn't time for further explanation before they crossed the railroad tracks and reached the spur where the crew had placed the chapel car.

Eager to see the inside of the railcar, Luke followed the preacher and his daughter up the steps. "As you can see, this is the portion where we hold our meetings." He chuckled. "I forgot, you saw all of this in Brookfield, didn't you?"

Luke shook his head. "No, the car was already full up when I arrived. I got a glimpse from outside but never was able to see much." He looked around, amazed at the sight. "This is really something. Looks like you can fit sixty or seventy people in here." He pointed to the wooden lectern and small organ. "Hard to believe you can get everything in here. It's just like a church, only a little more cramped."

The preacher laughed. "Folks are a lot more crowded in here, and when winter arrives, it's too cold for the children to have their classes outdoors. When I'm in a town for the winter, I try to find an empty building to use if there's no church." He gestured for Luke to follow him. "Is there a church in Finch?"

"There was up until about five years ago when we had a fire that destroyed it. There's nothing much left. Nobody made any effort to rebuild since we never could get a preacher to stay for more than a month or two. Outsiders aren't easily accepted in these parts, not even preachers."

The pastor pointed to one of the chairs tucked into their living quarters and motioned for Luke to sit down. Luke didn't want to gawk, but it was hard not to try to figure out how two people could live in such a small space. It appeared there was something tucked away above and below every piece of furniture.

"Why is that, Luke?"

His breath caught when Hope passed by him. The preacher cleared his throat, and Luke pulled his attention away from the young woman. "Why is what?"

The preacher's glance traveled to his daughter, then back to Luke. "Why don't folks trust outsiders?"

Luke bobbed his head. "Oh, right. Outsiders. Most strangers who show up in Finch are men looking for work in the mines. You've come from Pittsburgh so you must know there's not as much need for coal right now, meaning the owners have cut production. The men in the office tell us it's called a financial downturn and that it's all over the country, not just here in West Virginia. Anyway, most of us have had our hours cut and work only two or three days a week."

The preacher leaned forward. "Makes it hard to survive, doesn't it?"

"Sure does. And some men don't just get their hours cut, they lose their jobs. It's the same in all the mines around here. So when a miner loses his job, he goes looking at other mining towns. The miners in Finch don't want any outsiders coming in and maybe agreeing to work for lower wages than we're already making."

After taking a dose of headache powders, Hope sat down beside her father and lightly massaged her temple. Luke met her gaze, and she forced a feeble smile. There was no doubt she needed to rest, but where? If he stayed here visiting with her father, she couldn't possibly lie down. Luke gestured toward the doorway leading into the chapel portion of the railroad car. "Maybe your father and I should go in there to finish our talk so you can rest."

She immediately dropped her hand to her lap. "I'm fine. I don't need to rest. The headache powders will soon ease my headache and I'll be fit as a fiddle."

"I've discovered that if I rest after taking medicine, it works much more quickly." Luke leaned forward and rested his arms across his thighs. "I'm sure you want to be at your very best when you meet with the children and their parents for the first time this evening."

His heart warmed when she offered him a sweet smile and nod of her head. "Perhaps you're right. I wouldn't want anything to distract me this evening." Hope turned to her father. "If you don't mind moving into the chapel, Papa, maybe I should lie down for a half hour or so."

Her father bounded to his feet and looked at Luke. "Come along, young man. We'll finish our conversation in here." The two of them stepped into the compact chapel, then closed the door between the living quarters and the chapel. He settled beside Luke on one of the hard wooden pews. "You were telling me that the miners might think I'm here looking for work, but I can't imagine anyone would worry about that for long. I've never set foot in a mine, and a short conversation with me will confirm my lack of knowledge. I think folks will soon realize the only thing I want to do is spread God's message of hope and love."

Luke nodded. "Maybe, but we've had revenuers come into these parts pretending to be everything from bankers to lawyers to farmers. Just 'cause you're riding around in this chapel car and preaching from the Good Book doesn't mean you can't be a revenuer, too. If you stay here in Finch, it won't take long before you discover some of the men make moonshine back in the hills. Some make it for themselves or their neighbors, while others sell it to make money to help feed their families."

The preacher tipped his head to the side, his brow furrowed. "I didn't know West Virginia had passed a prohibition law."

"It's not the whole state yet, but that's what the lawmakers are hoping for real soon. Right now, it's decided by the counties, and more are dry than wet. We're one of the dry ones, so making moonshine is illegal. So is selling it. A few of the men have been arrested, and two revenuers were shot just last week. Although it's a dangerous business, the men won't stop. They need the money. With less work in the mines, most have decided they don't have a choice."

"Then I guess I better not act interested in the moonshine business." The preacher grinned.

Luke frowned. The preacher didn't seem to grasp the risk. If he crossed the wrong people at the wrong time, he could be in danger, and so could his daughter. The preacher needed to take this matter of bootlegging seriously. "Not asking about moonshine is a good start, Preacher, but you and your daughter shouldn't wander off in the woods by yourselves or show up to visit folks unexpectedly. The men might think such visits or walks in the woods are a way of spying on them. You'll win over the women and children first. The men will be slower to believe you're who you say you are." Luke hesitated a moment. "Don't ever let on you know anything about the moonshine business—not even to your daughter. Just tell her there's dangerous animals in the woods and it's not safe. A slipup of any sort could mean we'd find ourselves on the wrong end of a shotgun." He grinned. "And womenfolk sometimes get to chattering and share things they oughtn't. I learnt that the hard way with my sister."

"Well, it sounds like I've got my work cut out for me." Reverend Irvine leaned back in his chair. "Anything else I should know?"

Luke ran his fingers through his thick hair. "'Fraid so. You're likely gonna find that the mine owners won't be too happy to have you around, either. At least not until they're convinced you're not from the UMWA."

"What's the UMWA?"

Luke wasn't certain the preacher was being forthright. This was a man who had lived in one of the largest coal-mining areas in the state of Pennsylvania. "You lived in a coal-mining city, but you don't know about the United Mine Workers Association? That's hard to believe."

"Hope lived in Pittsburgh with her aunt, but my visits there were brief. I've been preaching in other states, moving around a lot. I never lived in the Pittsburgh area and never visited long enough to become familiar with anything other than matters that involved my daughter."

While Luke had no problem accepting the preacher's explanation, Mr. Finch and the other men at the main offices of Finch Mining and Company wouldn't believe a word of it. Luke imagined them drinking coffee and poking holes in the story while they sat in the windowed offices overlooking the mining operation. In the end, they'd be convinced the preacher was a union man who had come here to stir up the miners and convince them the path to higher wages and better working conditions was a strike.

The preacher withdrew a small Bible from his breast pocket and patted the cover. "Sounds as though I'm going to need the Lord's protection since I'm supposed to remain in Finch until I receive another assignment from the association headquarters."

"I don't mean to discourage you. I hope you'll stay here a long time, but you need to understand that folks around these parts are a little different from some—more guarded and slower to accept change." Clutching several of the tracts, Luke pushed to his feet. "I'll pass these out to the folks who live near my family. Like I said, I'm sure the young'uns and their mamas will come. Not so sure about the menfolk, but I'll do my best."

The preacher stood and extended his hand. "Thank you, Luke. Maybe their curiosity will get the best of them if you mention they'll get to come inside and see the chapel car."

Luke hiked a shoulder. "Never can tell." He shook the preacher's hand, made his way to the rear of the car, and descended the platform steps.

When he neared the depot, Luke glanced over his shoulder. He'd wanted to catch a final glimpse of Hope, but she was nowhere in sight. Most likely she was still resting. He wasn't certain what it was about her that had become so compelling to him. She was quite pretty, but it was something beyond her beauty that attracted him. Maybe her sense of independence. Yet it was that spirit of self-determination and freedom that worried him.

From what he'd observed thus far, she was a woman who wouldn't be deterred, one who might disregard warnings. Her encounter with the ruffians back in Brookfield only reinforced his belief that she would bear watching. If she happened upon a moonshine still while wandering around the hills, she could find herself in a terrible situation. He doubted she'd believe moonshiners shot first and asked questions later.

Luke stood outside the depot, his eyes fixed on the chapel car. Whether she liked it or not, Miss Irvine was going to need a protector.

For the first time in months, he was glad that his hours at the mine had been cut.

CHAPTER

6

Hope stared into the small hand mirror that had once belonged to her mother, then turned toward the afternoon sunlight shimmering through the train window. Luke had been partially correct. Although she didn't have a black eye, there was a distinct bruise on her temple. She was thankful, though, that the headache powders had given her some relief. She yanked the pins from her unruly curls and pulled her hair forward to hide the purplish mark. The style wasn't particularly becoming, but if all went well, she'd avoid any embarrassing questions.

Wearing a white lawn blouse and a tailored navy skirt accented at the hem with two bands of gray piping, Hope stood beside her father to greet each person who stepped onto the chapel car platform.

Luke and his family were among the first to arrive. He beamed at her as he introduced each of them. His mother, a weary-looking widow, had been escorted by her deceased husband's brother, Luke's Uncle Frank. Neither had a great deal to say before they hurried inside to take a seat in one of the pews, but Luke had been pleased he'd convinced his uncle to attend.

Luke's sister Nellie lingered by Hope's side while Luke directed his two younger brothers and a little sister who looked to be four or five to the stand of trees, where Hope had spread blankets and would meet with the children.

"I think my brother has taken a liking to you." Nellie's hazel eyes shone with mischief. "He'd be mad as a hornet if he knew I told ya." She giggled. "He talked long and hard to convince Ma she could do her mending another time, but he didn't have to convince me. I wanted to come and meet you. He said you were mighty pretty. He was right."

Hope could feel the heat rise in her cheeks. "Thank you, Nellie. You're very pretty yourself. I hope we can become friends."

Nellie bobbed her head. "I'd like that. I'm seventeen, so I'm thinkin' we're about the same age."

"Close. I'm nineteen," Hope said. "The next time you come to town, why don't you stop for a visit?"

"Oh, I'd like that a lot. Luke said the living quarters in the chapel car are really something to see." Nellie rubbed her hands together like a small child anticipating a rare treat. "And maybe you could show me how to fix my hair like yours. I really like it. Is that the latest style in the city?"

Hope swallowed hard. "Not exactly, but some of the women are wearing their hair shorter and pulled forward a bit. I'm glad you like it."

Before she could ask any more questions about Hope's hair, another family scrambled to the platform. Her father remained at her side until the last of the attendees arrived. There hadn't been as large a turnout as they'd hoped, but the car was two-thirds full of adults and there were at least thirty children waiting outside.

Hope followed her father down the narrow aisle to the slightly raised platform at the front of the chapel and took her place at the organ. Her heart fluttered when she looked out at the crowd and was met by Luke's broad smile. Nellie sat beside him with her hands folded atop her faded brown-checkered skirt.

Her father cleared his throat as Hope perched her fingers over the organ keys. She stifled a giggle when Nellie jabbed her brother in the ribs. It appeared Nellie was eager to reveal what she'd earlier confided to Hope was true: Luke had taken a liking to her. It also appeared she didn't care if she embarrassed Luke in the process. Hope grinned when Luke pinned his sister with a hard glare.

After leading the group in singing several hymns, Hope disappeared through their living quarters, descended the steps leading from the rear exit, and joined the children. The group was large, but they were all wide-eyed and eager to learn the hand motions to several songs she taught them. With the exception of a few of the youngest children and one or two older boys, they remained attentive as Hope told them of Moses being placed in a basket and floated in the Nile River where he was found by Pharaoh's sister. One of the older boys said he'd like to try that with his baby sister, who continually cried all night. His remark had caused raucous laughter and also required some lengthy enlightenment from Hope before she continued with the story of Daniel in the lions' den.

Knowing her father would soon conclude his preaching, she pulled out a list of questions. She hoped the children would recall a bit of what she'd taught them. Like popcorn exploding over a hot fire, a plethora of small hands shot into the air. Their enthusiasm was contagious. "I know, I know!" several shouted while waving in her direction. With each new question, they bounced up and down and flapped their arms. The child selected to answer would beam with pleasure when Hope proclaimed the response correct.

She caught sight of the adults descending the steps of the chapel car, quickly reached into her crate of supplies, and removed a paper sack. "You've all been so good that I have a treat for you." She instructed the children to walk past her in a single line and repeated the same comment to each child as she placed a piece of hard candy in each small palm. "Jesus loves you, and so do I. Please bring your friends tomorrow night so they can learn about Jesus."

A boy wearing a ripped pair of overalls and worn plaid shirt called out, "Do we get candy every night?"

Hope smiled and nodded as she continued to repeat the invitation, dropping sweets into their small hands. But when a large palm suddenly appeared, she stopped short and looked up. "Luke!" She smiled at him. "Sorry, no candy for the adults."

"But I was very good and listened to every word. Would you like me to tell you about the sermon your father preached?"

She tipped her head to the side and met his twinkling green eyes. "You are most welcome to tell me, but the candy is to encourage the little ones to listen—not to satisfy the sweet tooth of adults."

Nellie bounded to her brother's side and grasped his arm. "You're a smart woman, Hope. My brother shouldn't receive a reward for his knowledge of the Bible or listening to a sermon. He already knows more passages from the Good Book than most preachers, don't ya, Luke?"

He shook his head. "That's not true, Nellie. I know a little, but I'm no equal to the Reverend Irvine."

Undeterred by her brother's stern look, Nellie perched her hands on her hips. "He don't want to appear too proud, but he uses more than his share of coal oil reading the Bible late into the night." She pointed her thumb in Luke's direction. "And he's got a fine singing voice, too."

Hope stooped to tuck the sack of candy back into the crate. She peeked up at Luke as she stood. "That's good to know. I may need help with the children from time to time, and now I'll know who to call upon. They become restless waiting for me to finish the singing at the beginning of the meetings. You could lead them in a few songs."

Nellie jabbed her brother's arm with her index finger. "I never said he was good with young'uns. I just said he knows his Bible. I'm the one who's good with the young'uns."

"Is that a fact? Well, who's taught the boys to trap and fish? And who carries the little girls down the hill on his back?" Luke looked at Hope. "Now I ask ya, does that sound like a man who isn't good with young'uns?"

He beamed when Hope acknowledged that he'd revealed some excellent qualities. "It sounds as though both of you could help if our Sunday school expands. All of the children said they were going to bring friends."

Nellie glanced toward the children, who by now had scattered off to find their parents. "The young'uns will do what they can, but it all depends on whether their pa will give 'em permission. Some folks 'round here don't cotton much to strangers, and that includes preachers. That's why the few who have come here before leave after a few weeks."

The young woman's comment echoed what Luke had told Hope's father earlier in the day. Hope wasn't pleased by the idea of living in a town where she'd need to be constantly on guard. Still, she'd find a way to gain the acceptance of the older folks. While winning over the adults might take longer than it had with the children, she was determined to succeed. "Where there's a will, there's a way," she whispered. Long ago she'd taken that old saying to heart.

Over the weeks that followed, Luke frequently escorted Hope up the hillside to visit with his mother, as well as some of the nearby neighbors. While he was certain she expected to do the same today, he'd decided to surprise her with a change in their usual routine. During their brief times alone, he learned enough about Hope to know he wanted to discover more about her past. Yet each time he thought he might have her to himself, someone would appear and interrupt them. This afternoon would be different. He caught sight of her crossing the street and waved when he arrived at the bottom of the hill.

She pointed to his hand as she approached. "What's this? Are you going fishing?"

"I am. And I hope you'll agree to join me. There's a pond not far off where I like to try my luck with a fishing pole. I don't catch a lot of fish, but it's peaceful. I brought an extra pole for you."

"You were sure I'd say yes, were you?" Mischief danced in her eyes.

"I recall you mentioned feeling discouraged by the unwelcome reception you received from some of the folks on the hill, so I thought a change was in order for today. But if you'd rather not . . ."

She reached for the fishing poles and placed her hand atop his. "Which one of these is mine?"

His gaze settled on her hand, and she retracted it as quickly as she'd taken hold. The moment she lifted her hand, he regretted his reaction. He cleared his throat and shifted the poles so she could have a better look at them. "You can have your pick."

"I suppose I'll take the shorter of the two." She tapped the longer pole. "I don't think I could handle that one."

He bent down and picked up a large can. "You want to carry the worms?"

She laughed and shook her head. "I'll let you do the honors, but thanks for giving me the opportunity."

He rested the poles against his shoulder, held the can close to his chest, and crooked his free arm. "There's no path, so you'll need to watch so you don't step into any chuckholes. You might want to hold on to my arm. Don't want you to sprain an ankle."

"Some of the young boys have talked about fishing at the river, but I don't recall anyone mentioning a pond. Is this a secret spot no one else knows about?"

"It's not a secret, but most of the fellas like to fish down at the river. Truth is, there's not many fish in the pond, and most folks who go fishing want to come home with their dinner, so they go to the river."

"And you don't want to catch any fish?"

He shrugged. "Not when I go to the pond. When I go out there, it's mostly when I have something I want to think on without being disturbed. I can do my thinking and get closer to God out at the pond. That's hard to do when the young'uns are running around wanting you to bait their hooks." He shook his head. "And if I don't keep a close watch on Susie, she'd jump right in the water. That girl loves to get herself soaking wet."

"She's a sweet child. Your brothers are lots of fun, too." She hesitated a moment. "There's quite a gap in age between you and the little ones."

He nodded. "Ma had another baby between me and Nellie and then two other babies between Nellie and Joey. They died. Losing them was hard, and when Pa died while she was still carrying Susie, well, I think she would have sat down and died if it hadn't been for Uncle Frank. He made her face the fact that Pa wouldn't have wanted her to give up on life or on their family. Took a while for Ma to get back to her old self, but by the time Susie was a year old, she was doing better. Uncle Frank spent a lot of hours reading the Bible and praying with her—with all of us. He's the one who encouraged me to search and memorize God's Word."

"So he never married?" Hope arched her brows when he didn't immediately answer. "Your Uncle Frank, was he ever married?"

"Yes. Both his wife and only child died in childbirth about a year after their wedding. He never married again. When I asked him why he'd stayed single all these years, he told me that after Aunt Louise died, he vowed to stay single unless the Lord pushed him to the altar. So far that hasn't happened." He inhaled a deep breath. "Guess it's selfish of me, but I've always been glad he didn't remarry. I don't know what we'd do without his help."

"I'm sorry. I didn't mean to bring up unpleasant memories."

"No need for apologies. Besides, all those memories aren't unhappy, and there's lots of laughter in our house nowadays." He shifted the fishing poles. "What about you? What was it like growing up without any brothers or sisters?"

"Lonely. I always wanted a sister. There was a girl about my age who lived next door to Aunt Mattie for a couple of years. We had fun together, but then they moved away." She looked up at him. "Speaking of sisters, where's Nellie today? Didn't she want to come along? She told me she liked to fish."

"She does like to fish, but whenever she's around I can't get a word in edgewise." He hesitated a moment. "I wanted you to myself for a little while." He chanced a quick look at her.

"So you didn't ask her?"

He shook his head. "Do you mind?"

"I'm sure her feelings will be hurt if she thinks she wasn't wanted. I know mine would be."

"She couldn't have come even if I'd asked her. Ma needs her to help with the canning the next couple days."

"I feel much better knowing she couldn't have come along."

He pointed to a spot along the edge of the pond. "Always thinking of others, aren't you?"

"No, not always. My thoughts right now are only on enjoying your company—and maybe catching a fish." She grinned and looked into his eyes.

Could she hear his heart thumping beneath the fabric of his shirt? He wanted to tell her how he adored her laughter and how he loved the way her hazel eyes seemed to change color each time he looked into them. He wanted her to know how much he'd come to care for her since they'd first met. And yet she'd likely think him a fool for speaking his feelings so soon. After all, she wasn't from these parts where men didn't wait long before speaking their piece and staking their claim on a gal. Luke couldn't be certain, but he figured things were different in big cities. Men likely courted for months and months before stating their affections to a woman.

He cleared his throat and shifted his attention to the fishing rods. "You bait your own hooks or do you want me to do it?" He moved the can between them, then picked up his rod. "There's a lot of good night crawlers in there. They work best." He dug his fingers into the dirt, pulled out one of the wiggling worms, and threaded it onto his hook before glancing up at her.

"Since I've never baited a hook, why don't you go ahead? I wouldn't want to cause the worm more pain than necessary."

He laughed heartily. "Never in my life have I heard anyone worry about the pain of a worm. You do confound me. I didn't realize your concern for others would extend even to a worm being used as bait."

"Well, they're God's creatures too, and while I don't know if they feel pain, the process looks like it would hurt." Splotches of pink inched across her cheeks, and he longed to snatch back his laughter and words. He'd obviously embarrassed her.

He quickly baited the hook, stepped close, and extended the rod. "I'd be glad to help you cast if you'd like."

"Let me try on my own first." Before he could move, she swung the rod in a wide arc. Luke dove for the ground. Instead of casting the line, the rod went flying into the pond. Hope let out a yelp and pointed at the slowly sinking rod.

Without thought to his shoes, Luke jumped up and ran into the pond, high-stepping his way through the murky water that splashed around his legs. When he finally captured the rod, he lifted it high in the air and slogged back to the bank holding it like a prize catch. Water sloshed in his shoes, and his pant legs were soaked through when he made his return to dry ground.

"I think you might need a lesson or two before you try that again, but you do have a good throw." He smiled as he went to her side.

"Oh, Luke. Look at you." She pointed to his feet. "Your shoes are going to be ruined."

"They'll be fine." He dropped to the ground, removed his shoes and socks, then glanced up at her. "Don't worry. I won't remove my pants."

"Oh, my! I hope not." She covered her mouth with her palm.

He placed his shoes in the sun and hung his socks on the branches of a nearby bush. "The socks will dry in no time, but we may have to stay here a day or two for the shoes to dry." Seeing the look on her face, he burst into laughter. "I'm only joking. They'll dry out soon. Besides, I can always go barefoot." He reached for the fishing pole. "How about I give you your first lesson?"

She nodded. "I think that would be helpful." He stepped to

her side and then, after a few verbal instructions, moved behind her. She glanced over her shoulder. "Why did you move?"

"To provide a little more instruction." He glanced to be sure her hands were properly placed on the rod, then reached around her and wrapped his hands over her own. He lowered his head and spoke into her ear. "Just keep your arms loose enough for me to help you cast the line into the water." With a slight turn of her head, she gave him a sideways look that caused his pulse to quicken. "Here we go."

Holding her from behind, he directed her arms in an arc while the two of them watched the worm fly in the air, skip across the water, and lower into the depths of the pond.

"Let's hope my earlier mishap didn't scare the fish away," she said.

"Like I said, no one has much luck in this pond, so there's no need to be concerned if we don't catch anything. Besides, I don't much enjoy cleaning fish." He nodded toward the pond. "If you feel like something is tugging on your line, jerk back and then reel it in."

He'd just prepared to cast his own line when Hope jerked her pole and squealed. Luke dropped his pole and once again assumed his position behind her. "That's it. Pull back and turn the handle on your reel."

She was doing her best but making little progress. He moved forward to help her, and together they hoisted a large turtle into the air. No sooner did they pull the turtle from the pond than it broke the line and dropped back into the watery abyss.

Hope sighed. "I don't think fishing is ever going to be one of my talents."

When she made a quick turn toward him, his lips unexpectedly brushed her cheek. "I-I'm sorry. I didn't mean . . ."

She smiled and shook her head. "No need to apologize."

Luke's pulse quickened. Did she already have feelings for him, too? Maybe city and hill-country courting weren't so different after all.

..............·�֍·..............

Hope's excursions up the hillside had soon become the bright spot in her days. Even though the men still considered her an interloper, the women and children welcomed her visits. At least Luke's Uncle Frank had been quick to accept her. He'd done his best to convince the other men that she had no intention of wrongly influencing their wives. But even Uncle Frank's words didn't ease their attitudes. They considered her a varmint that needed shooing from their door.

Her father hadn't met with much more success. The men weren't totally convinced her father wasn't a revenuer with a smooth tongue who'd brought along a young woman to lessen suspicion. Mistrust further heightened when her father had been seen speaking to one of the managers of the mining company at the general store. A story soon circulated that he'd been hired to flush out miners favoring a strike. Little did they know that the manager had accused her father of being a representative of the union and warned him against stirring up trouble. It seemed Hope and her father were met with resistance and wrongful accusations at every turn.

Every week a new tale spread among the locals, though a few families had been approachable. Along with the Mintons, Burnses, and Winters, Luke's family, including Uncle Frank, had accepted them. But even with Luke and those four men vouching for Hope and her father, they'd had little success winning over other men in the small community. Most of the men now accompanied their families down the hill, but rather than attend meetings, they gathered in a grove on the other side of the chapel car and typically rejoined their families afterward. At first her father had been encouraged by their appearance, except the men hadn't relented in their decision to remain at a distance.

While her father continued to pray for the men's acceptance, Hope took a more ambitious approach. Invited or not, she believed that going to the homes of the locals was more beneficial. Although her father's uninvited appearance might be met with a shotgun, her knocks were met with squeals of delight from the children who'd learned to expect a piece of candy when she appeared. And the women became as animated as their children when she produced a spool of much-needed thread or a packet of sewing needles.

After a glance out the train window, Hope picked up a small basket, tucked a handkerchief into the pocket of her skirt, and kissed her father on the cheek. He looked up from his writing. A slight frown wrinkled his forehead. "Going up the hillside again, are you?"

She nodded. "Yes. Nellie and Luke are going to walk me up. I want to visit Celia Fisher's family. She's a sweet little girl who's been at every meeting since we arrived. Neither of her parents has attended, but they live near Nellie and Luke. Nellie brings Celia with her each evening. The little girl is quite withdrawn. I've been somewhat concerned because several of the children are unkind to her, and I've had to come to her defense. I think their unpleasant behavior may be the cause of Celia's shyness."

Her father folded his hands in his lap. "I hope you had a talk with the children who have been unkind to the girl. They need to learn how to treat others with love and compassion."

She smiled down at him. "I've corrected them, but a few of the older boys brushed off my remarks. If they don't obey, I'll have you visit with them."

"Just let me know. I'll be glad to have a word with them." He cocked an eyebrow. "Did Nellie think the child's parents would welcome a visit from you?"

"I know Mrs. Fisher wants to meet with me. She sent a note with Celia and asked me to call on her. I'm not sure about Mr. Fisher. He works for the mining company, so I don't think he'll be at home." She squeezed her father's shoulder. "You don't need to worry. I'll be back in plenty of time to prepare dinner."

"Wait!" A look of sudden realization flashed in her father's eyes. "Did you say Luke was going to meet you?"

Hope nodded. "Yes, Luke and Nellie." She edged toward the door. If she didn't hurry, they'd think she wasn't coming.

Her father leaned back in his chair. "Why isn't Luke at work?"

She tipped her head to one side, surprised by the question. "Because he was laid off again. I assumed you knew. Miners with the least seniority were laid off a few days ago. I thought he'd told you."

"No, he never mentioned it." His tone of disbelief affirmed she'd caught him unaware. Her father hesitated a moment. "He did say he'd be available if I needed any help with my carpentry projects, but I figured he'd been assigned a different shift at the mine. He probably thinks me completely insensitive."

"I don't think he'd believe you uncaring, Papa. He knows you want only the best for the people who live here. I'm sure he simply doesn't want to burden you with the problems going on at the mine. He hasn't told me much, but Nellie confides in me. I think there's growing unrest among the men." She stepped to the door. "I really must go. We can talk more when I return." She pushed the iron door handle and shoved her hip against the heavy door before her father could further detain her.

By the time she arrived at the stand of elderberry bushes near the path leading up the hillside, beads of perspiration were trickling down the side of Hope's face. "Sorry I'm late." She gasped for air after sputtering the words. "Thank you for waiting." She clamped her palm to her waist.

Nellie's gaze followed the movement. "Got a stitch in your side from walking so fast?"

Hope bobbed her head. "My father stopped me on my way out the door." She turned toward Luke. "He didn't know you'd been laid off at the mine."

Luke's brow furrowed. "I thought he'd figure it out when I told him I could help out with his carpentry work."

Hope shook her head. Folks took it for granted that outsiders understood how things worked in the mining camp, but Hope wasn't certain why. Most of the families remained uncommunicative, especially the men. When her father inquired about their work, they immediately turned the conversation to talk of the weather or crops. Nellie said it was because some folks still believed she and her father were company spies who passed information to the mine manager.

Though she hadn't pressed Nellie for details, Hope had difficulty believing the girl's explanation. After all, they'd been here for more than six weeks, and other than her father's one brief conversation with a mine manager at the general store, they'd not had contact with the hierarchy at the mining company. To her knowledge, none of the managers or supervisors had ever visited any of their chapel car meetings. Perhaps that wasn't enough to convince folks; perhaps they never would win the trust of these people. Then again, maybe rebuilding the church would help persuade them.

She pushed aside the thought when Nellie skipped ahead of them toward the path, her faded print dress swishing and catching on bushes as she led the way. "Come on, you two."

She and Luke dutifully followed behind. Nellie was much

more accustomed to climbing these hills, and Hope soon found herself gulping down air in her attempt to keep pace. Thankful that Luke had remained by her side, Hope smiled at him when he guided her around a muddy hole in the path, then slowed his pace.

Once her breathing had returned to a normal rate, Hope cleared her throat. "My father may need your help before long. He wrote to the association headquarters and asked if they would fund the rebuilding of the local church. The one that was destroyed by a fire."

When he grinned and nodded, she immediately realized there'd been no need for her explanation. The only church in the town was the one that had been destroyed by fire. She could feel the heat climbing up her neck. No doubt her cheeks were now a bright shade of pink.

"That's wonderful news. I'll be praying the association will decide to help. We've tried to raise money to rebuild several times, and folks want a new church. Problem is, for most of us, it's hard making enough money to put food on the table, much less having any extra to give toward building a church."

"My father explained that the miners and their families didn't have additional funds to help with the rebuilding. The board of directors were to meet this week, so he's hopeful he'll hear from them soon."

Nellie, who had slowed her own pace, shifted and looked over her shoulder. "Did you say your father is going to rebuild the church? Folks are going to be so excited!" She clapped her hands together. "I can't wait to spread the word."

Hope sighed. This was how inaccurate chatter spread among the families. One person heard only bits and pieces of a conversation and spread it as gospel. "Wait, Nellie. That's not what I said, so please don't tell anyone the church is being reconstructed." Hope reached out and gently caught the girl by her arm while she detailed what she'd told Luke. "So you see, nothing is certain, and we don't want to give rise to hope until we've heard back from the association. I know they don't have an excess of funds, so there's a possibility my father's request will be denied. All three of us need to pray they'll understand the importance of helping the residents of Finch."

Nellie's smile faded. "I'm willing to pray, but I have to admit I have my doubts they'll want to help. Seems we're pretty much forgotten by everyone."

Luke placed his arm around his sister's shoulder. "Come on now, Nellie. Don't be such a doomsayer. Let's put our faith in the Lord." He held her tight until she smiled at him. "That's the sister I know and love." He released his hold as they neared the top of the hill. "You go ahead and take Hope to meet Mrs. Fisher. I need to get back out to the field and weed the garden."

Nellie nodded, and the two young women watched him lope off. "I'm surprised he's letting me take you to meet Mrs. Fisher." She lowered her head close to Hope's ear. "You're all he talks about, you know. He thinks the sun rises and sets on you."

Hope couldn't withhold a smile. The words warmed her heart, even if she was certain Nellie was prone to exaggeration. "I'm fond of you and Luke, too."

Nellie giggled. "I have a feeling you'd rather be with him than me, but you don't need to say so. I know you wouldn't want to hurt my feelings." She reached down, grabbed Hope's hand, and swung it as though they were schoolgirls. "Come on, we'd better get a move on or Mrs. Fisher will think we're not coming."

As she expected, Mr. Fisher wasn't at home when they arrived, but Mrs. Fisher greeted them with a work-worn smile. Dark circles rimmed her eyes, and strands of hair sailed free from the loose knot pinned at her nape. Weariness oozed from the woman. "Come on in and sit a spell. Can't offer you anything more than a cup of weak coffee, but . . ."

Hope stayed the woman with a shake of her head. "Thank you, Mrs. Fisher, but there's no need for refreshments." She waited until the older woman gestured to the straight-back chairs that surrounded a marred metal table.

"I'm gonna go on home. Ma said she needed some help hanging out the wash." Nellie looked at Hope. "Come get me when you're done and I'll walk ya back to town."

"There's no need for an escort, Nellie." While Hope appreciated the girl's offer, any real threat to strangers arose only if they attempted to gain entrance into the hillside community without an escort or proper invite. The miners and their families had no problem with the departure of outsiders. Truth be told, they often encouraged it with a strong warning and a shotgun. Hope was touched by Nellie's concern, yet there was no need to keep the girl from her chores.

The flimsy door clacked shut, and Hope turned her attention to the older woman. "Celia is a delightful child, Mrs. Fisher. I'm sure you're very proud of her."

The woman wilted. "I worry 'bout Celia. She cries a lot, says the other kids make fun of her 'cause she ain't learnt to read real good. Trouble is, I can't help 'cause I got the same problem myself." The woman pressed her hands together. "I was thinkin' maybe you could help her. The teacher at the school says she don't have time for special teachin', and I can tell Celia likes you a lot. She talks 'bout you all the time."

Hope leaned forward and grasped Mrs. Fisher's callused hands in her own. "I would be pleased to help Celia with her reading, but we'd need to decide on a time when I could meet with her. Would you want me to come here?"

Mrs. Fisher's brow puckered. "Only if her pa ain't here. He

don't take to having strangers around. If'n you could come 'bout this time a few days a week, he'll be at work. Think you could do that?"

After they'd talked a little longer and completed their plans, Hope bid the woman good-bye. Instead of stopping for Nellie, she headed off toward the path leading down the hill with a lightness in her heart. Maybe this would be the first step toward acceptance among the miners and their families.

When she neared the base of the steep path, she stopped at the sound of rustling underbrush. The noise ceased, and she inhaled a fortifying breath. Probably a small animal scurrying through the woods that bordered the trail. She took a tentative step.

"Who might you be?"

The booming voice cracked behind her. Heart thumping, Hope gasped, turned on her heel, and backed against a tree.

Kirby Finch settled his gaze on the young woman who'd pinned herself against a large oak. She stared at him like a wide-eyed, frightened rabbit caught in a snare. He didn't close the short distance between them for fear of causing her further alarm. He smiled and said, "Let me offer my deep apologies for frightening you. I am so sorry."

The moment he uttered the words, the look in her eyes changed from fear to anger. She waited what seemed an eternity, then gave him the slightest of nods. "You shouldn't sneak up on a person like that."

"Again, I apologize. It wasn't my intention to frighten you. The truth is, I was as surprised to see a lovely young lady on this path as you were to hear me call out to you. I'm Kirby Finch. My father owns the mine. I was on my way up the hill to check on damage to a few of the vacant houses the company owns."

"And repair them?" She glanced toward his empty hands.

He chuckled. "No. I don't count house repair among my skills. Maintenance needs are performed by our employees."

"Or not," she said.

Her tone bore a hint of contempt that captured his attention. The sun slanted across her face, and he tilted his head to gain a better look at her eyes. "Excuse me? Did you say 'or not'?"

"I did." She gave a firm nod. "I've been told your company owns all the housing where the miners and their families live. If that's the case, you should be ashamed. Those houses were shoddily constructed, and it doesn't appear your company has done anything to maintain them since they were first built." She shook her head. "And what about paint? Has your company ever considered the idea? Or furnishing the families with supplies so they can paint their houses?"

Who was this impertinent young woman? Never before had any resident of Finch been so critical of the company or its owners—at least not to his knowledge. Then again, maybe things had changed since he was last in the town. "And you are?"

"Hope Irvine. My father is the preacher assigned to the chapel car located near the depot. We've arrived to hold church meetings and help the residents of Finch wherever needed."

He shouldn't egg her on, but he couldn't stop himself. With a quick movement, he gestured toward the upper portion of the hill. "Since you've come to assist wherever needed, I assume you were up there helping folks paint and tidy their houses."

Her mouth dropped open, and she planted her feet in the soft dirt. "I was not helping with repairs, but both my father and I would be happy to do so if your company will supply the materials. My father is an excellent carpenter and I know he would welcome the opportunity."

"And you, Miss Irvine? Are you an excellent carpenter, as well?" He grinned at her. Perhaps living in Finch for a while wasn't going to prove as bad as he'd anticipated. This young lady might prove to be a much-needed diversion. After all, he did like his women a bit feisty. And a preacher's daughter might

90

prove a real challenge. And he did love a challenge. At least where women and good times were concerned.

"No. I'm here to lead classes for the children during my father's church services, play the organ, and direct the singing."

He cleared his throat. "I've just—"

"Let me finish, Mr. Finch." She waved him to silence. "Although I've come here to lead Bible school classes, I would be more than willing to learn any skills that might help provide the miners and their families with a better life." She stared at him with unwavering candor. "Can you say the same?"

"That's very admirable, Miss Irvine. After assessing the needs and available funds, the management may take you up on your offer of free labor." He inhaled a deep breath, prepared for her to interrupt him once again, but her lips remained clamped together. "As I was going to tell you earlier, I've just arrived in Finch. Though I've been at the mine for various visits, the last time I climbed this hill was when I was a boy of eleven or twelve." He sighed. "This time I'll be in Finch for more than a visit." He dropped his voice to a mere whisper before he added, "If my father has his way."

She pursed her lips. He was certain she was weighing his every word, and right now it didn't appear as if he'd won her confidence. Still, he'd do his best to win her over. She might prove useful as well as entertaining. Yet lovely as she was, he continued to hold out hope his father would relent and permit a return to Pittsburgh.

Hope arched her narrow brows. "So rather than a hired manager, your father has sent you to be his personal representative in Finch?"

"I suppose you could call me a company representative, since Mr. Daniels has been the local manager for many years. My father and I didn't discuss an actual title for the position."

Rather than a title for his new job, Kirby's time had been consumed in attempts to change his father's mind. He'd failed. Judging from Miss Irvine's desire to help the residents of Finch, he doubted such a confession would sit well with her. "I'll be helping wherever needed."

"I'm pleased you've decided to take stock of the homes your company rents to the miners." She perched her hands on her hips. "I suppose you know that they're forced to live in company housing." She inhaled a quick breath. "That being the case, I do think the company should perform proper maintenance. Don't you agree?"

He needed to sidestep her question. Even if he committed to the obligation, his father would overrule any decision to spend money on the miners or their housing. "How long have you and your father been in Finch, Miss Irvine?"

"Just over two months. I've been saddened by the deplorable conditions the miners must endure, Mr. Finch. I truly hope you plan to lend as much help as possible. Beyond the poor housing, they go further and further into debt each day and are forced to remain in the company's employ because they can't pay their obligation at the company store."

"I'll look into the complaints, Miss Irvine." He did his best to appear concerned. "I'm doing what I can to learn more about the mining operation, but it will take some time. This is a new job for me, so I hope you'll be patient."

He didn't mention that while working in Pittsburgh, he'd been appointed vice-president of the mining operation but had completely ignored the business. If Miss Irvine learned of his lackadaisical attitude, he wouldn't succeed in winning her favor. Had he given Finch Mining and Company the attention it deserved back then, he would still be living in Pittsburgh. But instead of attending to business, he'd enjoyed himself at the gaming tables and late-night parties. Now he was paying the price for his indulgent behavior.

His father, determined to mold Kirby into a powerful leader of the company, had been merciless when Kirby begged for one more chance to assume his duties in Pittsburgh. His father's refusal had been swift and harsh.

"You don't sound particularly enthusiastic about your new assignment, Mr. Finch."

Her comment brought him back to the present, and he pulled a wry smile. "Adjusting to life in Finch is going to be difficult after living in Pittsburgh."

She shrugged. "I suppose it depends upon the person. Frankly, I was pleased to leave Pittsburgh."

"You lived in Pittsburgh? When was that, Miss Irvine?"

"Prior to our arrival in Finch." She hesitated a moment. "My circumstances changed in Pittsburgh, and I was able to persuade my father to let me come with him. We made a few stops along the way, but I'm pleased we're going to be remaining in Finch for a time. There's a need for a preacher here. And a church building. We've learned that a fire destroyed the church a while back, but you probably knew that."

He didn't know about either the church or the fire, but she looked at him as though she expected some kind of response. "Fires are a terrible thing. Sad, very sad." He shook his head.

"Indeed." She tipped the brim of her hat to block the sun. "I'm hoping we'll be able to host some fund-raisers to help re-build the church. My father is seeking financial assistance from the association headquarters, but it would be a fine gesture if the mining company donated funds toward such a cause, don't you think?"

Kirby swatted at a pesky fly that whirred near his slick-backed brown hair. Miss Irvine's requests were as persistent as the insect that had been buzzing near his left ear. First she wanted the houses painted and repaired, and now she hoped to secure donations for a new church. He grinned at the thought. Miss Irvine was charming and downright pretty, and he didn't want to do anything that might offend her. Enjoying her company would likely be the only thing that would make life bearable in this one-horse town.

"You'll need to give me some time to see what I can do, Miss Irvine. I haven't yet had the opportunity to go through the books and check our resources. I do know the mine hasn't been doing as well as projected over the past year." He extended his arm to her. "Let me escort you back to town. The path is steep, and I wouldn't want you to take a tumble. While we walk, I'd like to hear more about your life in Pittsburgh."

She lightly grasped his arm. "I'll accept your invitation if you'll accept mine."

A rush of anticipation coursed through him as he patted her hand. Perhaps this young lady was more worldly than he first thought. "I'd be delighted to escort you anywhere, Miss Irvine."

The hint of a smile played at her lips. "I won't need you to escort me. I'm extending an invitation to attend our church meeting at the chapel car this evening."

The request caught him off guard. He hesitated as he pictured himself sitting in a church service next to the men who worked in the mines. Discomfort assailed him. He'd need to frame an answer that would let him avoid the church service but keep the door open to further contact with Miss Irvine.

He cleared his throat. "While I would very much like to attend, I believe my appearance would cause discomfort for the miners and their families. I'm sure you've already learned that there's some hostility between the workers and management."

"Perhaps you can help overcome those issues, Mr. Finch."

Her enthusiasm was infectious, but rather than close the divide, his attendance would likely expand the chasm. He shrugged. "We'll see. For now, I think it's best I stay away from your meetings."

She clapped her hands together. "I know! You can attend the late-night service we hold for the railroad workers. There's a train due in late this evening, and my father always holds a late meeting for the railroaders. It's well attended, but none of the families from up the hill ever come to that meeting."

If he was going to stand a chance with Miss Irvine, he'd need to do more than reveal a bit of gentlemanly comportment. Even if he had the money to purchase gifts, he doubted Miss Irvine would be impressed with such offerings. No, if he was going to impress her, he'd need to accept her invitation. That thought pained him. He had hoped for something more intimate than attending a church service, but he'd go—at least this one time. "Thank you for the invitation, attending with the railroad workers will be perfect."

As they continued to pick their way down the hill, he quizzed her about life in Pittsburgh: where she liked to shop, the names of acquaintances, and functions where they might have met. He soon discovered they had little in common. That revelation might have mattered back in Pittsburgh, but in Finch there was no need to concern himself with social standing. The only things that required concern were the happenings at the mine.

After bidding Miss Irvine good-bye, Kirby trudged back to the hillside. He didn't relish the idea of sniffing out recent threats of a strike at the mine or weeding out the possibilities of a union movement. He would need help, and the most likely source would be a desperate miner in need of immediate cash or credit at the company store to feed his family.

Before approaching the first house along the hill, Kirby removed a handkerchief from his pocket and swiped the perspiration from his forehead. Three small children played in the dirt outside the ramshackle house. A weary, worn woman in a cotton print housedress sat on the porch snapping green beans. When she caught sight of Kirby, she pulled her sweater tight around her neck and watched his every move.

The moment Kirby called out a greeting, the children scrambled to the porch and circled around the woman, clinging to her arms with dirty fingers. Her face registered unwavering suspicion, and a hint of fear.

She wrapped an arm around the smallest of the scruffy children. "Who are ya, mister, and what you doing up here?"

"Kirby Finch. Your husband around?" He hadn't met any of the miners' families on his limited visits to the town, but Kirby had heard his father and some of the managers discuss life "on the mountain." He'd heard enough to know he shouldn't approach the womenfolk when their husbands weren't around.

"You must be kin to the mine owner." As she spoke, her gaze traveled the length of his body. Both her look and tone bore undeniable contempt. She didn't wait for an answer. "He ain't around right now. Don't know when he'll be back. He's off lookin' for work ever since you cut his hours." Her lip curled. "Again!"

Kirby flinched and took a backward step. "I had nothing to do with his hours, ma'am. I just arrived in town a couple days ago, but I'm planning to do what I can to help."

She lifted the pan of green beans from her lap and shoved it beneath the decrepit chair and grunted. "We done heard them promises afore. 'Specially when there's threats of a strike. You come to find out for yerself? I'm thinkin' you're afeared the men are gonna strike."

Kirby blew a long breath. This woman might not look like

much, but she was shrewd. Coming up here to find a miner who would be his eyes and ears among the other workers was foolish. Unless he could say or do something to quell rumors, his appearance would likely affirm the miners' belief that the company feared another strike.

He finally gathered his wits and shot a broad smile in the woman's direction. "No, nothing like that. I heard that some of the houses up here were in need of repair. I was going to take a look around for myself, see what needs to be done and report back to the managers."

She stared at him as if weighing whether she should believe what he said. He forced himself to meet her steady look. Never letting her gaze waver, she pulled her young son close and wiped his runny nose with the corner of her apron. "I'm not sure I trust what yer sayin', mister, but I know Miss Hope's been busy makin' a list of repairs that's needed. She's the preacher's daughter. Might save ya some time to get back off the mountain and ask her for a look at what she's already wrote down."

Kirby nodded. "I believe you've got a good idea. I'll go back to town and see if I can speak to . . ."

"Miss Hope." She finished his sentence before he could decide if he should refer to Hope as Miss Irvine or Miss Hope. The woman pointed in the direction of the railroad yard. "You'll likely find her at the chapel car. They're parked on a spur close to the depot. Tell her Nora Selznick sent ya. She'll know who I am."

"Thank you for your help, Mrs. Selznick." He probably should have mentioned that he'd already met Hope, but decided the less he said, the better.

She leaned down to retrieve the pan of green beans. Then, almost as an afterthought, she gestured to him. "If'n you're genuine in what you done told me, you might want to talk to the preacher, too. Hope says her pa is mighty good with a hammer and nails." She grunted. "Says he can paint, too. The good Lord knows these shacks could use some paint. Screens for the doors and windows would help keep the flies and skeeters outside where they belong. These young'uns get all bit up with skeeters."

"Hadn't thought about that, Mrs. Selznick. We'll see what we can do."

Kirby hurried off before the woman could ask for anything else. When he arrived back in town, he glanced up the hillside and wondered if Mrs. Selznick would mention that he'd spoken to her about possible repairs. Even more, he worried the woman would tell Hope that he acted as though he'd never met her. No doubt such a remark would give rise to suspicion. He raked his fingers through his hair. Should Hope question him, he'd need to have a believable response at the ready.

In the meantime, he'd continue to look for someone willing to act as his connection inside the mine. Someone who would tell him if a strike was imminent or unionization was on the horizon.

CHAPTER

8

Hope placed her fingers on the organ keys, ready to begin the evening meeting for the railroad workers. Unlike the earlier service, the pews weren't completely full, but the railroaders who weren't needed at work were in attendance. Her father had formed friendships with some of the men and was quick to inquire if a regular wasn't present—a fact that pleased the railroaders. The miners, on the other hand, frowned upon being questioned. Queries into their lives or whereabouts were sidestepped and met with looks of suspicion.

When Hope asked Luke about the apprehensive behavior, she learned the miners didn't like to be asked a lot of questions. "But why? What has happened to cause such distrust?"

He'd told her that wariness of outsiders was a feeling long held among the hill people, not just miners. They were clannish in nature, and outsiders were viewed as folks who wanted either to take advantage of or force change upon them. The hill people had experienced both types of intrusion in the past and now guarded against such happenings. "They keep to themselves and want others to do the same," he said.

Fortunately, the children weren't as secretive as their parents. The younger ones hadn't yet learned to be cautious. While Hope didn't take advantage of their trusting nature, she did want to learn ways she could help the struggling families. If a child who regularly attended was absent for more than a day or two, she would send a note home with another child, asking if there was sickness or if assistance was needed. At first her notes had been met with silence, but finally she'd developed a friendship of sorts when one of Nora Selznick's children became ill. Though uninvited, Hope ventured up the hill with a kettle of chicken and noodles for the family. Initially, Nora refused the offering, but the children were so insistent that their mother finally relented.

Once she won the confidence of Mrs. Selznick, Hope began taking note of the repairs needed on the shoddy homes owned by the mining company. Rent for these homes was withheld from their wages, and those who couldn't pay were evicted. Paying excessive rent and being forced to purchase their necessities from the company store had caused ongoing strife between the miners and the company, a situation that continued to create strikes and threats of unionization.

Though Hope had met Kirby Finch only a few hours ago, she'd already begun to anticipate he might prove to be different from his father. A man who wanted to do right by the folks living in this town—a man of his word.

Eager to see Kirby's face, she scanned the group of men inside the railcar. Had she misplaced her hope in him? He said he'd attend the evening meeting with the railroaders, but he wasn't among the attendees who'd taken their seats in the wooden pews. No doubt he'd never intended to accept her invitation and had forgotten his promise before they'd parted company.

Disappointment assailed her as she struck the chords of "Come

Ye That Love the Lord." They had sung the first stanza, the men's deep, throaty voices raised in unison as they continued to the chorus: "'We're marching to Zion, beautiful, beautiful, Zion; we're marching upward to Zion, the beautiful city of God.'"

Hope scanned the roomful of men and was unable to withhold her smile when Kirby entered the coach and took a seat near the door. He tipped his head in recognition, and she broadened her smile. As she returned her attention to the music, Hope caught sight of Luke, who now attended both the early and late-night meetings in order to learn as much as possible from her father's preaching. Luke had followed her gaze to the rear of the car. For the rest of the meeting, his features remained creased in a frown.

After the benediction, her father stepped from the platform and moved to the center aisle to greet the railroaders. Luke remained seated on the front pew, his eyes fixed on some unknown object in the distance. Once her father had stepped farther down the aisle, Hope pushed away from the organ and made her way to Luke's side. "You look gloomy. Was there something in the sermon that caused you discomfort?"

He shook his head. "No. Your father presented a good lesson in his sermon." Luke shifted and glanced over his shoulder. "It's that fellow in the last row." He turned back toward Hope and lowered his head. "That's Kirby Finch. His father owns the mine. Mr. Woodbine over at the general store pointed him out to me. I'm surprised to see him here. I hope he came for the right reasons."

Hope sat down beside Luke. "I don't know Mr. Finch very well, but if he needs to change his life, this is the place where he can find help. This is where he should be."

"That's true enough." He hesitated before adding, "Exactly how well do you know him? I didn't know you'd ever met him."

He sounded a bit like a jealous schoolboy. "We only just met earlier today when I was coming down the hill after visiting with Celia Fisher's mother."

"Nellie never mentioned seeing any strangers today. I thought she was walking the hill with you today. Did she forget to meet you?"

"No, we walked up together, but she was busy helping your mother when I was ready to return home. Besides, I didn't think I needed her to accompany me on my way back to town. You're the one who told me strangers didn't have a problem if they were going down the hill."

"That's usually true, but . . ."

Hope held up her hand to stay him. She didn't want Luke to think she had anything to hide. In as few words as possible, she described the events that had culminated in her recent meeting with Kirby. "So you see, I don't know him very well, but I did invite him to attend the meeting this evening." She glanced toward the rear pew. "You might be interested to know that he rejected my invitation to attend the earlier meeting because he didn't want to create discomfort among the miners and their families." When Luke said nothing, she sighed. "I believe it was a thoughtful gesture."

"That's because you don't know how men like the Finches think and act. They're like a robin in springtime. They sing a pretty song, but it's always the same tune. You can't trust a word that comes from Mr. Finch, his son, or any of his other men who get paid to keep us under their thumbs." He leaned back against the pew. "I know my words are harsh, but you haven't lived through years in mining camps and seen how the families suffer while the owners become rich and tightfisted."

Hope flinched at his encompassing statement. Since her arrival in Finch, she'd come to know Luke as a man of deep faith, a compassionate man, a man who desired to serve God. Yet he was now willing to lump a group of men together because of their positions with the mining company—without genuine knowledge of their personal beliefs. Even though she'd seen for herself how the miners and their families had been treated through the years, it seemed unfair to judge the entire group of managers as if they were one. Then again, perhaps Luke knew all of them more intimately than she'd thought.

She folded her arms across her waist. "How well do you know Kirby Finch?"

"Not well at all, but you know what they say, like father, like son. I don't think Kirby Finch plans to do things any different from what his pa has done."

"I'll have you know that he's already planning improvements up on the hill." She looked again in Kirby's direction and hoped he wouldn't leave before she could thank him for keeping his word. She silently willed him to remain in place and was pleased to see her father extend his hand and engage Kirby in conversation.

Luke squared his shoulders. "What kind of improvements?" His tone bore a note of disdain that inexplicably heightened her resolve to defend Kirby.

"Repair and paint the houses owned by the company, and I'm sure he'll agree to do even more once he's been here long enough to learn exactly what's needed." She leaned toward him. "Please come and make him feel welcome to attend our meetings."

He stared at her for a long minute before finally pushing to his feet. "I want to believe he's going to do what he says. I'll do my best to welcome him, but don't expect too much." He looked down at her. "You don't understand how things work in these parts. If I take up with a company man, the other miners are going to look at me sideways. They won't trust me or my family and will shun all of us. I can't let that happen."

When he gestured toward the aisle, she took his cue and led him to where her father now stood talking to Kirby. Upon their approach, her father beamed at Luke and waved them onward. "Luke, I don't know if you've met Kirby Finch. He tells me he's going to be acting as his father's representative at the mine, and he's interested in gathering ideas from the miners and their families on what's needed to improve conditions, but he believes he'll need someone to act as a connection until he's viewed as trustworthy by the miners. I told him you'd be an excellent choice to work with him." Her father turned to Kirby. "This is the fellow I've been telling you about. Luke Hughes, meet Kirby Finch."

Instead of looking at Kirby, Luke kept his eyes on the preacher. "I know who he is, Preacher. Mr. Woodbine pointed him out the day he arrived."

"But we've never formally met." With his hand extended, Kirby leaned toward Luke. "I'm pleased to meet you, Luke."

For a moment, Hope wondered if Luke was going to accept Kirby's hand. A small sigh escaped her lips when Luke reached out, briefly shook Kirby's hand, and gave him a slight nod. "Mr. Finch."

"Ah, now, Mr. Finch would be my father, Luke. You should call me Kirby."

"That's kind of you, but I don't think it would be fitting, Mr. Finch." Luke eyed the door leading to the platform with obvious longing. If he hadn't been pinned between her father and her, Hope was sure he would have bolted and run like a spooked horse. "Besides, I don't know that there's much I can do to help you. Feelings run deep around these parts. Best you try to build trust with the men on your own."

Hope gave a little tug on Luke's sleeve. "I'm sure you could do something to ease hard feelings a bit, especially since Kirby is already planning to paint and repair the miners' houses."

"That's not exactly what I said, Hope." Kirby gave a tight smile. "I first need to check the books and make certain there are sufficient funds for the project." He turned to Luke. "I do plan to do everything in my power to better the living conditions for all our employees, and as soon as possible."

Luke gave her a look that said *I told you so* before he spoke. "We've heard all those promises for years, Mr. Finch. Until you're ready to put action behind your words, you'll make no inroads with your workers."

Kirby arched his brows. "I hope that doesn't include you, Luke. With both Miss Irvine and her father speaking so highly of you, I'd like to think you'd at least give me a chance to make a difference here."

"Of course he will." She flashed Luke a smile that she hoped would melt his resolve. "Won't you, Luke?"

"I'll give it some thought, but I'm not makin' any promises." He tapped the preacher on the arm. "If you'll let me by, I need to be on my way home. It's late and I'm sure you and Hope want to get some rest, too."

Kirby nodded his agreement. "I didn't think about the time. We all need to get to bed."

Her father stepped aside, and Luke hurried toward the door, with Kirby close on his heels.

Hope's shoulders sagged as both men departed. She had hoped for a few minutes alone with Kirby. She'd quickly assessed him as an insistent fellow, but if he was going to gain Luke's help, Kirby needed to give Luke what he asked for—a little time to think.

As he was stepping from the rear platform of the car, Kirby stumbled forward and caught Luke by the arm. "Sorry, Luke. I lost my footing and couldn't regain my balance."

Kirby immediately released his hold when Luke looked down at Kirby's hand on him. Kirby forced a smile. "How is it you attend the late meeting? Hope told me the miners and their families attend the first meeting, so I waited. Didn't want to be the cause of any problems."

"The preacher holds only one meeting except when the railroaders are in Finch or there's something special going on. When he holds two meetings, I try to attend both. I feel the Lord is leading me to become a preacher."

Kirby looked surprised. "That so? Well, I hope there's no hard feelings between us. I'd really like to spend some time with you and get a better idea how to improve things around here."

A faint light glowed from inside the railroad roundhouse. The pale light slanted across Luke's face and revealed suspicion in his eyes. It was going to be difficult to win him over, but Kirby had acquired the art of persuasion a long time ago. Throughout his childhood, he'd gained a variety of techniques by observing his father, who'd become a master at swaying the opinions of others. In time, he'd become even more masterful. At least until this latest debacle, when nothing he'd said or done would deter his father from sending him to this dreadful town.

The suspicion in Luke's eyes diminished ever so slightly. "I said I'd think about it, and I will. But you need to remember what I told you. If you set to work getting some repairs done to the houses, it might ease hard feelings a little. And if you take my advice, don't follow your good deed by raising the rent. If you do, any good you accomplish with a coat of paint will be lost—probably tenfold."

Luke turned to leave, and Kirby took a step toward him. "When can I expect to meet with you again?"

The young miner gave a shake of his head. "Maybe right after you've finished some projects up there." Luke gestured toward the hill. "I gotta go."

Kirby expelled a long breath. For most of his life, being a member of the Finch family had been advantageous. Now, in this town that bore his family's name, he'd been confronted with a new reality. A reality that was going to be difficult to overcome. How could he find an expeditious way to gather information that would prevent a strike and unionization of the miners if he couldn't make inroads with at least a few of the men who worked for the company? He strode toward the boardinghouse where he'd spend another night in the rented room decorated with floral wallpaper and oversized, marred furniture. How had his life regressed so far in such a short time? He'd believed his indifference to the company business and his roguish behavior would be tolerated by his father for at least another few years. He'd been terribly mistaken. Now he must find a way out of this situation. And find one, he would.

First, he'd step up his efforts to gain Hope's friendship. While Luke might eventually prove helpful, who could say how long he might take to arrive at a decision? He'd given no indication if it would be one day or ten, but he was now certain Hope could be useful.

...............⚬ℕ⚬...............

Luke trudged up the hill with the evening's events weighing heavily on his mind. He'd been harsh and quick to judge Kirby and his intentions. Truth be told, Luke still thought the man nothing more than a lot of bluster, yet he should have reflected Christ's love rather than behaving like a spoiled child. *Help me, Lord. You know my pain runs deep.* He swallowed hard, remembering the day his father's broken body had been pulled from deep within the mineshaft after an explosion. Even the passage of time hadn't healed all the wounds his death had inflicted upon their family. Luke wasn't certain what they would have done without Uncle Frank's continuing commitment to them. He was an answer to Luke's prayers.

Unfortunately, Luke had observed little change in attitudes or management of the mine since his father's death. Over and over they had heard promises of improvement in the mines, of better pay and living conditions, but none of those promises came to fruition. Using the company store and low wages, the owners continued to hold the workers in a viselike grip. Luke wanted to believe Kirby's words held a kernel of truth, but years of broken promises did little to advance thoughts of trust or forgiveness for anyone who represented the company.

Luke's shoulders slumped in defeat as he topped the hill and spotted the orange glow of his uncle's pipe from his front porch.

Frank waved the pipe in a welcoming arc. His brows dipped low as Luke approached. "You look like you just lost your best friend, boy."

Luke dropped onto the step and leaned against one of the porch posts while he related his encounter with Kirby. "I know the preacher and Hope both are thinking I'm not much of a witness for Jesus." He sighed and shook his head. "And I guess I got only myself to blame, but every time a company man comes 'round here, it's more lies and heartache."

"I can't deny most of 'em have been a bad sort, but it ain't fair to be faultin' a man afore he has a chance to prove hisself." He pointed the pipe in Luke's direction. "'Course that don't mean you shouldn't watch him real close, neither. Right or wrong, everyone living on this hill has a grudge or two against the company. Thing is, we all got the choice to leave if'n we're too unhappy."

"That's not true, and you know it. How's anyone gonna leave this place when we can't ever get outta debt to the company store?"

His uncle hiked a shoulder. "Now, that there's not quite true, Luke. There's a few of us that ain't in debt, but we stay for other reasons. And then there's those who sneak off still owing the company."

Luke nodded. "Yeah, but they can't get a job at another mine, what with the owners refusing to hire without a reference. They got this whole thing figured out so they can keep the miners under their thumbs."

Frank leaned down and knocked the ashes from his pipe. "Are you looking for an excuse to keep feeling ornery about Kirby Finch, or are ya wantin' to do the Lord's bidding, Luke? That there's your choice, too."

"You're right, Uncle Frank. I think I best get on home and spend some time praying. Besides, Ma's gonna begin to worry if I don't get back."

Frank pushed up from his chair and patted Luke's shoulder. "You're a good boy, Luke. One day you're gonna be a fine preacher and make us all proud. Ain't easy turning loose of heartache. Sometimes we take a step forward and then fall back to our old ways. When that happens, you jest gotta admit it and try again."

As he closed the distance between his uncle's house and his own, Luke considered his uncle's words. Luke believed overcoming heartache and anger was a long process for most folks, and he'd been able to achieve both in most instances. But this was different. Accepting the Finches at face value would require heavenly intervention.

...............✿...............

The following morning, Kirby took his place at the breakfast table with three other boarders. The eggs were cold, the biscuits overbaked, and the oatmeal pasty. He ate only a few bites, but downed two cups of the strong coffee before he pushed away from the table.

The landlady gestured to his plate and frowned. "There's folks who'd give their eyeteeth for the food you're leaving on that plate."

He merely shrugged and pushed the plate toward her. "Feel free to give it to them. I'm not fond of cold eggs or burned biscuits."

Kirby stood and left from the dining room while the landlady muttered her displeasure. He strode out the front door without a response. For years he'd ignored his father's disapproval, so disregarding the landlady's remarks had been quite simple. He bounded down the front steps. Instead of arguing over eggs and biscuits, he would use his powers of persuasion for more important matters.

CHAPTER

9

Kirby entered the dilapidated brick edifice that contained the offices of Finch Mining and Company. Years ago his father had waged a battle with the surrounding landowners and succeeded in the purchase of the vast acreage that adjoined the mine. Those brutal proceedings had included the decrepit mansion that now made up the company offices. Loose bricks and crumbling mortar presented the appearance of a business in trouble. A look that might persuade employees the company couldn't afford to give them raises or bargain with a union. Neither was correct, but his father was a shrewd businessman who used every means at his disposal to keep the company money in his own coffers. If it meant operating the company from a neglected structure, so be it.

After inhaling a deep breath, Kirby pulled open the heavy front door and entered the once-elegant foyer. Inside, peeling wallpaper and a frayed carpet runner perpetuated the impoverished theme. These offices were a far cry from the towering structure that contained the Pittsburgh offices, which had been well-appointed with expensive furniture and amenities to meet the wants of every wealthy visitor.

Kirby stepped to the doorway at his right and nodded to a bald man poring over a leather-bound ledger. He offered a nod before looking around the room. "Good morning. I need to speak to Mr. Daniels. Is he around?"

The bookkeeper pushed his spectacles onto the bridge of his nose before he returned the nod, then glanced over his shoulder. "I don't see him."

Kirby didn't miss the look of disdain or the sarcasm that colored the man's response. "Do you know who I am?" He moved forward two steps and pinned the man with a hard stare.

"No." The older man shrugged. "But no matter who you are, I think you can see that Mr. Daniels isn't here."

Kirby cleared his throat. "I am Kirby Finch. My father owns this company." His mouth curved in a condescending smile. "So if it isn't too much trouble, can you tell me where I might find Mr. Daniels?"

The older man blanched. "A pleasure to meet you, Mr. Finch. I didn't know who—"

Kirby waved him to silence. "No need for an apology. Just tell me where I can find Mr. Daniels."

"He's over by the tipple. Some kind of problem earlier this morning. You can wait in the office across the hall if you like." He pointed with the tip of his pen.

"No thanks. I'll go over to the mine." Kirby turned on his heel and strode from the room. He didn't relish the idea of meeting with Henry Daniels, and waiting in his office would only increase his uneasiness. Kirby would likely have trouble convincing Daniels to give him the money he wanted. There was little doubt Kirby would need to speak with authority.

Otherwise, Daniels wouldn't believe that Kirby's father had given his son permission to speak on his behalf.

He hadn't gone far when he caught sight of the manager walking up the hill toward him. Kirby removed his hat and waved it overhead. The manager shaded his eyes with his hand and then waved in return. Kirby couldn't be certain at this distance, but it appeared as if the manager's face had tightened into a scowl.

Kirby continued toward him and forced a smile. During his earlier visits to the mine, Kirby discovered the level of power entrusted to the manager. In addition, he observed Mr. Daniels's loyalty to his employer. Both Kirby's father and Mr. Daniels shared the same goal—to see Finch Mining and Company increase its profits by any means possible. Of course, Mr. Daniels's paycheck was hefty. Large enough that he could easily overlook the poverty of the miners and their families. No doubt he even slept well at night.

Kirby approached with his hand outstretched. "Good to see you, Mr. Daniels."

"I'd heard you were in town. Wondered if you were ever going to show up for work."

Kirby chuckled. "I haven't been here but a few days. Just long enough to get settled and begin checking into a few projects." He met the older man's gaze. "Related to the mine, of course."

"I didn't know we had any *projects* that needed checking into." He pushed an overhanging tree limb out of his way and continued walking. "Guess you better fill me in since I haven't had any word from your pa about these projects."

Kirby kept pace with the older man. "That's why I'm here. I'm going to need . . ."

Mr. Daniels pointed toward the house. "Let's get inside before you start explaining. I want to give you my full attention while I hear about the important work you're here to do." He shot a wry grin in Kirby's direction.

Kirby stiffened at the man's mocking behavior. He had anticipated resistance from Daniels, but he hadn't expected his condescending conduct. Well, Kirby had come prepared for this meeting, and when it was over, he doubted Henry Daniels would still have that smirk on his face.

A short time later, Kirby followed Daniels into the foyer of the old house and waited as he halted in the doorway of the bookkeeper's office. "I'll be in my office with Kirby. We're going to have a brief meeting. If you need me, don't hesitate to interrupt."

Kirby clenched his jaw and bit back a scathing retort. He didn't want to make their conversation more difficult than need be. He followed the manager into his shabbily furnished office and waited until Mr. Daniels indicated the empty chair opposite his worn desk. "Take a seat. Now, let's hear about these projects of yours."

The wooden chair creaked and gave a slight shift when he sat down. After a quick downward glance, he sighed. "Hope I don't land on the floor."

"You should be just fine. Besides, it's not far to the floor." Daniels leaned back and waited.

"I need some cash so I can purchase supplies and paint. Or if you'd prefer, we could set up an account at the bank. Whichever's easier for you, or I suppose I should say whichever's easier for your bookkeeper." He was careful to hold a steady eye on Daniels. If Kirby appeared nervous, the manager would spot his fear and go in for the kill.

A slow smile spread across the manager's face. He leaned forward and rested his arms atop the desk. "Is this your idea of a joke? You must know that the only allotment ordered by your father is payment to the boardinghouse and a small stipend for your expenses."

Kirby nodded. "Of course, but this isn't for me. This is for the repair of houses up on the hill. The miners' homes are owned by the company. Since you've been able to purchase a home on the edge of town, I'm sure you don't realize the condition of those houses. I've been up there recently, and the places are in ruins. They need major repairs, although right now I'll do my best to mollify the men with minor maintenance and a coat of paint."

"Mollify the men?" Daniels's knuckles turned white as he clasped his hands together. "What are you talking about? I doubt there's any unrest among the miners that's gone undetected by me. There's been no strife regarding unpainted houses or needed repairs. This is nonsense. I have work to do." He waved a dismissive hand in Kirby's direction.

"You might be surprised to know that there's talk of a strike in the near future, and even more talk about unionization."

Before he could make his point, Daniels guffawed. "I know your pa is worried about a strike and that he thinks you can gain information about that possibility, but I told him there's no reason to worry." He shook his head. "There's been talk of strikes and unions for over a year now and nothing's happened." His brows dipped low. "To be frank, your request for paint isn't making any sense. As I said—"

"Why don't you let me finish before you decide I don't know what I'm talking about." When the older man gave a nod, Kirby continued, "From what I've heard, paint and lumber would go a long way toward creating goodwill among the miners. A show of concern by the company that would help out their families and ease the unrest around here."

"Now who mighta told you that bit of nonsense?"

Kirby cocked his head to the side. "If you really think it's nonsense, why do you care who told me?" He leaned back in the chair. "Besides, if I told you how I was able to dig up the information, you wouldn't need my help, now, would you?"

"I didn't ask you to come down here, and I don't need your help to run this operation. I've been doing it for years." Daniels picked up a stack of papers and shoved them aside. "Ain't much that gets past me, so I think you're blowing smoke where there ain't no fire."

Kirby stiffened. He'd been annoyed when he was forced to listen to his father's account of happenings at various mines in the region, but now he was thankful for the knowledge. Along with what Hope had told him, he'd let loose a few of his father's remarks at Daniels. Maybe then the man would release his tightfisted hold on the company's bank account.

"You go ahead thinking you know it all," Kirby said, "but we both know the UMWA is a lot stronger now. Word has it they've been able to get union men hired on to stir up trouble in a lot of the mines in these parts without management knowing a thing until it's too late and there's a walkout. But I suppose you know all about that, too."

"'Course I do, except we ain't hired anybody in over six months. Fact is, we're laying off, not hiring." He folded his arms across his chest. "Anything else you feel you need to warn me about?"

Kirby shrugged. "Guess not. You already told me you don't need my help."

Daniels clenched his jaw and edged forward in his chair. "If you know something important, you need to tell me instead of playing these silly games. Having the union stir up the men means trouble for your pa and this company—and that means trouble for you, too."

"I *am* telling you. You're not listening." He lowered his voice a degree. "There's trouble brewing. If you're smart, you'll head off the trouble before it starts. I already told you my plan."

"Painting houses? That's a plan?"

For the next hour, Kirby argued his idea with the manager. It had taken every trick in his arsenal to finally convince Daniels that a little lumber and paint would be a cheap way to ward off a possible strike.

Daniels heaved a long sigh. "I don't s'pose it would cost that much. I'll send a telegram to your pa and get his approval."

Years ago, that remark would have sent a chill racing down Kirby's spine. But not now. He was prepared. Truth be told, he would have been disappointed if Daniels hadn't mentioned the need for his employer's approval. Kirby reached into his jacket and removed the carefully folded note he'd written and forged with his father's signature.

"No need to send a telegram. This will take care of your worries. My father gave it to me at the train station before I left Pittsburgh." Kirby pushed the message across the desktop.

Daniels unfolded the handwritten note that had been penned on company stationery. He stared at the communication for a long moment, then reached for the stack of papers he'd moved aside during their earlier conversation. After placing Kirby's note alongside another document signed by the company's owner, the manager frowned. Milton Finch's signature appeared identical.

Kirby slouched and yawned. "You look troubled, Mr. Daniels."

"I'm a little surprised your pa would be so free with—"

"As I said, my father's deeply concerned about the threat of a strike or unionization. He believes I can be of help unearthing more information about those risks. Besides, my father realizes I've had a change of heart regarding the mining operation and that I'm eager to learn more. After all, one day this will all belong to me."

A hint of skepticism remained in the manager's eyes. "I'm glad to know you want to learn more about the operation, but this goes against previous orders I've had from your pa. I'm feeling real uneasy about this."

"Then maybe you should send a telegraph to my father that you don't believe he sent this note."

This was one of the few times when Kirby was glad the coal mining town had only limited telephone service. The infant service consisted of no more than local calls between a few business owners. Having the ability to make a long-distance call would have given Mr. Daniels an opportunity to immediately speak with Kirby's father, but sending a telegram required more effort, as well as the waiting time for a reply.

Still focused on the signatures, Mr. Daniels massaged his forehead. "I don't s'pose your pa would have given you this note unless he meant for me to follow what it says. Still, it goes against everything he's been tellin' me about keeping costs down." He blew out a breath. "He's been so set against extra expenses, it's hard for me to—"

"I understand. My father has always spoken of your loyalty and ability to keep this place running when he wasn't around." Kirby forced a chuckle. "Which has been most of the time. I mean, you've always been the one who's kept this place going, and I know my father is grateful to you. He holds you in high esteem. In fact, right before I left Pittsburgh, he told me he hoped I would become as dependable as you have been."

Kirby's words hit the mark. With each accolade, Mr. Daniels's smile had grown wider and his shoulders squared. The man was more malleable than a child. A few syrupy words of praise and he'd likely agree to most anything.

"That's mighty nice to hear. I do work hard, but your pa has always been fair to me. I count it a real honor to work for him." He folded the note and set it aside. "He's a great man."

Kirby attempted to stifle a cough. "So . . ." The legs of the chair scraped on the wood floor as he rose to his feet. "How do you want to handle my purchases? Probably be easiest to give me cash or deposit money in a personal account at the bank."

If Daniels would simply instruct the bookkeeper to set him up with a bank account, he could use the money for gambling. In no time he'd end up with sufficient funds to get out of this town. Winning against these backwoods miners would be easy. All he needed was an invite to wherever they gathered to do their wagering and a little money to throw in the pot. He'd use every dirty trick he'd learned over the years and soon be on his way out of here. *Success!* He could feel it in his bones.

When Daniels didn't immediately respond, Kirby cleared his throat. "Either cash or the bank account would work fine for me."

Mr. Daniels shook his head. "I don't like the idea of a separate bank account. It's more work for Mr. Farragut and ties up extra cash." The manager scratched his head. "I think it's best if we set up credit accounts at the stores where you'll be purchasing goods. You can get most everything you'll need at the hardware store, but you might need a few things from the general store. I'll go with you and speak to Ned Berry and Doug Woodbine. Ned owns the hardware and Doug runs the general store. I don't want there to be any confusion about the accounts. I've got a little time. Why don't we go right now?" He pushed back from the desk and stood.

The suggestion hit Kirby like a sucker punch to the midsection. Things had been going so well. Using the back of his hand, he wiped away beads of perspiration that had formed on his upper lip. He needed time to think, to come up with another suggestion that would deter Daniels from the idea of credit accounts. But there was no time. Daniels was moving around the desk toward the office door.

He stopped beside Kirby. "You all right? All of a sudden you look kind of pale."

"I'm fine." It took everything in his power to choke out the words.

Daniels led the way into the hall and then stopped outside the bookkeeper's office. "I'll be gone for about an hour, Mr. Farragut."

The bald man cast a wary look in Kirby's direction before turning his attention to Mr. Daniels. "I need you to look at the pay records when you get time."

Daniels nodded and grabbed his cap from the hall tree. "I'll look them over when I return." He turned, gestured to the front door, and arched his brows at Kirby. "Let's get a move on. Once we have this set up, you can get things going up on the hill."

Kirby nodded. "I can hardly wait." Mr. Daniels gave him a sidelong glance. In an effort to hide the sarcasm still dripping from his curt response, Kirby forced a smile. "I know the miners and their families will be thankful."

"Let's hope so. And let's hope your idea will halt any more talk of strikes or unions. Otherwise, your pa is gonna be one unhappy man."

Kirby grinned at the older man. Mr. Daniels may have way-laid Kirby's plans for now, but he'd come up with a new one. One that would give him the money he wanted. For now, he would play along and gain the trust of some of the miners. He'd supply the goods needed to fix their houses and get the preacher to do the work. There were parts of this that would be advantageous to him. He could get out of doing much at the mine itself by saying he was helping the miners with their homes on the hill, and he could tell the preacher he was needed at the mining operation. His time would then be freed up to do whatever he wanted, whenever he wanted, with whomever he pleased.

Though the meeting with Daniels hadn't gone as planned, a silver lining was on the horizon. He was sure of it.

CHAPTER

10

Hope and her father had just finished breakfast and she was clearing the dishes when a knock sounded on the door of the chapel car.

Her father met her inquiring gaze and shrugged. "Early for callers. I wasn't expecting anyone. Luke said he'd come down about eight, so I doubt it's him."

She doubted it, as well. Luke had mentioned he needed to work in the family garden plot and cornfield before his morning visit. Since Luke's layoff at the mine, he'd been meeting with her father for morning Bible study. When Luke expressed his desire to become a preacher, her father had been eager to share his knowledge with the young man. While the two men studied and discussed the Bible, Hope busied herself with laundry and cleaning their living quarters. Occasionally she overheard one of their discussions and would join in, but usually she and Luke would visit afterward and they'd become fast friends. Both Luke and Nellie had introduced Hope to residents on the hill, and she'd gained acceptance—at least among the women—and for that she was most grateful. Even more, they'd both offered their friendship, though she secretly hoped Luke might one day become more than a friend.

Her father stepped around her and opened the door leading into their quarters. "Kirby! This is a surprise. Come in."

"I know it's early. I hope you'll forgive me." He stepped into the compartment and stopped short. Although Kirby had attended meetings in the railcar, he'd never seen the living quarters. He made a quick survey of their tight living space and swiped his hand across his forehead. "Whew! I don't know how you two can live in here. I'd go stark raving mad if I had to stay in something this small. How do you do it?"

The preacher directed Kirby to one of the chairs. "We're happy in our little home." He glanced at his daughter. "Aren't we, Hope?"

"Of course. We have everything we need right here in this small space." She directed a hard look at Kirby. "Our accommodations are better than those shanties your company owns up on the hill. At least we're able to keep warm during the winter and have screens for the windows and doors on the train. That's more than can be said for your company houses."

Her father frowned. "No need for a lecture, Hope. I don't think Kirby would be here so early in the morning unless there was some sort of problem or he needed assistance." He looked at Kirby. "Am I right?"

Kirby shifted in his chair. "I hope we can talk about a solution rather than a problem, Preacher, but I am in need of your help."

The preacher rubbed his hands together. "I'll do whatever I can. What kind of assistance do you need?"

Hope wiped her hands on a dish towel. If Kirby had a personal matter to discuss, her presence would likely cause him discomfort. "Should I leave while the two of you talk?"

"No, please stay. This whole thing started with you."

Kirby's tone hadn't indicated irritation, but there may have been a hint of accusation in his words. She couldn't be certain, so she stepped to her father's side to gain a better look at Kirby's face. He didn't appear angry. She tipped her head to the side. "What whole thing started with me?"

"Fixing up the houses up on the ridge for the miners and their families."

She clasped a hand over her heart. "You've come with good news?" Excitement bubbled in her chest until she thought she might explode. "Hurry and tell us!" She sat down on the sofa and stared at Kirby.

"The company is going to purchase supplies and paint to begin refurbishing some of the houses. I can't guarantee how many. We'll need to be thrifty, and there won't be any money to pay for labor." He hesitated and looked at Hope's father.

The preacher reached forward and patted Kirby's arm. "I told you I'd be pleased to assist with the repairs. I think Luke will lend a hand when he can, and we may be able to enlist workers from among the other young men. When can we start?"

"The sooner the better, I suppose. From what Hope tells me, fixing up the houses may ease some of the tension that's been on the rise between the miners and the company."

Her father's smile faded a modicum. "I appreciate what you're doing, but there's no guarantee a few boards and a little paint is going to heal all the wounds among the folks living up on the hill. If you're going into this with that idea, I'd caution you to set your sights a little lower. I think it will help, but . . ."

"But what, Preacher? Don't expect miracles? I thought you and God were in the business of miracles." He elbowed the older man and grinned.

"I believe all things are possible with God, but I don't believe He can be manipulated to suit our fancy. While it's true God is faithful to answer our prayers, there's something you need to remember." The preacher leaned toward Kirby. "His answers aren't always the ones we seek. Only He knows what's best for us."

Kirby's grin vanished. "Oh, I know about those prayers that don't get answered the way we want. When I was a kid, I prayed my brother wouldn't die. Guess God thought it would be better for my mother to spend the rest of her life grieving and for me to grow up without a sibling, right? Want to elaborate on that, Preacher?"

His anger was palpable. The earlier excitement had escaped the room like air releasing from a burst balloon. "I can't tell you why some people die and others live, Kirby. All I can tell you is that we live in a sin-filled world where both good and bad happen. Sometimes good happens to bad people; sometimes it's the other way around. But I know God loves me. His Son died for me."

"Yeah, I've heard all that before, but it doesn't change the fact that my brother died and then my mother died two years later." He stared into the distance, but then jerked back to the present when a nearby engine whistled. "Sorry, didn't mean to bore you with my life story." Bright splotches colored his cheeks.

"You're not boring us," Hope said, "and you never need to apologize for sharing the particulars of your life with my father or me. I think most everyone has been touched by death and sadness. We all need to talk about it sometimes."

She doubted her words adequately reflected the compassion she felt for him right now, but she did understand his emotions. When her mother had died, she felt betrayed by God. Had it not been for Aunt Mattie, Hope might have wallowed in her sorrow and become bitter.

She scooted forward on the sofa and met Kirby's pained expression. "When I was a young girl and my mother died, my aunt Mattie told me only I had the power to choose whether I would dwell on the unhappy circumstances in my life and eventually become a bitter, disagreeable young woman who would be liked by few or embrace the blessings I receive each day and become an affable, kind woman with a host of friends. I pondered her words for several days and decided I didn't want to become bitter and unlikable. I'm sorry to admit it took me more than a few minutes to make that choice." She pressed her hands down her skirt as she recalled that time in her life. "When pain runs deep, we sometimes need time and advice to guide us toward the right decision."

He inhaled a deep breath. "I'll think about what you said, but maybe we should get back to the business of fixing up those company-owned houses. Whether it eases tension or not, I've got the go-ahead, so we might as well see when we can get it done. While up there, I'm hoping I'll get to spend some time with a few of the men."

Hope's father patted Kirby's shoulder. "Good idea. I think the men will be quicker to let down their guard when you're on the hill rather than at the mine. We should make a list of supplies. Hope already knows where repairs are most needed." Her father flashed a smile in Hope's direction as he removed a sheet of paper from his desk.

Moments later, a knock sounded at the door, and all three of them turned. Hope stood and glanced at the clock. "That will be Luke. It's eight o'clock already."

She heard her father mention the morning Bible study to Kirby as she was crossing the short distance to the door. Opening the door, she greeted Luke with a bright smile. "Come in. There's good news to share."

Luke had barely cleared the doorway when he stopped short, narrowed his eyes, and whispered, "What's he doing here?"

Kirby swiveled around. "Good morning, Luke."

Luke nodded. "You joining us for Bible study?"

"Naw. I came to tell the preacher that the mining company is going to purchase paint and carpentry supplies to repair some of the houses up on the ridge."

Hope lightly grasped Luke's arm. "Isn't that wonderful news? I can hardly wait to tell the women they'll soon have screen doors and fresh paint. Some will even have repairs made to the roofs and siding on their houses." She bounced from foot to foot while delivering the news.

Kirby nodded toward the door. "Since your father and Luke are going to be busy with their Bible study for a while, why don't you go with me and we'll deliver the news together?"

Hope turned to her father and arched her brows in question. She wouldn't accept Kirby's invitation without her father's approval.

Her father smiled and gave a nod. "I think you should have the pleasure of delivering the good news with Kirby. After all, you're the one who's pushed to have the company provide the finances for the repairs. Besides, the ladies might not believe Kirby if he's the one who tells them." He looked at Kirby. "I'm told the company has broken some of their promises in the past."

Hope listened to her father's comments, but it was Luke she watched. His eyes had turned dark, his mouth stiffening into a taut line. There was no doubt he was unhappy. Surely he realized she'd done nothing to elicit Kirby's invitation. More than anyone, Luke should understand her excitement and be elated the company was going to repair the miners' houses. Yet he appeared as sullen as a child who'd been denied a piece of candy.

She stepped around Kirby. "Let me get my hat and then we can leave Luke and my father to their Bible study."

Her father gestured to Kirby. "While you're up on the hill, let folks know that you and I will head up the work teams and we're looking for volunteers to lend a hand."

"Whoa!" Kirby held up his hand. "I don't think I should be included as a leader of any work team, Preacher. I have my duties at the mine to consider. I don't possess enough carpentry skills to be in charge of anyone with a hammer, but I'll be up there supporting you every chance I get." He directed a wry grin at Luke. "Maybe Luke would be willing to take over as your second-in-command. What do you say, Luke? You willing to spare some time to make things better for your neighbors?"

"I'm willing to do everything I can to fix up those houses, but I don't think you should let your lack of skill with a hammer stop you from taking charge. As far as I know, you don't have any mining skills, but you've taken charge of the company, so this shouldn't be any different."

The exchange between the two younger men charged the air with an uneasiness that threatened to erase Hope's earlier excitement. She jabbed a pin into her straw skimmer and motioned toward the door before Kirby could respond. If they didn't depart right this minute, she feared the two men would end up in a bout of fisticuffs.

·············· ❧ ··············

Kirby followed Hope out of the railcar and offered his arm. When she didn't immediately accept, he nodded at the rutted terrain. "I don't want to be responsible if you trip on this uneven ground." He extended his bent elbow closer to her side. "Please."

She grasped his arm, and a sense of glee shot through him.

Not because he particularly wanted to win Hope's affections, though she would certainly prove a nice distraction while he was in town. Rather, he was glad to know his charming ways remained effective. He would need every ounce of appeal in his arsenal if he was going to accomplish his goal.

"I'm pleased you agreed to come with me, but I don't think Luke was too happy." He directed her around a furrow in the soft earth. "Is he calling on you? I mean, do you consider him a suitor?" They approached the path leading up the hillside, and he grasped an overhanging branch and held it aside for her.

"Luke, Nellie, and I are friends. If not for them, I doubt any of the folks on the ridge would have accepted me."

He grinned. "But do you consider him more than a friend?"

"He's . . . he's a very dear friend."

She'd struggled to answer his question. Given Luke's behavior, Kirby surmised there was more than friendship involved between Luke and Hope. While it wouldn't be wise to annoy Luke too much, he was going to find it difficult to ignore Hope. He'd not discovered many good choices among the women in this town, but Hope possessed both beauty and intelligence. And unlike most of the pretty girls Kirby had known, Hope didn't attempt to use her looks to gain an advantage. He doubted she even considered herself pretty. And while he wouldn't give her a second thought once he was out of this desolate town, she could provide a little amusement and usefulness while he was here.

Kirby was breathing hard when they arrived on the ridge. He'd hate to think of working in the mine all day and then having to climb this steep hill to get home. Hope jerked on his arm when they neared the first house, the one where he'd met Nora Selznick. He wondered if the woman had told Hope of their conversation. If so, Hope had never mentioned it to him.

"I'd like you to begin work on the Selznick house first. Their home needs a great deal of work. Nora said all the houses up here need screens. If one of the men could make screens for windows and doors before the heat sets in, I know that would be appreciated. The mosquitoes and flies are a real nuisance, and it gets too warm to keep the windows closed all summer."

"I'll stop at the hardware store and see how much screening they have on hand. They may have to order more." He scanned the area. "There are quite a few houses up here."

She waved to several children playing in the dirt a short distance from the dilapidated porch. "Is your mother inside?"

A little boy with disheveled hair sprinted toward them, his hands crusted with dirt. "She's feelin' poorly, but my pa's here. He don't have to go to the mine today, but he's goin' out to the woods pretty soon. Best hurry if you wanna talk to him."

Kirby stooped down in front of the child. "Your pa going out in the woods to go hunting?"

The child's eyes filled with curiosity. "Huntin'?"

"Billy!" A man shouted from the porch, and the boy ran back toward the house.

Kirby looked at Hope. "Is that Mr. Selznick?"

"Yes. Nora says he doesn't like me coming around, so I don't stop if I know he's home."

"Maybe he's afraid you'll put strange ideas into his wife's head." He chuckled. "You stay here and I'll go talk to him. I don't think he'll try to run me off since the company owns his house and the land it sits on." He hesitated a moment. "What's his given name?"

"His wife calls him Alvin. I refer to him as Mr. Selznick."

Kirby didn't expect a hearty welcome, but if he was going to make inroads with the men, he had to begin somewhere. "Good mornin', Alvin. I've come up here with Miss Hope to let you and the other families know we're going to begin repairs on some of the houses. Yours is first on the list." He drew closer and extended his hand.

Alvin swiped his hand on his breeches before accepting Kirby's. "Ain't no denyin' it needs work, but I ain't got money for supplies."

"The company's going to purchase the supplies, and the preacher and Luke Hughes are planning to head up the work teams. Of course, I'll help when I'm not needed down at the mine. We're hoping some of you men might lend a hand, too."

Alvin took a backward step and let his gaze wander over his shoulder. "That's good to hear. Don't know how much labor you can expect from any of us men. When we're not down at the mine, most of us got to look for other ways to earn a few dollars to feed our young'uns."

Kirby patted Alvin's shoulder, and although the older man flinched at the gesture, Kirby didn't remove his hand. "I understand that earning a living has to come first, but if you have a little extra time, I know it would be appreciated."

"Me and the missus will do what we can, but right now I gotta get to work in my garden plot."

"Garden? I thought your boy said you were going to the woods."

Alvin's eyes narrowed. "That young'un don't know what he's talking about. Ain't got much up here." He tapped the side of his head with his index finger. "You might as well move on so you can tell the others about the repairs. I'm guessin' they'll be happy for the news." Alvin turned and strode toward the children.

Kirby didn't share Alvin's assessment, especially since Alvin hadn't appeared thrilled by the plan. Were the other men going to prove as standoffish?

Kirby stared at the miner's back as he approached the young

boy and slapped him on the side of the head. "Don't you be tellin' no one I'm out in the woods. Ya hear me?"

The child ducked and covered his head. "I hear ya, Pa. I'm sorry. I didn't mean no harm."

Alvin ignored the boy and stomped onto the porch and inside the house without a backward glance.

Kirby grimaced. While he'd hoped to gather some information that might prove useful, he hadn't expected the boy to suffer because of the inquiries. He stepped to Hope's side. "Appears Alvin has a quick temper. I don't know why he became angry over something as trivial as a comment about going to the woods."

Hope matched his stride, and they continued on to the next house. "I'm sure it's because there's activity that goes on in the woods that's secret. At least that's what Nellie has told me."

"What kind of activity? Some sort of gambling house or speakeasy?"

"I'm not sure. She told me it wasn't safe for me to go in the woods. I guess there have been a couple of strangers who've been shot at when they went out there uninvited." She shivered. "Isn't that terrible?"

Kirby nodded and mumbled his agreement while his thoughts raced. He wasn't sure what might be going on out in the woods, but given Alvin Selznick's reaction when his son mentioned it, and Nellie's warning to Hope, it had to be something illegal. Something that might provide the money he needed to get out of this town. Excitement pulsed through him like a hammer striking an anvil.

CHAPTER

11

Hope grasped a damp dishcloth in her hand and walked over to a rope clothesline her father had strung between a towering black walnut tree and the chapel car. She pegged the towel to the line and then went back to the railcar. In this humidity, she figured the towel would remain damp until early afternoon.

She hiked her skirt a few inches, climbed the rear platform steps, and poked her head around the doorway leading into the living quarters. "Are you ready to go, Luke?"

He pushed back his chair and stood. "Good timing. We just finished." Luke patted her father on the shoulder. "Good study this morning. You gave me a lot to think about."

"If you want to discuss those thoughts tomorrow, we'll take time to do that." Hope's father turned toward her. "I want to work on my sermon before I continue with my carpentry duties. Why don't the two of you stop by the hardware store and see if that screening arrived that Kirby ordered. I thought it would be here last week. If so, it would be wise to get the screening cut and nailed to the window frames before we start on the roofs. I'm hearing complaints about mosquitoes and flies."

Luke nodded. "We'll be sure to ask. If it's come in, I should be able to get some of it up the hill this morning." He hesitated a moment. "Depending on how it's bundled, of course, but I should be able to hoist it up the hill on my shoulder."

"Don't hurt yourself trying to carry too much," the preacher said. "We can't afford to have you laid up with injuries. I don't know what I'd do without your help."

Luke immediately stood a little taller. With each word of praise from her father, Luke seemed to gain a modicum of confidence and pride in his workmanship. Perhaps he'd received little respect in the mine.

Together, they crossed the weed-filled patch between their railcar and the depot. Hope held Luke's arm as they rounded the depot and prepared to cross the street. A horn honked, and she jumped backward as a green flatbed truck sent a plume of dust flying in their direction.

"You okay?" Luke's eyes shone with concern when he turned to look at her. He frowned and pointed at her dust-covered skirt. Hope brushed her palm down the front of her skirt. "Kirby's a bit of a show-off when he's in that truck, but I don't think he saw us."

Luke raised an eyebrow, but didn't reply. She was thankful he hadn't let Kirby's behavior spoil their time together. She remained close to his side as they crossed the street and continued on toward the hardware store. The owner, Mr. Berry, stood near the entrance of the store and waved when they entered.

"Morning, Ned." Luke's work boots clattered on the wood floor. "We stopped by to see whether the screening Kirby Finch ordered has come in yet. Folks up on the hill are asking about screens more than anything else."

Mr. Berry's bushy brows dipped low on his forehead. "Yep. Kirby picked up the order not more than ten minutes ago. I loaded everything onto the bed of his truck." He chuckled. "Not sure how he's gonna get those supplies up to the ridge. I had to load the whole order; he never lifted a finger. Maybe he was saving his energy so he could carry everything up the hill. I told him he wouldn't get that truck up there unless he tried to cut through the woods, but going through the woods wouldn't be smart." The older man shrugged. "He said he'd been up the hill before and knew he couldn't drive up the path."

"Might've been best if you hadn't mentioned going through the woods. If he gets lost, there's a chance he could get shot."

The store owner laughed. "Didn't think about that. Might take a bit of starch outta him if somebody starts shooting." His smile disappeared when he glanced at Hope. "That wasn't kind. I don't want him to get hurt, but he's sure a hard fella to like. Pretty full of himself."

Luke nodded and gave the owner a mock salute. "Thanks for your help, Ned."

They weren't far from the store when Hope tugged on Luke's arm. "What's the big secret about the woods? Nellie told me it wasn't safe, but she wouldn't say anything more."

"Some of the men like to spend their free time out there. They don't like uninvited guests, so Kirby or you or anyone else who doesn't live on the ridge wouldn't be welcome. That's why you should always use the path. Those men are known to shoot first and ask questions later."

Hope frowned. "I think you know more than you're telling me. Why would they shoot someone just because they're walking through the woods?"

"The less you know, the better. These men consider the woods their stomping ground to do as they please, and they don't want intruders." He pointed to a spot near the bottom of the path. "Looks like Kirby took Ned's advice. I kind of expected him to do just the opposite, but I'm glad he didn't."

She smiled at him. "I'm delighted to hear you say that."

"Why's that?"

"Because I feel as though you're somewhat unwilling to accept Kirby. The fact that you're glad he didn't cut through the woods shows you don't want him to get hurt."

He lengthened his stride when they drew near the truck. "I'd rather talk about something other than Kirby." He walked to the side and peered over the wood slats. "Looks like he left the whole order right where Ned put it."

Hope walked to the back of the truck and sighed. "I can carry some of the smaller items. If you take one roll of screening, maybe my father will see the other roll and bring it up when he arrives."

"I can make a couple trips. I don't want your father carrying one of those rolls." Luke shook his head. "And you wonder why I haven't shown a real liking for Kirby. You have to admit, he's pretty lazy."

"I'm sure he thought one of the men would come down and get the supplies. Most of them are stronger, and I'm sure he thinks that if he's purchasing the items to repair their homes, the least they can do is carry them up the hill."

"Maybe, but they're *his* houses. Since the company owns them, they should be the ones to fix them. If we can't pay the rent, they kick us out." He inhaled a deep breath and blew it out. "Why do you feel the need to constantly defend him?"

"I could ask you why you feel the constant need to criticize him. Nothing he does suits you."

He stopped and wiped the perspiration from his forehead. "Maybe you're right. There's nothing Kirby Finch or his pa could ever do that would bring my pa back, but if they would have made the changes they promised years ago, other men wouldn't have died in that same mineshaft. When mine owners know there's problems and they do nothing to fix things, I hold them responsible for each man who dies in their mines. Kirby worked for his pa back in Pittsburgh, and that tells me he knows the problems we got in this mine just like his pa knows." Luke shook his head. "Greed. That's what causes men to die in these mines."

She lightly grasped his arm. "I'm sorry for the pain you and your family have suffered, but unless we give Kirby a chance, we'll never know if he'll be the one to make a difference."

The smile he offered didn't quite reach his eyes, but she hoped her words would ease some of the tension between the two men. She reached inside the truck bed and removed a box filled with sacks of roofing nails, tacks for nailing screens, screws, nuts, bolts, and a variety of other fasteners. "I can carry this."

Luke lifted the box and gave it a jiggle. "It's pretty heavy. Maybe you should take a few of the sacks out. It's a long walk up the hill." He grabbed two of the larger bags.

"Leave them. I'll be fine."

"Whatever you say." He swung around and placed the box in her extended arms.

The thrust of weight caused her knees momentarily to buckle, but she managed a quick recovery. Not quick enough that Luke hadn't noticed. She'd seen his eyebrows arch as if to accentuate his warning, but she didn't heed it. Even though the box was heavier than she'd originally thought, she was determined to make it up the hill without complaint.

Luke grunted as he hoisted a sizable roll of screening onto his shoulder. He shifted the weight to gain his balance, then looked at her. "Ready?"

139

Instead of telling him the box was too heavy, she gave a nod and trudged to the bottom of the path. "Ready."

Climbing the hill was going to test her mettle, but she didn't want to yield to Luke's advice. Was it pride, anger, or plain old stubbornness? Perhaps a combination of all three? Aunt Mattie had sometimes accused Hope of being stubborn when things didn't go her way. So had her father. While she admitted she could sometimes be stubborn, Luke had tapped into a burst of unexpected pride with his suggestion that she was weak. However, her determination was foolish. If she fell while carrying the supplies, not only would she injure herself, but she'd also leave the hillside scattered with nails and screws they'd never recover. With each painful step, she silently rebuked herself for the rash decision.

They had made it only halfway up when her shoulders began to ache and her arms trembled with weakness. "I think I'll set this down and take a short break. You go ahead. I'll see you when I get up there."

Luke hefted the roll of screen from his shoulder and placed it on the ground. "I'm not leaving you." He lifted the box from her arms and placed it beside the screening. "There's a stump over there. Why don't you sit down for a few minutes?"

Though she disliked admitting to her weakness, she pushed aside her pride and did as he suggested.

Once she was seated, Luke lowered himself to a small mossy patch alongside the tree stump and folded his legs in front of him. "I'm glad you suggested we stop. Carrying that roll of screening was causing my arm to cramp." He dangled his right arm in front of him and shook his hand.

Hope doubted he was in need of a break, but she'd keep that thought to herself. There was no need to accept his gesture of kindness with words that might provoke an argument.

They hadn't been there long when Hope stood. "We can't waste any more time sitting here. I'm fine now."

Luke pushed to his feet. "I'll agree to go on if you agree to leave that box right where it is. Since Kirby is still up there, maybe he can come and get it." He folded his arms across his chest and waited.

The steepest portion of the path remained ahead of them, and they both knew she couldn't make it while carrying the box. Finally she nodded and said, "Fine. I won't be mulish. It would only waste more time."

He chuckled. "Thank you."

He'd been more talkative since she agreed to his request, his mood lightening as they continued on. Luke came to a halt when they rounded the end of the path. She followed his gaze to the Selznick house, where Kirby was stooped down and talking to Billy Selznick.

"It looks like Kirby has befriended Billy. That little fellow is always seeking attention from adults, especially men. I've watched him follow after my father when he's up here. I think it's because Mr. Selznick is so harsh with the boy, don't you?" Hope tipped her head to the side when she noticed Luke's deep-set frown. What had she said to create such an unexpected reaction? "What's wrong, Luke?"

"Nothing, in particular. I'm just wondering why Kirby's taken such an interest in the children who live up here." Luke dropped the roll of screening to the ground and turned toward Kirby. "Hey, Kirby! Could you come help us?"

Kirby looked in their direction, then stood and waved. "You bet. Be right there." He leaned down near Billy's ear and appeared to slip something in the boy's hand before he sprinted toward them. "What can I do?"

Luke motioned to the path. "There's a box of supplies

near a large stump about halfway down the hill. Could you fetch it?"

"Sure. Be glad to. I need to go to the mine for about an hour, but I'll bring it on my way back up, if that's okay." He flashed a charming smile at Hope. "Unless you need it right away. If so . . ."

Hope tucked an unruly auburn curl behind her ear. "Of course not." She glanced at Luke. "You won't need those items until later, will you?"

"No, but I'll probably run out of tacks to nail the screens in a couple hours."

Kirby drew near and landed a light slap on Luke's back. "Not a problem. Glad to lend a hand."

"Thanks." Luke shifted his shoulder away from Kirby's hand. "Surprised to see you talking to Billy after hearing Alvin shout at him for talking to strangers the other day. I hope Alvin didn't see you. He's got a short fuse, and I'd hate for the boy to get in trouble again."

"No need to worry. I saw Alvin leave the house before I spoke to Billy." He reached for Hope's hand. "Looks like you've scraped your fingers. What happened?"

Heat flamed in her cheeks, and she pulled her hand from his grasp. "I was trying to carry a load that was too heavy. When I shifted the box, my hand scraped on the wood. It's nothing serious."

Kirby aimed a harsh eye in Luke's direction. "I wouldn't think you'd permit a lady to exert herself in such a manner." His tone changed to one of sympathy when he looked at Hope. "Don't you worry. I'll take care of getting that box up here when I return. You should see to getting a bandage on your fingers so they heal properly. Do you want me to stop at the doctor's office and see if he can send some ointment?"

Hope lowered her eyes and hid her hand behind the folds of her skirt. "My hand will be fine. I don't need any medical attention, but thank you for being so kind."

After a slight nod and wave, Kirby headed toward the path, and Hope gave Luke a sideways glance. "See? All you had to do was ask. He's willing to help. And his offer to stop at the doctor's office was very thoughtful, don't you agree?"

Luke gave the roll of screen a light kick before hoisting it onto his shoulder again. "Yeah, he's one thoughtful guy."

Luke went to an empty patch of ground not far from the Selznick home and dropped the roll of screen, his thoughts skittering like hot grease in a skillet. He wanted to believe Hope had begun to care for him as more than a friend, that her feelings would soon match his own. Yet it now seemed it was Kirby who had captured her affections. He clenched his jaw at the thought, removed a tape measure from his pocket, and stepped toward the windows of a nearby house.

Kirby remained at the forefront in Luke's mind as he continued around the house, measuring and jotting figures on a piece of paper. "You gonna stand there all day staring at that window?"

Luke startled and dropped the tape measure at Bertha Fredericks' feet. She stood in front of him with her worn hands perched on her hips. "I hung out a week's worth of wash while you been out here lollygagging."

"I've been working ever since I got here, Miss Bertha." He leaned down and retrieved the tape measure, then moved to another window. "You might think I'm wastin' time, but I need to measure the windows before I cut the screen."

"Seems like you had plenty of time to get done with your

measurin'. My young'uns is gonna be eat alive by skeeters if you don't get to movin'."

"I'm doing my best, Miss Bertha. If some of the other men would help out, things would get done a lot faster." He held the tape measure to the window. "You might mention that to your husband. Haven't seen him lend a hand since we started."

Luke's comment was enough to send the woman scampering back inside and provide peace and quiet while he completed the measurements on several houses and cut the roll of screen. He would have preferred making frames, but that would be a monumental task. If they were going to complete all the necessary repairs, they'd have to take a few shortcuts. Like Mr. Fredericks, the other men who lived on the ridge disappeared into their gardens or out to the woods on their time away from the mine, offering no apologies.

Then again, neither had Kirby. Luke figured most of the company men would starve to death if they truly had to work for a living.

The afternoon sun beat down on his back while Luke continued cutting and tacking screens. His fingers ached from the cutting shears and he'd nearly run out of tacks. Kirby should have returned long ago. He'd said he would be gone for only an hour. Luke trudged toward the path and blew out a long sigh. If he wanted those supplies, he'd have to get them himself.

Hope stood a few houses away with her hands cupped to her mouth. "Where you going, Luke?"

He stopped and turned around. "Down the hill to get the supplies. Looks like Kirby wasn't as willing to help as you thought."

CHAPTER

12

K irby stared out the dirty window of the small room he'd claimed as his office in the old house owned by the mining operation. Every day for the past week, he'd crept into the woods trying to discover what Alvin Selznick and the other men were doing out there. He decided it must be some sort of gambling or other illegal activity. Otherwise there was no reason for the men to be so secretive. Kirby had remained unwavering in his decision to find out what they were doing and, more important, become involved in anything that might yield him some cash, enjoyment, and a little excitement.

After scouring the area for three days, he'd returned to the Selznick house and enticed Billy with the promise of another quarter for better directions. The boy had scratched out a rough map of where his pa supposedly spent his time in the woods, but the map hadn't proved any more helpful than the boy's earlier instructions. By now, Kirby was beginning to doubt Billy had ever been in the woods with his pa. Any attempts to befriend another child who might offer better information had proved futile. They'd all run off like frightened rabbits when he approached.

Kirby pulled his thoughts back to the present and read the letter he'd scratched out to his father. Hopefully, he'd given the older man just enough news to hold him at bay. If his father didn't believe he was doing as instructed, the older man might make an unexpected appearance in Finch, and Kirby didn't want that to happen. It would take his father only a short time to learn Kirby hadn't been using his time to discover information about strikes or unions.

With a sigh, Kirby leaned back in his chair, viewed the coal tipple from his window, and curled his lip. Henry Daniels had mentioned they needed to talk about the mine, yet Kirby was tired of waiting on him. He pushed up from the chair and strode into the hallway. "I'll be out the rest of the day, Mr. Farragut. Tell Mr. Daniels I have other matters that need my attention up on the hill."

The bookkeeper looked up from his ledgers. "I believe Mr. Daniels wanted to have a meeting with you this morning." He reached to his left and tapped a calendar. "Yes. It's written down for nine o'clock." Mr. Farragut glanced at the clock hanging on the far wall. "It's only eight thirty."

Kirby stiffened at the man's patronizing tone. "I know the current time, Mr. Farragut." He pinned the older man with a hard look. "Problem is, I need to be up on the ridge by nine o'clock. Besides, I thought when he said 'first thing in the morning,' he meant first thing. Not nine o'clock."

The bookkeeper's eyes flashed. "He never has meetings before nine. Mr. Daniels spends the early part of his day down at the mineshaft. He's been here since six o'clock."

Kirby shrugged his shoulders. "That's good to know, but it doesn't help me today."

"Maybe if you spent more time around here, you'd know

what his schedule is." Bright red splotches colored Mr. Farragut's cheeks.

"No need to get yourself agitated over a missed meeting. Mr. Daniels won't be angry with you. He can look at your calendar and see you had it properly scheduled. Feel free to tell him it's all my fault. Put it down for another day and let me know."

The older man slid the calendar to the center of his desk and picked up his pen. "Would you care to tell me what would fit into your busy schedule, Mr. Finch? I wouldn't want Mr. Daniels to encounter this problem again."

Kirby glared at the man. How dare he act in such a brazen manner! "Let's remember who owns this company, Mr. Farragut. I'm sure you wouldn't want to find yourself looking for another job in the near future."

Mr. Farragut jerked back in his chair. "I'm only trying to make certain I perform the job I was hired to do, Mr. Finch. I apologize if I offended you in any way."

The bookkeeper's apology created an unexpected rush of satisfaction, and Kirby straightened his shoulders, giving the man a tempered smile. "Your apology is accepted. I'll meet with Mr. Daniels on Friday morning at eight o'clock."

"But . . ."

Kirby waved his hat at the bookkeeper. "Tell him he can go to the mine either before or after we talk, his preference. I don't want to meet at nine." He turned on his heel and walked out the door, enjoying a momentary sense of power.

He drove the company truck to the path leading up the ridge. For a moment he stared at the woods flanking the jumble of houses that clung to the hillside. Maybe he shouldn't go up to the ridge at all. Maybe Billy had given him incorrect directions on purpose. Maybe he should try a new passage into the woods.

Yes, that was it. He'd ascend the trail for a short distance, then enter the woods at an entirely different level.

He trudged up the dirt path until he neared the stump where Hope had left the box of supplies last week. That was the first day he'd gone into the woods. Kirby had become so set on locating Alvin or any other man who might be in the woods, he'd wandered around until he came to the frightening realization he was lost. When he finally returned to the footpath, it was nearly dusk, the box of supplies gone. He'd returned to his boardinghouse and that night attended the late church service at the chapel car. After the meeting, Hope expressed disappointment that he hadn't proved to be a man of his word.

Fortunately, his quick thinking and prognostication skills changed her mind. She'd become apologetic when he lied and said he'd become violently ill after he departed. Tears had formed in her eyes when he said he'd forced himself out of his sickbed to attend the service and request prayer for healing. He'd momentarily felt guilty for lying to her, but the feeling soon passed—especially when she asked him to remain so she could brew him some tea.

A smile tugged at Kirby's lips when he remembered her ministrations that evening. A squirrel scampered across the path and pulled him back to the present. He cast a glance at the wooded expanse. There didn't appear to be any sort of path, but maybe that was the secret. The men knew how to hide themselves out here without leaving any clue of their whereabouts. Of course, he hadn't seen any clues when he'd gone in the direction Billy gave him, either. He pushed aside the hanging pine branches and stepped into the thicket. He'd need to keep his bearings or he would never find his way out of here. He pulled a knife from his pocket and made a V on the side of a tree. If he marked trees as he moved deeper into the woods, he'd surely get out just fine.

Hours later, Kirby wiped the perspiration from his forehead and dropped to the ground. He hadn't seen or heard anything except for the occasional squirrel or rabbit scurrying through the brush. He should have brought food and water with him. Then again he hadn't expected to be here so long. He blew out a sigh and pushed to his feet. At first he'd done his best to move silently through the thicket, but after aimlessly wandering with no sign of another human, he'd quit worrying about each footstep.

Now all he cared about was locating the chinks he'd cut into tree bark and finding his way back to the path. He slapped a mosquito that circled in front of him, then landed on his forehead. "Confound it! This place is swarming with insects."

A second later, an earsplitting report was followed by a whizzing rush of sound. Buckshot tore through Kirby's shirtsleeve, and blood trickled from his upper arm. He clasped his right hand across the wound and dropped to his knees. When he opened his eyes, a pair of worn work boots and the metal barrel of a shotgun were all he could see. Sticky blood glazed his hand, and he forced his gaze upward. He was met with Alvin Selznick's angry scowl. Kirby mustered his resolve. He didn't want to pass out. If so, Alvin might finish what he'd started and bury him out here in the woods. No one knew he'd come out here. No one would even look for him out in these woods. Pain shot through him. He stared down at his bleeding arm. "You shot me!"

Alvin spit a stream of tobacco juice near Kirby's crouched figure. "Yep." He hoisted the gun and rested the barrel against his shoulder. "Guess I better check the sights on this thing. Looks like I only grazed ya. Don't appear you're bleeding much."

Kirby looked up with angry eyes. "You could have killed me!"

Alvin gave a slight nod. "Still could, if I'm a mind to." His brow furrowed, and he pointed a thumb over his shoulder. "There's signs posted all over warnin' folks to stay outta here. Them that choose to ignore 'em get shot."

Kirby couldn't deny he'd been warned, but he'd managed to ignore such admonitions all his life. Of course, his father and college friends had never carried guns. This place was different.

He shifted to a sitting position and leaned his back against the tree. "Signs or not, a person doesn't expect to get shot."

"What did ya think it meant when it said 'enter at your own risk'?" Alvin reached into his pocket, pulled out a dirty cotton square, and tossed it at Kirby. "You can tie this around your arm. You ain't got nothin' more than a scratch. It'll stop bleeding soon."

Kirby glowered at him. "If this is a scratch, I'd hate to see what a direct hit would have done."

"Mighta kilt the likes of someone that ain't got no more starch in him than you."

Kirby wasn't certain what Alvin had meant about "starch," but he did understand he'd been ridiculed by the miner. Using the tree trunk to steady himself, Kirby pushed to a standing position and looked in the direction where Alvin must have been only a short time ago. He caught sight of a lean-to that had been constructed into the hillside, partially hidden with vines and branches. A tarp strung between wood stakes hung above several wood casks, a couple of washtubs, and a variety of metal coils and receptacles. A low fire smoldered in a makeshift fire pit.

Realization hit like a bolt of lightning and his mouth dropped open. "You're making moonshine out here." Prohibition had been legislated by most counties in West Virginia. The miners weren't gambling; they were making and selling bootleg liquor.

"Unless you want more than a grazed arm, you'll keep your

mouth shut." Alvin tapped the barrel of his gun against his shoulder.

Alvin's menacing words created a seething indignation that quickly replaced Kirby's earlier fears. How dare this lowly miner stand there and threaten him! He was Alvin's employer, his landlord, his superior in every possible way. Yet Alvin stood there thinking he had a right to threaten Kirby for walking through property that belonged to his family.

"For your information, Alvin, this land is owned by my family. In truth, I *own* that still and all the moonshine in those casks over there. And before you aim that gun at me again, you ought to know that I didn't come out here without telling someone where I'd be. If anything happens to me, you won't get away with it."

Alvin laughed. "All I gotta say is that I was out in my garden working when you went missing. My old lady will vouch for me."

"Trouble is, other than Luke Hughes, you're the only man who isn't working at the mine today. I looked at the schedule this morning before I came up here. Won't take the sheriff long to figure out who shot me, especially since most of the women on the ridge will vouch that Luke was there all morning repairing their houses." Kirby's voice hadn't wavered, and his steely gaze had held Alvin's attention. He hoped his skill at fabricating half-truths and lies would prove good enough to get him out of this jam.

Alvin narrowed his eyes until they were mere slits. "I ain't sure I believe anything you said, but I admire a man willing to argue against a shotgun with nothing more than a few words." He lowered the weapon and aimed it at Kirby's belly.

The tree bark bit into Kirby's shoulders as he shrunk back and gasped.

Alvin swung the barrel toward his still. "C'mon. I ain't gonna shoot ya. Least not right now."

Kirby remained pressed against the tree and watched Alvin stomp away toward the still. The miner stopped and looked over his shoulder. "C'mon afore I change my mind."

Kirby drew a shallow breath and followed, still unsure he'd exit these woods alive.

When he neared the still, Alvin pointed to a piece of lumber balanced between two tree stumps. "Sit down." He immediately shook his head. "In the middle. That piece of wood ain't nailed down. If you sit close to one end, you're gonna wind up on the ground."

Kirby did as he was instructed. He didn't ask any questions, but while Alvin put out the low-burning fire, Kirby attempted to memorize his surroundings.

He startled when Alvin tossed a pebble that landed near his shoe. "I know what you're doing, but you ain't gonna find this place on your own."

"I found it today, so that means I could likely find it again." Kirby met Alvin's lopsided smile.

"Ha! You didn't *find* it—you was as lost as a bear cub separated from its mama." Alvin finished dousing the fire, then moved to the bench and dropped down beside Kirby. "I think what's best for both of us is if we come to a meetin' of the minds."

"Such as?" Kirby asked.

"Such as, I don't shoot you, and you keep yer trap shut."

"I can offer a better idea, one that will give us both some financial gain and provide protection for you and your operation."

Alvin snorted. "*You're* gonna protect me. Now, that's downright funny."

"You won't think it's so funny once you hear what I have in mind."

"I'm listening." Alvin didn't appear convinced, but at least he hadn't picked up his gun.

"I like your operation. I want to become a partner. I think—"

"I don't need no partner."

"Let me finish, Alvin. I think you'll soon change your mind." Kirby knew he'd need to talk fast and keep it simple or Alvin wouldn't hear him out. "If we join together, you can double your income. I can make sure you're off work whenever you want, and you can be out here making more liquor." He sucked in a quick breath. "The best part is you'll have more time because I'll take over delivering the moonshine. I can use the company truck. I don't know how or where you're selling your liquor, but I can make that part of the operation a lot faster and easier for you. I won't be suspected by the sheriff or revenuers, and if I use the company truck, we can figure how to raise the truck bed and hide it in a compartment underneath." He drew in another breath. "What do you think?"

Alvin rubbed his stubbled jaw. "I don't know. You could be working for the revenuers right now. I'm not sure I trust you enough to be your partner."

"That makes us even. I'm not sure I can trust you, either." Kirby forced a smile. "This could make us both a lot of money."

Alvin stared at him for a long minute. "Hard to decide if I'd be better off shootin' you right now or waitin' until I catch ya in a lie."

Hope dipped the bristles of her brush into a can of thick pea-green paint. Little wonder Kirby had been able to secure a special price on the outlandish shade. Given a choice, nobody in his right mind would have chosen such an ugly color. When they'd first seen it, the women had complained the shade reminded them of many things—all of them vile—and that they didn't want such reminders every time they looked out the window.

Eventually, Luke's uncle exclaimed, the color would darken once it was covered with a layer or two of coal dust. "The houses will turn the shade of the hillside in spring and summer," he'd told them. "The houses will blend into the woods and look like part of the landscape."

The women soon agreed, and the painting had begun. Right now, the hills more closely resembled a kettle of split-pea soup. At least Hope had been able to convince Kirby to purchase enough beige paint to cover the trim.

"Want me to paint around the door?" Luke stepped to her

side, holding a can of the tan paint in one hand and a paint-brush in the other.

She glanced toward the path. "That would be wonderful. My father said he'd be up to paint the trim this afternoon, but I don't know what's happened to him."

Luke stepped onto the front porch. "He probably got busy preparing his sermon or went to help someone in need. Then again, he may have gone to work on the church building."

She nodded. "You're probably right. He's been excited about the building project, but I'd rather he took some time to rest. I fear he's working too hard."

"I should ask Uncle Frank to lend him a hand when he's not down at the mine. He's pretty good with a hammer."

A week ago, her father had received permission and funding from the association to begin rebuilding the burned-out church in Finch. Since then, his sermons had been filled with words of encouragement and praise for answered prayer. There were excited responses from folks living in the main portion of town, those on the hillside, and even the railroaders had shown enthusiasm and a willingness to help with the project. After Bible study with Luke each morning, her father went to work clearing the debris from the church site. During the afternoons he climbed the hill to assist with repairs on the miners' houses before returning to the chapel car to preach at both the seven o'clock and the late-night meetings for the railroaders when they were in town.

Luke drew his brush down the narrow wooden frame. "I don't think you need to worry about your pa. Even so, I can go down and check on him if you'd like."

"Thank you, Luke, but I'm sure he's all right. He tells me I fret about him far too much. I know he's right. I try to remember that he traveled without me for many years."

156

Luke grinned. "And he did just fine. I'm more troubled by Kirby's failure to be up here helping with more of the work."

"Sometimes it helps that he's not around." Hope giggled as she continued brushing on a second coat of paint. "If he was here working, I'd have to get permission to put more than one coat of paint on the houses."

Luke wheeled around. "He's already said one is the limit. I thought you were just touching up some spots you missed."

Hope waved her brush in the air. "Look at this place. The first coat has already disappeared into the wood. I don't care if Kirby approves. I'm going to put at least two coats on the front of each house."

Luke pointed to the stacked paint cans. "We better make sure there's enough. Some houses don't even have a first coat yet."

"There's going to be plenty. I've discovered I overestimated when I told Kirby how much to order."

"I thought your father did the estimates."

"He did, but I increased the figures on a few things before I gave the list to Kirby. Father wanted to be frugal so that Kirby wouldn't change his mind about paying for the supplies."

Luke laughed. "Hope, I'm surprised at you."

"Are you disappointed?"

"Quite the contrary."

Luke dipped his brush and wiped the excess on the edge of the can. "What would you have done if Kirby had objected?"

"I think I could have convinced him to keep his word." She looked up at Luke. "But it wasn't necessary. He didn't object at all. In fact, he asked if there was anything else we'd need."

"Guess it's good he was generous with the materials since he's not doing much to help with the work."

Hope shrugged and continued painting, wishing Luke wouldn't press the issue. Kirby possessed little ability to swing a hammer, but at least he'd tried to complete a few of the minor jobs. Still, counting him as a member of their workforce added little value. "I suppose he needs to put his position at the mine first. He can't do that and be up here painting houses or tacking tiles on roofs."

Luke crouched to complete the bottom portion of the doorframe. When he stood, he turned toward her. "Maybe so, but he needs to actually be at the mine to do that work."

She arched her brows. "What do you mean? I'm sure he's busy in the office. Work at the mine entails more than digging coal."

"You're right, but he's not in the office. I saw Mr. Farragut the other day, and he said something about Kirby spending all his time up here helping us." Luke straightened his shoulders. "I think Kirby has been telling everyone a different story. I wonder what he's really doing with his time." He shook his head. "Maybe he goes back to the boardinghouse and sleeps all day."

Hope weighed his words, uncertain what to think. "Did you tell Mr. Farragut he hasn't been helping us?"

"Naw. Not my place to get in the middle of that mess. I did say that if he was needed at the mine, we could get by without him."

Hope chuckled. "Since we're doing just that, at least you didn't have to tell a lie."

"True." Luke reached for a screwdriver to pry the lid off a can of beige paint. "But I don't want to talk about Kirby anymore."

"Oh?" Hope stepped away from the house and turned to Luke. "What do you want to talk about?"

Luke cleared his throat. "Us."

"Miss Hope! Miss Hope!" Hope spun around and caught sight of Ned Berry waving his handkerchief overhead. "Come quick! It's your pa."

The paintbrush dropped from Hope's fingers and she ran

toward the hardware store owner. "What's wrong? What's happened to my father?"

"He's quite ill." Mr. Berry panted, then drew in a deep breath. "The doctor is with him and said you should come right away."

Luke placed a protective arm around her shoulder. "I'll come with you."

"You should stay . . ."

He shook his head. "I'm coming with you. The work can wait."

She leaned into his shoulder, longing to draw strength from him. Never before had she felt so fearful and helpless. What would she do if anything happened to her father? "Thank you."

"Can you tell us what happened?" Luke hugged Hope close. "Was he in an accident of some sort while working at the church?"

Mr. Berry shook his head. "No. He was over there clearing away the burned wood, but then came into the hardware store to check on some supplies he'd ordered last week. We visited for a few minutes, and then I left him at the counter and went into the storeroom to get his order. When I returned, I didn't see him. There was no answer when I called his name, so I headed toward the front door to see if he was outside. When I got near the front of the store, I saw him on the floor. I called his name and shook him, but he didn't respond so I ran for the doctor."

Hope took a steadying breath and swallowed the lump in her throat. "What did the doctor say?"

"He's not sure what's wrong, but he said I should fetch you. I figured it must be kind of serious since he wanted me to come all the way up here."

"Thank you, Mr. Berry." Hope was concerned by the man's heavy breathing. She didn't want him to suffer some sort of medical problem because of climbing the hill. Then the doctor would have two patients to tend to. "If you need to sit down and rest, we can go ahead without you."

"No, I'll be fine." Mr. Berry straightened his shoulders. "Let's get going." He hurried toward the footpath with Luke and Hope close on his heels.

They'd descended only a short distance when Luke lifted his hand to shade his eyes. "That looks like Kirby farther down the trail, doesn't it?"

Hope squinted at the figure descending the path at full speed. "I think so. At that pace he'll be back in town before we make it halfway down the hill. Wonder where he came from and where he's going."

Luke looked at her. "Either he started up the hill and turned around or he was out in the woods and now he's headed back to town."

Mr. Berry grunted. "I don't think that city slicker would be out in the woods. He's not the sort of fellow who'd be looking to shoot his next meal. He probably forgot something and turned around. I gotta say I'm glad his pa sent him to work at the mine—sure has been a help for my business."

Right now Hope was more concerned about her father than Kirby's comings and goings. "Is my father at the chapel car or the doctor's office?"

Mr. Berry shrugged. "I don't know. When I left, he was still on the floor in my store."

Hope half walked, half ran down the remainder of the hill, then headed toward the hardware store. They'd gone only a short distance when she pointed down the street. "That's the doctor and Kirby carrying my father on a stretcher." She shouted and waved in their direction.

Kirby glanced over his shoulder while they continued walking. "We're taking your father to the doctor's office," he called.

Mr. Berry waved them forward. "You two go on. Let me know how he's doing as soon as you know something."

Hope didn't take time to answer. Instead, she quickened her pace, and soon she and Luke caught up with the men. She clasped her palm over her mouth when she caught sight of her father. His complexion bore a gray pallor and he appeared unconscious. Luke hurried to help carry him, taking one end of the stretcher from the doctor's hands.

"Thanks, Luke. I was beginning to wonder if the two of us were going to be able to carry him the rest of the way to my office." The doctor shot a half smile in Luke's direction before glancing at Hope. "Why don't you go ahead of us and open the door, Hope. My wife should be in our living quarters at the rear. Knock on the door and ask her to prepare the examination room."

Hope hesitated. "Is he going to be all right? Do you know what happened?"

The doctor shook his head. "I'll be able to tell you more once I get him in the office and complete an examination. Go on now."

She wavered a moment longer. She wanted to help, but a part of her wanted to remain at her father's side. After one more look at her father's lifeless form, she ran and did as the doctor asked.

Mrs. Burch bustled about, insisting there was nothing Hope could do to help other than stay out of her way. She pointed to the other room. "Just take a chair in the outer office, my dear."

Hope paced back and forth until she finally heard the men approach, but their first words were for her to step aside. She felt like an unnecessary appendage. Once the men had placed her father on the examination table, Dr. Burch ordered them out of the room, and his wife closed the door with a firm click.

Hope dropped to one of the chairs and looked at Kirby. "Did he speak at all while you were with him?"

Kirby shook his head. "No. He was out cold the whole time I was with him. I was on my way to the mine when the doctor called to me from the hardware store and asked for help."

Luke frowned. "From where?"

Kirby lifted an eyebrow. "What do you mean?"

"I mean, the hardware store wouldn't be on your way to the mine if you were leaving the boardinghouse, so where were you coming from?"

"It's the middle of the afternoon. Why do you think I'd be leaving the boardinghouse?"

Luke stiffened. "'Cause it's where you live."

Hope pressed a knuckle to her lips to keep from shouting at the two men. Clearly, Luke was trying to bait Kirby or catch him in a lie. Right now, she didn't want a petty argument between the two of them.

"We saw you coming down the path a few minutes before us." Luke's voice had an edge to it. "Since you hadn't been up on the hill helping with repairs . . ."

Kirby twisted around toward Luke. "I had started up the hill, but once I was about halfway up there, I recalled I needed to stop at the hardware store and order something we need at the mine. Does that answer your question, Luke?" His earlier defensive tone was replaced with a defiant one.

Hope removed a handkerchief from her pocket and twisted it between her fingers. "Gentlemen, the only thing that matters right now is my father. You should both be ashamed."

Luke's gaze dropped to the floor. "You're right, Hope. I'm sorry. The only thing that matters is your father. I'm going to do everything I can to help you through this." He reached over and touched her arm. "You can depend on me."

Kirby cleared his throat. An air of discomfort surrounded him as he took a backward step toward the door. "And you can depend on me, as well. Whatever you need." He glanced over his shoulder at the door, seemingly eager to be on his way. "I need to get back to the hardware store. I never did place my order with Mr. Berry."

"Kirby, don't go just yet. I thought perhaps the three of us could pray before you leave." Luke gestured to one of the chairs.

Kirby winced and shook his head. "I'd like to stay, but I need to get that order placed. Can't afford to wait too long for those supplies." He turned to Hope. "I'll stop back later to see how your father's doing."

Hope stared after him. Why couldn't Kirby take a few minutes to pray with them? Could Luke be right about the man after all?

⁕

Near the base of the path that descended the hillside, Luke stooped down and picked a bright pink bloom and tucked it into his hand. This one would give the wildflower bouquet a little more color. The handful of flowers wasn't much to look at. His choices had been limited due to a late-night storm that had beaten the blooms off most of the foliage dotting the hill. Limp though they appeared, he hoped they would cheer up Hope.

He hurried across the railroad tracks and knocked on the door of the chapel car. Hope smiled when she appeared in the doorway. "Luke! What a nice surprise." Her attention shifted to the flowers.

He wasn't certain if her pleasure was due to the bouquet or his arrival, but it didn't matter. He was pleased to see her smile. He extended the bouquet. "Sorry they aren't in better condition, but maybe they'll perk up after they have time to recover from last night's storm."

"They're lovely. Thank you." She took the bouquet and

gestured for him to follow her inside. "I'll put them in one of my beautiful vases." She grinned and held up a glass quart jar that had been filled with canned peaches his mother had sent with Nellie a few days ago. She filled the jar with water, tucked the stems into the container, and placed it on her father's desk. "They brighten up the place, don't you think?"

He nodded. "Not near as much as you, but they do add color to your father's desk."

"Why, thank you. You do know how to make a lady feel better." She ran her index finger beneath one eye. "I don't think these dark circles brighten up much of anything." She sat down opposite him at the small table.

"Not sleeping well?" he asked.

"I'd like to blame the storm, but I find myself worrying about Pa. I know he'd tell me that worrying doesn't change a thing and I should spend more time in prayer, only it's hard to control my thoughts when I go to bed at night."

"Don't be so hard on yourself. You've been through a lot since you left your home in Pittsburgh." He hesitated a moment. "And even before that, what with the death of your aunt Mattie." He reached across the table and covered her hand with his own. "I don't think your pa would fault you for worrying a bit. Nellie said you were fretting because you couldn't get your washing and ironing done, what with spending so much time with your pa over at Doc Burch's place, so I was thinking I could go and spend the rest of the morning with him." When she brightened at the offer, he continued, "If you like, I could spend time with him on the days when I'm not scheduled to work at the mine."

"I could sure use the time here at home to get some things done, but I don't want to take you away from your work at the church building. I know Papa would want to keep things moving, and with him laid up, I'm guessing most of the men won't want to take charge."

Luke smiled. "Don't you worry yourself about that. So long as we have the needed supplies, I can make sure the men keep working on the church." He gently squeezed her hand. "Does that ease some of your worries?"

"Yes. Thank you, Luke."

He pushed up from his chair and nodded toward the wicker basket. "Then I better get myself over to the doc's so you can get started on that washing of yours."

............♒️............

Hope washed the few dishes she and Nellie had used last night, but her thoughts were elsewhere. Luke had been true to his word; Kirby had not. While Luke had been her stalwart companion and assistant during the weeks following her father's injury and ongoing recovery, Kirby had done little to help. She couldn't have managed without Luke. In truth, she still couldn't.

Dr. Burch assured her that soon her father would return to normal, yet as the weeks passed, she wasn't so certain about that. The doctor provided excellent care and had insisted her father remain with him during the early weeks of convalescence. Hope had reluctantly agreed, mostly because their quarters were cramped and holding meetings in the chapel car while her father regained his strength and memory would have likely proved impossible.

The doctor was vague in his answers concerning her father's accident. Since there had been few injuries other than a cut and large lump on his head, the doctor had surmised her father either suffered a seizure, apoplexy, or a heart attack, although her father had never mentioned any sort of pain in his chest. In his fall, he'd taken a blow to the head, and the jolt had resulted in memory loss. While he'd quickly regained a portion of his memory, much had not yet returned.

Hope convinced Luke that his daily Bible studies with her father over the last several months, together with his personal knowledge of the Bible, had prepared him to stand in for her father as an interim preacher. At first he'd objected, but then finally agreed that if folks continued to attend, he'd preach until her father regained his ability. That still hadn't occurred, and she'd recently begun to wonder if it ever would.

Every time Luke stepped up to the pulpit, Hope found her feelings of admiration growing for him. Not only did he possess a deep faith, he also lived that faith in his actions every day. He was steadfast and devoted, especially to the Lord.

She touched the tiny feather he'd given her, which she now carried in her pocket. He'd told her it was to remind her of Psalm 91:4—"He shall cover thee with his feathers, and under his wings shalt thou trust." Yes, God was covering her, but as her friendship with Luke continued to blossom into much more, she also felt he was covering her with protection and prayer.

He was sitting in one of the pews in the chapel car when Hope stepped through from the living quarters. He glanced up when she appeared. She offered a bright smile. "Preparing your sermon for this evening?"

"Yes." He gestured for her to sit down on the bench. "I always do better when you're close by."

She settled beside him and leaned close to see what he'd been writing. He laid his hand atop hers and created warmth that radiated through her body. Besides being her protector, he'd become her adviser, confidant, and problem-solver. When Hope had expressed fear over staying alone at night, he suggested his sister Nellie spend her nights with Hope in the chapel car. His suggestion had been met with quick agreement by both women.

That first night, Nellie appeared with a few bedtime necessities, along with Luke's rifle propped over her shoulder. She greeted Hope's look of disbelief with laughter. "I'm a good shot, and Luke says if there's anyone lurking about at night, I should shoot first and ask questions later."

Nellie had taken her brother's admonition seriously. On two separate occasions she'd fired the weapon. On the first, she killed a raccoon; on the second she scared the daylights out of Mr. Jeffries, one of the railroaders who'd attended a late-night meeting and had forgotten his cap inside the chapel car.

His hands were shaking when Hope handed him his hat. "In the future, it would probably be best to holler out to us if you come around after the meeting has ended. You might tell the other men, as well." She inclined her head a little closer. "Nellie doesn't hesitate to use that rifle."

"So I noticed. I'll be sure to tell the others, and if I forget anything else, I'll wait until morning to fetch it from ya." Then he'd hurried off toward the flickering lanterns at the railroad station while she and Nellie quietly giggled for at least half an hour.

In spite of the incident, Luke had convinced Mr. Jeffries and a group of other railroaders to continue working on the church building during their time off in Finch. They were men accustomed to hard work, and most possessed carpentry skills they were willing to put to use. They'd said it was the least they could do after all the late-night meetings he'd preached just for them.

Her eyes remained fixed on Luke's work-worn hand, enjoying the warmth of his touch. "I talked to Dr. Burch this morning. He thinks Papa is continuing to make good progress, but I'm not as confident. There's still so much he doesn't remember, it's frightening." An unexpected tear slid down her cheek.

Luke gently wiped it away with the pad of his thumb. "He's going to be all right, Hope. He just needs more time."

"After my mother died, I was so lost. If my father . . ." Her voice trailed off.

He stroked her cheek. "You're not alone."

"I know I have the Lord." She lowered her chin. "I should have more faith."

"That's not what I meant." He lifted her chin. "I meant you have me."

His gaze dropped to her lips, and his eyes seemed to darken to a deeper shade of green. Did his eyes always change like that or was it this tender moment?

"Hope." Luke's voice was husky. "May I kiss you?"

Words refused to form. She nodded, then closed her eyes and waited.

It seemed like forever before his lips met hers. The first kiss was everything she dreamed it might be—sweet, breathtaking, and reverent. But the second kiss surprised her. Their friendship had caught on fire, and her father would certainly not approve of kissing like this inside his chapel car.

But since he wasn't here, maybe it would be all right just this once.

Mr. Daniels rounded the marred desk, his face the purplish-red shade of a beet. "Weeks ago, when you insisted on changing the time of our morning meetings, I thought we'd come to an agreement."

Kirby gestured to a chair. "Sit down. You need to calm yourself."

"Don't tell me to calm myself, and I don't need to sit." His jaw twitched. "Do you even recall our agreement?"

Kirby shook his head. "Not really. What did we agree?"

"You promised that if I scheduled any future meetings with you at eight o'clock, you would be in my office at the appointed time." Mr. Daniels pointed to the clock. "It's almost noon and you're just arriving. I don't know anyone whose workday begins at noon."

"You do now." Kirby dropped into a chair, stretched his legs in front of him, and crossed his ankles. "What was so important that you need me here at eight o'clock? Looks like things are operating just fine."

"Does it?" Henry glowered at him. "They may appear to be

just fine, but they aren't. There are mine inspectors due here later today. I got a telegram yesterday after you left the office." He paused, then added, "Early, as usual."

Kirby bristled. "I can leave any time of day I want. I'm not a miner who's been assigned a hangtag."

Daniels might be the manager of this mine, but he sure wasn't going to force Kirby to maintain scheduled work hours. Each miner was assigned a number that was engraved on a metal disk attached to a thick piece of chain. The tags were picked up from a board inside the office when the miner arrived for work and returned when they left in the evening. The method allowed Mr. Farragut to keep track of the men's arrivals and departures each day. More important, in case of an explosion or cave-in, Mr. Daniels could tell at a glance which men were in the mine.

Daniels continued to glare at him. "Believe me, I know you're not one of the miners. If so, you would have been fired after your first week."

Kirby returned Mr. Daniels's harsh look with one of his own. He'd listened to about as much of Daniels's denigrating talk as he cared to. "You may be in charge, but you need to remember my name is *Finch*. I don't—"

Henry jerked forward. "I know your name is Finch. But you? You don't seem to care about this mine. You can't even get outta bed before noon." Daniels curled his lip and leaned back against the edge of the desk. "I don't have time to wipe the snot from your nose, Kirby. Truth is, you don't care about no one except yourself. You can go ahead and tell your pa whatever you want. I got real problems that need my attention. If you're supposed to be sniffing out talks of strikes or unions, you haven't told me one thing I don't already know. But I'm guessing there's gonna be a lot more talk since the inspectors found we had those problems in number four." Daniels pushed away from the desk and nodded toward the door. "Go on and get outta here. When you write your pa, be sure you tell him I kicked you out of my office, 'cause I'll be telling him the same thing the next time I see him. 'Course I'll be telling him why, too."

Kirby grasped the arms of the chair and tucked his chin low to his chest. He'd gone too far. He loathed the idea of an apology, but sometimes that was the only option. His father valued Henry Daniels and would heed the manager's words.

Kirby lifted his chin and forced a contrite expression. "I am very sorry, Henry. My behavior is inexcusable. I knew I was in the wrong. Instead of immediately offering an apology, I attacked you with a lot of bluster. Please forgive me." He'd used his most conciliatory tone and was pleased to see the stiffness slowly disappear from the older man's shoulders. "I'm here now, so let's quit arguing and talk about the inspectors. What's the big worry?"

"What's the big worry?" Daniels's words oozed contempt.

In any other circumstance, Kirby would have taken the offensive, but right now he had to remain calm and appear mollified. He swallowed hard and tightened his grip on the arms of the chair. Otherwise he might jump to his feet and punch Daniels in the nose.

"The *worry* is that we're not going to pass the inspection. I'll be surprised if they don't close us down. And while we're closed down, you can be sure union men will be sneaking into town, telling the miners the union can protect them in the future."

"I can keep an eye out for strangers coming into town and let you know about any meetings the miners might have with union organizers." Kirby didn't know how he'd learn of any such meetings, but he'd let Daniels believe there were a few miners who would confide in him.

Instead of acknowledging Kirby's remark, Daniels massaged his forehead. "We need better ventilation in the number-four shaft, but the miners don't want to quit digging since they get paid by the pound. Working on the ventilation means no pay."

Kirby frowned. "That's easy enough. Have Mr. Farragut average out what they make an hour and go ahead and pay them to get the better ventilation put in."

Daniels shook his head. "Already tried that. Your pa won't agree. He says nobody pays miners for anything except the coal they dig, and he's not going to do any different. Truth is, those men would rather go out in the woods and hunt or work their cornfields than go into the mines and work for nothing. Gotta say I don't blame them, but not having proper ventilation puts their lives in danger."

Kirby considered Mr. Daniels's comment for a moment. "So they'd rather go in there and take their chances of an explosion than work for a few days without pay?"

"Yep. And your pa would rather take a chance of being shut down than pay them for their hours putting in the better ventilation that's needed." Daniels folded his arms across his chest. "Your pa didn't think the inspectors would ever show up here. I didn't either, but I think someone wrote a letter and stirred things up."

"Does my pa know the inspectors are coming?"

"I sent a telegram, except that don't matter. He'll just tell me I'm being paid to handle any problems that come up in the mine."

"I say we tell the inspectors we're starting to put in the improved ventilation and that we've decided to pay the men to do the work. I can talk to them if you'd like. I think I can convince them." Kirby smiled, feeling like he'd redeemed himself. "I've been told I'm good at the art of persuasion."

Mr. Daniels didn't return the smile. "These are seasoned men who won't be fooled by groundless promises. If you tell them we're going to upgrade the ventilation, you can be sure they'll either have one of their inspectors remain behind, or they'll come back within a month to see if we've done what we promised. If we agree to upgrade and don't carry through, we'll be in even more trouble." Henry stroked his jaw. "Be honest with me. Do you really think you can convince your pa to pay the men so we can get the job done?"

He'd burned a lot of bridges with his father before coming to West Virginia. Right now, other than news of strikes or unions, Kirby wasn't sure his pa would listen to anything he said. Yet one thing was certain. He wouldn't divulge that fear to Henry Daniels.

Henry arched his brows, still waiting for an answer.

Kirby gave a firm nod. "I do. I wouldn't suggest telling the inspectors we'd begin work unless I was sure I could convince him."

Henry blew out a long sigh. "Then that's what we'll do. Both of us will meet with the inspectors, and you can tell them we have a plan. In the meantime, I need to meet with some of the men and tell them what we've decided. They'll need to know in case the inspectors question them."

Kirby nodded. "You do that." He was willing to meet with the inspectors at the office, but he sure wasn't going to go down into the mineshaft to spread word among the miners—or for any other reason. He'd *never* venture into those shafts. He leaned back in his chair and sighed. Had his father ever gone into one of those dark, dangerous mines? Probably not. The Finch men called the shots. They didn't get their hands dirty.

Several hours later, Kirby leveled his gaze at the inspectors sitting across the desk from him. Henry had been correct in his assessment. When the inspectors returned to the office, they'd already posted signs in front of number four. Both men insisted the shaft be closed until the ventilation was upgraded and inspected again. Henry had accompanied them to the mine, yet it was Kirby who took the reins upon their return.

"We completely agree that the ventilation is insufficient, and I'm sure Henry told you we've already agreed to pay some of our men to begin work on the upgrade. We would have started by now, but we thought we'd reach some kind of agreement with the men before now."

Mr. Summers, one of the inspectors, removed a pipe from his pocket and filled the bowl with tobacco. Using his thumb, he packed the tobacco tighter into the bowl before he looked up and thrust his chest forward. "I'm sure you'll forgive me if I don't entirely believe you, Mr. Finch. We hear that same story from all the mine owners and managers when we appear for our inspections. Unfortunately, nobody actually agrees to get things done until we arrive and close them down."

Kirby jutted his jaw and decided to use his college debate skills. "I won't forgive you if you're insinuating we are liars, Mr. Summers. I find such a notion repugnant. We care about the well-being of our men and their families. Even as we speak, this company is financing improvements to the homes where our miners live. You can't lump all owners into one category any more than we can lump all inspectors into one group." Kirby glanced toward Mr. Daniels. "Why, I'm sure there are many inspectors who have been paid off to forget what they've seen at a mine. Would you be offended if I insinuated you and Mr. Wayfair would remove that Closed sign if I handed you a sum of money?"

Mr. Summers took a backward step. "It wasn't my intention to insult you, Mr. Finch, but I take my position as an inspector seriously. If I fail to require necessary corrections and men die, I must bear the guilt for those deaths."

"And we take our position as owners seriously, as well. Without good men willing to go into those shafts and bring out the coal, our land is useless. Finch Mining and Company is going to correct the ventilation problem immediately. You have my word." He patted the man on the shoulder. "I'd be happy to drive the two of you over to the next town in our company truck. You'd be able to catch the train there."

Mr. Summers nodded. "I'll take you up on that offer, but Mr. Wayfair will be remaining in town until the work is completed on that shaft." He tucked his pipe into his pocket. "We know you have good intentions about getting the ventilation in, but we know what they say about that road and good intentions, don't we, Wayfair?" Mr. Summers elbowed his partner, who nodded.

Kirby bit back a scathing retort and forced a crooked smile. "You do whatever you need to, Mr. Summers, but I have to say it seems wasteful to pay a man's wages while he sits in a hotel room. Mr. Wayfair, maybe you'd like to help our men put in that new ventilation shaft? I'm sure your days will be mighty long with nothing to do."

Wayfair glanced at Summers. "You're right, Mr. Finch. I'd be glad to help. That way we'll be sure it's done right the first time." He chuckled. "And I won't even charge you for my work."

Kirby gulped. He'd let his tongue get ahead of his brains. There'd be no backing out or changing plans now. Whether his father agreed or not, they had to get men into that shaft and begin work on the ventilation.

Mr. Wayfair rubbed his hands together. "I'll go over to the

hotel and get settled and report for duty first thing in the morning. What time are your men set to begin?"

Henry cleared his throat. "They report at six. You plan to be here that early?"

Wayfair nodded, then turned to his partner. "How soon are you and Mr. Finch leaving?"

Mr. Summers hiked a shoulder. "Up to Mr. Finch, but hopefully soon enough to catch the next train." He arched his brows when he looked at Kirby.

"I have a few things I need to take care of before we leave. Why don't I meet you at the hotel in half an hour? That should get us to Longview before the train is scheduled to leave." He nodded to Mr. Wayfair. "And we'll see you in the morning."

The inspectors realized they'd been dismissed and hurried from the office. Once certain they were out of earshot, Kirby dropped into a nearby chair. "We're going to need to move forward without my father's approval. I'll send a telegram from Longview, but the fact remains, we have no options." Kirby massaged his forehead. "Let's speak to Mr. Farragut and make certain he understands he'll need to record the time and pay the men who work in the number-four shaft." He jumped up from the chair and strode toward the hallway leading to Farragut's office.

The older man didn't attempt to hide his misgivings. "Without your father's approval, I'm . . ."

Kirby stopped short and spun on his heel. "We have no other choice. I'm making the decision, not you, so push aside your worries. My father may write me out of his will, but he won't fire you, Henry. He needs you to continue managing this place."

Henry continued to fidget after they'd entered Mr. Farragut's small office. "There won't be a mine to manage if we spend our profits."

Mr. Daniels's quavering voice captured Mr. Farragut's attention, and his eyes widened. "What's this? You think Mr. Finch is going to close down the mine?"

"No! The mine isn't going to close." Kirby blew an exasperated breath and frowned at Mr. Daniels. "There are going to be a number of miners going into number four to repair the ventilation. You need to go through their records and average how much each man is paid per hour and then pay at that rate."

Mr. Farragut gaped. "But . . . that would be a very difficult reckoning, Mr. Finch. The men's wages are calculated by pounds of coal removed each day. Trying to—"

"Never mind." Irritation took hold, and Kirby waved the man to silence. He shifted to face Mr. Daniels. "Go and talk to the men and offer them an hourly wage. One that's as low as you think they'll accept."

Mr. Farragut shook his head and reached for his ledger book. "I'm not sure that's a good idea, Mr. Finch."

"I didn't ask for your opinion, Mr. Farragut. I don't have time to argue with you and Mr. Daniels. The ventilation in number four must be repaired or the inspectors will shut down our entire operation." Kirby clenched his jaw. "Pay the men," he ordered through gritted teeth. He glanced at the clock, then stomped out of the room. His plans for the afternoon had been ruined, and he'd have some tall explaining to do when he got back to town.

<hr />

The ride to Longview with Mr. Summers was proving dreadful. The man could talk about nothing but mining. If he wasn't discussing the methane leaks and floods that had occurred in various mines, he was revealing the horrors of the many explosions he'd investigated over the past ten years.

Kirby longed to tell the inspector that he thought conversations about mining were mundane and boring, but he forced himself merely to nod or grunt when required to respond. Near the end of their journey, Summers asked Kirby about various techniques used in their mining operation. He appeared eager to hear Kirby's response.

"You know, I'd like to tell you all about that, Mr. Summers, but the truth is, I've never stepped foot in any of our mineshafts."

The man's face contorted in horror. "You're joking with me. Never? None of them? How can you run an operation and not go into the mines?"

Kirby shook his head. "I came to Finch at my father's request, but I know very little about the operation. I'm sure you understand that it takes a long time to learn all there is to know about mining."

"Well, of course it does. Years and years of experience and accumulated knowledge are needed in such an operation. With your lack of knowledge, I'm surprised your father would entrust you with such a huge undertaking."

"My father knew I could rely upon Mr. Daniels and Mr. Farragut. They've been with him for years and know the operation very well. Mr. Daniels could have answered all your questions with great expertise, but I fear I can tell you very little about the inner workings of the mines."

The inspector leaned against the truck door, his jowls sagging with disappointment, and his voice silenced for the remainder of the journey.

...............❧...............

The moment he returned to Finch, Kirby parked the truck near the path leading up the hillside. He raced to the cutoff that would take him deep into the woods, then slowed his pace as he ducked beneath low-hanging branches. His senses heightened as he trudged through the undergrowth. The sun was beginning to set, and he wanted to get in and out of these woods before dark.

A branch crackled, and Kirby swung around. His heart thudded at a rapid pace beneath his jacket as he scoured the area.

"Where you been?" Alvin stepped from behind a large oak tree, his rifle resting against his shoulder. "I been waiting out here all afternoon. If you brung the law, I swear I'll shoot ya." He slowly lowered the weapon from his shoulder.

"Don't do anything crazy, Alvin. I didn't bring the law. I'm alone."

The words had barely escaped Kirby's lips when a shot rang out.

CHAPTER

15

A bullet whizzed by Kirby's ear. He ducked behind a tree, his heart pounding. He heard someone stomping through the underbrush, but he dared not risk a look. If it was a revenuer and they caught Alvin, so be it. His presence in the woods could be easily explained, although being spotted out here could prove to be Kirby's undoing.

"Carl Lee!" Alvin's voice echoed in the forest's valley. "What in tarnation are you doing? You coulda kilt me."

"Weren't shootin' at you, Alvin. I seen a revenuer sneaking around. You should be thankin' me for scaring him off. He was so close to you, he coulda snatched you by the arm and hauled you off to jail. I can't believe you didn't hear him." Carl tugged on his ear. "You going deef?"

"I'm not going deef and that ain't no revenuer you seen. Come on out here, Kirby."

Kirby removed his hat before he stole a quick glance from behind the tree. He wasn't about to make any hasty moves that might startle Carl. "Afternoon, Carl!" Kirby waved his hat, and when Carl didn't shoot it from his hand, Kirby cautiously ventured from his hiding place.

"What's *he* doing out here?" Carl Lee jabbed Alvin in the side with his elbow. "You crazy?"

Kirby edged a little closer. "He's not crazy, Carl Lee. The two of us have a working arrangement." He waved his hand back and forth between Alvin and himself.

"Right." Carl Lee spit a stream of tobacco juice that landed in front of Kirby's shoe. "He works in the mine and you own it. That ain't no reason for you to be in our woods."

Kirby wanted to tell Carl Lee the woods belonged to his father, not the men who lived on the hill, but he bit back the retort. "You tell him, Alvin."

Alvin didn't mince words. "Kirby's using his truck to deliver my moonshine. Safer for me, and I can stay here and make more while he worries about the revenuers stopping him on the road."

Carl Lee hoisted his gun to his shoulder. "How come you didn't tell me?" His eyes turned dark. "Looks like y'er set on taking over the moonshine business and leaving me out."

"That ain't the way of it, Carl Lee." Alvin pushed his floppy-brimmed hat back on his head. "You been knowin' me for most all my life, so you know better than that." He gestured toward Kirby. "I wanted to be sure I could trust him afore I said anything to you. That's the truth, ain't it, Kirby?"

Kirby nodded. "Alvin said it would be best to make sure things ran smooth before we included you." He shot a quick glance at Alvin. "The truth is, we're about ready. I've got my truck rigged up and I could make an extra run with your shine whenever you need me."

Carl Lee frowned. "How come you wanna take a chance running shine? We make and sell it 'cause we need the money, but you—you got all the money a man could ever need."

Kirby shook his head. "My pa's got all the money he could ever need. Trouble is, he doesn't share it with me. I'm working at the mine for next to nothing. I'm trying to get enough money so I can leave Finch and get started on my own."

Carl Lee tipped his head to the side. "You best not be lying to us or . . ." He grasped the barrel of his rifle and eyed Kirby with a look of warning. "You understand?"

Kirby nodded. "Understood."

He'd let Carl Lee and Alvin think they were in charge of the moonshine business, but they weren't going to be Kirby's main source of revenue. Two months ago he'd experimented with making moonshine on his own. Disappointed when his efforts had resulted in a dark, fetid liquid that would have killed a large horse, Kirby enlisted the assistance of Jimmy Ray Malloy, a young fellow who sorted coal from rock outside the mine. What Jimmy Ray lacked in intellect, he overcame with the moonshine-making skills he'd learned from his father. The boy was easily persuaded to construct and operate a still for Kirby. And while Kirby told Jimmy Ray they were partners, the young man was no more than an employee he paid a pittance for his knowledge and labor at the still. Making runs for Alvin had gained Kirby introductions and acceptance by owners of the nearby speakeasies.

Kirby would haul the moonshine and take a cut, but delivering his own product and earning far more cash would remain his primary objective. Once the West Virginia legislature carried through with its plan to make the entire state dry, Kirby planned to cross state lines and make even more money. If his plans went well, he'd stay in Finch and ride this money train until the law came sniffing around, and then he'd be gone. Jimmy Ray, Alvin, and Carl Lee could take the heat.

Carl Lee shifted his gun and pointed it at Kirby. "He don't

look or talk at all like us, Alvin. One of us needs to go to the speakeasies and tell 'em we got a new deliveryman or they'll think he's a revenuer."

Deliveryman. Kirby flinched at the term. While he was pleased that Carl Lee noticed he didn't act or talk like the miners, having Carl refer to Kirby as a deliveryman tested his mettle. He clenched his jaw and silently reminded himself that he didn't want to anger Carl. The man was too eager to use that rifle of his.

Alvin shook his head. "I already talked to most of 'em."

Carl Lee arched a bushy brow. "You sure the two of you weren't planning to cut me outta this?"

"Naw. I told ya I was gonna talk to ya once I was sure Kirby could be trusted, but sounds like you ain't believin' me." Alvin balled his hands into tight fists. "If you ain't happy 'bout things, Carl Lee, we can settle this between us right now."

"There's no need to fight," Kirby said. "We can all work together and make a lot of money. Save your fighting for the revenuers, Alvin." When Alvin slowly nodded, Kirby blew out a breath. "Why don't you two decide how you want to do this? Pick when you want me to deliver and then each of you mark your crates with a letter of the alphabet—not your own initials. We don't want anyone to figure out who's making the shine." He glanced back and forth between the two men. "We need to decide on one spot where I'll pick up the crates. Of course, it would help if we make it somewhere I can hide the truck while I load up."

Carl Lee stroked his beard. "I know a good spot where you could back the truck in and out of a grove of trees at the edge of the woods. The truck would be out of sight while you're loading. You gotta make sure no one's around when ya move in and outta the spot." He directed a ridiculing look at Kirby. "Think you're smart enough to do that?"

Kirby bristled and wished he were the one with a loaded gun slung over his shoulder. "I can handle it. You think you can figure out how to hide the crates somewhere near the spot?"

Carl Lee curled his lip. "If there weren't no place to hide the shine, what good would it be? You take me for stupid?"

"No. I'm sure you're one of the brightest fellows I've ever met, Carl Lee."

Carl narrowed his eyes as if weighing Kirby's response. "Yeah, well, I'm smart enough to know you need us more than we need you. We been running shine for years without you, and we can keep doing it if we need to, so don't get no ideas 'bout trying to take over or cheat us."

Kirby clenched his jaw. If only he'd gotten set up with Jimmy Ray before making plans with Alvin. Running shine would have been so much simpler with Jimmy Ray as his only partner. Now he not only had to deal with Alvin, but he also had to tolerate Carl Lee's rude remarks and aggressive behavior. "I have no intention of cheating anyone. Like I said, if you mark your crates when you put them in the hiding place, I can keep track of it in a notebook so each of you receive what he's owed after I deduct my share."

"Hold up a minute. Just how much you gonna charge?"

"I get a third of whatever the speakeasy pays per crate." Kirby looked at Alvin for confirmation. "That's what Alvin and I agreed on."

Carl Lee shook his head. "That's too much. I'll give ya a fourth or nothin'."

Kirby shrugged. "Then it's nothing. You can haul it yourself. A third is fair. It's my truck, my gas, my risk. If you'd rather haul your own, that's fine with me. I'm not going to argue with you, Carl Lee." He extended his hand. "I wish you good luck."

Carl's hand remained on his gun. "If you told him the same

thing as me, Alvin, he'd have to agree to drop his cut to a fourth. Whaddya say?"

Alvin hesitated. "We already agreed, and he's made a run for me already. Not sure I can go back on my word, Carl Lee."

"Ain't like you give it to one of us'uns. He's an outsider. You can break yer word and it don't matter none. I ain't gonna tell no one, and he sure ain't gonna jabber 'bout you changin' your mind." Carl Lee leveled a hard look at Kirby and stroked the rifle. "Lessen he wants to meet up with a painful accident."

Kirby experienced a sudden lightness in his chest. "You do whatever you want, Alvin, but I'm not agreeing to cut my payment to a fourth. If you and Carl want to run your own shine, it's fine with me."

"Well, Alvin?" Carl shuffled his heavy work boots in the dirt. "Ain't no reason we can't keep on like always." He jabbed his thumb at Kirby. "He needs us. We don't need him."

Alvin turned to Kirby. "Guess he's right about that. You sure you don't want to change your mind?"

Kirby shook his head. "I'll find some other way to make some cash. Sorry it didn't work out, Alvin." He offered a mock salute to the two men and walked out of the woods, feeling as though a weight had been lifted from his chest. The terrible meeting with Carl Lee couldn't have gone any better than if he'd planned it. Alvin had already introduced him to the owners of the surrounding speakeasies, so continuing to make his own deliveries wouldn't be a problem.

Kirby would have to make certain he wasn't around when Carl Lee or Alvin was at a speakeasy making a delivery, but he could solve that, too. He'd simply be sure they were at work in the mine when he was making his rounds. Besides, making deliveries in daylight would subject him to less scrutiny from the law. They expected runs at nighttime, not in the middle of the day. And he need not worry about the owners of the speakeasies telling Alvin or Carl Lee about his deliveries—they protected their sources at all costs.

.... ❧ ....

Kirby had been mistaken about the revenuers. He'd been on his second run during the middle of the afternoon when two men in suits carrying rifles and wearing badges on their lapels jumped into the road and waved him to a stop. They were the same two men who had stopped him outside of the small town of Denton only days before.

They approached the truck, one man on each side, and peered into the windows. The one with a cigar between his lips leaned against the truck door. "Ain't you the same fella we stopped a few days ago in this here truck?" He looked at the lettering on the side of the rear panels and nodded his head. "Yep. Finch Mining and Company." He looked at the other revenuer. "This here's the same truck and might be the same driver, too."

The man at the far window stuck his head inside the window. He appraised Kirby and the vehicle, then straightened. "Sure enough. Same truck, same driver. You going to Denton again?"

Kirby nodded. "Is there some law against going to Denton twice in one week?"

"Ain't no law against it unless you got moonshine in your truck."

Kirby's stomach tightened like a hangman's noose. He needed to remain calm. Last time he'd packed the crates in a hidden compartment beneath the truck's bed, covering them with a load of coal. The revenuers hadn't wanted to dig through the coal and had let him pass without checking. This time he hadn't been as careful. Instead of loading the crates into the hiding place, he'd shoved them onto the flatbed and covered them with a layer of coal.

If the revenuers decided to dig through the coal this time, it wouldn't take much before they discovered the crates, and then Kirby would quickly find himself inside a jail cell. He gripped the steering wheel with a ferocity that turned his knuckles white and forced a weak smile.

He nodded toward the rear of the truck. "You didn't find anything back there last time and you won't find anything now. You can see I'm carrying a load of coal. Might as well save yourself the time and let me get back to making my deliveries."

Using the barrel of his rifle, the revenuer near Kirby's window pushed his hat up from his forehead. "I got a couple questions." He leaned down until he was eye to eye with Kirby. "First off, how come the owner of the mining company is making coal deliveries?"

"That's a good question, Harry." The other man bobbed his head.

Harry smiled at the compliment. "Second, why you delivering coal in the heat of summer?"

"Another good one, Harry."

"Thanks, Joe." Harry narrowed his eyes at Kirby. "Well? You got answers for me before we start unloading that coal?"

Kirby pushed down the bile that rose in his throat. No matter what, he needed to appear calm and respond with nonchalance. A tremulous voice could signal fear and result in dire consequences.

"First of all, I'm not the owner. That title belongs to my father. As to why I'm making the deliveries, my father wouldn't approve just anyone driving the company-owned truck." He forced a half smile. "Not that any of the miners know how to drive." He furrowed his brow. "What was the second question?"

"Why are you delivering coal in the middle of summer?"

"Oh, right. You probably didn't think about the fact that the women use coal in their cookstoves out here in the hill country. And the amount of coal I'm delivering wouldn't be enough to keep their houses warm in the winter. One of my men heard there was a shortage of coal in Denton, and I had some of the breaker boys pick up what fell off the coal cars and load it into my truck." He forced himself to lean back, release the steering wheel. "Anything else I can answer for you?"

This time it was Joe who peered through the truck window. "I'd think two loads would be about as much as the ladies in Denton would need for their cookstoves."

Kirby swallowed hard. If he was going to get away without the men inspecting the truck, he'd best agree. Yet giving Joe an affirmative answer meant he'd need a new plan if he was going to make future runs. "I don't think they'll need any more coal until winter. Of course, there may be some other small towns that have a need."

Joe nodded. "That might be true. Tell you what—me and Harry will check on that, and if there's a shortage in any of the towns around these parts, we'll send word to the mine." He reached into the truck and shook Kirby's hand. "That's the least we can do to help out."

Kirby forced a smile. "You do that. I'll be glad to make deliveries if any of the folks are in need."

Harry swung the barrel of his rifle toward the road. "You can go on. Some of the womenfolk may need that coal to cook supper. Wouldn't want to be the cause of cold food being served to their young'uns."

Kirby nodded to the men, put the truck in gear, and slowly pulled away. Moments later, he let out a long sigh. He'd need to find some other ruse, or delivering the shine was going to be much more difficult than he'd thought. Maybe he should have remained friendly with Carl Lee and Alvin. They'd likely be able to give him some ideas.

No. He shoved the idea from his mind. He'd come up with a plan on his own, one that those revenuers would never suspect.

CHAPTER
16

Her father's recovery had been slower than Hope anticipated, but the doctor finally had agreed he could return
to the chapel car the previous week. She'd been delighted. Nellie
did her best to appear pleased by the news, but Hope knew her
dear friend was going to miss spending nights at the chapel car.
And Hope would miss Nellie, as well. They'd shared their lives
with each other and created an inseparable bond. Yet they both
realized things would be different, going back to the way they'd
been before—and they had.

After a few minutes exchanging happenings of the day, Nellie would return up the hill and Hope would help her father
prepare for the late service. Luke continued to preach at the
early service, although conducting both meetings, working his
shifts at the mine, and helping with repairs on the miners' homes
had taken a toll on him. Hope insisted her father could lead the
late meeting. Besides, the railroaders were aware of her father's
condition, and when he occasionally forgot a word or addressed
one of the men by the wrong name, they were always forgiving.

Even Kirby had overlooked her father's inability to recall who he was for several nights.

Hope sat beside her father, reading the sermon he'd written earlier that day. "This is quite good." She beamed at him. "You've made wonderful progress. You're getting better with each day that passes."

Her father shrugged. "I'm still not feeling confident during meetings, but the doctor says eventually I'll feel like myself again. He says recovering from a head injury is different for everyone."

"And you have been particularly fortunate, Papa. I know it's answered prayer. And I'm thankful I was with you."

"As am I. If you wouldn't have been with me to keep things going, I don't know what would have happened." He shook his head. "And to think I tried to talk you out of coming with me."

"I did my part with the children, but Luke was the one who was able to keep the adults sitting in the pews each evening. At first I thought I should write to the headquarters and tell them what happened to you, so they could send another preacher. But after hearing Luke preach his first few sermons, I knew they wouldn't send anyone who could do a better job." She reached over and squeezed her father's hand. Her father grinned. "I doubt headquarters could have found someone willing to come here, even on a temporary basis. Fortunately, we didn't need headquarters. The Lord took care of matters for us."

"Miss Hope! Miss Hope! You inside?"

She leaned toward the open window of the railcar where she caught sight of Jed King, one of the railroaders loping toward the spur. She called out to him and then walked to the rear door and met him near the small platform. "Something wrong, Mr. King?"

He gulped for air, leaning against the metal railing of the

platform. "Got a big delivery for your pa over at the station. Lots of large crates. Some of us was gonna bring 'em over, but then we got to thinking maybe you wouldn't have room for whatever it is in all them crates." He inhaled another breath. "What do you think? Should we bring 'em?"

While Jed was telling her about the delivery, her father stepped outside and Hope turned to him. "Were you expecting a delivery, Papa? Did you order something before you had your accident?"

Her father kneaded his forehead. "I don't recall ordering anything." He looked at Jed. "Was there any information on the shipping tags?"

Jed frowned. "I think it said some kind of headquarters or something like that. You want to come and take a look? We could open one of the crates."

Her father nodded. "That would probably be easiest. Once I know what it is, I can make a decision." Jed descended the steps, and her father followed.

"Wait for me." Hope scurried down after them. The huge wooden boxes sitting on the station platform caused a stirring excitement, the same anticipation she'd experienced as a young child on Christmas morning.

She grasped her father's arm as they stepped onto the station platform. "Look at all of them, Papa. What do you think is inside all those crates?"

He traced his finger along the printed tag. "They're from the association headquarters, but I have no idea what all of this can be."

"The crates got numbers on 'em, Preacher. Want me to open number one? I got a pry bar right here." Jed picked up the bar that was leaning against one of the crates.

"Makes sense. They're probably numbered for a reason."

Jed didn't need any further encouragement. He pried off the top of the crate and peered inside. Reaching in, he pulled out an envelope. "Got your name on it, Preacher." He handed the envelope to Hope's father, then pulled out a Bible. "This one looks like it's full of Bibles. No wonder these crates are so heavy. Maybe they all got Bibles in 'em."

Her father shook his head and flapped the letter in the air. "Only this one has Bibles, Jed. One has hymnbooks, and the rest are filled with Sunday-school materials."

Hope's mouth gaped. She gestured to the remaining crates. "All of those?"

"The letter says the ladies throughout the state raised funds and wanted the money used toward teaching materials for children."

Jed scratched his head and stared at the crates. "The young'uns will be full growed before you can use all of this, Miss Hope."

Her father placed his hand atop one of the crates. "I'm more concerned about where we're going to store the contents. We have no room in the chapel car, and we can't leave the crates sitting outside. The contents will be ruined."

"You can leave 'em under the eaves here on the platform for a day or two until you decide, Preacher. Maybe one of the folks who attend the meetings will have an idea where you can store the crates. Won't hurt to ask."

"Thanks, Jed. Good idea, I'll do that."

Hope clasped her hands over her heart. "God will provide, Papa. I just know it."

.... ❧ ....

Kirby rolled out of bed with a smile on his face. The preacher had announced he was in need of storage space for several crates of supplies during a late-night service earlier in the week, and Kirby had been quick to offer an area in the mining company offices. If he could convince the preacher and Hope to go along with his latest plan, he'd solve the problem of delivering moonshine. Hope, along with those church supplies, would provide him with the perfect cover. Of course, he'd need to make an exceptional pitch to the preacher, but he doubted he'd have any trouble convincing Hope. She seemingly couldn't do enough to help unfortunate children.

Instead of making his usual trek to the still he and Jimmy Ray had located in the woods about a mile from the mining office, Kirby ate breakfast and ambled toward the railroad spur. He whistled a soft tune, his mood much improved now that he had a plan.

Hope was hanging wet clothes from the makeshift line she'd strung between a couple of trees not far from the railcar. He smiled at the sight of her. She would be a delightful conquest. He didn't know which he'd enjoy more, winning her affection or besting Luke.

He waved his hand in greeting as he approached. "Good morning! Looks like it's going to be another warm day."

She stood on tiptoes and peeked over the clothesline. "Good morning, Kirby." She pegged a dish towel to the line, then walked over to him. "What brings you over here this morning? If you've no work to complete at the mine, we can always use help with repairs up on the hill. Neither Luke nor I have been able to devote as much time as we had before my father's incident."

His good mood soured a bit. He didn't want to think about repairs needed to the company houses up on the hill. "I wanted to speak to you and your father about the crates of supplies he received."

"I hope you haven't decided against storing them. I truly don't know where we'd put them, and yours was the only offer we received."

"No, there's plenty of room for them. But instead of storing them, I've thought of a way you could put those children's materials to good use. Of course, it's up to your father and you, but . . ."

Her face brightened. "Truly? I'm curious. Tell me what you've come up with."

He extended his arm to her. "It's probably better if I tell you and your father at the same time, since the idea would need his approval."

"Now I'm even more curious. I'll be only a minute more." She bent down and lifted one of her father's damp shirts from the basket at her feet. The fabric snapped as she gave it a quick shake, then hung it on the line. She grasped the basket handle and gave him a nod. "All right. Let's go and talk to my father."

The preacher arched his brows when Kirby entered the railcar a few steps behind Hope. "Kirby! Not used to seeing you at this time of day. Sit down." He indicated a nearby chair. "I hope nothing's happened that requires extra prayer."

Kirby shook his head. "No, nothing like that, Preacher." He waited until Hope was seated and then sat opposite the preacher. "Last night I had an idea about how you might want to use some of those supplies you received from your church association."

The preacher folded his hands together. "I'm eager to hear what you've got in mind. Those supplies don't do anyone a bit of good sitting in your offices."

"Exactly!" Kirby nodded his agreement. "I've made several trips to some of the small towns around here and a few farther away, and I discovered that even though a couple of them have churches, they don't have the kind of teaching material Miss Hope uses when she teaches the children here in Finch. Folks in those little towns would feel beyond blessed if they received some of those items. Of course, they'd need Miss Hope to provide them with a bit of training on how to use the materials, but she'd know about that better than me."

Hope's eyes gleamed with anticipation. "Oh, Papa! Kirby's solution is an answer to prayer. Isn't that a marvelous idea?" Before her father could reply, she turned to Kirby. "We've been praying the Lord would reveal how we could put those materials to good use, and now you've given us the perfect solution."

Kirby leaned back and let Hope sell the idea to her father. She thought him to be a knight in shining armor, who was going to help her save the needy children of the countryside. All the material that made for a good fairy tale. But women, especially the young ones, liked the idea of a handsome prince or valiant knight coming to their rescue. By the time she realized she was the one coming to his rescue, he'd be out of town.

Her father stroked his chin. "Now, hold up, Hope. We need to talk this through before you get all excited. I think Kirby's idea is fine, but there are some problems, as well."

"What problems?" Hope said.

"First off, we'd need to come up with a way to get the supplies to the folks and then locate someone willing to help put them to use with the children in each little town. You can't just dump a basketful of materials on someone's doorstep and believe it will do the good work for which it was intended."

Kirby cleared his throat. "I can help with the delivery portion, Preacher. I'd count it as an opportunity to serve the Lord and the folks of West Virginia if you'd accept my offer." He ducked his head. "I can't offer to teach them about how to use the materials, but I'd be willing to take Miss Hope along with me, and perhaps she could offer her help. We could promise to stop back in the towns every so often so she could provide any added assistance the folks might need."

"You see, Papa! It's perfect."

"I don't think your plan will work, Kirby. Please don't take offense, but I couldn't allow Hope to travel alone with a man. It simply wouldn't be proper, and I don't think I'm up to such travels just yet. Your willingness to help is greatly appreciated, but—"

"Wait, Papa. I'm sure we can find a solution if we give it some thought. We don't want the supplies to sit in a building unused without giving Kirby's suggestion more consideration."

Kirby leaned forward and looked at the preacher. "Is traveling alone with me your only objection to the idea?"

"I'm not sure. What time of day would you be making the deliveries? I need Hope here to help with meetings in the evening. Besides, I wouldn't want her traveling through the hills at nighttime."

"I understand. We could leave Finch as early in the morning as she'd like, and we could plan to return by midafternoon at the latest. Do you think that would work?" He glanced back and forth between Hope and her father.

Hope bobbed her head, but her father immediately disagreed. "No. Even though the time of day works, we still haven't solved the problem of Hope traveling alone with you."

"I know!" Hope clapped her hands together. "I can ask Nellie if she'd go with us. You wouldn't object if Nellie was with us, would you, Papa?"

Her father smiled. "That would solve the problem." He looked at Kirby. "What do you think, Kirby? Would having Nellie along be all right?"

He hiked a shoulder. "Whatever will make it possible to get those materials to the children. I just want them to have the same opportunities Hope has given to the children in Finch. I know their families will be grateful, as well."

He'd done his best to sound nonchalant, but his insides

churned at the thought of having Luke's sister ride with them. Of all the people Hope might have suggested, Nellie would have been far from his first choice. No doubt the girl would report everything that was said and done to her older brother.

"Before we decide on when we'll make our first trip, you should make certain Nellie will be able to go with us. I think you mentioned she helps care for her younger brothers and sisters. Her mother may not want her to come along." He forced a weak smile. "If that should happen, you could always see if one of the other girls could accompany us." He pushed up from the chair. "I should be getting to work now, but I'll be at the late meeting tonight."

Hope jumped to her feet. "I'll walk as far as the street with you and then go up the hill and talk to Nellie. I should have a definite answer for you this evening."

She brushed a quick kiss on her father's cheek. "I'll help with some repairs while I'm up on the hill, and then I'll come back in time to prepare lunch. You can work on your sermon in peace and quiet."

A pang of jealousy shot through Kirby as he watched the exchange between father and daughter. They shared a special bond, something he would never experience with his father. He shook off the dark thoughts of his past and assisted Hope down the platform steps.

She was giddy with excitement. Shouldn't he feel the same? After all, he'd succeeded in what he intended. Why then did he feel this might prove to be a mistake?

uke trudged up the hill from a long day at the mine. He'd been on the schedule more of late and wondered if Kirby was making certain he'd be at the mine so he couldn't work alongside Hope doing repairs to the houses. He'd told himself it was a silly thought and he should be glad for the paid hours. They could certainly use any extra money he could earn, even if he'd not see any of it.

Between rent and their credit account at the company store, his wages would be held back for payment owed. Mr. Farragut always made certain the company was paid before the miners ever saw a penny. Only the miners who worked every day still received a bit of cash in their pay envelope. The rest of them received an empty envelope with scribbled calculations on the outside—usually telling them they'd earned less than they owed. Escaping the vicious cycle had become impossible for most of them.

Nellie ran toward him as he topped the hill, her hair flying loose behind her. "Guess what, Luke!" She pranced alongside him, her face alight with pleasure. "I had something wonderful happen today."

Luke pushed his hat back on his head and looked down at her. "I'm glad to know someone has some good news, but I doubt I'll be able to guess. Why don't you just tell me?" He didn't want to spoil her happiness, yet he was too tired for guessing games. As soon as supper was over, he'd need to clean up and get back down the hill to help with the evening meeting.

Nellie frowned for a moment, then clutched his hand. "I'm gonna get to go all over the countryside with Kirby Finch and Hope, delivering the church supplies that were sent to the preacher. That means I'll get to ride in that nice company truck he drives and get to see places I ain't never been." She tugged his arm. "Ain't that grand, Luke?" She giggled, tightened her grasp on his hand, and tried to swing his arm back and forth.

Luke shook loose of her hold and stopped in his tracks. He didn't want to believe it. "You're joshin' with me, ain't ya?"

Nellie's laughter died. "No, I'm telling you the truth. Why would I joke about something like that, and how come you're looking mad as a hornet?"

Luke's jaw quivered with a slight tic. He didn't want to say anything he'd regret, yet he couldn't remain silent. The thought of Hope traveling with Kirby Finch set his blood to boiling. "When did all of this happen? I was with Hope last evening and she didn't say anything to me." Disappointment washed over him. How could Hope agree to such a plan?

"She didn't know until today. Kirby stopped at the chapel car and talked to Hope and her father. Hope thought his idea was a good one, and her pa agreed so long as she didn't travel alone with Kirby." Her wide smile returned. "So she thought of me, and Ma said it would be fine if I went along with her. Ma says she'd never stop me from doing the Lord's work."

202

A stab of guilt shot through him. How could he find fault with such a noble cause? He shifted his metal lunch pail and let the idea settle into his consciousness. Only a moment passed before he'd formulated an answer to his own question: Kirby Finch. Even though the man attended most of the late meetings, Luke questioned his motives. The only times he appeared truly attentive was when Hope was playing the organ and singing.

Was Kirby's offer because he wanted to spread God's truth, or was it merely an opportunity to have Hope sitting close at his side? He suspected it was the latter, but when he quietly mentioned that possibility to his mother, she'd pinned him with a hard look. "You best be rememberin' what the Bible says about judging one another." She squeezed his shoulder and leaned close. "Sounds to me like that gal's sent your heart a quiverin' and now you got yer dander up for the wrong reasons."

His mother was right about judging others, but she'd never been around Kirby Finch. The man was a sneaky wolf. Luke wasn't passing judgment—he was stating fact. At least that was what he told himself as he descended the hill a few hours later.

Hope's eyes widened when she opened the door of the chapel car. "You're early. I was washing the dishes, and Papa went over to the depot to talk to a few of the men."

He pointed to the platform. "Can you leave that for a minute and go for a short walk with me?"

She smiled and bobbed her head. "Of course. I'd like nothing more." When she descended the steps, she lightly grasped his hand.

Luke's heart quickened at her touch and erased his earlier disappointment. He remained hopeful he'd convince her to set aside her plan to travel with Kirby. They stopped near a large oak and sat down in the grass.

He turned and looked into her eyes. "There's something I need to ask you."

"About delivering the Sunday-school materials with Kirby?"

The mere mention of Kirby's name caused a return of Luke's earlier displeasure. "Yes. Nellie told me about the idea, and I—"

"It's more than an idea, Luke. It's a plan. We're going to begin deliveries this week." She smiled, though he thought it appeared forced. "Isn't it wonderful?"

"No, I think it's a lousy idea. I can't believe you and your pa agreed to it. Kirby Finch is a sorry, good-for-nothin' sort who—"

"Luke! Listen to yourself. You're a man who has dedicated his life to the Lord. How can you say such terrible things about another man who has done the same?"

"What?" The thought of Kirby Finch dedicating his life to anything other than money and a good time was preposterous. "You really think Kirby has devoted his life to God?"

"I do." She reared away from him and pushed back until her shoulders were ramrod straight. "Kirby has made a generous offer to help the less fortunate living in the small communities throughout the area. He's going to use his truck and contribute his time to this project for as long as we need him. If that isn't a man who wants to serve God, then I don't know what is."

Luke grimaced. "I think Kirby is a man who has pulled the wool over your eyes. I doubt his offer is because he cares about the young'uns."

She frowned. "Why else would he make such a generous offer?"

Luke released an exasperated breath. "So he can be with you. I've seen the way he looks at you when he thinks I'm not watchin' him."

Her cheeks flushed bright pink. "You're wrong. If that were true, he wouldn't need to go to such lengths. He could ask me to join him for a picnic or dinner at the restaurant. That would be much easier, don't you think?"

"You think I'm making a mountain out of a molehill, but you're wrong. I know Kirby better than you, and he doesn't do anything unless there's something in it for him." Luke raked his fingers through his hair. "I think you should refuse his offer."

"Refuse? And deprive the children of an opportunity to hear about Jesus?" She sprang to her feet. "I can't believe you'd make such a suggestion, Luke. And unless you have some idea how to deliver the supplies without Kirby's help, I'm not going to change my mind."

He'd expected Hope would ask him to come up with an alternative plan before she would agree. Unfortunately, he'd been unable to think of one. He didn't have a vehicle he could use, and even if he did, Kirby would be sure to object if Luke asked for time off at the mine. Losing his job, even if the work was irregular, wasn't an option. Luke and his family would be booted out of their company housing if that occurred. Luke couldn't risk it, not even if that meant Hope would spend much of her time with Kirby.

"I wish I had some other idea, but I can't compete with Kirby." He bowed his head in defeat.

Hope reached for his hand and covered it with her own. "This isn't a competition between you and Kirby. It's about serving the Lord and teaching the children about His love." She looked into Luke's eyes. "I begged my father to bring me along with him so I could help with his ministry. I believe this is what I'm supposed to do, Luke. I believe that's why those unexpected supplies arrived. We need to help other folks living in these hills when we have the ability to do so."

He studied the blanket of green beneath him as it swayed in the mild breeze. Why had this happened? There was no doubt in Luke's mind that God could have provided him with an answer for this dilemma. Yet He hadn't. The truth was, God could have prevented the entire happenstance. Yet He hadn't. If there was a lesson to be learned from all this, God surely would have shown him. Yet He hadn't.

Hope had spoken the truth. He was being selfish. Nothing about his attitude was right. Instead of being pleased there was a way to help others, he was worried about losing Hope's affection.

The wind whispered through the overhanging tree branches, and Luke lifted his eyes toward the heavens. Where was his faith? Where was his trust? Was his faith no stronger than a blade of grass, easily tugged to and fro by the slightest wind? He didn't want to think his belief could be so easily shaken. And where was his trust in Hope? If she truly cared for him, she wouldn't be easily swayed by any advances Kirby might make toward her.

With a sigh, he said, "You're right. We need to help however and wherever we can. In my heart, I know it's gonna be good for you to deliver those Bibles and supplies." He forced a smile. "I've got to remind myself that God gave you a fine singing voice for a special reason, and I'm not the one who should say where you should use it." He pulled a blade of grass from the ground and ran it through his fingers. "Everyone 'round these parts sees how much the young'uns love you and listen to your teaching. Who am I to say you shouldn't use your talent wherever God leads?"

"Thank you, Luke. I was sure you'd see things this way." She squeezed his hand.

He gave a slight nod, unable to meet her eyes. Though she took his words to mean he'd accepted her decision, he still held out hope that something would prevent the arrangement. It was wrong of him, he knew, and he would pray for God to change his heart, and more important, to protect Hope's.

............·%·............

Much to Luke's disappointment, nothing had happened to prevent Kirby's arrangement with Hope. Even worse, the folks in the small towns begged Hope to return and continue to teach the children. Of course, Kirby had been more than willing to agree to supplying the transportation for her return visits.

Although Luke had continued to pray God would change his heart, he still bore resentment each time he watched his sister and Hope climb into the truck with Kirby. He didn't miss the fact that Kirby somehow made certain it was always Hope sandwiched in between Nellie and him. Luke had briefly considered telling Nellie she should sit in the middle, but he was sure his sister would repeat the request to Hope and she would think he was being mistrustful. So he silently brooded and watched the threesome depart several times a week. He'd begun to wonder if Kirby had intentionally scheduled him to work at the mine each time they made a run. While he was pleased for the work, even some of the other miners questioned why he was suddenly on the schedule more often than the rest of them. A few had even lodged a protest with Mr. Daniels in the office, who'd told them all the same thing. They'd need to speak to Kirby since he'd recently taken over that part of the operation. That piece of news had affirmed Luke's suspicions.

Luke carried his lunch pail down the hill with Nellie at his side. "We're going to Fern Hollow today. We ain't been there before. It's always fun when we go to a new town. The young'uns always love hearing Hope's teachin'. I been helpin' with the singin', and she's even having me help her when we have a real big group of young'uns." Her face beamed with undeniable pride.

"That's good. I'm real proud of you, Nellie. I hope you have a wonderful day." He couldn't deny her a bit of praise. Being with Hope had changed his sister. She'd gained more confidence and had been in better spirits since beginning her work with Hope, and he wouldn't do or say anything to ruin her happiness. "I'm going over to speak to the preacher before I head to the mine."

Nellie shaded her eyes with her hand and stared down the road. "Tell Hope to hurry or we'll be late. Kirby's truck is already in front of the boardinghouse, so he'll be here any minute."

"I'm sure he won't leave without her." There was an angry edge to his words that he hadn't intended, and his sister's mouth dropped open. "All I meant was that there's no reason for Kirby to make the trips unless the two of you are along to hold your meetings and hand out the church supplies. Otherwise he'd stay in Finch."

"If you say so," Nellie said, "but you sounded kinda mad to me."

He ignored her words and pointed to the grassy expanse beside the train depot. "There's Hope, so you can quit your frettin'. I'll see you later." After a quick wave, he ran off in Hope's direction, longing for a few minutes alone with her.

He was panting when he stopped in front of her moments later. "Mornin'." He gestured to her pale-green frock. "You look mighty pretty in that color."

She glanced down at the dress. "Thank you, Luke. Well, I better hurry—Kirby doesn't like to wait."

"Sounds like the two of you are getting mighty familiar."

"Just because I said he doesn't like to wait? Don't be silly." She moved to one side and stepped around him.

He crossed his arms over his chest. "Hurry on, then. I wouldn't want you to keep Kirby waitin'."

Hope squinted and looked over her shoulder. "Or Nellie." She frowned, but said nothing more before rushing off toward the truck.

Luke silently chastised himself as he trudged across the field and stepped into the chapel car.

The preacher glanced up from his Bible. "You look like you lost your best friend. What's bothering you, Luke?"

He couldn't talk to Nellie about his feelings, and he sure couldn't tell the preacher about the green-eyed monster lurking around every corner. "Just tired. Didn't sleep too good last night." That much was true. He never slept well on the nights before Hope and Nellie were leaving with Kirby, and last night had been no different.

The preacher nodded. "I know about that. I've had trouble sleeping lately, too." He waved to the chair opposite him. "If you've got a few minutes before you head off to the mine, I've got something I want to talk to you about."

"I'm all ears," Luke said, moving to the chair.

"Seems someone around these parts has been buying up a lot of corn. Story goes that whoever it is has been making moonshine and selling it to speakeasies around these parts." The preacher sighed. "I can't blame any of the men who are selling their corn. They need money to care for their families, and they aren't going to ask questions if someone is willing to buy their whole crop—especially at a higher price than they're used to getting."

Luke frowned. He hadn't heard anything about such dealings. Nobody had offered to buy his crop, and he hadn't seen any strangers on the hill. "Who told you about this?"

The preacher shook his head. "Can't say. I promised I wouldn't tell, but I believe it's true. Seems there's also been some folks coming into the area selling shine for less than some of the locals.

Anger is building among the local men who sell moonshine. Not only that, but they figure the extra activity is going to bring more revenuers into the nearby counties. I'm worried that a dangerous situation could arise. I don't hold with anyone selling bootleg liquor, but if there are outsiders getting involved, I think it could make things a lot worse. I was hoping you knew something about it and could tell me there's nothing to worry about."

Luke leaned back in the chair. "Since I haven't heard anything yet, I don't think you need to be too concerned right now. Let me see what I can find out. I promise I won't mention that we've talked." He ran his fingers through his thick hair. "Trouble is, where there's smoke, there's usually fire."

"Thank you, Luke. You'll tell me what you find out?"

"You can count on it." Luke stood and turned toward the door. "I best be on my way. Don't want to be late." He headed off to the mine determined to sniff around and see who'd been selling all their corn. If he was lucky, he might find out who was doing the buying. He'd need to take his time and be careful or he'd tip his hand before he got any good information.

Throughout the day, his thoughts remained in a jumble. He'd had little chance to talk to anyone, but he'd had plenty of time to think about Nellie and Hope out on the road. Every man on the hill knew what danger any moonshine feuds could pose, and if the moonshiners were looking to discover who was infringing on their territory, they wouldn't hesitate to shoot first and ask questions later.

Now that he'd heard this latest news, he didn't care if he was scheduled to work or not. He wasn't about to let Nellie and Hope become possible victims caught in the middle of a feud. One thing was certain—he'd be in that truck with them on their next run.

CHAPTER

18

The truck bounced along the rutted road toward Fern Hollow, each pothole seeming to toss her body closer to Kirby. She gave him a sideways glance and frowned. "Are you doing that on purpose?"

"Of course not. I don't want to ruin the tires. If you were driving, you'd soon learn that it's hard to avoid all those holes." He leaned the upper portion of his body over the steering wheel and looked past Hope. "Doesn't seem to be bothering Nellie. She's able to sleep through every bump."

Hope glanced at Nellie. Using her sweater as a pillow, she'd positioned her head against the back of the seat and had fallen asleep. She smiled at the girl. "You're right. I guess I shouldn't complain."

Kirby slid his hand from the steering wheel and slipped it across the back of the seat. The truck bounced and his hand dropped onto her shoulder. When he made no move to lift his hand, she jostled her shoulder.

After an interminable pause, he returned his hand to the steering wheel. "There's something I've been wanting to talk to you about when we have some time alone." He lowered his voice to a whisper. "Even though she seems to be asleep, I'd rather not talk when Nellie's around."

Hope had no idea what he might want to talk about, but this was their first visit to Fern Hollow and there was much to accomplish. "Why don't you stay after the evening service tonight and we can talk then?" His shoulders slumped, so she explained her reasoning. "If my father is present, no one can consider our meeting inappropriate. I know you would always want to protect my reputation."

He frowned. "That's true, but I wanted to speak to you alone. This isn't something I want your father to overhear, either. You'll understand once I've told you of my concerns."

"Father will be in the living quarters, and we can talk in the chapel car. He'll be nearby, but I know he won't attempt to eavesdrop. He's an honorable man." She hoped the added explanation would put an end to his objections.

His shoulders sagged, but he nodded. "That's fine."

She'd barely heard his mumbled response. While there was little doubt he was unhappy with her decision, at least he'd agreed. She couldn't imagine what he might want to discuss. Her stomach knotted. What if Kirby wanted to talk about courting her? If she refused, would he discontinue their trips to teach the children in the outlying communities?

Her thoughts tossed about like a leaf in a windstorm until they arrived in Fern Hollow. Throughout their time in the small community, she and Nellie were so busy leading singing and telling Bible stories, there wasn't time to think of anything else. The attendance had been greater than they'd anticipated, and the children had begged for a return visit.

On the journey home, the two young women held an excited conversation about the day's events. Nellie leaned forward and looked at Kirby. "I'm so glad you picked Fern Hollow for a visit. The young'uns can hardly wait for us to come see them again. I told 'em we'd be returning every week. They promised they'd be waiting for us."

Anger flashed in his eyes as he turned to Nellie. "Why'd you tell them that?"

Nellie's head snapped as if she'd been slapped. "'Cause we come to each of the towns once a week? Ain't nobody said Fern Hollow would be any different."

"Well, *ain't* nobody asked." His lip curled as he mimicked her. "I'm the one who does the driving and decides where and when we go to each town."

"Kirby!" Hope stared at him, shocked by his mocking response.

He cleared his throat. "Sorry, but she can't take it for granted that we'll return to a town every week just because we came for one visit."

"It isn't me you owe an apology." Hope grasped Nellie's hand and gently squeezed.

Kirby shrugged. "I apologize, Nellie."

He didn't sound sorry, but Hope doubted Kirby was capable of much more. He was a man of privilege who seemingly felt little need to apologize for anything he did or said.

"Now that you've stressed the fact that you're the one in charge, why don't you tell us when and how often we'll be returning to Fern Hollow?" She directed a piercing look at him.

"Maybe in a couple weeks, but we won't ever be going there every week."

Hope frowned. "Why not?"

"Too far out." He focused his attention on the road.

Hope rubbed her temple. Fern Hollow was located no farther from Finch than some of the other communities they'd visited, but voicing that argument would likely have an adverse effect right now. Still, she planned to mention it when they had their talk later this evening.

The moment they arrived in town, Nellie leapt from the truck, hollered good-bye, and scurried to the hillside. Hope scooted across the seat toward the open door, but Kirby lightly grasped her wrist before she could step out of the truck.

"Wait just a minute, Hope. I want to tell you that I'm truly sorry about the way I spoke to Nellie and I plan to tell her so. I got a lot on my mind right now." He lowered his head. "That's why I said I needed to talk to you." He glanced about. "There's nobody around, but if it'd make you feel better, I'll get out of the truck and you can stay inside while I talk. I don't want to hurt your reputation, but I can't wait until tonight to get this off my chest."

His distraught tone tugged at her heart and she couldn't refuse. "You stay inside the truck and I'll step outside." She stepped down, closed the door, and leaned her forearms against the open window frame of the truck. She gave a nod. "Go ahead. Tell me what has you so worked up."

He cleared his throat. "There's talk of a strike at the mine. Could happen soon."

Relief washed over her, only to be replaced by a fresh, even deeper worry. She frowned. "I thought all the whispers of a possible strike or formation of a union died down once things were set to rights when the inspectors were in town."

"Well, talk has picked up again. Mr. Daniels caught wind of it earlier this week. He's sure some of the UMWA men have been sneaking into town. I've been keeping a close watch, but I haven't seen any strangers."

"Then maybe Mr. Daniels is mistaken about what he heard. If he wasn't privy to the entire conversation, the comments he heard could have been misinterpreted. When that occurs, falsehoods and gossip can spread like wildfire." She straightened her shoulders and peered down the street. If Luke saw her leaning too close to the open truck window, he'd likely be unhappy. "I wouldn't worry too much, Kirby."

He beckoned for her to remain. "Wait. Don't go just yet. The truth is, things have been stirred up ever since the inspectors paid their visit. Seems some of the men think I paid them off, and we didn't fix the ventilation the way it should be. Not true, of course, but those thick-skulled miners wouldn't know the truth if it walked up and punched them in the face." He gritted his teeth. "Which is exactly what I'd like to do to some of them."

She took a backward step. "Is this why you wanted to talk to me? You felt I needed to know you want to hit some of your employees?"

"No, of course not. I just get discouraged when the men won't believe the truth." He hesitated, then added, "And when they go behind my back trying to stir things up by going on strike."

Rather than discouraged, he seemed angry. She supposed talk of a strike could create a little of both, especially when Kirby's father would likely hold his son accountable if there were a strike.

The afternoon sun slanted through the window, and she tilted her head to block the glare. "I'm not sure why you wanted to talk to me about a possible strike. None of the men who work in the mines share that sort of talk with me."

He arched his brows. "Don't they?"

His question stunned her. "What does that mean?"

"Don't get all upset with me, but I've heard Luke is involved in the movement and is encouraging other men to join in." His jaw twitched. "There's talk that they've been meeting out near the Hughes cornfield. I don't know that to be a fact just yet, but I do know the Bible instructs workers to be loyal to their employers. What these men are doing goes against the Bible's teachings, and that's why I'm asking you to help me find out as much as you can."

She clasped a hand to her throat. "You want me to spy on folks living up on the hill?"

"No, no." He shook his head. "That's not what I said. I said I'd be grateful if you'd find out what you can about a possible strike. You and Luke are good friends. I'm sure he confides in you from time to time. All you need to do is ask how things are going at the mine. If he doesn't say much, you can push him with a few more questions. Maybe tell him you heard one of the wives up on the hill say she's worried there might be a strike and see if he tells you more."

She glared at him and said, "I won't do that, Kirby. I could never betray Luke or any of the folks who have talked to me, whether in confidence or otherwise. I don't share that sort of thing and I'm surprised you would even ask me."

He gave a crooked smile and wagged his index finger. "Don't get too uppity with me, Hope. You need to remember I've done a lot to help your ministry in these parts. You've been happy to ride in this truck owned by the mining company, and you encouraged me to use company money to purchase food and other supplies for the folks living in those towns we visit. If it weren't for Finch Mining and Company, you wouldn't have been able to help any of those folks."

She pressed her lips together. "That's true, but when I accepted your help, I didn't know it came with strings attached. I didn't expect you'd ask me to spy on your behalf."

"You need to look at this from my position." His tone softened. "It's true I want to prevent a strike, but I'm doing it for good reason. Not just to help the mine, but to help the miners and their families. The UMWA gets them all stirred up by saying things are going to be better if they go on strike. Well, that's not what will happen. The mine doesn't make enough money to pay the wages the UMWA will demand. That means a long strike, and do you know what that will mean for the miners and their families, Hope?"

She lowered her gaze. "They can't pay their rent or buy food for their families."

"Right. It also means the mine will close down. This operation doesn't make enough money for my father to get into a long battle with the UMWA. He may be able to sell it, but if that fails, he'll just close it down and count it as a business loss. I know my father. He won't give in to the UMWA and their outrageous demands. He simply can't do it. The mine won't support higher wages right now." He inhaled a deep breath and slid closer to the door. "I know I sound harsh, but I'm doing this only because those folks on the hill will end up without anything except hungry young'uns and no place to go. Help me before things get out of hand. Please, Hope."

His final words wrenched her heart. She couldn't bear the thought of folks being forced out of their homes or children crying from hunger, yet the idea of disloyalty to Luke weighed heavily on her. Would she be helping or hurting the residents of Finch if she heard talk of a strike and passed it along to Kirby? There was no way to be certain, but one thing was sure. If she didn't agree, Kirby would withhold any future trips to the outlying towns, and she didn't want that to happen.

"Fine. If I hear anything, I'll tell you about it. But don't get your hopes up. After all, you've already heard rumblings, yet I've heard nothing. I doubt I'll learn anything you don't already know."

At least that was her hope, and would soon be her prayer,

because she wasn't sure she could betray Luke's trust—even if it meant keeping food on the table for the children of Finch.

............⚬⚬............

Two days later, Luke tromped down the hillside with his coonhound Blue sniffing and trotting along on one side of him and Nellie keeping pace on the other. He shouldered his shotgun and called to the dog when it picked up a scent and started to wander off. When Luke called after him, the dog whined and loped back to his side. Luke reached down and gave the dog a pat on the head. "Good dog." They continued on a short distance farther before Luke stopped and turned to Nellie. "You might as well quit your pouting. I'm not about to change my mind."

She frowned and said, "I don't want you tagging along, and I bet Kirby ain't gonna be none too happy to see you, neither." She pointed at the dog. "Or Blue. There ain't gonna be room for either of ya in the truck." Then after a brief pause, she asked, "Does Hope know 'bout this?"

"No. I didn't say a word. Thought it would be a nice surprise." He'd been careful not to say anything to anyone except the preacher. He might not have told him either, but since they had their Bible time together each morning, Luke didn't want to cause undue concern.

Both Hope and Kirby were waiting near the truck when Nellie and Luke appeared. Kirby nodded when they approached. He glanced at the shotgun and then looked at the dog. "Taking that coonhound with you for a Bible lesson, or you going hunting?" He chuckled and leaned against the truck.

Luke shook his head. "Won't be having any Bible study this morning. I'm gonna ride along with the three of you. I heard talk there's been some revenuers around these parts. Thought I'd ride shotgun for you."

Kirby perked to attention. "I haven't heard anything about revenuers, but I did hear tell there's been a few strangers around town. That what you're talking about?" He cast a quick glance at Hope.

"I ain't seen any strangers in Finch," Luke replied. "Like I said, there's talk of revenuers in the area looking for bootleggers carrying shine. I don't want the three of you to get caught in any crossfire between moonshiners and revenuers, especially since you don't even tote a gun." He gestured down the road. "Anything could happen out there."

Kirby appeared unconvinced, yet he could see a flicker of worry in Hope's eyes. Moments later, Kirby pushed away from the truck and told the ladies to get in. "Sorry, Luke, but there's only room for the three of us in the truck. There's no way for you to ride along with us."

"Sure there is." Luke placed his foot on the running board and jumped onto the bed of the truck. He slapped his hand on his thigh and let out a whistle. "Come on, Blue, get on up here." The dog bounded in front of Kirby, nearly knocking him to the ground. Luke scooted to a corner of the truck bed and smiled. "See? No problem at all. I can keep a good lookout from back here."

"Too bad you didn't get here early enough to help load the truck." Kirby's mouth became a thin line. "I thought you were scheduled to work at the mine today."

"I was, but I switched with one of the other men."

Kirby bristled. "Since when do we let the men change the work schedule?"

"Been doing it ever since I can remember. Long as there's a man who knows how to do the work, it's never been a problem." He directed a hard stare at Kirby. "I don't think you'd want to mess with trying to put a stop to what's been allowed by the supervisors for years. Could stir the fellas up, if you know what I mean."

His remark was a bit of a stretch. The supervisors had allowed the men to switch out if they had an emergency of some sort, but mostly they didn't like the schedules changed—said it made for too much trouble in the office. Luke viewed this as an emergency, so he figured he hadn't told an outright lie. Besides, he wasn't so thickheaded that he hadn't checked and found the schedules were being manipulated so that he was working at the mine each time Kirby left town with Hope and Nellie.

Kirby climbed into the truck and shut the door rather hard. He started the ignition and steered them out of town. Soon the sounds of chattering from inside the cab carried on the warm breeze, and Luke shifted his position to gain a better look through the small rear window. Kirby's arm was stretched across the back of the seat, his hand occasionally dropping to Hope's shoulder. She would shrug, he would grin, and then he'd lift it from her shoulder. The boorish conduct seemed a game to Kirby, but Luke's anger escalated as he observed Kirby continue the unseemly diversion. Luke clutched the stock of his shotgun as he looked on. When he could stand it no longer, he knocked on the cab's rear window.

Kirby glanced over his shoulder, then leaned toward the door and shouted out his window, "Got a problem back there, Luke?"

Luke slid across the truck bed closer to Kirby's window. "It would be best if you kept both hands on the steering wheel."

Kirby laughed. "You'd better sit down or I'm liable to hit a pothole and throw you from the truck."

"And I'd sure hate for this shotgun to go off while it's pointed at your head, Kirby. Best be *real* careful of those potholes."

Hope looked at him, her eyes wide. Maybe that threat was

a little too much. He flashed a smile to let her know he had no intention of shooting Kirby—at least not yet.

Kirby didn't say anything more, but he kept his hands on the steering wheel until they arrived in Muskrat Creek. After driving down a lane leading to a ramshackle church building, he stopped and got out. Nellie and Hope followed suit, and when his sister waved for him to get down, Luke jumped from the back of the truck. Blue followed his master and remained close at his side.

Kirby strode to the rear of the truck. "Since you're along, Luke, you can help unload and carry the supplies into the church."

Luke lifted a crate of Bibles. "Glad to be of help wherever I'm needed."

"And wherever you're not wanted."

Luke stopped short. "What'd you say?"

Kirby shook his head. "Nothing. Let's get this stuff inside before folks start gathering."

They'd barely uncrated and arranged the supplies when folks began to arrive. One or two wagons appeared, their beds filled with children of various ages. A few swayback horses plodded into the churchyard, each bearing several children who held tight to the horses' manes or to each other, and the remainder arrived on foot. Mothers and older daughters carrying infants and toddlers on their hips, and others toting the youngest in slings tied around their shoulders.

Luke tied Blue to an oak near the rear of the church and walked inside. "I didn't know there were so many folks living in Muskrat Creek. Where'd they all come from?"

Hope peeked out the front door. "I'm not sure. This is the third time we've been here. Each time there's more folks. They seem to be spreading the word." She looked at Luke. "There are a lot of boys out there. Maybe you could take over teaching them? It sure would help since we've got such a large crowd, and Nellie will need to spend time handing out the extras to the womenfolk."

"I wondered what was in all those bags and boxes. Didn't figure you'd need that many Bibles and papers. What kind of extras you got?"

Hope glanced at the far corner of the building. "Kirby gets end pieces of cloth and a few other things from the general store in town. The rest he ordered the last time a requisition was sent to supply the company store."

Luke crossed the short distance to the other side of the room and peered into the crates. "You telling me the mining company is buying coffee and beans and piece goods in each of these towns?"

Hope nodded. "Nobody gets much, but they're thankful for anything we give them."

Luke scratched his head. Why would the mining company give handouts to folks in outlying areas when they'd never done the same for the miners when they were in need? It didn't make sense, especially when Kirby was always talking about how the company was in such bad shape and couldn't afford to pay the miners a living wage. He didn't begrudge these folks a few meager supplies, but there had to be something more to this. Kirby's pa wasn't the generous sort.

And even if Hope thought differently, neither was Kirby.

Luke caught sight of Hope pointing to a group of boys. "Why don't you take the boys over to that corner for their lesson?" she asked. She held a stack of papers in her hand and thrust them toward him as he drew near. "There are Bibles for those who can read. They can pick them up at the table." She leaned closer. "If they say they don't have a Bible and haven't received one at a previous visit, be sure they get one to take home. I've asked them to bring their Bibles when they attend, but sometimes they forget."

He glanced at the papers she'd handed him. "Joseph and his coat of many colors. There are lots of lessons to be learned from this Bible story. If I know boys, as soon as they hear that Joseph's brothers left him to die in a well, they'll tell me they'd like to toss their younger brothers into a well, too."

"Let's hope none of them actually try it." Her laughter swept through him like a summer breeze.

"When they hear the entire story, I'm sure they'll change their minds." He hesitated a moment. Although Kirby had expressed his dissatisfaction when Luke jumped into the truck and joined them, Hope had said very little. "I hope you aren't feeling cross toward me for coming along. What I told Kirby is true. With all the bootlegging goin' on, traveling these back roads isn't for the faint of heart. Betwixt the moonshiners and the revenuers, there are men out here meaner than a passel of striped snakes."

"I'm glad you came along, but mostly because we need your help with the children, not because you're carrying that shotgun." She pointed toward the boys, who'd begun taunting one of the younger children. "Better get over there before that little one ends up down in the well."

He laughed and tucked the stack of papers under one arm. "You still hand out candy if they sit still and listen?"

"I do." She turned to a small box and removed a paper sack. "Most of them know about the candy, so if they get loud or become unruly, just wave the sack in the air."

"I'll do that." He grinned. "And do the teachers get a piece of candy if they're on their best behavior?"

She nodded. "They do. Especially if they've been teaching the boys."

"And what if the teacher would like something even sweeter than candy?"

"Such as?" She arched her brows.

"A kiss from the sweetest girl a teacher ever met."

"It might be arranged if the teacher does an exceptional job."

"Hmmm. I'm feeling quite inspired." Luke gave a salute and made his way to where the boys had congregated.

The boys, though louder than the girls, had listened and were quick to answer questions after he'd told them the Bible story. When Hope signaled it was time to finish, he lifted the sack of candy in the air and glanced at Hope. Her bright smile and the twinkle in her eyes warmed his heart.

Hopefully her look of pleasure confirmed that she'd welcome him on all their future visits, or at least the ones when he didn't have to be at the mine. In truth, he worried Kirby would find some way to make certain he couldn't join them. The thought immediately annoyed him, but before he could dwell on the idea for long, Hope called to the children.

She stood at the front of the sanctuary and waved them forward. "Come to the center of the room and sit down, children. We're going to sing and have one more story before you're dismissed. I have lots of papers to send home with you."

Luke remained inside, enjoying the sound of her voice as she and Nellie led the children in several hymns. Afterward, Nellie read the story of the loaves and fishes from the Bible and spoke of how one young boy and his meager lunch had been used to feed thousands.

His sister earnestly looked at the group of children before she spoke to them. "God can use all of us no matter where we live, no matter if'n we're young or old, and even if we think we ain't got any special gifts. Pray and ask what you can do for Him, and He'll show you. Maybe not right away, but one day you'll find your answer. I know I did."

Luke swelled with pride as Nellie finished her talk. Her friendship with Hope had proved to be a good thing. He packed the remaining papers into a crate, carried it outside, and stopped short when he didn't see Kirby's truck. He walked to the road, placed the crate in the grass, and shaded his eyes with his hand. The truck was nowhere in sight.

He frowned and turned back toward the church. Now that he thought about it, he hadn't seen Kirby since they'd unloaded the truck. Where had he gone? Other than the general store that also served as a post office, there wasn't anything to see in this tiny town. Kirby wasn't the type who'd make friends among the locals, so he surely hadn't gone out in the country to visit anyone.

Using his thumb, he gestured toward the road when he entered the church. "The truck's not out there and neither is Kirby." He drew near to Hope. "Any idea where he might be off to?"

She shook her head. "No. He doesn't stay here to listen."

"Or to help." Nellie stooped down to pick up a crate. "He said he gets enough preachin' at the chapel car every night."

"He's usually back to meet us by the time we're done, but once in a while we have to wait on him." Hope patted one of the passing children on the head. "I'm grateful he's using his truck to drive us around the countryside, so I don't complain if we have to wait once in a while."

Luke's eyebrows drew tight as he considered her answer. "Only when you're in Muskrat Creek, or does he go off by himself at all the stops?"

Her shoulders raised and lowered in a shrug. "At all the stops. He uses the time to deliver items to the needy."

Luke didn't question her further, but he sure planned to find out more about Kirby and his disappearing act. He couldn't imagine Kirby driving through these back hills looking for folks who might need a handout. Besides, most of the folks living back in the hills would shoot any stranger who came onto their land uninvited.

Nellie walked outside with one of the girls and her mother while Hope and Luke finished packing up the remaining items. He was still mulling over likely reasons for Kirby's disappearance as they stacked the remaining boxes outside the church.

"We might as well sit down out here where it's cooler." Hope moved toward the rickety church steps.

"You think they'll hold both of us?" He chuckled and held out his hand to her. "Better let me hold your hand so I can catch ya if we fall through."

She gave him a sideways glance. "Is that just a trick so I'll let you hold my hand?"

"I'll admit it. You caught me." He chuckled and reached for her hand as they sat down. "I'm glad I got to come with you today. It's wonderful seeing what you and Nellie are able to do for the young'uns and their families."

"Thank you, Luke." She gently stroked the back of his hand with her thumb. "I hope we're making a difference in their lives and in the lives of the people who live in Finch, too."

"I know for a fact that folks are glad to have you and your pa in Finch. And if we can ever finish getting the church rebuilt, that's gonna be a double blessing."

"Once my father is better, he'll be able to return to work on the church. The railroaders are willing to help, but none of them can take charge, especially with their changing schedules. Most of the men living on the hill are too busy working in the mines and raising crops. So Papa understands he's the one who's got to lead. In the meantime, we need to assure folks that we're not giving up on getting it completed."

"I'll sure do my part to spread the word. I can talk to the men over at the mine, and I know Nellie will tell the womenfolk."

Hope nodded and asked, "Have the miners been talking more about joining the union or going on strike? I noticed some of the men have been gathering over near that stand of trees by the chapel car after church services. Anytime I get near, they quit talking. I mentioned it to Nellie. She said they were probably discussing the union because they get real private when there's talk of the union or strikes."

He was startled by the question. Why the sudden move from talk of rebuilding the church to questions about the union and a strike? In the past, they'd briefly discussed the UMWA and the occasional strikes that had occurred before Hope and her father arrived in Finch, but he and Hope hadn't talked of such things in recent weeks. The gatherings to discuss the possibility of a strike had been kept very quiet—at least he thought they had. Now he wondered if someone had leaked information. The union men had been brought in under cover of night, and he was sure they hadn't been seen by anyone other than the miners who'd attended that meeting. Yet Hope's questions raised his suspicions that the word had spread.

An icy shard cut into his core. "Why are you asking about a strike, Hope?"

She shifted and removed her hand from his. "Because I know it would be a terrible hardship on the families if the men went out on strike."

He lifted her chin with his thumb and looked into her eyes. "It would be a greater hardship if men died in an unsafe mine. Kirby and his family have made a fortune off the backs of miners who go into those mineshafts each day. Mr. Finch knows the conditions are unsafe and so does Kirby. The only time they do anything is if an inspector threatens to close them down."

"But now that they fixed the ventilation, everything should be fine, shouldn't it?"

How little she understood. He shook his head. "The ventilation system was only one problem. There are lots of other dangers down there." He looked deep into her eyes. "Are you asking because you care about the families or because Kirby Finch wants to know if we're going to strike?"

"You know I care about the families, Luke. And I care about you. As for Kirby, I'm certain he would be delighted to know if there are plans for a strike." She jutted her chin toward the road, then jumped to her feet. "Here comes Kirby now. Let's get out there so we can load the truck." She glanced over her shoulder and waved to Nellie. "Come on, Nellie. The truck is here."

Hope's heart pounded a loud, unsteady beat. She had avoided a lie, but the thought of what she'd done caused bile to rise in the back of her throat. Even if she knew with certainty there would be a strike, she couldn't betray Luke.

Tears threatened as she remembered Kirby's recent warning. She lifted a crate from the grass and knew there would be no more visits to these communities if she didn't comply with his demands. Yet how could he fault her if she was unable to gather any information for him? Luke hadn't given her an answer that would satisfy Kirby, and she was sure none of the other miners would reveal their plans to her. So, no matter the consequences, she wouldn't ask any more questions.

Kirby leaned against a tree while Luke lifted the final boxes into the rear of the truck and the two women settled inside the vehicle. "Sorry I'm late. I fell asleep."

Luke jerked around. "I thought you were out delivering supplies to needy folks who live in these parts."

"I-I was. I mean, I did. Deliver supplies. But when I got done, I was on a winding road that went near the creek, so I parked the truck and sat down for a bit." He jammed his hands into his pockets as he sputtered the explanation. "It was so peaceful, I lay back and fell asleep. When I woke up and looked at my pocket watch, I couldn't believe the time."

Luke gave a slight nod. "So who were the families you paid a visit to?"

Kirby hiked a shoulder. "I don't ask their names. Most places, I just drop the goods on their porches and leave." He looked down at the ground. "Don't want to embarrass them."

"Is that a fact? I'm surprised you don't get your head blown off."

Eyes wide, Kirby pushed away from the tree. "Why's that?"

Luke untied Blue, jumped into the bed of the truck, and whistled for the dog to join him. Kirby stood nearby, still staring at him, obviously wanting an answer. "Folks in these parts don't cotton to strangers, Kirby. You should know that by now." Luke glanced from Kirby to Hope.

She tilted her head, considering the possibilities. "Well, the Lord must be protecting you, Kirby."

"Yes, Luke." Kirby chuckled. "The Lord's taking real good care of me."

⁕

Luke cocked his ear as they neared town. He leaned over the edge of the truck bed and shouted toward the open window. "The bell's ringing. There's an accident at the mine! Hurry up!"

The truck surged to a higher speed, yet it felt as though they'd never get there. When they entered the far end of town, Kirby slowed the truck. "Keep going, Kirby. Get to the mine."

He continued to slow the truck. "I'm going to let Nellie and Hope out."

Luke couldn't believe his ears. Was Kirby out of his mind? Didn't he realize what that bell meant? "No! Just get over there. They can walk back to town."

Nellie leaned forward and shouted at Kirby to keep driving. The truck gained speed as the bell continued to reverberate through the surrounding hills. Women and children appeared like ants scampering down the hillside, each one intent on reaching the disaster, each one frightened they might discover their father, brother, or husband dead or missing in the yawning void beyond the mine entrance, each one praying their loved one would be spared.

Luke jumped from the truck with Blue following close on

his heels. He raced toward one of the men covered in coal dust and dirt, a gash on his arm spurting blood. Luke ripped off a piece of his shirt and tied it around the miner's arm. "What happened, Mort?"

"One of the coal pillars give out. Daniels is blaming us— saying we stayed in there and dug too deep into the pillars. But we had moved into the other room like he ordered." He looked over Luke's shoulder. "You seen anything of the doc? I think I'm gonna need him to sew this up."

Luke waved, and Hope came running to his side. "Did you see the doctor?"

"He's over near the entrance." Her focus remained on Mort's arm for a moment. "I'll go get him."

Luke shook his head. "Stay here with Mort. I'll go. I don't want you moving any closer to the mine."

Hope knelt beside Mort and held his head in her lap. "I can't believe this has happened."

His eyes remained at half-mast when he tipped his head to look at her. "Ain't no surprise to any of us. We ain't been able to get that good-for-nothin' owner to make things safer in there, but now they're gonna blame us for the cave-in."

Luke's earlier comments replayed in Hope's mind, and she shivered at the thought of him returning to such dangerous work. No doubt, the wives and mothers living on the hill faced the same thoughts every day. How did they manage the constant fear?

Mort winced and adjusted the makeshift tourniquet. "Maybe a walkout will get 'em to change a few things."

Before she could answer, Mort's wife appeared and touched Hope's shoulder. "Here, let me hold him. I'm sure there's others needin' ya." Once she'd knelt on the ground beside her husband, Hope moved aside.

She stood and took in the disaster. Men lay on the ground groaning in pain, women and girls knelt at their sides, and crying children wandered through the mayhem, their eyes radiating unspeakable terror.

Surely now Kirby would make the necessary changes, wouldn't he?

Hope's eyes widened when a few days after the cave-in, Kirby appeared at the late-night chapel meeting and took his place in the back pew. She'd seen nothing of him since the disaster, and her visits to the hill revealed he'd done little to help the injured miners. Unrest remained high among the men, and several of the wives had urged their husbands either to call for more inspections or join the union and strike if the owners were unwilling to do something to improve safety in the mine.

For Kirby's sake, she was glad there weren't any miners at the late meeting, but even the railroaders looked at him with disdain as they departed after the service. When he made no move to get up, Hope stepped down the narrow aisle between the pews and stopped near his side.

"How are you doing? I haven't seen you on the hill and I didn't want to go to the mining office, but I want you to know my father and I have been praying for a swift resolution to the problems at the mine."

"We'll do what we need to in order to shore up the timbers

and get the men back in there. We're hoping it won't take too long to get them back to work."

Her brow furrowed. "I'm surprised to hear that. I thought it would be some time before the miners could go back in."

"The women on the hill been talking to you?"

"A little. Mostly they're worried about the welfare of their husbands and sons. And I don't blame them. If I had a husband or son or brother, I wouldn't want him going into your mine until there was some assurance it was safe."

"We can't ever assure complete safety in the mines. Mining will always be dangerous, and I can't change that fact. The miners know there's danger, and when they accept the job, they take that on." His smile was stiff as he blew out a sigh. "I didn't come here to talk about the mine. I just wanted to make sure you were planning on going to Fern Hollow tomorrow."

Her mouth dropped open. Had she heard him correctly? Was he truly going to drive to Fern Hollow and make deliveries to the needy when families on the hill weren't yet able to earn their pay? What was he thinking?

"I thought you'd want to devote your time to work at the mine and helping folks up on the hill. With some of them not working, I'm sure they're going to need some assistance."

"Like I said, Daniels is taking care of matters at the mine, and I'll speak to Mr. Farragut about helping folks on the hill if it's necessary. So you need not concern yourself about my job or Finch Mining and Company." There was an edge to his voice. "If you don't want to go to Fern Hollow, that's fine. I just wanted to let you know you're welcome to come along since I'll be leaving at the usual time."

Her thoughts turned fuzzy as she attempted to sort through his suggestion. Would the folks on the hill think her insensitive to their needs if she went to Fern Hollow? Where could she provide the most help, and who needed her more? On her recent visits to the hill, the women thanked her but turned down offers of help. They'd seemed intent on providing all the care themselves.

She jarred to attention when Kirby pushed to his feet. "I'll plan to go with you. I know folks will be waiting at the school-house in Fern Hollow. I don't want to disappoint them, but I'll need to talk with Nellie early in the morning and see if she can come along. I'd already told her I didn't expect to be going, and she may have gone ahead and planned to help someone up on the hill."

He leaned across the back of the pew and picked up his hat. "Well, you go ahead and check with her and let's hope she's able to join us. If not, I'd be happy to speak to your father and see if you could make this one trip alone—especially given the circumstances."

She shook her head. "He wouldn't agree, but he might feel well enough to come along if Nellie can't."

His smile disappeared, and she noticed a slight tic in his jaw. "That would be fine, too. I'll see you tomorrow."

Questions about Kirby swirled in her mind. How could he be so generous one moment and so selfish the next? Was Luke right to be suspicious of him? Did she really know Kirby at all?

Maybe tomorrow she'd get some answers.

..............ॐ..............

Kirby trudged back to the railroad station where he'd parked the truck, climbed inside, and headed toward the mining office. He parked the truck, then picked up a lantern from a shed near the office building. He wouldn't take a chance of anyone seeing the glimmer of light, but he'd need it when he arrived at the still. He stepped into the thicket at the edge of the woods and waited for his eyes to adjust to the cavernous darkness that blanketed the hillside at night. These past few days had been one problem after another. As soon as one was fixed, another needed attention.

Anger had burned deep inside his chest when Daniels told him the miners hadn't followed instructions to leave the pillars of coal at the thickness he'd ordered, and that had been the cause of the cave-in. Kirby questioned a number of the miners. Of course, they all denied they'd cut too deep into the pillars and swore they'd been digging in another area when the cave-in occurred. Kirby didn't know who to believe. On the one hand, there was Daniels, a man his father trusted who possessed years of experience. On the other, there were the miners, men who'd worked in the mines for years and knew the danger of weakened pillars. Still, the miners' pay depended on how many pounds of coal they sent out each day. Digging a new seam took time, and yields were much lower, so they might not tell him the whole truth.

Thankfully, the entire roof of the room where the cave-in occurred hadn't collapsed, but the slowdown was costing the company money. And if the inspectors arrived and found in favor of the miners, there would be large fines to pay. Kirby could only hope he'd have enough money to leave Finch before the inspectors got there.

Along with worry about the accident, he'd had to fend off Daniels's and Farragut's demands to notify his father. Realizing Daniels would send word to his father if he didn't, Kirby promised to send a wire from Longview. He'd done his best to sound calm and composed when he told Daniels he'd pass through Longview on his way to Fern Hollow the next day. Initially the manager had been taken aback when Kirby mentioned he would be traveling to Fern Hollow so soon after the accident.

However, a promise to notify his father while on the excursion seemingly set Mr. Daniels's concerns to rest.

On the evenings before making runs to the small outlying settlements, Kirby would leave the company truck parked near the mining office. Then, after he was sure everyone was gone for the evening, Jimmy Ray would load the jars of moonshine into the hidden compartment beneath the truck bed. Today that had been impossible, and now he could only hope Jimmy Ray hadn't gone home. Loading all the jars into the truck by himself was the last thing Kirby had wanted to do, but he couldn't risk doing it in the morning light.

Perspiration crept down his neck, and his heart raced at the sound of every snapping twig and rustling branch. He stopped short when a skunk swished through the undergrowth and crossed his path. He instinctively held his breath until the animal was well out of sight, then blew it out. Lucky for him the nasty little creature hadn't lifted its tail and sprayed him. Once certain the skunk was gone, he continued to push his way through the thicket. They'd been careful to hide their tracks each time they came through. And although that action provided an extra layer of protection from revenuers, it also made it difficult to traverse the hill at nighttime.

Kirby stopped near a towering pine and took stock of his surroundings. Had his memory betrayed him? He'd been up here at night only one other time, but he was certain he should have reached the still by now. His breath caught when he heard what sounded like breaking glass. He squinted his eyes and slowly moved toward the sound. Finally he glimpsed a flickering light. Moments later, a figure leaned near the lantern and illuminated Jimmy Ray's features. Kirby sighed, then hissed Jimmy's name into the darkness.

The boy went still, then straightened and peered into the night. "That you, Kirby?"

Kirby answered the boy, now moving forward at a quickened pace. "I'm sure thankful you didn't go home, Jimmy. We need to load the truck tonight."

"Figured we would, but I shoulda been home at suppertime. My ma's gonna whoop the tar outta me."

The boy was only thirteen, but his height and broad shoulders belied his age. Kirby couldn't imagine a woman giving Jimmy Ray a beating. "Tell her I needed help at the mining office because of the cave-in, and I asked you to stay late. I'll talk to her if you need me to."

The boy grinned, his uneven teeth appearing dull and yellow in the lantern light. "I'm obliged to ya." He pointed to a wheelbarrow with a long bed and large front wheel. "I got the first load on here. Need to strap it down before starting back through the woods."

Kirby looked at the contraption. "Where'd you get that?"

The boy shrugged. "I made it from parts of an old small wagon I found down at the mine. They wasn't using it no more, so I tore it apart and made this." He gestured to the crates he'd filled with jars of moonshine. "Ain't no way I wanted to carry each crate through the woods."

Kirby helped him strap the crates onto the wheelbarrow, and then the boy bent down, grabbed the handles and stood. The crates remained steady. Kirby chuckled. "Good job, Jimmy Ray."

The boy grinned and straightened his shoulders. "Thanks. My ma says I ain't the sharpest knife in the drawer, but I got me some good ideas once in a while." He nodded at the wheelbarrow. "Ya want to take it down or do ya want to stay here and fill them other crates with jars?"

Jimmy Ray's mother was right. He wasn't very smart. Otherwise he would have known Kirby would accept the job requiring the least amount of effort. "I'll stay here and fill the crates.

Once you get those in the truck, come on back and we'll do another load."

When he hoisted the last crate onto the bed of the truck, Jimmy Ray's cheeks puffed out like a muskrat with a mouthful of lily roots. He settled the crate in place and blew out a long breath that flattened his cheeks. "That there's the last of it." The boy stood back and admired the truck. "Sure wish I could earn me enough money to get me a truck like this."

"If you keep up the hard work," Kirby said, "I think you'll be driving the best truck in the county one of these days." He reached in his pocket, removed a dollar bill, and handed it to the boy.

His mouth gaped, and his eyes glimmered in the moonlight. "You're giving me a whole dollar just for helping you load tonight?"

"And for keeping your mouth shut in case your ma catches you coming home late." Kirby placed his hand around the back of the boy's neck and applied a little pressure. "You know you'd be in big trouble if you ever let it slip what we're doing, don't ya?"

The boy wriggled free and bobbed his head. "I done told ya there ain't nobody can get nothin' out of me lessen I wanna tell. You ain't got to worry 'bout me."

"Just make sure it stays that way." Kirby gave him a nod, and the two of them walked side by side until Kirby neared his boardinghouse. "Get on up the hill now. While I'm gone tomorrow, see if you can locate some more corn for us to buy. We're getting low."

The boy shoved one hand in his pocket. "You want me to go lookin' somewhere off the hill? I don't know if there's much left to buy from the miners' plots. I've asked most everyone, 'cept Luke and his uncle Frank. You want me to see if they want to sell any of their corn?"

Kirby shook his head. "I already told you, we don't ask either of them for their corn." Luke could likely charm the boy into saying something that would tip his hand. Kirby was certain Luke would want to know why Jimmy Ray was buying corn and where he'd gotten the money to buy it. Jimmy Ray wasn't bright enough to withstand a lengthy interrogation.

Kirby sighed. There was always another problem to solve. Why was life so difficult? "See how much you can get from right around here without asking Luke or Frank."

The boy shuffled his feet in the soft dirt near the edge of the road. "Thing is, last time I tried to get more, there was lots of questions. The men said there'd be a feud for sure if someone else was selling shine to their regulars. I told 'em I was selling the corn for livestock feed, but I ain't sure they believed me."

"Just do your best, Jimmy Ray. I'm not selling to their regulars so there's no reason to worry." Kirby wiped the perspiration from his forehead. "Go on home. I've got to get some sleep before I leave in the morning."

Once the boy disappeared into the darkness, Kirby plodded up the boardinghouse steps and inserted his key into the lock. Surely tomorrow would be better.

.... ❧ ....

Luke walked a short distance behind Nellie and Hope as they descended the hill. He squinted in the early morning sun as he patted Blue on the head. Maybe he was being overprotective of Nellie and Hope, but he didn't think so. Every time he thought about the two of them traveling in the midst of a possible moonshine feud, an uneasy feeling settled in his gut.

When Kirby caught sight of them as they approached, Luke shifted his shotgun and waved. "Morning, Kirby. I'm surprised you're heading out this morning. Hope says you're going to Fern Hollow."

"I am." Kirby rounded the back of the truck, his jaw rigid. "You have some problem with what I'm doing?"

The challenge in his voice surprised Luke. "Nope. Just thought you'd be over at the mine."

Kirby's gaze settled on the shotgun resting on Luke's shoulder. "I thought you'd be over there, too. I'm sure you're on the schedule for today, and I don't think you'll need that shotgun unless you're expecting to do a little hunting before you go home after work."

Luke shook his head. "Nope. I switched with Bill Withers. Mr. Daniels said it was fine. I'm going to ride shotgun in the back of your truck again. I sure was glad 'cause I don't want no harm coming to my sister and Hope—or to you."

"I don't think there's any need." Deep lines formed between Kirby's brows. "There hasn't been any sign of revenuers for a long time. I think we'll be fine without you."

Luke gave a shrug. "I'm not as sure as you. Besides, I've got nothing better to do." He jumped into the back of the truck and signaled for Blue to join him before Kirby could voice any further objection. Like it or not, he was going along. From here on out, no one was going to hurt his sister or Hope.

As for Kirby, well, he'd decide on protecting him if and when the situation arose.

............ঞ............

Kirby sat down at his desk in the mine office to compose a letter to his father. Instead of sending the wire he'd promised after the cave-in, he'd decided to wait until the inspectors concluded their investigation. Though he hadn't anticipated waiting a full week before informing his father, the inspectors had, in

Kirby's opinion, been painstakingly slow in completing their task. And while he doubted his father had received any inkling of the cave-in, he needed to post this letter to the main offices in Pittsburgh before such a thing occurred. Wanting to be certain the wording would have the desired effect, Kirby had written and rewritten the letter several times. As always, the need to update his father was imperative. No communication would bring the man to Finch as quickly as unresolved problems in the mines.

As in the past, Kirby had carefully waited for what he considered the proper time to send a letter. Just one more irritating thing about his life in Finch. Dealing with the mine and his father's expectations were proving problem enough, but having Luke tail along on his trips with Hope and Nellie grated on his every nerve. Could nothing go easy here? At least there'd been no sign of revenuers, which had made gun-toting Luke look a bit foolish.

But how could he word this letter so that his father understood things were well in hand? He detailed the cave-in, then immediately explained that his delayed notification had arisen from a desire to free his father from concern until the inspectors had completed their examination. Now that he'd received the report, Kirby was elated to inform his father that the inspectors had declared it was impossible to be certain whether the miners had disobeyed orders and dug into the pillars or whether Mr. Daniels had failed to give the order. They'd found notches in the pillars that seemed to prove digging had occurred deeper than what was safe, yet they declared the notches could have taken place during the collapse. Therefore the inspectors had concluded the miners' statements and Mr. Daniels's statement had nullified each other.

Kirby didn't include the fact that the inspectors had voiced their disbelief that a miner would put his own life in jeopardy by digging too deep into a coal pillar, or that they had listened when Mr. Daniels declared it occurred frequently because the miners hoped their loads would weigh more for higher pay at week's end. At Daniels's remark, the inspectors grunted and claimed such an incident wouldn't happen if the miners were paid a livable wage. Kirby decided there was no need to include information that would either anger his father or possibly cause him to pay Finch a visit.

In the end, the inspectors determined the company couldn't be held at fault. The miners had been unhappy with the decision. And if Kirby was any judge of attitude, the inspectors' dour faces revealed they would have much preferred to find the company at fault. Mr. Wayfair's parting words still rung in Kirby's ears. "This is the kind of thing that causes miners to unionize or strike." He'd pointed his finger at Kirby. "We didn't level a fine against you, but mark my words. You may be in for more trouble than just a fine when this is all said and done."

Kirby hadn't included the warning in the letter to his father, either. Instead, he'd written that he continued to befriend as many miners as possible and that he'd attempted to be thorough in his investigation. Although untrue, Kirby further declared there was no evidence of a possible strike or unionization. His father would expect to read those reassuring words. He'd ended the letter with a caveat that though he'd been doing his best to uncover any unrest, the hill people didn't trust outsiders, so there was always the possibility they weren't being completely honest with him.

He hoped his final words would vindicate him if either event should occur before he left town. And leaving couldn't happen soon enough.

CHAPTER

21

Hope stepped down the narrow aisle to the last pew, where Kirby sat after the late-evening meeting. His attendance had become sporadic over the past weeks. When she questioned him about his absence, he mentioned the need to keep late hours at the mining office. By the time he finished his work each day, he was just too weary to attend chapel meetings.

She'd considered his response and drawn the conclusion that their daytime runs to surrounding communities must be the cause of his late office hours. With that in mind, she presented him with a solution. Since her father was making good progress, she suggested Kirby teach him to drive the truck. That way he could deliver the supplies and also minister to any in need in the surrounding towns.

Kirby's refusal had been immediate and abrupt, but he'd returned the next day to explain and apologize. His father, Kirby lamented, wouldn't grant permission to drive the truck to anyone except Mr. Daniels, Mr. Farragut, or him. His apology was profuse, though she somehow felt he hadn't been completely honest with her. Still, she accepted his apology. Since then, he'd been present every night. Each evening she wondered if he appeared at the church service in order to prove he didn't need help or desire her interference.

He smiled when she approached. "Good evening. I thought your singing exceptional this evening."

"Thank you. That hymn is special to me." She'd sung "A Mighty Fortress Is Our God," a hymn that had been one of her mother's favorites.

He glanced toward the front of the chapel car, where her father was deep in conversation with several of the railroaders, then gestured to the pew opposite him. "Please, sit down. We seldom get a chance to visit without anyone else around."

"That's true, but I do enjoy Nellie's company, and she's a great help to me. If she's not handing out tracts and Bibles, she's helping with the younger children. I don't know what I'd do without her." Kirby had been quite clear about the fact that he didn't particularly enjoy Nellie's company, and so she felt the need to defend the girl. In truth, Nellie had taken a bit of a liking to Kirby, yet he rebuffed her every time she attempted to gain his attention. "Besides, if Nellie hadn't agreed to make these trips, I wouldn't be able to travel with you."

"I know." He scooted to the end of the pew, closing the distance between them, and tipped his head to the side. "I was wondering if you'd heard any more about the possibility of a strike? The other day I was sure I overheard some of the men talking about a union meeting. Ever since the cave-in, the men seem to be gathering in groups and whispering among themselves. I feel certain they're planning something and I'd like to avoid a strike. The day after the cave-in, you said the women on the hill had been talking about encouraging their husbands to strike. Have you heard anything more? Surely Luke has said something to you. I see the two of you together all the time."

"That's not true, Kirby, but even if it were, who I spend my time with isn't any of your concern. And if you're worried about a strike, I suggest you talk to the miners. I'm not going to carry tales for you or anyone else. It simply isn't proper." She'd maintained an even but firm tone. She wanted to put an end to his questions about strikes and unions.

He'd been somewhat distant on their most recent trips, and this latest disagreement might create an even greater chasm. At times she thought it was because she hadn't given him information about rumors of a walkout, but at other times she thought he was angry that Luke continued to travel with them—at least most of the time. Luke was certain that Kirby did his best to juggle shifts at the mine so Luke couldn't come with them. Hope remained uncertain why Kirby had become so aloof, but even Nellie had mentioned his lack of affability.

He nodded. "Well, I wouldn't want you to do anything that wasn't proper." His words came out stilted.

"Are you still planning on going tomorrow?" Hope asked.

He tucked the hymnal in the metal rack beneath the pew, then looked up at her. "I am, but you may need to adjust a little. I want to make a stop at Hopkins Fork, as well as Muskrat Creek and Denton."

"Three stops?" Her breath caught as she considered the number of supplies she'd need to pack. "Two is the most we've made in the past, and you always let me know in advance."

He shrugged. "We can cut down on the amount of time while we're in Denton if we need to. I don't think folks will complain if you let them know we're trying to help as many folks as we can."

"I've never heard you mention Hopkins Fork. How did you happen to decide to make a stop there?" Truth be told, she'd never heard of the place and had no idea how many people might live in the area or even where it was located. "And where is it?"

He appeared to study the pew in front of him for a moment. "One of the families in Muskrat Creek has relatives in Hopkins Fork. They said folks were in need of help and asked if we'd stop over there."

"But they won't know we're coming, and we don't even know if there's a church or school where we can meet with them. Maybe we should stop at a few houses and pass out some tracts and see about setting up for a regular teaching visit in a couple of weeks."

"You can do your visiting however it suits you, but I can't drive you and Nellie from house to house. The folks I'm going to talk to asked for a private visit with me." Kirby pushed up from the pew. "Just take along a few extra flyers to pass out, and maybe you and Nellie can find someplace to sit under a tree near the side of the road until I return."

His inconsiderate attitude surprised her. Surely he must have known of this meeting before tonight. Would he have even mentioned the additional stop if she hadn't approached him? She certainly didn't like his suggestion that she and Nellie sit by the side of the road in Hopkins Fork, yet the folks in Denton and Muskrat Creek were expecting their weekly visit and she didn't want to disappoint them.

He stepped toward the door of the chapel car. "I'm planning on leaving at the same time in the morning."

She nodded. "I'll be there."

She offered up a silent prayer that Luke didn't have to work at the mine tomorrow. If she and Nellie had to sit by the roadside, she'd feel much better if Luke were there.

⚬

The following morning, Luke descended the hill alongside his sister. His shotgun rested on his shoulder as they approached the truck. Hope greeted him with a bright smile, and Kirby pinned him with his usual scowl. The first morning he'd joined Kirby and the two girls on their run, Kirby had been clear about not wanting Luke with them. Since then his attitude hadn't changed, but he'd been unsuccessful in his attempts to control Luke's work hours without raising suspicion with Mr. Daniels and the other miners. He constantly brushed aside Luke's worries over danger lurking on the road, but Luke was undeterred. He'd lived in these parts all his life and he knew trouble could appear when it was least expected.

Luke hoisted himself into the rear of the truck and whistled for Blue. The dog leaped in and settled between Luke and the crates of flyers, Bibles, and Sunday-school papers. Kirby shook his head and directed a disgusted look at the dog before opening the door for Hope and Nellie.

The stop in Muskrat Creek had gone as usual. Once the girls and Luke had unloaded their supplies, Kirby disappeared on his mission of mercy delivering sacks of supplies. Luke remained baffled by a man who could extend generosity to the people of these outlying areas, yet ignore the needs of the families who worked for his family's mining business. He had asked God to reveal Kirby's reasoning, but that hadn't happened. He then asked God to stir Luke's sense of right and wrong, but that hadn't occurred, either. Desperate for answers, Luke went to Hope's father seeking answers.

"I'll do my best to answer your questions, Luke, but I'm not sure the answer will satisfy you." The preacher had sat opposite Luke with his Bible open on his lap. "We may not understand anything that happens on this earth until we get to heaven, but don't become bitter over what Kirby is doing. You must remember that the people Kirby is helping may not be as important to you as the folks who live on the hill, but we are all important to God. Don't begrudge the good work Kirby is doing. We have to trust he is doing what God has called him to do. If he isn't, we need to let God take care of that, as well. Trust is a difficult thing, but God has a plan. Of that you can be sure."

In spite of his misgivings about Kirby, Luke had listened to the preacher. He tried to believe that Kirby's intentions were good and that God would provide for the people of Finch, even if Kirby didn't.

Kirby was leaning alongside his truck when they completed their meetings in Muskrat Creek. Luke carried several boxes that had contained Sunday-school materials back to the truck while Nellie and Hope packed some of the remaining papers and then bid the children and their mothers good-bye.

With a loud grunt, Kirby pushed away from the side of the truck and glowered at them. "We need to get moving. Tell the girls to hurry up. I told Hope I was making three stops today. She should know I don't have time to wait around."

His tone grated on Luke, but upon his return inside, he passed along Kirby's message, then looked directly at his sister. "He's got his dander up, so don't say anything that's gonna make matters worse."

Nellie frowned and dropped a pile of papers into one of the boxes. "Why you lookin' at me? Kirby don't pay me no mind."

"Because you forget to mind your tongue no matter what anyone tells you." He lifted the crates, looked around the room, and gave a nod. "Looks like this is the last of it. Go untie Blue while I load these up, Nellie."

His sister wrinkled her nose at him, but she did as he asked. Hope matched Luke's stride as he walked toward the truck. "He said he told you we'd be making three stops today. Why's that?"

"I don't know. He didn't tell me until last night, but he did tell me we'd need to cut short our time in Denton."

Luke lowered his voice as they neared the truck. "Did he say where else we're stopping?"

"Yes. Hopkins Fork." She looked up at him. "Do you know it?"

"About as well as I know Muskrat Creek or any of these other outlyin' areas. Not much there. As I recall, there's a one-room schoolhouse and a small general store. That pretty much makes up the town. Just like here, folks live in the hills that surround the school and the store."

Blue loped past them and buffeted Kirby. The dog hurtled into the back of the truck, unaware that Kirby had almost landed in the dirt. Kirby's lip curled. Keeping his voice low, he leaned close to Luke's ear. "Don't keep bringing that animal with you, or the first chance I get I'm going to run him over with this truck."

Luke glared at him. "You so much as harm a hair on that dog's head and you'll be facing the wrong end of my shotgun. We clear on that?"

Kirby wheeled around, jumped into the truck, and slammed the door. Without another word, he took off with a jolt that nearly caused Luke to come unseated. When they arrived in Denton, Kirby sat in the driver's seat and rushed them to unload the truck. "Don't forget to be out here a half hour early."

"We'll try our best, Kirby." Nellie's tone was syrupy sweet. She glanced over her shoulder. "And you try to be on time, too."

Kirby leaned toward the open window. "Unless you plan on walking home, Nellie, you best not use that tone with me."

Luke glared at his sister. "I told you not to do anything to cause a ruckus with him."

Nellie squared her shoulders. "I'm not afeared of Kirby Finch, and I don't need you tellin' me what to do." She marched off with a crate held tight beneath her arm.

Hope went to the back of the truck to help Luke unload. "Don't be too hard on her. I think Nellie is finally accepting the fact that Kirby isn't the kind of man she had hoped."

Luke frowned. He didn't know how his sister could have overlooked Kirby's many faults for so long, but he'd learned that women sometimes view things different from men. Then, as if someone had jerked him to attention, his eyes opened wide and he stared at Hope. "Are you tellin' me that Nellie thought Kirby might ask to court her?"

"She never said as much, but I got the idea she would be happy if he did. Now that we've been traveling with him, I think she's seeing the real Kirby with all his shortcomings, and what she sees doesn't please her." Hope lightly grasped Luke's arm. "Don't tease her. She's unhappy enough."

"I won't tease her, but if she thought I'd ever agree Kirby was a good match for her, she's dumber than a coal bucket."

"Luke! That's not—"

"I know, I know, but it's the truth. Kirby isn't good enough to clean the mud off my sister's shoes."

"Well, I can agree with that much." A group of children ran toward them, and Hope enlisted their help carrying the supplies inside. She looked at Luke as they neared the church door. "Remember—don't say anything more."

He nodded, and the three of them fell into their usual routine. Luke was careful to watch the time, making certain everything was packed and they were waiting by the road when Kirby returned.

Kirby had remained inside the truck while the three of them began to load. Moments later, he stepped out, removed his pocket watch and clicked open the gold case. "We're running late. Hurry up!" He stood by the truck door and barked the order, but made no move to help load the remaining boxes.

"You're the one who wasn't here on time, so don't yell at us." Nellie shoved a box onto the truck bed and glared at him. "If you're so worried about the time, put that watch away and help us load."

Luke stepped close to his sister's side. "Stop it, Nellie. Don't be cuttin' off your nose to spite your face. You keep it up and he won't be willing to bring the two of you along to hold your meetings." She caught her bottom lip between her teeth and nodded. "I don't mean to be harsh with you, but that's what big brothers are for." He winked at her.

Once they'd finished loading, they climbed into their respective positions. Kirby shifted into gear and steered the truck out of the small town. Once they were a short distance away, the truck picked up speed. Luke's chest tightened as Kirby pushed the truck faster. He tapped on the rear window and shouted for Kirby to slow down, but Kirby ignored him. Instead of slowing the truck, he tromped on the gas pedal, and Luke grabbed for the wood side rails that surrounded the truck bed. His back slammed against the cab of the truck, then slid in the other direction as Kirby attempted to navigate a sharp curve.

A horn blared from an oncoming vehicle, and Kirby swerved. The tires spun, loose gravel and dirt flying in all directions. The back end of the truck veered out of control, which caused it to careen toward a ditch beside the road. Blue jumped from the truck. Luke followed, his landing softened by the thick undergrowth and bushes. The side of the truck struck an oak tree, swung around and came to a halt with its front in the ditch.

Unharmed, Kirby jumped from the truck and rushed toward the rear. "Look at what you've done!" He glowered at Luke. "If you hadn't distracted me, this never would have happened."

Nellie and Hope had climbed out the driver's side of the truck and rushed to Luke's side. "You have a cut on your forehead. Did you break any bones?" Hope knelt on one side of Luke with Nellie on the other.

"I'm fine. If I hadn't jumped, it might be a different story." He pushed to his feet and leaned against a nearby tree to gain his balance. "Appears I'm in better shape than the truck."

"I'm not so sure that's true." Hope yanked a handkerchief from her skirt and dabbed at the blood trickling down the side of his head.

Kirby had retrieved a crowbar that was thrown from the truck and was frantically yanking at the truck fender with it. "I've got to get this fender off the tire or I won't be able to drive the truck."

"Looks like you're doing a good job," Nellie said, "and there's only the one crowbar. Besides, Luke's got a cut on his head so he shouldn't lean over. Let us know when you're ready to leave."

Kirby glowered in their direction, but he continued to work on the fender. A short time later, he rounded the truck and opened the door. "If you're coming with me, you better get in."

He stood by the open door. Blue jumped into the rear of the truck while Hope helped get Luke settled into position. She paused and sniffed the air, then looked around. "Whatever is—?" Before she could finish the question, Luke pulled her close and kissed her on the lips.

He backed away ever so slightly. "Don't say anything more. I'll explain later." He kissed her once more before releasing her.

"I said you need to get in the truck, Hope." Kirby glared at Luke as Hope scurried around the side of the truck and got in. The truck swayed when he slammed the door.

There was no doubt Luke's brash behavior had increased Kirby's fury, but it was the only way he could quiet her. He smiled. Yet what a lovely way to gain her silence.

When they arrived at a fork in the road, Kirby turned the truck toward Finch. There would be no stop at Hopkins Fork today. With all that had happened, he couldn't take the risk. Jimmy Ray was always careful to pack straw around the jars of moonshine to keep them from rattling or breaking if Kirby hit a deep rut in the road, but he worried that some of the jars had at least cracked in the accident. He needed to get Luke out of the truck before he suspected anything.

Nellie leaned forward as they made the turn. "We could still stop in Hopkins Fork long enough to tell folks—"

Kirby lifted his hand from the wheel and quickly waved the girl to silence. "We're not going to Hopkins Fork. I've already made the decision, so just be quiet."

"Kirby! There's no call to be rude." Hope crossed her arms tight around her waist. "I understand you're upset about the accident, but that wasn't Nellie's fault. If you hadn't been driving so fast, it wouldn't have happened."

Her criticism was like salt in a wound and further ignited his anger. "I don't need nosy Nellie telling me what I should or shouldn't do, and I sure don't need a bossy woman telling me how to drive my truck. I don't need an opinion from either of you."

Hope stiffened beside him. "Fine."

He stared straight ahead, his hands tight around the steering wheel. For the remainder of the ride, Hope leaned away from him at every turn. When they finally neared town, he gave her a sideways glance. "I'm sorry. I shouldn't have been so abrupt, but I'm concerned about the damage to the truck. My father is going to want an explanation as to why I'm driving you to these meetings during work hours and using the company truck. Especially since the company will need to pay to have it repaired."

Nellie shifted toward him. "It still drives just fine, so it shouldn't cost much to fix that dented fender. Luke can probably use a mallet to pound it out. With a little paint, it should be fit as a fiddle."

Kirby swallowed back his frustration. He didn't want Nellie's opinions, and he certainly didn't want Luke's help repairing the truck. He had hoped his apology would melt Hope's icy behavior, but her arms remained frozen around her waist.

When she didn't respond, Kirby searched for something that might break the barrier between them. "I can't take back what I said. All I can do is tell you I'm sorry and hope that you'll show me some of the grace your father is always preaching about." He needed to keep her as an ally for as long as possible.

She sighed, and the tightness in her shoulders eased. "I accept your apology. In the future, I hope you'll remember to think before you speak. You can't take back hurtful words after they've been spoken. Painful words can remain etched on a heart forever. They can do irreparable harm."

Kirby nodded. "I'll remember that." While he might need a reminder to think before he spoke, he'd need more than a minute or two if he was going to win Hope's favor. After all, he'd been given little opportunity to exhibit his courting demeanor. Either Nellie, Luke, or both of them appeared every time he might have had a few minutes alone with her. Even after the late-night meetings at the chapel car, the railroaders or her father were close at hand. Maybe if she'd give him a few minutes alone, he could change her mind about him.

He pulled the truck to a stop near the path leading up the hillside. Nellie had opened the door and jumped down when Kirby touched Hope's hand. Maybe he could use this time to his advantage. "I thought I could walk you back to the chapel car."

She frowned and shook her head. "I couldn't possibly leave Luke. I'm sure that cut on his forehead should be seen by the doctor. It may require stitches. You go on back to work. I know you have a great deal that requires your attention." She slid across the seat, stepped down, and quickly rounded the truck.

He didn't move. Every muscle in his body turned taut. He angled the mirror attached to the dashboard and watched Hope and Nellie position themselves on either side of Luke once he had wriggled from the back of the truck. Blue edged between Nellie and Luke and whined at his master.

Luke patted the dog's head. "I'm okay, Blue."

Hope reached for the handkerchief she'd placed on his forehead and lifted a corner. "You should let the doctor see if this needs stitches." When Luke hesitated, she grasped his arm. "I insist."

Nellie pointed toward the path. "I'm gonna go back up the hill and let Ma know what happened while you go see the doc." She snapped her fingers. "Come on, Blue. You can't be in the doc's office."

When Blue refused to leave, Luke said, "Go on, Blue. Go home with Nellie." The hound whined and nudged Luke's leg before he trotted off toward Nellie. "Don't get Ma all riled up. Be sure you tell her I'm fine. I don't want her comin' down the hill to check on me."

Kirby remained in the truck as the twosome walked toward the doctor's office, then shifted the truck into gear and hit the gas pedal. He roared past them, leaving a cloud of dust and flying gravel in his wake.

.... ❧ ....

Hope turned sideways to avoid the dust and gravel. "I don't know what's gotten into Kirby. That was downright rude. He had to know we'd be covered in dust." She swiped her hand down the front of her dress.

"I'm guessin' the green-eyed monster has got ahold of him. He was mad as a hornet when I kissed you." He grinned. "And you looked mighty surprised, too. I know it wasn't proper, but I needed to keep you from saying anything about the smell in the back of the truck."

She cocked her head and smiled. "So you really didn't want to steal a kiss. You just kissed me so I'd be quiet. Is that right?"

"Well, I sure enjoyed the kiss, but I wouldn't have done it in front of Kirby except that I was afraid you'd give it away."

"Give what away?"

"The smell. I'm sure he's haulin' moonshine in the truck. When we wrecked, I think some of the bottles either broke or leaked. I know the smell of shine and that's what I smelled in the back of that truck."

Hope gasped. "You really think Kirby would sell moonshine?"

"Sure do. I don't know who's makin' it for him, but I think he must have that truck all rigged up special to hide the shine. Worst of it is that he's puttin' you and Nellie in a lot of danger having you two in the truck with him while he's makin' those deliveries."

Hope shook her head. "But we only go to the churches and schoolhouses, while Kirby goes and delivers supplies to . . ." As her eyes widened, Luke nodded. "So you think when he drops us off at the church, he goes to deliver moonshine? He's not going to help the needy?"

Luke hiked one shoulder. "He might be stopping at a few houses and leaving some fabric or a sack of coffee, but his reason for leaving you and Nellie is so he can go to the speakeasies hidden out in the woods and deliver shine."

"I'm not saying you're wrong, but why would he take such a chance? He could have most any opportunity he wants. His father must know every influential person in several states."

"I'm not one to give you an answer to that. Maybe he likes the excitement of doing something illegal, or maybe he's tryin' to get his pappy's attention. I don't claim to understand the likes of Kirby Finch, but I'm thinkin' he's playing with fire. If he's cuttin' in on the moonshine business of some of the men who live in these parts, he's gonna find himself in deep trouble—and it won't be just with the law."

Every word Luke spoke made sense, yet Hope didn't want to believe Kirby would be so scheming and reckless. Her thoughts spun as she considered the many trips they'd made and the possibility they could have been stopped by revenuers or moonshiners.

She gasped. "I just realized that if the revenuers had stopped Kirby and discovered the moonshine, Nellie and I could have been arrested." She clapped a hand to her mouth and shook her head.

"Don't faint on me or the doc will need to take care of both of us." Luke opened the door to the doctor's office and followed her inside. "Besides, there's no need to worry. You won't be going with him again. As soon as we're through here, we'll go and talk to your father and seek his advice. Agreed?"

"Agreed," she said.

The cut had required only a brief doctor visit and a couple of stitches. When they left Dr. Burch's office, the two of them made their way to the railroad station and then crossed the stretch of grass and thicket to the spur where the chapel car was situated.

Her father's eyes widened when they entered the chapel car. "Luke! What happened?" Before either of them could answer, he pulled out a chair for Luke. "Sit down. Was there trouble on the road? Not revenuers, I hope."

"No, no revenuers or moonshiners. Kirby took a turn too fast and we had a small accident, but I'm fine." He glanced at Hope. "Thankfully, nobody else was injured."

Her father turned and looked her up and down. "You sure you're not hurt?"

"I'm fine. Luke needed a few stitches in his forehead, but the doctor said he'd be all right and even promised there wouldn't be a scar to spoil Luke's good looks."

Her father chuckled. "Well, I'm certainly glad to hear that. I wouldn't want your handsome appearance ruined, Luke." He inhaled a deep breath. "So, tell me what happened."

When Luke completed the tale, he leaned back in his chair. "There's no doubt he's haulin' moonshine and selling to the speakeasies."

"You're probably right, but the authorities would need more proof than a sniff test." Her father's brows knit together and he leaned forward to rest his elbows on the table. "You think Kirby would know how to make shine, or do you think he's selling for someone else?"

Luke pondered the question for a minute. "I don't think he'd know how to set up a still and make shine, but I don't think anyone in these parts would trust someone like Kirby to haul and sell their shine. I don't judge him to be the kind of fella who'd want to take orders from anyone else—especially one of us hill folk. Maybe he got friendly with someone, who showed him how to set up a still." He shook his head. "I'm just not sure 'bout none of it except that he had shine in that truck today."

Her father nodded. "Then we need to get some evidence and put a stop to whatever he's doing before Kirby or someone else gets seriously hurt."

Luke swallowed hard. "Or killed."

.............⧆.............

Kirby drove the truck to the rear of the boardinghouse, parked, and then walked back to the mine. He couldn't risk having Daniels or Farragut decide to drive the truck. They might smell the moonshine and search the vehicle. Though they'd been surprised to see him, neither man questioned his early return.

Instead, Mr. Daniels asked his usual question. "Any word from your father? We keep hoping he'll pay us a visit."

That was Daniels's cloaked remark that really meant he wanted to visit personally with Kirby's father. Although Daniels had been the manager for many years, he'd never made decisions without the owner's approval. With Kirby's arrival, Daniels seemed at a loss. There was no doubt he wanted to contact Kirby's father, yet Kirby had given both of the men explicit orders they were not to call on his father. And since Kirby was Daniels's acting superior, he hadn't written the Pittsburgh office. Still, he never failed to let Kirby know he had misgivings.

"My father has every confidence that, with you and Mr. Farragut, everything is being well managed here at the mine. He's not planning any travel in the near future." Kirby offered a half smile. "Rest assured, I've told him that you have matters in hand. I've kept him advised that you're doing a fine job managing the men and he need not worry about a strike or unionization."

"W-what? I never said we didn't need to worry about a walk-out or unions. We've always had those concerns, and they've only increased since the cave-in." He stared at Kirby, his expression one of confusion. "You know that. Why would you give your father a false report?"

"Rumors of a walkout aren't any greater now than they've been for the past several years, so there's no need to worry my father." Kirby touched his fingertips to his chest. "My father's heart condition. The doctors say too much anxiety isn't good for him."

Mr. Daniels's eyes widened. "Your father has problems with his heart? I didn't know." He glanced at Mr. Farragut, who merely shrugged and shook his head.

"My father is a private man when it comes to his health. I'm sure you understand that he wouldn't want such information bandied about. The truth is, he'd be quite angry if he knew I'd told the two of you, but I know I can trust you both to keep a confidence."

Mr. Daniels stepped closer. "You can rely on us. And you're absolutely right. We shouldn't bother your father with our concerns here at the mine."

Kirby strode off with a wave and a smile of satisfaction. Those two old men were so easy to manipulate, it eliminated some of the fun. Even if someone held fire to their feet, they'd never mention his father's supposed heart condition. While he himself had never possessed that level of loyalty, Kirby appreciated it in others. It made life so much easier for him.

The remainder of the day passed with greater tedium than

usual. Though he didn't like to admit it, Kirby was still worried about the moonshine in the company truck. If there were leaking bottles and someone happened to pass nearby, they'd surely investigate. Yet it was the safest place he could park the truck. If he'd returned it to the usual spot near the office, his chances of being discovered were far greater. Besides, he'd never even seen anyone behind the boardinghouse.

When the final bell rang and Mr. Daniels and Mr. Farragut departed for the day, Kirby released a sigh and headed for the door. He locked the office, then walked back to the boardinghouse. He hurried to the rear of the building and, after looking around, stooped to look beneath the bed of the vehicle and whispered an expletive. The ground was wet.

While driving the truck back to the mine, Kirby silently reproached himself for his careless driving earlier in the day. He'd let anger get the best of him, but Luke should have known better than to try to tell him what to do. And now Luke had probably made him lose a customer. The owner of the speakeasy near Hopkins Fork was still without shine and might decide to do business with someone else unless he could make a delivery before morning. Even more worrisome was the nagging possibility that Luke had smelled the odor of moonshine. No telling what Luke might do if he thought Kirby was selling shine. Then again, maybe the two lovebirds had been too busy kissing to notice. Even so, he'd need to be extra careful.

Kirby parked the truck and trudged through the thicket leading away from the company office. As he neared the still, he spotted movement in the brush. He quieted his breathing and stopped behind a pine tree. "Psst. Jimmy Ray! Is that you?" His voice was no more than a whisper.

"Yep, it's me." The boy waved his hat in the air. "What you doin' out here? Wasn't expectin' ya till later."

Kirby crossed the short distance between them. "We got a few problems. Come down to the truck with me."

While they were walking, Kirby recounted the day's events. "We need to see how many bottles are broken and then see if you have enough to replace them. We can make a run over to Hopkins Fork as soon as we refill the crates."

Jimmy Ray began sniffing like a hound dog hunting a rabbit when they neared the truck. "Sure 'nuf. Ain't no denyin' that's shine we're smellin'. Better get to it." He leaned down, unhinged and removed the cover of the hidden compartment, then leaned back. "Um-hum." He shook his head. "Must be quite a few broken. You musta really hit that tree with a thud. I got lots of straw around them bottles."

Kirby ignored the remark and loosened the lids as Jimmy Ray removed each crate. Thanks to the young fellow's packing method, none of the jars was completely shattered. Six needed to be replaced. They'd cracked around the lids, and some of the liquor had seeped out. Kirby sat back on his heels and surveyed the bottles and crates.

This was all Luke's fault. If he hadn't been trying to give orders, Kirby would never have wrecked the truck. There had to be a way to get Luke out of his life once and for all.

CHAPTER

23

Early the next morning, his shotgun resting on his shoulder, Luke cut through the grassy thicket on his way to the chapel car. Today, Luke and the preacher would set out in search of Kirby's still. Both men were certain it must be hidden deep in the woods. Luke surmised Kirby would have located the still on company property so there'd be less chance of anyone nosing around. Luke wasn't scheduled to work at the mine today, but Kirby should be there. He usually drove the women to Fern Hollow on Thursdays, which would give Luke and the preacher several days to search before Kirby made another run. At least that was their hope.

Before he had an opportunity to knock, Hope opened the door into the living quarters of the chapel car and greeted him with a bright smile. She stepped to the side and gestured for him to come in. "You're nice and early. Coffee?"

He removed his cap as he entered. "Already had my breakfast and two cups of coffee. That's my limit." He nodded to the preacher. "Mornin', Preacher. You all set?"

Hope's father pushed to his feet. "Believe I am." He turned

to face his daughter. "You remember what I told you, Hope. You stay away from Kirby until we get things sorted out. I don't want to think he'd do anyone harm, but sometimes folks react just like animals. Get 'em trapped and they come out fighting."

Hope picked up a dish towel and began drying the breakfast dishes. "There's no reason to worry. I don't see Kirby during the day unless we're going on one of our trips out of town. You two are the ones who need to be careful. You may find some unexpected moonshiners out there while you're looking for Kirby."

"More apt to get ourselves shot by revenuers than moonshiners. I don't think the moonshiners are brave enough to set up in the woods behind the mine. Most of 'em have their stills in the woods on the hill. The Finches own all the land 'round here, but the men living on the hill consider the woods up there to be theirs." Luke shrugged his shoulders. "Not sure why, but it's always been thataway."

Her father grabbed his hat and followed Luke to the door. "Remember what I told you—keep your distance from Kirby."

She stepped onto the platform. "I'll do that. And you two remember to keep a good lookout. I don't want anything to happen to either one of you."

Luke waved his hat overhead as they walked off, then glanced toward the preacher. "One good thing, we got us a fine day to go out in the woods." He tipped his head back and inhaled a deep breath. "You can smell the air changing. Fall will be here afore we know it."

Reverend Irvine followed Luke's lead and took several sniffs. "Believe you're right. Seems like a big part of summer slipped right on by while I was recuperating. Nothing like living in the mountains during the fall season."

"That's true enough. It's downright pretty in the winter when

266

the snow's falling too, but the blowing wind and cold means keepin' fires burnin' day and night. That sure can take away from the pleasure." He grinned. "'Course when I was a young'un, I couldn't wait for the snow to fall. Me and the other boys would slide down the hillside on big ol' pieces of cardboard we'd get from the general store." He stared into the distance. "That seems like a lifetime ago, but not a whole lot has changed since then—leastwise not in these parts."

The two men continued talking until they'd drawn near the road leading to the mine when Luke motioned to turn in the opposite direction.

The preacher glanced toward the mine, then back at Luke. "Did they move the mine? Last I knew, it was that way." He pointed to the gravel road.

Luke chuckled. "It hasn't been moved, but we don't want to be seen heading out to the woods. We're gonna end up in the woods behind the mine, but we'll be getting there a different way. Although it'll take us a little longer, it's safer this way."

The preacher nodded and said, "I'll follow your lead. You're the one who knows what's best out in these woods."

Luke moved slowly through the thick underbrush and noted no signs of disturbance. He looked over his shoulder. "Hard to be quiet with all this overgrowth. It's clear no one has cut through here. Even so, try to be as quiet as possible. I doubt we'll come across the path being used by Kirby out this way, but you can't never be sure."

"I'm doing my best." The preacher kept his voice low.

It was clear the preacher hadn't grown up hunting in the woods. If there was a dry branch, it was tromped down by his heavy boot. The resulting cracks of wood caused Luke to flinch, but he said no more. The preacher was doing his best. They'd gone deep into the woods, then circled around. Now they cut back toward an area Luke thought might be a good space to hide a still.

He turned around and waited until the preacher drew near. He pointed toward the spot. "I'm going to go down there and have a look around. Why don't you stay here and keep a lookout? Watch from over there." He nodded toward the left. "The mine is down that direction, and I'm guessing Kirby would come that way. I don't expect him this time of day, though you can't be sure. I won't be able to see him coming when I'm down there."

The preacher narrowed his eyes. "You want me to holler if he comes? How can I warn you without . . . ?"

Luke tapped the gun resting on his shoulder. "Turn in the other direction and shoot. Whoever's out there will shout to get your attention. You holler back and apologize. Tell 'em you're hunting squirrel and didn't expect to see anyone this far out. That'll give me time to get out of there and hightail it back to town. Then you do the same as soon as you're able."

The preacher appeared a little worried, but Luke didn't stick around long enough for the older man to object. Being careful not to slip, he descended the sloping hillock and surveyed the surrounding area. He studied a pile of branches that appeared somewhat out of place, then turned his attention to examining the damp ground. There were footprints throughout the space, one set larger than the other. The larger set appeared to have been created by thick-soled work boots, while the other set looked as if it had been made by shoes rather than boots.

Luke walked over to the mound of branches and carefully pulled aside several limbs. He sighed. This looked like quite an operation. An area had been molded into the hillside, and once the branches were placed over the opening, the still was protected from sight on all sides. The interior was larger than Luke had anticipated and not only housed a large still, but it provided storage for stacks of crates, jars, and heaps of corn. He shook his head. He doubted any of the locals would have established anything this large—or permanent. Fearing revenuers who stalked the woods, most of the local moonshiners moved their stills frequently and carried their supplies with them each time they made their shine.

From the looks of this place, Luke surmised shine was being made most every day. Considering the supplies and location, he was sure Kirby owned the still, but who was making the shine? Most likely, Kirby didn't possess the knowledge or have the time to come out in the woods every day and make shine.

Luke dragged the branches back across the opening, then took one final look. He hoped his presence would go undetected. For now, he needed to get out of here. Whoever was working for Kirby could show up any minute.

.... ❦ ....

Once she'd finished drying the dishes, Hope stepped from the living quarters into the sanctuary portion of the chapel car where she could sort through teaching materials. She raised a few of the windows to allow for fresh air to blow through. Then, using the pews to hold the papers, she divided the materials according to the children's different age groups. With both Nellie and Luke helping her when they visited the small communities, it had become much easier for her to divide the materials into separate boxes for the visits they would make in the coming week. Of course, she couldn't be certain there would be any more visits, not if Luke's suspicions proved true. And even if Luke was wrong, unless Kirby could get over the anger he'd exhibited upon their recent return from Denton, she doubted he'd be willing to provide their transportation any longer or that she and Nellie should accompany him.

Although he'd been angry when they parted, she had thought he might come to the late service. In truth, she'd fully expected him to appear. She'd even been a bit disappointed when he didn't. Not because she wanted to see him, but because she wanted an apology for his behavior when he'd driven off yesterday. And perhaps she wanted to believe he wasn't who he now appeared to be.

She picked up one of the papers and moved it to another pew as a knock sounded at the door of their living quarters. "Just a moment." She pushed a wayward curl behind her ear and hurried to the door. "Kirby! What are you doing here at this time of day? Is something wrong?" She peered around his shoulder in the direction of the mine.

"No. Not unless something happened in the last half hour." He moved a step closer, and she backed away, permitting him just enough space to pass by. Before she could object, he was inside the living quarters. He nodded to the stove. "Coffee?"

"I'm afraid not," she said.

He glanced toward the other end of the car, then sat down. "Your father in there going over his sermon for tonight?"

"No." She hoped he wouldn't ask her to elaborate. "He's gone for a while, so you really need to leave. It isn't proper for us to be alone together."

A slow smile spread across his face. "Where is he?"

"He went squirrel hunting with Luke, but they should be back any time now." The first part of what she'd told him was the truth; she prayed the second part would be true, as well. "If you want to talk to him, you should wait outside, or I can ask him to pay you a visit at your office when he returns." She remained standing near the door, but he didn't get up.

"I hope you aren't angry with me about my reckless driving yesterday. I know I was going too fast when I made that turn. I think the fender can be repaired so my father will never know it happened." He leaned back and met her gaze. "What did Luke say about the wreck?"

She frowned. "He had to have a couple of stitches to close up that cut, and I'm sure he's thankful he jumped out of the truck before it hit the tree. Otherwise he might be dead."

Kirby chuckled. "I think you're exaggerating just a little. The accident wasn't serious enough to kill anyone. Besides, I recall that Luke was feeling good enough to kiss you when you started talking to him."

Kirby's tone made her squirm. She peered out the window, but there was still no sign of her father. "I want you to leave, Kirby. My father wouldn't approve of your being here."

He stood and drew closer. His eyes dropped from her face down the length of her figure. "And what about you? Do you approve enough to let *me* kiss you?"

"No, I do not." The hair at the nape of her neck prickled. She needed to get him out of these tight quarters. She took another step toward the door, but he blocked the path. If she couldn't get him to leave, maybe she could escape through the sanctuary.

He offered an apologetic smile. "I'm sorry, that wasn't appropriate, but you can't fault me for trying. I promise it won't happen again. In truth, I'd already guessed that Luke stole that kiss. I knew a proper young lady such as yourself would never do anything to compromise your self-respect or that of your father." He leaned against the metal doorjamb, his stance now relaxed. His eyes shone with intensity, however. "What was it you were saying to Luke when he forced himself on you? I thought I heard you say something about an odor. Am I right?"

His sudden change of attitude and abrupt question jarred her. "W-what?"

"I heard you say something about an odor, and Luke mumbled

a reply before he kissed you. But I didn't hear what either of you said." He straightened and looked her in the eyes.

Her stomach churned. She couldn't tell him what they'd discussed, but he wasn't going to leave without a response. "You're right. I did say that I thought there was a strange odor and I wasn't able to distinguish it. I think Luke said it was likely some sort of fluid leaking from the truck. I'm not sure because I was so surprised by his unexpected behavior."

Kirby's gaze didn't waver. He seemed to be deciding whether she'd told him the truth. "So what kind of fluid did he think it was? He must have mentioned it after you went to the doctor's office with him."

His tenacity was beginning to frighten her. Did he suspect they knew the truth or was he seeking an assertion that proved he had nothing to fear? If she was going to get him to leave, she needed to reassure him.

She prayed her response would have the desired effect. "I've told you what little there is to relate about our conversation. I'm confused as to why you're so concerned about that silly conversation about an odd smell in the truck rather than Luke's injuries from the accident. I have to say I'm disappointed you haven't shown more compassion. I think your concerns are misplaced. You seem to care more about your truck than Luke's welfare."

"Luke's welfare? You've already told me the doctor stopped his bleeding with a couple stitches and that he's out hunting. I don't think his condition requires any further inquiry."

"Truly? Then why does my mention of an odor in your truck require so many questions?" She'd decided to try a new tactic and put Kirby on the defensive. Maybe that would force him out the door.

Instead of heading off, he dropped to a chair and folded his arms across his chest. "Oh, I don't know. Once I found out you were alone, I thought it would be a good time for us to visit. As I've said before, we never get much time alone." He pointed to the opposite chair. "Sit down and let's talk some more. I promise I won't ask any more questions about the accident. Truth is, I've been thinking about going back to Pittsburgh for a visit, and I thought you might like to join me on the train. You could come along and meet some of my family and visit a few of your old friends. I was going to ask your father if he'd approve. That's the real reason I came to see him this morning."

Hope's mouth dropped open and she stared at him. There must be something wrong with him. Maybe he'd hit his head in the accident and didn't realize he'd injured himself. His behavior was making no sense, and now she worried he might actually hurt her if he didn't like her response.

She sent up a silent prayer asking God to deliver her. Her father had warned that a man who felt trapped could come out fighting. If this was Kirby's way of fighting, not only was it underhanded, it was terrifying.

.... ❧ ....

Luke followed behind the preacher as they picked their way back to the road. They'd made the trek in silence, and Luke had been careful to cover their tracks during the descent.

When they were out of the woods, Luke detailed the operation. "Sure is a lot bigger than what I expected to find. If it's Kirby that's running it—and I'm sure it is since we smelled the moonshine in his truck—then he's bound to be putting some of the other bootleggers out of business. It's not gonna take long before they figure out what he's doin', and he's gonna find himself in more trouble than he knows how to handle."

The preacher pushed his hat back on his head. "But you still don't think it's Kirby who's making the moonshine?"

Luke shook his head. "Naw. There are two stills in there, and they both look to be like the others I've seen in these parts. He wouldn't know how to make a still, and there's nobody gonna teach him. Leastwise I don't think so. And like I said, he doesn't have time to sit on the mountain making shine."

"So how do we find out who's helping him?"

"I'm not sure about that just yet." Luke shifted his shotgun to his other shoulder. "I could plant myself up there and keep a lookout. Could be a might dangerous, but the only other way I know to find out for sure is if Kirby tells us. I don't 'spect he's gonna do that, but you never know. If he thinks it will keep him out of trouble, he'd likely turn on his own kin."

"That's a harsh judgment, Luke, but you may be right. Let's head on back. We can tell Hope what we found, and you can pick up the notes I made for you on tonight's sermon." He smiled. "You did a fine job. As usual, I didn't have many comments."

Luke hadn't received help with his sermons while the preacher was recovering from his illness, and folks thought he'd done well filling in for the preacher. But Luke wanted to prepare himself to be more than a substitute. He'd prayed long and hard about the future and believed that one day he would lead a church of his own. When that happened, he wanted to know he'd done everything he could to be prepared. They'd agreed that Luke would continue to preach at one of the meetings each day, yet Luke insisted the preacher examine his sermons. Even though Hope's father thought the review unnecessary, he'd agreed.

One of the miners was hunched on the boardwalk outside the general store. His face was covered by his hands, and his miner's hat was lying on the ground in front of him. The preacher glanced at Luke. "Let me go and talk to him. You go on over to the chapel car. I'll be along in a few minutes."

Luke didn't argue. There was little doubt the miner had problems that needed both prayer and advice. Luke knew the preacher would provide both, along with a strong dose of comfort.

Taking long strides, he walked to the depot, then crossed the tracks toward the spur. Several windows of the chapel car were open, and the sun glistened on the shiny brass rail that surrounded the rear platform. Eager to tell Hope what they'd discovered, he loped across the grassy thicket, but then stopped short when he neared the window of the living quarters.

Luke's heart started pounding. He sprinted toward the chapel car, straining for a better view. He clenched his jaw.

Kirby was alone with Hope.

CHAPTER

24

L uke charged toward the platform, his feet hammering the ground and his racing heartbeat pounding in his ears. He was reaching for the platform railing when a flicker of light on the tracks captured his attention. He released his hold and rushed toward it.

A lit fuse shot sparks into the air as it sizzled toward three bundled sticks of dynamite. Without thinking, Luke lunged toward the dynamite, grasped it in his hand, and hurled it into a gully behind the rail spur. Before he could hit the ground and cover his head, a thunderous explosion rocked the area. Windows in the chapel car shattered, rocks and gravel flew in all directions, branches broke loose from nearby trees, and the tangy-sweet odor of dynamite hung in the air.

Luke lifted his head from the rail spur and shook off the fog that had invaded his mind. Hope! He struggled to his feet, gained his footing, and rushed toward the railcar. "Hope! Hope! Are you okay?" He gasped for air. "Answer me!"

"Luke!" She appeared on the platform, her features twisted

in fear. Her auburn curls flew in countless directions, and a sleeve of her dress revealed a jagged rip.

He ran to the platform and extended his arms. Gently he lifted her down and held her close. He longed to erase the horror she'd experienced. "Are you hurt? Do you need the doctor?"

"No. What about you?" She brushed the dirt from his cheek. "I was so frightened, and then I realized you were out there on the tracks. I tried to get to you . . ." She coughed. "Kirby caught me when the explosion happened, but I fought myself free of him. I had to know you weren't injured."

"You don't have to say a word, Hope, but if I don't declare my love to you, I'll regret it forever. In those few seconds before that dynamite exploded, I regretted I'd never said those words to you. I know I'm not worthy of your love. You deserve a man who can give you a fine home in a big city, not a poor miner like me."

She touched her fingers to his lips. "Please don't ruin this moment by saying I deserve a man who is better than you, Luke. I could never find a better match. You're honest, kind, trust-worthy, and you love the Lord. How could I ask for anything more?" She leaned back and looked up at him. "I love you, Luke. I don't need a fancy house in a big city to make me happy. I need only you."

He leaned down, brushed a curl from her temple, and gently kissed her on the mouth. "I could hold you like this forever, but I s'pose we should check on Kirby and see if he's hurt. What was he doing inside with you, anyway?"

As he and Hope returned to the chapel car, she recounted Kirby's unexpected appearance and how strange he'd been act-ing. Before he could press for more details, Luke pushed open the chapel car's door and led the way inside the living quarters.

She stood in the doorway and glanced over her shoulder at Luke. "Kirby's not here."

Luke followed her into the living quarters. Using his boot, he pushed aside shards of glass scattered across the floor. His gaze settled on the books and papers that had been tossed from shelves and tables and now lay strewn on the floor. He shook his head. "It's a wonder you weren't hit on the head by falling books or cut by flying glass."

Hope gave him a weak smile. "I don't know why, but now that I'm back inside and see all this, I can't seem to stop shaking." Luke pulled her into his arms, and she leaned heavily against him. "I have no idea what happened to Kirby. I'm amazed he's gone." She looked up at Luke. "Did you see any sign of him before you came to the railcar?"

Luke smoothed her hair. "No. He must have gone out the door at the other end of the car. There's no way I would have seen him. I'm guessin' he's not hurt since he took off in such an all-fired hurry."

"I suppose, but I can barely hold my thoughts together. I don't know how he could jump up and run off like that. I feel like I'll never stop shaking."

"I understand. It's like hoping you'll wake from a nightmare, but having to accept what happened is real." Luke held her close. "I'll be more than happy to have you in my arms until you stop trembling." He smiled down at her, hoping his words would ease her fears.

She nodded. "Thank you, but I don't think it would be proper for you to embrace me quite that long."

He chuckled, pleased she'd been able to tease him. "I'd sure like to know who put that dynamite out there—and why. Nobody's got a bone to pick with you or your pa, so I'm thinkin' this has something to do with Kirby."

Before they had a chance to talk any further, the shouts of men and the sound of pounding feet could be heard through the open windows.

Luke released her and peered outside. "Looks like the off-duty railroaders are comin' to find out what's going on." The group of men ran toward the spur, some bearing weapons, others carrying picks and shovels. "From the looks of what they're bringing with them, I'm not sure if they're planning to shoot someone, plant a garden, or dig for coal."

Hope stepped forward to look for herself. "I'd say they grabbed whatever was close by that might be used as a weapon." She shivered. "I wouldn't want someone coming at me with one of those picks."

Luke smiled. "I don't think you need to worry about that."

One of the approaching men shouted at the railcar, "Anybody inside? Anyone need help?"

Luke stepped out onto the platform. Hope followed him outside, her hair blowing in a breeze that remained scented by the odor of dynamite. She waved to the men. "The railcar's a mess, but we're okay."

The two of them stepped down as the railroaders gathered around. One of the men leaned on the handle of his shovel. "What in the world happened out here? We heard a blast when we were in the roundhouse, but couldn't figure out what was going on."

Luke shrugged. "I can't tell you much." He quickly related what he'd seen and how he grabbed the dynamite and tossed it in the gully.

"Why in tarnation would anyone wanna dynamite the chapel car? Ain't nobody got hard feelings toward the preacher." He nodded toward Hope. "Or Miss Hope. Don't make no sense." He scratched his head. "I guess we ain't the ones needin' to figure it out." He gestured to the men. "C'mon. Let's see what we can do to help Miss Hope get things cleared up inside." He turned back to Luke and pointed to a large tree not far away. "You two had enough excitement for one day. Sit down over there by that tree and try to steady yourselves a bit." The railroader nodded toward the station. "Looks like your pa got wind of things."

Hope saw her father hurrying across the area. She waved her handkerchief, calling to him, "I'm fine, Papa! Don't run." She looked at Luke. "We're both fine."

Her father didn't heed her words. Instead, he picked up his pace until he'd reached her. "Someone in town said they heard there was an accident over here. I went up on the hill with a miner and didn't know until I got back to town." His eyes shone with panic as he looked her up and down. "You sure you're not hurt?" His gaze drifted to the railcar. "What happened?"

She grasped his arm. "I'm fine. Just a tear in my dress that can be easily mended. Come sit down. Luke and I will explain what we can."

The three of them settled beneath the tree while they told her father what had happened. Afterward he raked his fingers through his hair and said, "I have to think that someone was attempting to either scare or hurt Kirby. Whoever it was must have followed him. Makes me wonder if they would have set off dynamite near the boardinghouse if he'd gone in there." He shook his head. "I'm thankful you were able to pitch that dynamite away from the railcar before it went off, Luke. I don't know how I can ever thank you for saving Hope's life."

Luke grinned. "I might be able to come up with an idea in the future."

Hope squeezed his hand.

Her father sighed. "Who would do something like this?"

"I've been thinking about that," Luke said, turning serious

again. "It has to be someone riled up enough to want to make a point."

The preacher arched his brows. "Any ideas?"

Before Luke could answer, the railroaders who'd been working inside the railcar appeared, with Jed King taking the lead. "I think we done about all we can. You'll need to get things organized a might better, Miss Hope." He shifted around toward her father. "I'll send some wood over so you can board up the broken windows, Preacher."

"Thanks for your help, fellows. I trust you'll all be back for the preaching tonight?"

"We'll be here," several of them called as they headed back toward the roundhouse.

Luke hunched forward. "I do have an idea about who might have been angry enough to do this."

The preacher nodded. "Who's that, Luke?"

"Jasper Rollins and Mort Smalley have been pushing hard for a strike ever since the cave-in. I know it couldn't have been Mort 'cause he's still having trouble with his arm, but Jasper's rough as a corncob so I wouldn't put it past him. He and Kirby were in a ruckus just the other day over the conditions in one of the tunnels. I think I'll go find Jasper and see where he was this afternoon."

"Sounds like a good idea," Hope's father said. "Maybe I should come with you."

Luke shook his head. "Thanks for the offer, but I think Jasper would be unwilling to talk if anyone else is along. Besides, I think Hope could use some help inside." He motioned toward the roundhouse. "Looks like Jed's got some wood he's bringing over, too. I think you'll be plenty busy right here. I'll stop back after I talk to Jasper. Maybe you'll find those notes for tonight's sermon while you're going through the papers."

The preacher chuckled. "We'll do our best."

As Luke ambled back toward town, he decided he'd stop at the mine before going up the hill. Maybe Jasper had been working all day. If so, it would rule him out as the culprit. Besides, Luke could try to find out what had happened to Kirby after the explosion. Maybe he'd hightailed it, figuring there might be another detonation. Yet he'd given no thought to Hope before he'd run off. For a man who was supposed to be capable of running a mining company, Kirby sure acted more like a coward than a leader.

Luke strode toward several young men who were picking coal near the mine entrance. "Hey, fellas. I'm lookin' for Jasper. He in one of the tunnels or is he off today?"

Two large white eyes peered at him from a face layered in coal dust. "Ain't seen nothin' of Jasper today." The boy's flesh-colored lips and pink tongue appeared strangely out of place as he spoke.

"You sure?" Luke said.

Another young man looked up and bobbed his head. "We always know when Jasper's around. If he's at work, he's tryin' to get everyone riled up. Been pretty quiet today, so you kin be sure he ain't here."

Luke turned to leave and then stopped. "You seen anything of Mr. Finch today?"

"Ain't seen nothing of him neither, but he could be in the office. Don't never see him down here lessin' there's a problem."

"Thanks." Luke headed toward the office. He'd at least ask about Kirby before he went up the hill to locate Jasper. He pulled open the door, stepped into the hallway, and stopped outside Mr. Farragut's door.

The older man looked up from his ledgers. "Luke? Something I can do for you?"

283

Luke glanced toward the office down the hallway. "I was wondering if Mr. Finch was in today. I wanted to speak to him about something."

Mr. Farragut shook his head. "I can't tell you where he is. If it's important, you could stop by the boardinghouse. I wouldn't think he's there, but I can't say for certain." His brow creased. "Is the truck out there? He might be on one of those trips he makes with the preacher's daughter."

"I'm not sure about the truck, but he's not with the preacher's daughter. Thanks, Mr. Farragut." Luke tipped his hat. "If he returns . . ."

"I'll tell him you were looking for him." Mr. Farragut smiled and picked up his pen again.

Luke spotted the company truck parked in its usual place when he exited the office. No telling where Kirby might be. And he wasn't going to stop at the boardinghouse—speaking to Jasper was more important.

He climbed the hill quickly and went directly to the Rollins house. After he'd rapped several times on the rickety door, Jasper's young wife appeared. She pushed the hair off her forehead, then swiped her hands down the front of a smudged apron. She squinted against the afternoon sun as she pushed open the screen door. "What kin I do fer ya, Luke?"

"I'm looking for Jasper." Luke nodded toward the interior of the house. "He in there?"

"No. He should be out in the garden. If not, he's in the woods somewhere. I ain't too sure. You kin go back there and see fer yerself, if ya want."

"Thanks, I'll do that." He rounded the house and walked the short distance to Jasper's garden plot. He was about to leave when he caught sight of Jasper in a distant cornfield. He yanked off his hat and waved it overhead. "Jasper!"

Jasper turned, shaded his eyes with his hand, and waved in return. As Luke approached, Jasper stepped to the edge of the field. "What you needin', Luke?"

"Guess you know about the dynamite explosion over at the railroad spur earlier today." Luke waited, hoping Jasper's response would give some hint that he'd been involved.

Jasper shook his head. "Naw, ain't heard nothin'. Too bad it weren't Kirby's truck—with Kirby in it." He guffawed and spit tobacco juice.

The fact that he'd mentioned Kirby set off a silent alarm. "You sure you weren't down near the rail spur earlier today?"

"I said I weren't. I ain't got no cause to be at the railroad spur. It's you that's always sniffin' around that chapel car, tryin' to have a fling with that city gal."

"And it's you that's always talking about hurting Kirby Finch. Who do you think was in that chapel car when the dynamite went off, Jasper?"

"Dunno, and don't care. But since ya asked like that, I'm guessin' Kirby was there."

Luke lurched toward him, his anger flaring. "That's right. And so was Hope. You could have killed her. If I hadn't gotten to that dynamite before it exploded, you'd have killed her right along with Kirby."

"Whoa!" Jasper placed his large hand against Luke's chest. "Hold up, Luke. I weren't never off the hill today. You can ask around. I was over at Junior Harding's all mornin', and I been out here in the garden ever since. You check around. There's plenty of folks seen me up here, and you ain't gonna find a soul that can say I was anywhere else."

Luke drew a deep breath and forced down his anger. Jasper appeared to be telling the truth. Besides, it would be easy enough to check out his story. He couldn't have made it down the hill and over to the spur without someone seeing him come through town.

Jasper wiped the perspiration from his forehead and met Luke's stare. "I understand you being all fired up about that woman being hurt, but you need to look somewhere else. There's a whole bunch of folks who'd like to see Kirby dead or gone, and most don't care which it is. That man's got a long list of enemies and a short list of friends." He gave Luke a pat on the shoulder. "You been knowin' me a long time, Luke. I ain't one to mince words or raise my fists, but I ain't no liar. I had nothin' to do with whatever happened today."

Luke considered his words before finally nodding. But if Jasper wasn't the one who set off the dynamite, then who was?

Hope gathered the stacks of papers the men had piled onto the table and sifted through them while Jed helped her father board up the broken windows. Weary from her chore, she stood and walked into the sanctuary, where the two men were still hard at work.

She pointed to the door. "I'm going outside to pick up the pieces of glass around the car. Some of the children don't wear shoes. I don't want anyone to get cut."

After retrieving an empty box, Hope stepped down from the car. Pieces of glass sparkled in the bright afternoon sun. One by one, she gathered them into the cardboard box and continued to move along the spur. She'd gone only a short distance when she noticed a piece of dark blue printed fabric clinging to a bush not far from the tracks. Her brow furrowed as she drew closer. It appeared to be a man's handkerchief. She leaned down and pulled it from a thorny spike on the bush. Could this have belonged to the person who set off the dynamite? It was close to the spot where the lit fuse had been. She dropped it into the box with the shards of glass. Maybe it would prove helpful.

She'd ask Luke as soon as he returned. She turned and looked at the chapel car. Having been tattered by the explosion, it seemed to fit better in Finch now. She felt an odd kinship to the chapel car. She, too, felt battered tonight. The events of the day had not only bruised her body, but had also bruised her heart. Finch—the miners, the railroaders, the wives, the children, Nellie, and of course Luke—had become her home.

So who in her home had almost killed her?

CHAPTER

25

With Blue at his side and his shotgun over his shoulder, Luke returned to the chapel car a couple of hours later. His eyes widened and he smiled at Hope when he stepped inside. "You sure made short work of the mess that was in here. I thought it would take the rest of the day to clean up. You even got all the broken windows boarded up."

"Jed King helped Papa with that chore. I can't take all the praise for cleaning up. If the railroaders hadn't done so much work before I returned inside, I'd still be sorting through papers." She gestured to a nearby chair. "Sit down and tell me about Jasper. Is he the one who set the dynamite?"

Luke shook his head and told her what he'd discovered. "I believe Jasper's story. I stopped and asked a few folks on the hill and in town if they'd seen Jasper during the morning hours. Lots of the womenfolk said they'd seen him up on the hill, but I didn't find one soul who'd seen him in town. By the time I came back down the hill, I was sure he hadn't done it, but then I decided to go ahead and ask around in town just to be sure."

"I'm glad to know Jasper didn't do it, but . . ."

Luke nodded. "I know. It sure is a quandary. I don't know which direction to go now."

Hope pointed to the box of broken glass she'd carried inside. "I had time to go outside and gather the pieces of broken glass from around the rail spur." She bent over the box and, using her thumb and forefinger, picked up the bandanna she'd recovered and held it in front of her.

Luke's brows dipped low. "Why's that in there?"

"I found it on a bramble bush near the spur. Is it yours?"

"No, but there's quite a few men who wear those squares around their necks when they go into the mine. 'Course some use them as a handkerchief, too. Nothing unusual about it."

"Except that it was on a bush near the spur."

"Right." Luke sat down and continued to stare at the bandanna. "No doubt it belonged to whoever lit that fuse, but unless it's got some initials or a name stitched on the edge, it ain't gonna be any help to us."

A small flock of birds settled in a nearby tree, and Blue barked a loud objection. Hope leaned forward and looked out the window. "Blue!" The dog ignored her and continued to bark.

Luke chuckled. "Won't do any good to holler at him. He won't be happy till those birds are gone."

"No! I wasn't trying to quiet him." Her eyes widened. "Blue can follow a trail when you're out hunting. Could he sniff this handkerchief and maybe find the culprit who lit the dynamite?"

Luke slapped a hand to his forehead. "Why didn't I think of that? Can't say for sure if he'll be able to track the fella, but it's worth a try." He reached to take the handkerchief from her, but she pulled back her hand.

"I'm going with you."

"That's not a good idea, Hope. Let me take Blue, and you

stay here where you'll be safe. I promise to come back once I take him out huntin' for the culprit." He stood with his hand still extended toward her.

"You're not going to leave me behind, Luke. I promise to be quiet and do whatever you tell me, but I'm going along. It was me that almost got blown up in this railcar, and it's my idea to use Blue. If you refuse, I'll still follow behind, so you should go ahead and agree."

"You are one ornery, determined gal." He grinned. "Maybe that's why I love you."

She chuckled. "I hope you love more than my orneriness."

He nodded. "Yep. I said you're determined, too." He turned toward the door. "If there's no changing your mind, I guess we should get going." Luke followed her out the door, then stopped to untie Blue. "You going to give me that handkerchief so I can have Blue sniff it or are you thinking that's your job, too?" He tipped his head and smiled up at her.

"I'll let you take charge of Blue and his sniffing. I'll just follow along and do what you say."

"I'm gonna remember you said that." He held the fabric beneath Blue's nose and waited while the dog sniffed. "Go find him, Blue!" The dog's nose went to the ground, and the two of them followed as he moved to the position on the rail spur and then turned. Whenever Blue stopped, Luke would offer another smell of the bandanna, and the dog would begin once again to search out the scent.

At first, Luke thought the dog was going to the mine, but he turned and ambled into the woods instead, toward the still that Luke and the preacher had recently discovered. Luke's heart began pounding. He'd been certain that still belonged to Kirby, but Kirby had been in the railcar so he couldn't have lit the fuse to the dynamite. Who else would be brave enough to set up a still in the woods behind the mining office? Maybe Blue was following the scent. Maybe he was onto a rabbit or coon trail.

The dog continued deeper into the woods, still heading toward the location of the still. Luke stopped and turned to face Hope. "If Blue keeps going in this direction, we're going to come upon the still your pa and I discovered. That means it's dangerous for you to go any farther. Either we turn back or you stay here." When she hesitated, he frowned. "I mean it, Hope. I won't go any deeper in there unless you agree to stay right here."

She nodded. "Blue might not be able to find the scent if you have to wait until tomorrow. I'd rather go with you, but I'll do as you ask."

Luke sighed. "Thank you." He lifted the shotgun from his shoulder and extended it in her direction. "I'm leaving this with you."

"But I . . ."

"It's loaded. If you're in danger, fire the gun. Blue and I will come runnin'."

"I was going to say that I think you need to keep the gun with you. You're in more danger than me."

Luke shook his head. "I'll be just fine. Keep your eyes and ears open, and I'll get back soon as I can." Fear shone in her eyes, and Luke leaned forward and kissed her forehead. "We're both gonna be fine. I'll be back in no time. I'll whisper your name when I get close, so don't shoot me."

Hope gave a lopsided smile. "I promise."

He headed off with Blue on the scent. The dog continued to guide Luke toward the still. Worried the dog would be heard if someone was at the still, Luke commanded Blue to stay behind. Edging closer, Luke stopped when several voices drifted toward him. Careful of his step, he crept behind a stand of trees where he'd be able to hear the conversation.

He held his breath and listened. Kirby! He was positive one of the voices belonged to Kirby, but who were the other two? They both sounded familiar, yet he couldn't place either of them.

The men's voices elevated, the conversation turning angry. Kirby accused someone of being a turncoat, and then a deep voice responded, "He ain't no turncoat. He's one of us and he done the right thing. You got no business cashin' in on moonshine. Your pappy can buy and sell half the state and you come to these here hills and think you need to make money offa shine. I'm tellin' ya, that ain't gonna happen no more, Kirby. I'll see ya dead and buried first."

"You're the one who set that dynamite at the chapel car, aren't you? You thought you'd get rid of me earlier today."

"I'm the one all right, and this would have been a lot easier if you woulda jest died like I planned."

"You didn't tell me you was gonna dynamite the chapel car."

Luke frowned. This third voice wasn't as deep, more like a younger fella.

"Shut up, Jimmy Ray," the man with the deeper voice barked. "I told you I'd take care of things and that's what I'm doing."

And taking care of things apparently meant taking care of Kirby. Since the man had failed earlier, did he intend to finish the task now? Sensing Kirby's danger, Luke inched forward. Maybe he should have brought his gun along. The thought passed through his mind only seconds before his foot slipped on the damp moss.

A branch cracked.

A gunshot rang out.

..............❦..............

Hope startled at the gunfire. She held tight to the shotgun and rushed toward the sound. *Luke!* Had he been shot? More than anything, she needed to remain calm and keep her wits about her. She heard Blue yelp, followed by a man's harsh voice. The dog began to whine. Keeping low, she picked her way toward the sound. Once certain she was close enough to see, she stooped down and peeked through the thick brush. She covered her mouth to hold back a gasp.

Kirby was bound to a tree. Luke and a boy she recognized as Jimmy Ray Malloy were digging a hole while a larger man wearing a slouch hat trained a gun on Luke. Blue whined louder, and she caught sight of him tied near the still.

The large man holding the weapon turned on the dog. "Shut up, dawg, or I'll put ya outta yer misery."

The man swung around and pushed the slouch hat away from his forehead. Hope stifled a scream. *Carl Lee Williams.* Folks on the hill said Carl Lee was mean as a bear with newborn cubs. Her hands turned clammy on the stock of the shotgun. He'd threatened to shoot Blue, and she didn't doubt he'd do so. Would he do the same to Luke and Kirby? Her body trembled. Her thoughts skittered and her heart hammered in her chest. She needed to do something, but what? Maybe she should run back to town and get help. Could she possibly thwart Carl Lee by herself? She feared leaving Luke, but she also feared attempting to save him without the backing of several large men with guns. Her decision made, she slowly stood and turned in the direction of town.

"That hole's big enough for Kirby. Now dig another one, and make it big enough for yerself, Luke." Carl Lee's latest command brought Hope to a halt.

"You can't kill Luke, Carl Lee. He's one of us." Jimmy Ray's high-pitched voice trembled.

"Shut yer trap, Jimmy Ray, or I'll toss you in there with him." Carl coughed and waved the shotgun toward the hole.

Hope gulped down the lump of fear that had settled in her throat. There wasn't time to go back to town. She had to do something. And she had to do it now. Careful to avoid stepping on any fallen branches, she circled around to a spot where she might be able to descend the knoll without being seen.

Assured she could sneak down behind Carl Lee, Hope crept down the slope and situated herself out of sight near the still. Her breath caught when Blue ambled around the still and plopped down beside her. She offered a silent prayer that the dog would remain quiet, that she'd catch Carl Lee off guard, and that no one would be injured. Keeping her eyes fixed on Carl and holding the shotgun beneath one arm, she bent to the side and untied the rope that was fastened around Blue's neck.

The dog whined again. Carl spun around, and with the shotgun trained on the large man, Hope stepped from her position alongside the still and shoved the muzzle into his back. "Drop your gun, Carl Lee."

Carl glanced over his shoulder. Instead of dropping his weapon, he made a slight turn toward her and howled a boisterous laugh.

"Blue! Sic 'im!"

On Luke's command, the dog lunged at Carl's arm. He screamed in pain, and his gun fell to the ground. Luke sprang forward and scooped up the man's weapon. Blue's teeth remained implanted in Carl Lee's beefy forearm, the dog's guttural growl never ceasing.

"Call him off me!" Carl swung his fist in an attempt to wrest the dog from the painful hold. Sensing the danger, Blue jumped back. The movement yanked Carl's arm in another direction and caused him to scream again in pain.

"Leave it, Blue!" Luke shouted. Instantly the dog released Carl's arm, yet remained poised to strike if need be. Luke nodded at the still. "Hope, grab that piece of rope he used to tie Blue and bring it here."

She did as he requested and held the gun on Carl. "Put your arms behind your back, Carl."

"That dog of your'n hurt my arm real bad. I can't—"

Luke didn't wait for him to finish his excuse. He grabbed the man's arms, pulled them back, and tied his wrists together. Carl yelped when Luke checked to make sure he couldn't wiggle free of the rope. "I don't have any sympathy for you, Carl. You were planning to kill me and Kirby." He leaned around to face Carl. "Remember?"

Carl shook his head. "C'mon now, Luke. You know I woulda never shot you. I mighta gone through with shooting Kirby 'cause he sure enuf deserves it. And if you woulda jest kept your nose outta all this, things would be jest fine." He shifted his weight and tipped the upper part of his body toward town. "In fact, why don't you untie me right now and then you and your little gal can get on back to town? Fergit what you saw down here, and we'll fergit we ever saw you. Right, Jimmy Ray?"

Jimmy Ray sat hunched on a jagged boulder with his arms wrapped around his torso. "They ain't gonna let us go, Carl Lee. We done wrong, and now we gotta pay fer what we done."

Kirby cleared his throat. "I don't mean to interrupt Jimmy Ray's sad story, but could someone untie me?"

"Not just yet, Kirby. You don't deserve to be shot by Carl Lee, but before I untie you, I want to hear exactly what was going on. I can see this is a mighty fine operation." Luke swung his free arm in a wide arc. "I'm guessin' you'd be responsible for all this, Kirby, except I don't think you've got the know-how to make shine. Was it you and Carl Lee making the shine, Jimmy?"

The boy shook his head. "Naw. Jest me."

Luke turned to Kirby. "I already figured you were selling the shine outta your truck. Smelled it the day you wrecked into that tree."

Kirby appeared unshaken by Luke's remark. "You'll be hard-pressed to prove I sold it to anyone. You think the owners of those speakeasies are going to admit to buying moonshine?"

"I don't think there will be much of a problem convincing the revenuers what you were doing. Besides, I'm sure Jimmy Ray will be willin' to cooperate, won't you, Jimmy?"

Hope stepped to Jimmy's side and sat down beside him. "Your ma is going to be real disappointed in you, Jimmy. She told me you'd been bringing home a lot of money lately. She said she was worried because you were working so many long hours at the mine." She looked into his eyes. "You weren't working at the mine, were you?"

"No, ma'am. There weren't time to work at the mine and make shine, too. 'Sides, Kirby pays me lots more money to make shine than to pick coal."

Kirby strained against the ropes holding him to the tree. "Shut your mouth, Jimmy. Don't you say another word."

Luke pushed his hat back on his head. "Don't tell the boy what to do, Kirby. He's not gonna take all the blame for this." He frowned at Carl Lee. "So if you're not helping to make the shine, what's your part in all this?"

Carl Lee glowered at Luke. "Ain't you or no revenuers gonna tie me to this here still. This is all Kirby and Jimmy Ray. Let the revenuers haul 'em off and I'll git on home."

"You were threatening to kill me and Kirby a few minutes ago, Carl. I'm not about to send you home. Was Kirby holding out money on ya?"

"Naw. Worse than that. He tried to go into business with me and Alvin, but when I told him I wouldn't pay him what he wanted, he said he'd find some other way to make some extra money. Made us think he was gonna be shootin' dice or playing the horses." Carl glared at Kirby. "Instead, he set up his own still and got Jimmy Ray to make his shine. Then he went and sold his shine for cheaper. He thought we'd never figger out it was him, but we ain't as dumb as he thinks. Didn't take long afore we knowed what was goin' on. We ain't gonna let no city fella come in here and take over our business. 'Specially not one who's got a rich pappy and ain't got needs like the rest of us."

Luke strode to the tree and loosened the ropes around Kirby's body, but he didn't untie his wrists. Using the longer rope, Luke tied it around the waists of both men. He then stepped over to Jimmy Ray. "Do I need to tie you to these fellas or are you gonna come along peaceable-like, Jimmy Ray?"

The boy got to his feet. "I don't need to be tied up. I'm ready to go and take my punishment."

Luke shook his head at Carl Lee and Kirby. "That boy's more of a man than the two of you put together." He poked Carl with the end of his gun. "Now get moving."

Luke figured they made quite a sight coming over the hillside, him holding his shotgun aimed at Kirby and Carl Lee, who were tied together like a couple of wild horses, with Jimmy Ray, Hope, and Blue trailing along behind.

Little wonder they caused such a commotion when they marched through town.

CHAPTER

26

Luke stepped inside the small jail cell and leaned against the thick sandstone wall. Jimmy Ray sat huddled on the unforgiving metal cot attached to one wall of the six-by-six room. It was good the boy hadn't reached full height yet. Any taller and he would have had to sleep curled up like a dog. While Luke understood the purpose of jail was punishment, he feared this small, dank room with only a cot and a slop jar might be Jimmy Ray's ruination.

Along with Kirby and Carl Lee, Jimmy Ray had been jailed until the circuit judge came through Finch a couple of weeks ago. The revenue agents had visited the town and destroyed the still. They'd been delighted to testify that they were certain the moonshine had been sold at surrounding speakeasies. Along with testimony from the estranged wife of a speakeasy owner, there had been enough evidence to secure convictions. Neither Carl Lee nor Kirby would say where either of them had sold the shine. Carl Lee's refusal to provide any names or places didn't surprise anyone, but most of the locals, Luke included, had expected Kirby to disclose everything he knew to gain favor from the judge.

Soon after Jimmy's confinement, Hope's father had encouraged Luke to visit the boy in jail. "It's important Jimmy doesn't feel he's been forgotten. The Bible instructs us to care for those in need and those who have been imprisoned. I think you're better equipped to help the boy than I am." The affirming words had inspired Luke, and he'd visited the boy each day. He prayed he could make a difference in Jimmy's life, both while he was in jail and upon his release. "How you doing today, Jimmy?" Luke's words echoed in the musty stone cell.

The boy shrugged and peered up at him. "Not so good. This place is awful."

Luke nodded. "Sure is, but it's lots better than the place where Kirby and Carl Lee will be spending the next five years. The judge was kind to you because of your age, Jimmy. He realized a young fella like you is easy to influence." Luke squatted down in front of the boy. "I brought you a Bible and some of the papers Miss Hope uses when she teaches. You need to use this time to think about the future and decide what you want to do when you get out. The judge is giving you a chance to change things around."

"I dunno. Sittin' in this place for four months is a long time. I think I'm gonna lose my mind in here."

Luke shook his head. "Not unless you keep telling yourself that's what's going to happen." He placed his hand on Jimmy's shoulder. "Look at me, Jimmy. I care about you. I've been praying for you and so have the preacher and Miss Hope, and we're going to keep praying for you. God loves and forgives you for what you've done, and just like we want the best for you, He wants it even more. The thing is, you're the one who has to decide. Are you going to let what happened in the past control your future, or are you going to read the Good Book and make changes in your life? You can sit in here and wallow around about how hard you got it, or you can be thankful you got only four months and you've got time to pray and spend time with the Lord." Luke tapped his chest. "His Spirit's right there inside of you."

"Yeah, well that sounds mighty fine when you can walk out that door, but I'm in here by myself."

"There you go, heading back down that path of feeling sorry for yourself. I know Kirby led you astray, but you could have said no. You trying to convince me you don't know right from wrong?"

"Naw. The schoolteacher always said I was as dull as ditch-water, but my ma taught me right from wrong. I was jest tryin' to make enuf money so's my ma could get by a little better."

Luke nodded. "What you wanted was honorable, but the way you went about it was all wrong."

"I know, but how come Kirby's pa is such a bad sort and nothing happens to him?"

"Most would agree that the way Mr. Finch operates the mine and treats his workers is both dreadful and immoral, but it isn't illegal. You broke the law, and now you're paying for the choice you made." Luke sat down beside him on the narrow bunk. "Mr. Finch arrived in town yesterday. He says he's going to make some changes. We'll see what he does about the mine, but I have a feeling he's got some real regrets about sending his son down here."

Jimmy nodded. "My ma says she's got her some real regrets about not askin' me more questions 'bout the money I was bringing home. She said she shoulda knowed I wouldn't make that much money working at the mine." His lips drooped. "It was nice seeing Ma so happy when I'd hand her that money."

Luke smiled at the boy. "I know, Jimmy, but you've got to find ways to help that won't cause you to end up in here again."

"You think Mr. Daniels will give me a job back at the mine when I get outta here?"

"I can't speak for Mr. Daniels, but I'll put in a good word for you."

"Thanks, Luke. I promise I'll start doing some reading and praying on my own. Maybe you're right. The time will pass quicker if I keep myself busy and remember I'm not in here alone." He smiled. "I got Jesus right here with me."

"You certainly do, Jimmy." Luke stepped out of the cell and reached for the barred door.

"Will you come back and see me?"

"Every day." Luke stepped aside when the sheriff approached. The cell door clanged shut, and the sheriff turned the key in the lock. "And remember, you're not alone. You have your family, you have us, and you have Jesus."

.............✿.............

Luke and Nellie walked up the hill after the evening meeting, him carrying his Bible, and Nellie tucking her old umbrella beneath her arm. He gave his sister a sideways glance. "You might as well say whatever it is you've got on your mind. I can tell you've been itching to say something for the last couple of days."

Nellie paused a moment, then looked up at him and said, "Appears to me that you and Hope are moving past friendship into something more serious."

He grinned and blushed like a schoolboy caught stealing a kiss. "I'd say that's a pretty good guess. The fact is, I love her." He pulled a long breath. "And believe it or not, she loves me."

Nellie gasped. "She told you that she loves you?"

Luke chuckled. "I know it's hard to believe anyone could love your brother, but it's true."

She shook her head. "It's not hard for me to believe a girl would fall in love with you, Luke, but, well, I mean, Hope? She's used to a different kind of life than we have. It's one thing for her to come here for a time and help her pa with the music and teachin' the young'uns, but I don't know if she's the type of gal who'd find it easy living back here in the hills. And when her pa gets orders from his church to move on, what then? She couldn't stay behind. Where would she live?"

"I'd like to think she'd be living with me." Luke's smile broadened.

"W-what? You ain't jest talking about courtin' kind of love. You're talking 'bout marrying kind of love?"

"I didn't know there was a difference, Nellie. I thought when a man courted a woman and told her he loved her, it was because he planned on marrying her."

"Well, yeah, but you know, sometimes it's jest sweetheartin' and not the real kind of courting where you plan on getting hitched."

"If you're set on making a distinction, then you can be sure that this is courting. I love Hope and want to take her as my wife. My feelings for her go way beyond what you call sweet-heartin'." He frowned at his sister. "I thought you'd be happy. Way back you told me Hope was like the older sister you always wanted but didn't have. When we get married, she'll be just that, your older sister."

"I know what I told you and I do think of her like a sister, but . . ."

"But what?" He hadn't meant to shout.

Her features hardened and she stared at him like he was a dropped stitch that needed to be pulled back in place. "What about us, Luke?"

"Who is *us*? What are you talking about?"

Nellie stared at him and tapped her fingers to her chest. "*Us!* Your family! Me, ma, the other kids. Who's gonna take care of us? I can't go down in the mines, and Joey can't even work as a picker for two more years. How are we gonna get by without your pay and all the work you do in the fields? We need that food to get by, Luke."

His sister wasn't saying anything he hadn't already thought about. While he hadn't asked Hope if she'd consider living in Finch for the rest of her life, he was certain she loved him. And wouldn't she realize that they would remain here if she agreed to marry him? He'd even gone to Uncle Frank with a few of the same concerns Nellie had set forth.

"I know about my responsibility, Nellie. Truth is, all those same things worry me too, so I talked to Uncle Frank. Figured maybe he could give me a bit of advice about the future."

Nellie's eyes took on a glint of hopefulness. "What'd he say? Bet he thinks just like me."

Luke shook his head. "Not exactly. He said, 'You know I would never let your ma or the young'uns go without.'" Those words had soothed Luke. They'd been what he wanted to hear, but he doubted they'd be enough for Nellie. "He said I had those same thoughts when Pa died, but the family was still doing fine. He said he wouldn't let any of you do without." He shot her a reassuring smile. At least he hoped it would relieve some of Nellie's concerns.

"But we're not Uncle Frank's responsibility. Sure, he's family, but what if he goes off and gets married? There's always a chance some widow will snag him. Besides, you need to remember that Hope didn't grow up in these parts. I love Hope, but this ain't her true home. If her pa had to leave, I reckon she'd be aching to go, too."

He didn't want to admit it, but Nellie's words struck a chord deep within. He hadn't asked Hope if she thought she could live out her years in these hills.

Nellie placed her hand on his arm. "Any gal from up here on the hill would understand our ways and would be willing to move in with the family, if need be. We're all used to living cramped in tight quarters and feeling a gnaw in our stomachs from time to time. Hope's different. I'm not saying she wouldn't try to make do, but in the end I think you'd both be miserable. You because you couldn't give her the life she's used to, and her because she couldn't be happy with the life you could provide." She offered him a weak smile. "I don't mean to be hurtful, but truth is truth and you need to accept it."

Overhead, the skies had darkened, and a clap of thunder threatened a coming storm. They were almost home when thick gray clouds descended and a soft rain began to fall. Nellie opened her spindly black umbrella and held it toward him. Rain dripped down the side of the slick fabric and onto his shoulder.

He pushed the umbrella back toward her. "Use it to cover yourself. Otherwise we'll both get wet."

She turned to meet his gaze. "I'm sorry, Luke, but . . ."

"You don't need to say any more." He clamped his mouth shut as they stepped onto the porch.

Luke dropped into one of the damp chairs on the porch. He couldn't go inside just yet. He needed time alone to pray. He needed time to adjust his thinking. He needed God to reveal exactly what he should do.

Maybe Nellie was right.

......................✤......................

Hope trekked the distance between the railroad station and chapel car with her thoughts tossing about like leaves in a breeze.

She'd spent the afternoon on the hill, helping the children with their reading while their mothers stringed, snapped, and canned green beans. She'd been thankful to gather them under a shade tree rather than bear the heat inside one of the cabins where wood stoves burned hot and jars of green beans immersed in boiling water produced enough steam to wilt spinach.

Hope had planned to spend some time with Luke, but when she stopped by the cabin, his uncle Frank said he was working at the mine the next couple of days. She'd been careful to watch the time and had departed before the men would leave the mine. Knowing the miners would pass by the railroad station, she'd waited outside on one of the wooden benches. When she finally caught sight of Luke, she stood and waved. Her spirits plummeted when instead of coming over to talk, he merely waved and continued walking. For the life of her, she couldn't figure out what was wrong with him. If she didn't firmly believe he cared for her, she'd think he was trying to avoid her.

She trudged up the steps of the railcar and stepped inside. Her father was inside washing up and turned when she entered. He smiled and nodded toward the basin of water. "I thought I'd be finished before you returned. I'll be out of here in a minute and you can start supper." He picked up a cotton towel and dried off his face and hands before raking a comb through his hair. "We accomplished quite a bit over at the church today. If some of the men continue to help, I think we can have it completed before the weather turns cold. What a blessing that will be." When he turned to face her, his smile faded. "Why so sad? Are there problems up on the hill?"

She tucked a loose curl behind one ear. "No. The children are doing well with their reading, and their mothers, especially Mrs. Fisher, are thankful to have me helping them. Little Celia has truly blossomed and now loves to read. When school begins in a few more weeks, I think their teacher will discover the children can recollect most of what they were taught last year. At least that's been my goal." She forced a smile. "I've tried to make it fun so they don't feel like it's a classroom. I've been using lots of games to help them with their arithmetic, too. They beg to play the games. Probably because the winner gets a piece of candy."

"There's nothing better than sweets to inspire youngsters to listen and learn." Her father chuckled. "So if all is going well with the children and their mothers, what's the cause of your gloom?"

She picked at a nonexistent piece of lint on her sleeve. "Luke."

"Luke? What could that fine young fella do to cause you such misery?"

A long sigh escaped her. Given different circumstances, Hope would have chosen to discuss matters of the heart with Nellie rather than her father, but that was impossible. Over the past months, the two of them had become dear friends, but Nellie was Luke's sister. And Nellie had great difficulty keeping her lips sealed. She wasn't a girl who repeated secrets out of spite or to hurt anyone. Instead it seemed words slipped out of her mouth before she could think to stop them, especially when the secret included a family member.

Hope had become acquainted with many of the young ladies in town and considered them friends, yet she and Nellie had formed a special bond that linked them together like sisters. Hope had never shared any of her innermost thoughts with any of those other girls, nor had they with her. They would think her daft if she suddenly appeared at their doorstep and divulged her worries that Luke's attention had strayed. Besides, what if one of them secretly cared for him? Even worse, what if one of them was the reason he no longer cared for her? What if, unbeknownst to her, he'd begun courting one of the local girls? A lump formed in her throat. Could she bear to see another woman on his arm?

"Well? Are you going to tell me what Luke's done that has caused your usual smile to disappear?"

Her father's question interrupted her thoughts. "I think he cares for someone else." She'd blurted out the remark without giving it great thought.

"Cares for someone else?" He cleared his throat. "Has Luke declared his love for you?"

She caught her lower lip between her teeth and nodded. "And I have done the same."

Her father raked his fingers through his damp hair and mussed the careful combing he'd performed only minutes ago. "I realized the two of you were more than friends, but I didn't know it had gone this far. And he's asked you to marry him?"

Hope gasped. "Oh, no! I don't think he would be so bold without first gaining your permission." She turned away. "Given his recent behavior, I doubt either of us need concern ourselves about a marriage proposal." Tears threatened, and she swallowed hard. "I simply don't understand. I don't think I've done or said anything that would cause such a change in him. If I have, I don't know what it would be. I praised him for his visits to Jimmy Ray and even provided reading materials for Luke to give the boy. I've included his younger brothers and sisters in all the activities I've been conducting on the hill, and when I had some free time, I helped Nellie and his mother pick beans and shuck corn. I even worked alongside his uncle Frank when he was finishing up some painting inside the house." She removed a potato from the small bin and picked up her paring knife. "I truly don't know what has caused this change in him."

Her father settled in one of the chairs and watched her peel the dense potato skin. "I think that instead of talking to me or one of your friends, you need to ask Luke. He may be struggling with something that has nothing to do with you."

She peeled the last potato and began to cut them into thin slices. "I tried that before I came home today, but it didn't work. He wouldn't even cross the road to the railroad station and talk to me."

"Hmm." Her father stroked his jaw. "He'll be preaching this evening. I wouldn't try to talk to him before the meeting. He still gets a little nervous before he preaches. But afterward—that would be your best opportunity, I think."

She slid the potato slices into the hot grease, leaned down and kissed her father's cheek. She'd try to summon her courage and speak to Luke this evening.

But what if it confirmed her greatest fear?

CHAPTER
27

Hope's heart ached so much, she feared it would burst. None of her attempts to speak with Luke had proved fruitful. Though he assured her she'd done nothing to offend him and that he wasn't avoiding her, their relationship had changed. Instead of seeking her out after meetings, he was careful to have Nellie or some of the other children around him whenever she drew near. He'd canceled his morning Bible study with her father. Now, on days when he wasn't working at the mine, Luke went directly to the site of the new church building to help with the construction. When the workers stopped to eat lunch, Luke and her father conducted their Bible study at the work site.

For the past few days when he returned to the railcar, Hope would meet her father, eager to know if Luke had mentioned her name. Each day, her father would merely shake his head and give her a pitying look.

This afternoon her father once again shook his head as he entered the railcar. After washing his hands, he sat down and gestured to her. "I know I advised you to speak to Luke, but since he hasn't given you a satisfactory answer, I'm willing to ask him if there's a problem." He gathered her hand in his own. "But only if that's what you want."

She sat down opposite him and briefly considered the idea, then shook her head. "No. I don't want to draw you into this when it could cause problems between you and Luke. I do wish he'd at least give me an opportunity to talk to him alone. It seems there's always someone else around when I approach him."

Her father snapped his fingers together. "What about the box social? The fellows have been talking about it for days now, especially the unmarried young men. The day before the social I could mention to Luke that you were busy preparing your basket before I left and that you were pleased to find a pretty ribbon to tie on the handle." He winked at her. "You tell me what color ribbon you're going to use and then he can bid on your basket. What do you think? You'd have time to be alone with him while you eat your box lunch."

The idea was sound, but would Luke bid on her basket? Her stomach twisted. The thought that he'd know which basket was hers and still not bid would force her to accept that he didn't care for her anymore. At least not the way he'd professed in the past. Yet wasn't knowing better than spending each day wondering? She weighed that thought for several minutes. Did she truly want to be certain?

Hope inhaled a long breath. "Yes. That's a wonderful idea, Papa. You can tell him how I decorate my basket."

Once her decision had been made, a chill rushed through her each time she considered the consequences of her choice. Tears pricked her eyes, and she tried to remember that God had a plan for her future and she should trust that His plan would be better than any she might have in mind. Sometimes that worked for perhaps as long as half an hour. Other times it didn't work at all. She told herself that she should find pleasure in each day and not rush the future. That, too, worked sometimes, but usually not for long.

The day before the box social, Hope rummaged through the colorful buttons and pieces of ribbon in her sewing box. She removed only the ribbons that were long enough to make a bow, and wide enough to be seen at a distance. She stared at the two choices that lay before her. The larger was a long piece of black sateen that had been attached to a funeral wreath placed atop Aunt Mattie's burial plot. The thought of using the funeral ribbon to decorate her basket for a social wouldn't do. The other ribbon wasn't as wide, but it was long enough to make a double bow. Years ago, Aunt Mattie had removed the cream-colored ribbon and an ostrich plume from one of her fancy hats before she'd declared it beyond repair. The older woman had cautioned Hope to keep ribbons, buttons, and any other decorative pieces attached to her hats or garments before discarding them. While Hope followed a portion of her rule, she thought it imprudent to cut buttons off a dress before donating it to charity. She doubted the recipient would have the means or supplies to replace buttons, so she'd rejected that idea.

She lifted the basket onto the table and set to work on her bow. After several attempts, she smiled at the results. The bow looked brand-new. It was perfect from every angle, yet the color was indistinct. What if someone else tied a white or tan ribbon to their basket? Would Luke be certain which one was hers? She stared at the basket awhile longer and then turned back to her sewing box. She threaded her needle, removed the ostrich plume from the depths of the box, and tucked it into the bow, careful to tack it to the bow in several places. She didn't want it to come loose before the bidding began. Certain none of the other ladies would have such a decoration on their baskets, she tucked it away until her father returned home that evening.

When they'd finished supper, Hope removed the basket from the closet that held her clothes. She held it high in the air. "Well, what do you think?"

Her father gave a wide grin. "I doubt there will be another like it."

She swiveled the basket around and narrowed her eyes. "Do you think the feather is too much?" She didn't give him time to respond before continuing. "I wasn't going to use it, but the bow is such a neutral color, I thought he might mistake cream-colored for white or tan, and I have no idea what the other ladies may have on hand. Cream is such a common color that I—"

Her father held up his hand to stay her. "No need to explain further, my dear. I merely said I didn't think there would be another basket with an ostrich plume. It is lovely, and you're right. The cream color is quite common and could lead to confusion. I'll be sure to tell Luke about the ostrich feather." He chuckled. "That ostrich feather may entice more bids than the food inside the basket."

...............⚜...............

Her father had carefully selected the day they would hold the box social. He'd chosen a date when there would be an abundance of railroaders in town so that they would raise as much money as possible. Yesterday one of the men had told him one or two of the railroad managers might arrive in time for the box social. Great anticipation continued to surround the event as the churchgoing residents of Finch hoped to raise enough money for the purchase of a church bell. The preacher had been pleased by the folks' enthusiasm, but he feared the bell would arrive long before there was a steeple to house it. He was certain the men would be pleased to bid and spend their hard-earned money on the box suppers, and he was pleased for their participation in any form. On the other hand, he continued to pray more of the men would attend services in the chapel car and also help with construction of the new church building.

While pondering the need for more workers last week, he'd come upon an idea. He'd offered an incentive to gain the time and energy of the men. At the end of meetings in the chapel car, he announced that the man who worked the most hours during the week would have first choice and could choose any basket at the social without placing a bid. He'd told the men in attendance to spread the word.

The following day, and each day thereafter, the preacher had been delighted by the number of men who had appeared at the work site. He'd received a few good-hearted objections from the men who were assigned to be at their regular jobs in the mine, yet they remained determined to win and would appear at the construction site carrying their empty lunch pails after long hours in a dark coal tunnel.

As they had each day that week, Hope and several other women met the miners at the church site with jugs of water and cold sandwiches, for which the men lavished their gratitude upon the young ladies.

Nellie stopped beside the preacher and her uncle Frank. "We have a few sandwiches left, if either of you would like one." Both men nodded, and she lifted two paper-wrapped sandwiches from the basket. "Sorry, but the others chose the ham, so there's only these left."

Her uncle unwrapped the sandwich and lifted one edge of the bread. "The old men get jelly and the young'uns get ham. Somethin' seems wrong about that." He laughed before taking a bite of the offering.

She covered her mouth with her palm. "Oh, no. I'm sorry,

Uncle Frank. I should have given you and the preacher ham. We're handing out jelly sandwiches to the married fellas and ham to the single men." She grinned at him and dug into the basket. "I've still got a couple with ham. I can give them to you and the preacher if you'd like." She glanced back and forth between the two men. When they shook their heads, Nellie cradled the basket handle on her arm and skipped off.

Frank bent his head, unwrapped the sandwich, and murmured, "Best I keep this since I won't be single for long."

Hope's father leaned in. "What was that? Did you say you won't be single for long?"

Frank nodded. "I asked Myrna, Luke's ma, to marry me. I don't know why I waited so long. My brother's been dead and buried nigh on four years now, and there's no other woman I'd ever want. Me and Myrna love each other, and she and the young'uns need me. Truth is, I need her even more. The young'uns already think of me more like a pa than an uncle. And I don't think Luke or Nellie will have any objection."

"I think that's wonderful news, Frank. I'm happy for both of you. When are you planning to marry?"

Frank took a bite of his jelly sandwich and grinned. "Soon. Very soon."

..............ॐ..............

Luke flinched when his sister nudged him in the side. "You need to quit talkin' to Hope. She's confused 'bout what's goin' on betwixt the two of you, and it ain't fair to her."

Luke picked up his hammer and pounded a nail into the lumber before looking at his sister. "Why? What did she say?"

"She says you been acting strange. One minute you're smiling at her, and the next minute your lips are sealed tighter than a canning jar. The best and kindest thing to do is talk to her and move on and find a gal from up here on the hill. I care about Hope almost as much as you, but until you tell her it's best for the two of you to move on, she's gonna cling to hope. Maybe you could take up with Margaret McCray. She'd be pleased to have you court her."

He shook his head and glared at his sister. "Margaret Mc-Cray? That's the craziest thing I ever heard of. I've got no interest in Margaret. Or any other gal, for that matter."

"Not now, you don't, but Margaret has always liked you. A lot. She jest never knew how to show you. What you gotta do is bid on her basket at the social. You two can get to know each other better. Margaret would be a good match, Luke. She's one of us. She'd understand movin' in with the family and all after you get hitched."

"Are you pulling my leg? You got us married already? What's wrong with you, Nellie?" Using the end of the hammer, he pointed to the grassy knoll where the other women had gathered. "Go talk to the womenfolk and let me be. And don't use your time thinking up any more foolishness."

Undeterred, Nellie remained by his side for a moment longer. "I asked about her basket decorations. Margaret's basket will have a red-and-white gingham bow attached." She smiled down at him as though she'd presented him with a gift.

"Stay out of this, Nellie."

She flipped her hair over her shoulder and strode off as if he hadn't said a word. He stared after her, annoyed by her interference and lack of understanding. Did she truly believe he could so easily forget Hope? No doubt she did. Nellie had never been in love. How could she understand? He pounded until the head of the nail had disappeared into the splintered wood that surrounded it.

"I'm sure glad your thumb didn't get in the way while you

were pounding that nail." Uncle Frank smiled down at him. "You mad at the world or jest that nail?"

Luke hiked a shoulder and continued working. He didn't want to talk about his anger, or Nellie, or Margaret, or Hope. He wanted to go to bed tonight, wake up tomorrow and have this whole mess over with. He wanted things to go back to the way they were before. He wanted to forget the responsibility to his ma and the young'uns. Most of all, he wanted to ask Hope to marry him. She might not accept his offer, but now he'd never know.

Yet he couldn't live with himself if he didn't do what was right, what was expected. A future without Hope would be bleak, but once she left Finch, his wounds might begin to heal. He'd never forget her, never stop loving her, never cease missing her, but the pain of losing her would ease if he could no longer anticipate seeing her at every turn.

His uncle kneeled down beside Luke, picked up a nail, and began to work alongside him. "I'm thinkin' you're gonna ruin this piece of lumber if you keep hammering those nails so deep. What's eatin' at ya, boy? You know you can talk to me. Ain't that what kinfolk are for?"

Luke nodded. "I don't think it's anything you can help with, Uncle Frank, but thanks for the offer."

A pained look creased the older man's features. "I know I ain't got much book learnin' and such, but I do know a thing or two about life, and it's easy enough to see you got a problem. If you ain't thinking I could do anything, maybe the preacher could help. He's a right smart fella."

Luke remained crouched in front of the piece of lumber, then leaned back on his heels. He might as well talk to his uncle since the older man seemed unwilling to let the matter rest. If he told Uncle Frank he couldn't talk to the preacher, his uncle would suggest someone else, and then another, and another, until Luke finally agreed to reveal his problem to someone. He sighed. It might as well be Uncle Frank.

"I've got a problem with Hope."

His uncle slapped his palm against his thigh. "I knew it! Problems with womenfolk can eat at a fella like a squirrel gnawing an ear of corn. You needin' some money to bid on her basket? I kin lend ya a little if that's the problem." His uncle dropped his hammer and reached for his overall pocket.

"No." Luke covered his uncle's hand with his own. "I don't need any money, but I need to know how I keep from hurting someone I love. You see, I know Hope plans on me bidding on her basket. Her pa told me how it's decorated, so I can't say I didn't know which basket was hers. Truth is, I think she asked him to tell me, but he didn't say that."

"So what's the problem? You like her, she likes you, you got money to bid on the basket, and you know which basket to buy. How's that hurt her?"

"I can't bid on her basket. It wouldn't be fair to her or to me. I'm trying to stay away from her as much as I can."

His uncle pushed his hat back on his head. "You got me plum confused, Luke. I need a little more to go on if I'm gonna give ya any help."

Before Luke could respond, Nellie returned with a jug of water. She offered a cup to her uncle and then leaned close to Luke's ear. "I told Margaret you'd be bidding on her basket. She's so excited I thought she might cry."

Luke twisted sideways to look at Nellie. Anger churned in his belly until he thought he might explode. "I told you to stay out of this, Nellie. I'm not bidding on anyone's basket, so you can go and tell Margaret you made a big, fat mistake. If she cries or gets her nose outta joint, it's your fault for stirring things up. You're the one who's been running back and forth between us like a bow on a box fiddle."

Nellie grabbed the cup from her uncle and blew out a huff. "You'll change your mind." She hissed the words at him as she turned and stalked off.

His uncle nudged his arm. "I can't take no more of this, Luke. What's going on?"

"Nellie wants me to bid on Margaret's basket. She thinks we'd be a good match, but I told her I'm not interested. Now Nellie's trying to force my hand by telling me Margaret is expecting me to purchase her basket."

His uncle took off his hat and scratched his head. "You got two gals expecting you to bid on their baskets. You care for one, but not the other. You said you was tryin' to stay away from Hope, but if you care for her, why would you do that? I thought we hashed out the problems about caring for the family the other day. I'm true to my word, Luke. You ain't got no worries on that account. Don't let Nellie decide who you're gonna court."

"I'm not, Uncle Frank, but she's set me to thinking." He detailed his earlier talk with Nellie. When he finished, he met his uncle's gaze. "Nellie's right. Hope wouldn't be happy living in Finch for the rest of her life. I know you'd do your best for Ma and the young'uns, but it ain't fair to expect you to take over my responsibility. You've got a right to a life of your own, too."

His uncle laughed. "If that's your problem, then you can set aside your worries, boy, 'cause I'm gonna be taking care of your ma and the young'uns from here on out."

Luke stared at his uncle. "What does that mean?"

"We're getting hitched. I asked her and she said yes. The preacher said he'd say the words over us come Sunday afternoon."

Luke continued to stare at the older man as the words sunk into his consciousness. "Married? You and Ma?"

Uncle Frank nodded. "You don't look too pleased by the news. I thought you'd be happy. It solves your problem, don't it? I mean it frees ya up to court whoever you want. You don't need to worry 'bout supportin' your ma and the young'uns no more."

"Well, yeah, I'm happy, but I didn't know. I mean, she never said nothin' and . . ."

He guffawed again. "If'n you was 'round the house more, you'd have guessed, but you and Nellie been so busy with your own doings that neither of you paid your ma and me no mind. I love her and plan to do right by her, Luke."

"I know you will, Uncle Frank. I didn't hesitate 'cause I had any misgivings about you and ma getting married. I just never gave it any thought."

His uncle lightly slapped him on the shoulder. "I'm glad you ain't got no objection and that I could help ya with that problem of yours."

Luke drew in a deep breath and looked heavenward. Was this the answer he'd been praying for? Was he now free to follow his heart?

Luke glanced toward Hope, but a fresh fear made his throat tighten. He'd hurt her terribly in the last few days. Would she forgive him?

One of the railroaders who'd come to help with the construction was talking to her. She tipped her head and smiled at the fellow. Her laughter carried on the breeze. Maybe his problem wasn't solved after all. Maybe he was too late.

CHAPTER

28

On a sunny autumn afternoon, the ladies of Finch and the surrounding area arrived with their decorated baskets and placed them on a makeshift table that consisted of a wide board balanced on two sawhorses. The men arrived a short time later so as to avoid knowledge of who'd prepared what basket. Of course, the married men always knew and bid on the baskets prepared by their wives, and those baskets bore scant decoration. But the other baskets had been bedecked with ribbons, flowers, garlands, and even paper chains. The ladies paced in front of the table, examining the myriad baskets, with each unmarried lady hoping the young man of her dreams would win the bid for her basket.

Anticipation mounted as the men arrived and Hope searched the crowd for Luke. She caught sight of him as he circled the table with the other men. He couldn't possibly miss her basket. Not one was similar to hers. A few of the baskets boasted turkey feathers, but the only ostrich feather waved proudly from the handle of her basket.

Once the men had completed their walk around the table,

Hope's father stepped forward. "I promised the man who performed the most hours of work over the past week the right to choose a basket without the need to bid on it." He reached into his vest pocket and withdrew a small notebook. "I've kept a close calculation of the hours, and the winner of the contest is Thomas Ulrich."

When the announcement was made, several groans could be heard from the crowd. Undeterred by the reaction of the other men, Thomas jumped to his feet and tossed his hat in the air.

The young fellow pushed his way through the crowd, a wide smile on his face. When he arrived at the table, he extended his arms above his head with his palms toward the crowd. "I got lots of blisters to show for this, but it ain't gonna take me but a minute to pick the one I want."

Hope held her breath. What if he chose hers? She grimaced at the thought. Then again it would likely serve her right since she'd schemed to have Luke bid on her basket.

Thomas pointed to a box. "I'll take this one."

Hope watched as Thomas reached forward and picked up a wicker basket with a large red-and-white gingham bow attached. She let out a sigh as she glanced around the crowd to see who would step forward to join Thomas. Her attention was drawn to Nellie, who was frowning and whispering to Margaret McCray.

The girl pulled away from Nellie. "I'm here, Thomas." She ran toward him with a bright smile while waving to the crowd. She rushed to his side and grasped his arm, seemingly pleased that her basket had been chosen, though Nellie's frown remained intact. Hope momentarily wondered if Nellie had wanted Thomas to bid on her basket. Though she'd never heard Nellie mention Thomas, that didn't mean she wasn't hoping to catch his eye.

A few of the men pushed up the bids against friends who were eager to win a particular basket. But mostly the baskets were quickly retrieved, and the couples wandered off to find a quiet spot to eat. When only four or five baskets remained, her father held up Hope's basket.

She smiled when Luke called out a bid, but one of the visiting railroad managers who'd been talking to Hope earlier in the day immediately raised the bid. Luke raised the bid by ten cents, but the railroader again raised the bid. Back and forth it went until she feared Luke would have to end his bidding for lack of funds. She scowled at the railroader, who likely had more money than good sense, and was surprised to see Luke's uncle move to the man's side and whisper in his ear.

When Luke called out his next bid and her father turned toward the railroader, he shook his head. "I'm done. Let the other fella have it."

Luke strode to the table, withdrew the payment from his pocket, and gestured to Hope. As she moved toward Luke, she stopped beside his uncle. "What did you say to that railroader to get him to stop bidding?"

Frank grinned. "I told him I knew the lady who fixed the food in that basket and that she had a good eye for decoratin' and such, but couldn't boil water if someone pumped it fer her. I told him any of the other baskets would be a better choice. Hope ya don't mind, but I figured Luke was about to run outta money."

Hope laughed. "I don't mind a bit. Thank you."

When she drew near, Luke nodded at his uncle. "What were you and Uncle Frank laughing about?"

After she related what she'd been told, Luke chuckled. "Leave it to Uncle Frank to take care of things. He's been doing that a lot lately."

"Has he? How so?" she asked as she spread a blanket for them beneath a tree.

Once she'd sat down on the blanket, he took her hand. "It's a long story, but we've got plenty of time and I have a lot to tell you."

"Finally." She smiled nervously at him, and her voice held a tinge of hurt. "It seems like forever since you've wanted to talk to me at all."

"I know, and I'm hoping you'll forgive me once I explain."

While Hope lifted the food from the basket and placed it on a cloth, Luke explained why he'd been avoiding her. "I know I should have told you, but I wanted to believe there would be a solution. I felt so foolish for not having realized my family needed me to support them, and marriage to you would put an end to everything for them. No income, no house to live in, and I knew I couldn't do that. I have to admit I wasn't too happy with God, either. I felt like He'd abandoned me, like He wasn't hearing my prayers. All of it seemed so unfair. To have you come into my life, declare my love for you, and then realize we couldn't marry felt like a bad dream."

Her lips curved in a slow smile. "And now that bad dream has been replaced by a wonderful reality, but I do wish you would have come and talked to me rather than accepting Nellie's opinion that I could never adjust to a different life. I would have been understanding, and together we could have arrived at some solution."

He bit into a piece of crispy fried chicken. "This is delicious." He waved the drumstick in the air. "Best chicken I've ever had."

She shushed him. "Don't let that railroader hear you talking—not after what your uncle told him."

His eyes widened and he lowered his voice. "What do you think about marrying the fellow who knows you fry the best chicken in the state of West Virginia?"

"First, I would wonder if he'd asked my father for permission to marry me." Her voice quivered, her eyes shining with excitement.

"And if he said that your father had given his blessing?" Luke grinned, thankful he'd spoken to Pastor Irvine and asked for permission to wed his daughter.

She giggled. "I think I'd be very happy to marry him, but I must say that I had hoped for a more romantic proposal."

He picked up a cloth napkin and wiped his hands before taking her hand in his. "You're right. That wasn't very good at all. I love you very much, Hope, and I'd be honored if you'd agree to become my wife. You'd make me the happiest and best-fed man in all of West Virginia if you said yes."

"How could I refuse such a sweet request? I would be honored to become Mrs. Luke Hughes."

He cupped her cheeks between his hands, leaned forward and kissed her. "You, Hope Irvine, are the answer to my prayers."

............⚬⚭⚬............

The day dawned bright and crisp in late October with the sun glistening through the leaves that still clung to the trees, and all seemed right with the world. After Kirby's incarceration, his father had decided to sell the mine, and yesterday the new owner had arrived. He'd met with the miners and their families and answered their questions before announcing there would be an increase in pay for the miners and avowing their families would no longer be required to do business with the company store. The news had been met with enthusiasm, which spread throughout the town, and her father had offered a prayer of thanksgiving later that evening.

Hope placed an iron skillet on the small stove, then opened the rear door of the railcar to allow a breeze to pass through while she prepared breakfast. Her attention flitted back and forth to the window while she fried bacon and eggs. Luke had resumed his morning Bible study meetings with her father, and she'd insisted he join them for breakfast each day.

A smile played at her lips when she caught sight of him. Knees lifted high with each step, he tromped through the damp, calf-high grassy expanse. His boots and pant legs were wet with dew when he arrived at the rear door. He glanced down and then proceeded to remove his boots.

Hope shook her head. "No need to do that, Luke. The floor will dry in no time. Come and sit down. Breakfast is almost ready. I need to tell Papa." She stepped to the doorway between the living quarters and sanctuary, where her father sat on one of the pews. "Breakfast, Papa. Luke is here."

He looked up and smiled. "Smells good. My stomach is rumbling already." He stood and followed her into the living quarters. "Morning, Luke."

"Morning, Preacher. Looks like you were getting a head start on our Bible studying."

The older man chuckled. "Just trying to stay out of Hope's way while she's cooking. I was in there having a long talk with the Lord."

"Anything in particular you're trying to hash out?" Luke poured them each a cup of coffee.

"As a matter of fact, there's several things I've been praying about over the past couple months, and it seems the answer has arrived for at least some of those petitions."

Hope heaped their plates with bacon, eggs, and fried potatoes before she sat down. "Would you pray, Papa?"

"Why don't you, Luke? I'm sure the Lord gets tired of hearing me all the time." Hope's father chuckled and bowed his head.

Luke gave thanks for their meal and the bounty of God's blessings on the miners and their families and asked that He guide all of them through the coming day.

"Thank you, Luke." Her father tucked a napkin in his shirt collar. "I always enjoy hearing you pray—and I enjoy hearing you preach, too. I think I'm going to have you preach more often."

Hope glanced at her father. While she was accustomed to her father praising Luke for his increasing knowledge of the Bible and ability to preach when her father was ill or needed elsewhere, his comment seemed strangely out of place this morning. Besides, even though her father's health had returned, Luke continued to preach at one of the church meetings several days a week.

Luke's forehead tightened into thin lines. "You been feeling poorly again?"

"No, I'm doing fine. Even the doc agrees." He smiled and reached inside his vest pocket and withdrew an envelope. "I haven't told Hope about this. Thought it would be better to talk to the two of you together."

Her father's words could mean only one thing: bad news. The fact that he wanted Luke with her when she heard the news—whatever it might be—didn't bode well for them.

He laid the envelope beside his plate and tapped it with his fingers. "This is from the association headquarters, Luke. The association that sponsors the chapel car and our new church building. I received a letter from them back in September, requesting a report on the status of the construction, the number of regular attendees at our meetings, amount of debt we may have incurred, and other pertinent information about our mission here in Finch."

When he turned silent, Hope leaned forward. "And?"

"And I wrote and answered their questions. Yesterday I received a response from them." He smiled at his daughter.

"Were they pleased with the progress you've made? What did they say?"

He cleared his throat. "They say it will soon be time for the Herald of Hope to move on and help in another community."

Panic seized her. "Move on? Why? Because the church is being rebuilt? When do they want you to leave? Exactly what did they say?"

Luke reached for her hand and gently covered it with his own. "Don't get yourself all worked up, Hope. You're hitting him with more questions than a load of buckshot. Give your pa a chance to answer."

Hope exhaled a long breath and stared at her father. "Could we please have more details?" She turned toward Luke. "Was that better?"

He grinned and nodded. "Much."

"The association believes we've done a good job here in Finch, what with rebuilding the church at the—"

"But it's not complete yet." Hope couldn't stop herself. "Did you tell them the steeple isn't finished and we've got to get windows put in before winter? And that we only have benches to sit on until we can afford pews? And that the bell hasn't arrived yet?"

Her father directed a forlorn look at the congealed bubbles of grease that had formed on his bacon. "I should have finished eating before I mentioned the letter."

"You could eat while I read the letter." Hope extended her hand.

"Read it aloud so Luke hears what they had to say." Her father pushed the letter across the table.

Hope scooped up the envelope and withdrew the folded page. She cleared her throat and glanced at Luke as she spread open the creamy stationery.

Dear Reverend Irvine,

Thank you for your recent response to our earlier inquiry regarding your pastoral duties in Finch, West Virginia. Having examined your report, the association has made the following decision. The Herald of Hope will remain in Finch until April of next year in order to give you adequate time to complete construction of the church building and to make certain you have returned to full health.

As to your recommendation of a preacher for the church in Finch, we agree with your recommendation that Luke Hughes continue under your tutelage until you depart. At that time, we recommend he take over as pastor of the church there. If Mr. Hughes accepts the position, the association will pay him a monthly stipend and provide adequate living accommodations. Your letter stated that your daughter, Hope, is engaged to Mr. Hughes. Since she will no longer accompany you on the Herald of Hope, we will grant your request and donate the chapel car organ to the newly established church in Finch. You may return to use of the gramophone at your new assignment.

As the date of your departure draws closer, we will contact you regarding your new assignment. Please ac-

cept our grateful thanks for the good work you and your daughter have accomplished in Finch.

"Oh, Papa. This is all so wonderful." Hope clutched the letter to the bodice of her blue-print blouse. "Except for the portion about you leaving."

Her father patted her shoulder. "Whenever I go into a town, I know it will only be for a season. My work here is almost done, and I know I'm going to be leaving it in good hands. With Luke serving as pastor of the church and you by his side to help, I know the Lord will continue to do good things in this town."

"I'm honored you would submit my name to lead the church, but I'm not sure I'm qualified. I don't have all that seminary education like you. I'm not sure I've had enough training to be the preacher."

"I'm sure or I wouldn't have recommended you, Luke. There are lots of preachers who are called to spread God's Word who haven't attended seminary. You gained a solid knowledge of the Bible years ago, you've studied with me, you've been given a gift to preach, and you've expressed to me that you believe the Lord has called you to preach. The door has opened, Luke. You need only step through." Hope's father pushed away from the table. "Besides, it's only October. You have six more months to study and become comfortable with the idea." He turned to his daughter. "And you, my dear, have six more months to plan a wedding."

She nodded in agreement, yet his reminder of the wedding was also a signal that her life would forever change in six months. Would she adjust to life without her father nearby? Could she adapt to a permanent life in Finch? Would she and Luke be happy once they married? A knot of fear settled in the pit of her stomach, and she quietly excused herself and stepped into the sanctuary.

She sat down on the organ stool, rested her fingers on the keys, and began to play "Trust and Obey." Moments later, the deep baritone and tenor voices of her father and Luke wafted into the room. When they stepped behind her, she glanced over her shoulder and smiled at the two men she loved.

CHAPTER
29

APRIL 1914

Hope traced her fingers over the thin layer of dust that covered the old suitcase her father had removed from among his stored belongings. She'd never before seen this tattered bag and, with their limited space in the railcar, was surprised he'd kept it. He'd placed it in front of her with great reverence and now instructed her to open it.

"Shortly after your mother's death, your aunt Mattie made me promise to keep this and give it to you when you were preparing for your wedding."

Hope couldn't help but smile. "Was she so certain I would find a willing suitor way back then?"

"She was. And so was I, or I wouldn't have kept it all these years."

She unbuckled the metal clasps and lifted the lid. Tissue covered the contents, and Hope slowly peeled away the layers, then gasped in disbelief. "Oh, Papa. It's Mama's wedding dress."

Her chest tightened as tears welled in her eyes. How many times had she looked at the wedding picture of her parents, her mother wearing this delicate lace wedding dress and Papa in his fine black suit?

Hope lifted the dress with great care and held it in front of her body. "I think it will fit, don't you?"

Her father coughed and turned away for a moment. "Yes. You're much the same size as your mother when we married." Hope didn't miss the tears in his eyes. If he blinked, they would escape and run unchecked down his cheeks. "And there's no doubt in my mind that you'll be as beautiful on your wedding day as she was on ours."

"Thank you, Papa." She stepped forward and gently kissed his cheek. "You know I'm going to miss you, don't you?"

He offered a sad smile and nodded. "And I'm going to miss you. To think that a year ago I did my best to talk you out of coming with me, and now . . ." His voice trailed off, and he gave a slight shake of his head. "And now you're going to be a preacher's wife. You've been a real blessing to me and to the people of this community, Hope. I know they're pleased you'll be staying here." He brightened. "I didn't mean to sound so maudlin. After all, I'm not going to be so far away, and Jed tells me the railroaders are so happy you'll still be in Finch to play the organ, they've agreed to see that you get a railroad pass every now and again so you can come visit me."

"That's kind of them." She squeezed her father's hand. "I just wish you could stay in Finch a little longer."

"The association leadership has been very patient while I've regained my strength. Besides, I'm ready to move on and meet some new folks and face new challenges." He gestured toward the gown. "I'll leave you to try on the dress and see if it needs to be altered before the wedding. I have a few things that need my attention in town." He picked up his hat and gave her a quick wave before departing.

Hope spread the dress across the narrow couch. Using a light touch, she studied the scalloped lace sleeves, gently pressing the pale blue satin ribbon with her fingers. How she wished her mother and Aunt Mattie could be here for her wedding day. Yet deep within she knew they would be with her in spirit, and that thought alone would provide her with pure delight.

⚜

Earlier in the day, Hope had awakened with a smile on her face. Today was her wedding day. Even before breakfast, she'd been silently repeating those wondrous words. A bright April sun shone over the mountainside, promising a gorgeous day, and heightened her anticipation.

Nellie, along with her mother and some of the other ladies from the hill, had arrived a short time ago and decorated the sanctuary of the chapel car with fragrant lilacs, ox-eye daisies, and wild roses from their flower gardens. When they finished, they'd gone to the church to decorate for the reception that would follow the ceremony. Although the church had been completed, Hope and Luke decided there was only one place they wanted to join their lives—inside the chapel car. This itinerant church was what had brought them together.

After stepping from their living quarters, Hope sat down in one of the pews. Only God could have put all the pieces together to answer so many prayers—both said and unsaid. Her humble words of thanks hardly seemed adequate, but God knew her heart.

Moments later, she startled when Nellie threw open the door. "Sorry. Your pa said to go on in. You ready to get dressed? You know you don't have to marry that brother of mine if you're having second thoughts." Her eyes twinkled with mischief.

"I'm not." Hope stood. "And I can't wait to be his wife."

"You know he snores." Nellie giggled and then gave Hope a hug. "I'm glad we're going to be sisters."

"I am too." Hope motioned to their living quarters, where the wedding dress hung from a hook on the door.

"Oh, Hope, it's the purtiest thing I've ever seen." Nellie gestured to the thin gold chain with a cross that encircled Hope's neck. "And I ain't never seen that necklace before, either." She lifted the cross between her thumb and index finger. "That's sure somethin'. Was that your ma's, too?"

"No. Papa sent off for it after Luke and I got engaged. He said he wanted to give me something special on my wedding day." She choked back tears. "I have my dress from Ma, the necklace from Pa, and I'm carrying a lace handkerchief that belonged to Aunt Mattie. I think it's perfect."

An hour later, Hope stood in front of the tiny mirror in the chapel car's living quarters. She couldn't see the entire dress, but Nellie assured her she was beautiful. She fingered the delicate lace trim. What would her mother say if she were present? Would she kiss her cheek? Tell her about the secrets of the wedding night to come?

Hope felt her cheeks grow warm. Just then the familiar mellow tones of the gramophone began, and her pulse quickened. Nellie, dressed in her Sunday best, led the way down the narrow aisle.

Since her father was performing the ceremony, they'd agreed she would walk down the aisle alone. There wasn't room for two abreast, anyway. Hope stepped into the aisle, and everyone who'd squeezed into the pews of the chapel car stood. She studied their smiling faces. These townspeople had become her friends and her family.

She glanced at her father, who beamed with pride. God had

given her a wonderful father, and she silently thanked Him as she stepped forward.

Her gaze shifted to Jimmy Ray, Luke's best man who'd been released from jail a few months ago. The young man had grown so much in his love for the Lord.

And finally she looked at the handsome man who was about to become her husband.

Luke. God's greatest gift to her. A man of honor. A man of God.

How strange to realize that she'd come on the Herald of Hope chapel car thinking she could bring hope to the people of Finch. Her heart swelled with the knowledge she now embraced. Only God could truly bring the hope these people needed—the hope she needed. He was the hope that anchored their souls.

And He was the anchor that would hold the two of them, their children, and their children's children fast to Him.

Special thanks to . . .

My editor and the entire staff of Bethany House, for their devotion to publishing the best product possible. It is a privilege to work with all of you.

Carolyn Poe, for her generous spirit and willingness to loan me myriad materials to assist me in my research of the chapel car ministry.

Mary Greb-Hall, for her ongoing encouragement, expertise, and sharp eye.

Lorna Seilstad, for her honest critiques and steadfast friendship.

Mary Kay Woodford, my sister, my prayer warrior, my friend.

Justin, Jenna, and Jessa, for their support and the joy they bring to me during the writing process and throughout my life.

Above all, thanks and praise to our Lord Jesus Christ, for the opportunity to live my dream and share the wonder of His love through story.

Judith Miller is an award-winning author whose avid research and love for history are reflected in her bestselling novels. Judy makes her home in Topeka, Kansas.

More From Judith Miller

Visit judithmccoymiller.com for a full list of her books.

Ewan McKay came to West Virginia to help his uncle Hugh start a brickmaking operation. But when Hugh makes an ill-advised deal, the foundation Ewan has built begins to crumble. Can the former owner's daughter help Ewan save the brickworks—and his future?

The Brickmaker's Bride
REFINED BY LOVE

Rose McKay has plenty of ideas on how to make her family's newly acquired pottery business a success—too many ideas, in longtime employee Rylan Campbell's opinion. But can these two put aside their differences and work together to win an important design contest?

The Potter's Lady
REFINED BY LOVE

Ainslee didn't plan on running the McKay's West Virginia tile works alone. While her brother looks for a buyer, she hires talented artisan Levi Judson to keep the business going. But when she develops feelings for Levi, can their relationship survive the secrets they've been keeping?

The Artisan's Wife
REFINED BY LOVE

You May Also Enjoy . . .

Miss Permilia Griswold, the wallflower behind *The Quill* gossip column, knows everything that goes on in the ballrooms of New York. When she overhears a threat against the estimable Mr. Asher Rutherford, she's determined to warn him. Away from society's spotlight, Asher and Permilia discover there's more going on behind the scenes than they anticipated.

Behind the Scenes by Jen Turano
APART FROM THE CROWD
jenturano.com

Naval officer Ryan Gallagher broke Jenny Bennett's heart six years ago when he abruptly disappeared. Now he's returned but refuses to discuss what happened. Furious, Jenny has no notion of the impossible situation Ryan is in. With lives still at risk, he can't tell Jenny the truth about his overseas mission—but he can't bear to lose her again either.

To the Farthest Shores by Elizabeth Camden
elizabethcamden.com

The Boden clan thought their troubles were over with the death of a dangerous enemy. But with new evidence on Cole's shooting, Justin can't deny that the plot to steal their ranch was bigger than one man. While the doctor and his distractingly pretty assistant help Cole, Justin has to uncover the trail of a decades-old secret as danger closes in.

Long Time Gone by Mary Connealy
THE CIMARRON LEGACY #2
maryconnealy.com

⬥BETHANYHOUSE

More Historical Fiction

After being unjustly imprisoned, Julianne Chevalier trades her life sentence for exile to the French colony of Louisiana in 1720. She marries a fellow convict in order to sail, but when tragedy strikes—and a mystery unfolds—Julianne must find her own way in this dangerous new land while bearing the brand of a criminal.

The Mark of the King by Jocelyn Green
jocelyngreen.com

After a night trapped together in an old stone keep, Lady Adelaide Bell and Lord Trent Hawthorne have no choice but to marry. Dismayed, Adelaide finds herself bound to a man who ignores her, as Trent has no desire to connect with the one who dashed his plans to marry for love. Can they set aside their first impressions before any chance of love is lost?

An Uncommon Courtship by Kristi Ann Hunter
HAWTHORNE HOUSE
kristiannhunter.com

Cassidy Ivanoff and her father, John, have signed on to work at a prestigious new hotel near Mt. McKinley. John's new apprentice, Allan Brennan, finds a friend in Cassidy, but the real reason he's here—to learn the truth about his father's death—is far more dangerous than he knows.

In the Shadow of Denali by Tracie Peterson and Kimberley Woodhouse
THE HEART OF ALASKA #1
traciepeterson.com, kimberleywoodhouse.com